VLAD

THE DARK PRINCE

COLIN MARTIN

SCRIPTOR HOUSE
THE EPITOME OF GREATNESS

Scriptor House LLC

17434 Bellflower Blvd Ste 200-188 Bellflower, CA 90706

www.scriptorhouse.com

Phone: +1209-554-8271

Published by Scriptor House LLC

Paperback: 979-8-88692-482-4
eBook: 979-8-88692-494-7

'For land and people, Prince of Wallachia he reins;
Honouring the Dragon Order, his pride remains.
But his army depletes, upon the earth their blood stains;
So, if conjured, a dark evil pertains.
And then shall enemies, come deliver their pains;
He will drink the life-blood from their veins.'

CONTENTS

Acknowledgements

Kristina

Thanks to you my dearest friend. Your pretty face and gorgeous smile has again helped me conceive a feminine character for this story. I think that you may differ somewhat from the eastern European gypsy girl – *Tariana (Tatyana)*, but I am ever inspired to develop characters like her based on your beauty.

People, Events and Presentations

Thank you to all friends and family that give constructive criticism or provide positive words about my writing. Thanks to all the people who have attended events, such as presentations, where I have endeavoured to promote my novels and writing. During my research vacation to Romania in 2017, a sincere thank you to the hotel, history museum, bookshops and library staff in *Braşov*. Big thanks also to *Dan* (a tour guide), who gave information during my trip to *Bran Castle*.

Publishing Teams

Big thanks again to the publishing team(s) who helped in the publication of my fourth horror-fiction novel. This story diverted somewhat from pursuing the *Call Stone* trilogy of *Rain Maker*, *Dream Master* and *Dream Daughters*, as at the time I needed to focus back on writing to bring some hope and positivity in my life.

MAP OF VLAD'S WALLACHIA

CHARACTER LISTING

Vladimir Dracul… .... *Vlad Tepes, Prince of Wallachia*

Tatyana (Tariana) Alekseevna.................... *Ukrainian gypsy girl*

Radu Bey.. *Vlad's younger brother*

Jusztina Szilagyi… .... *Vlad's first wife from Moldavia*

Henrik Vasile......................... *Vlad's second-in-command soldier*

Kateryna Rabanek… .... *Half-Hungarian woman from Braşov*

Sorin Gabor… .... *Gypsy giant and Russian Cossack*

Andrei and Lydia… .... *Market peasants from Braşov*

Mihnea Dracul… .... *Vlad's son: was to be named Mircea*
 after older half-brother killed in battle with father

Lucian Dumitru… .... *Chief Councillor in Poenari castle*

Sultan Mehmet II......... *Turkish leader and Ottoman opponent*

Petru, Remus, and Simion.............................. *Gypsy camp males*

Mariana and daughter Alina....................... *Gypsy camp females*

Sabina… .... *Elder woman in gypsy camp*

Tibor… .... *Other gypsy Russian Cossack*

PART ONE

ONE

It was a sound quashed in the din of such battle, but the clash of his blade against the Turk's rang through Vlad's ears. His right arm also shuddered to the shock and vibration of metal against metal, but Vlad had experienced such combat many thousand times. Then as the curve of the Turkish blade scraped down his longsword, he knew it would slice past his armoured glove and into his wrist; his flesh exposed at such an angle.

At the last second Vlad twisted the handle of his sword. And although feeling his wrist pained by such action, was relieved to see his opponent's blade wedge against the cross-guard of his longsword. From here Vlad knew he had the advantage of height over his enemy, but froze momentarily to consider his enemy's origin.

This young soldier not only stood somewhat taller in comparison to the usual Turk, but his glaring eyes shone a piercing blue against the sunlight. They were not the dirty, murky brown of a usual Turk. And from his years enslaved as a boy, Vlad knew exactly the makeup of the Turks; not just their appearance, but their contempt, their vicious temperament – their cruel religion.

Taking advantage of Vlad's hesitancy, the soldier dug his heels into the mudded earth, trying to stand tall and use his weight to push down on Vlad's sword – try and turn his free. But he too stood tall, and having extra height, Vlad pivoted his weight against the young man's strength. The foreigner grimaced as he felt his feet slipping, knowing the Wallachian was pressing him to the ground.

Surprisingly the soldier relaxed and turned aside, using his curved blade to fling Vlad's longsword to ground. As his grip slid and his forearm armour caught against the pommel, Vlad felt his longsword slice deep into the long grass. Grimacing against the numbness of his elbow and forearm, Vlad threw back his weight to see his opponent wield free his sickle-like sword; the young man now grinning as he took a step to strike at him.

Vlad reeled back, leaving his cherished longsword anchored tall in the earth like some silvery cross swaying above his Christian grave. He stumbled and had hardly the time to notice blood ooze from beneath his leathery undergarment, when the soldier swung again. Sluggishly he dodged the attack but luckily the Turkish sword only caught the metal of his chest plate armour. As the soldier's attack thrust him forward,

Vlad took advantage of his opponent's unsteady footing and reached for his secret weapon.

From just beneath the right-side of his chest plate and holstered in thick leather, Vlad pulled out a straight, little dagger – edges sharp and pointed to almost eight inches. Swapping it quickly between hands, he gripped the dagger firmly as his opponent faltered to keep balance. The young man cowered, trying desperately to locate Vlad to maintain his defence, but Vlad was too quick for him. As the young soldier stumbled upon the muddied earth, Vlad thrust the dagger into his throat.

Momentarily Vlad was blinded by the squirt of red liquid over his face, but squinted to observe his opponent's silence. It was only when he pulled the dagger from the soldier's throat that he heard his wailing above all else. Stunned, Vlad wiped the blood from the side of his face; realizing now that his head was unprotected after previously losing his helmet. But he had to keep alert; not only should he end this soldier's life, but be aware of all others about him.

After swiftly replacing his dagger, Vlad raced to pull his longsword from the earth, and with rejuvenated strength lifted it to the sky as he turned swiftly to locate his injured opponent. As the young man recoiled in agony, staring up into rays of sunlight whilst holding a hand to his throat, he noticed how swift a longsword blade came down against his shoulder.

And then he was giddy; a numbness wreaking his left side, his legs unsteady and his feet slipping. At first his blurred vision only noticed the speckled red covering the long, green grass below. But then, lying next to his feet was his severed arm. After seeing his enemy fall, Vlad would have ended the young man's agony, but wielding his longsword again above his head, saw another soldier come from behind.

And another Turk was running at him, the slope of the field providing momentum.

Vlad met the Turkish sword with his own just in time and quickly thrust the cross-guard up into his enemy's face; the soldier dazed easily without the usual protective lapels from a metal collar. Unlike most, this soldier was scantily dressed for battle. And now, as Vlad's boot met the man's groin, the soldier's turban tumbled into the long grass. He raced forward to pierce his longsword's blade through the grounded soldier's throat, but another Turk was on his back.

Maybe it was the advantage of height he had on the Turk or just sheer power from his turn, but Vlad felt his longsword rattle the circular sword of his next opponent and dislodge it from the soldier's hand. Bemused and frozen, his enemy just stood there – the man evidently petrified at losing his weapon. And so Vlad took his opportunity, stepping heavily forward to thrust his longsword into the soldier's feebly protected stomach. But as his longsword lodged deeply into his screaming opponent, he noticed another soldier already upon him. Surely he could not free his weapon in time?

Using his longsword, Vlad motioned the stabbed soldier just in time to block the other. And thrusting the stabbed soldier forward, together he knocked both of the Turk's back, the uninjured now hindered by the weight of his dying comrade. But then from the corner of his eye, Vlad again noticed danger. Another Turk was running toward him, his curved sword wielded above his head, the soldier frantically yelling foreign dialogue. Perturbed at seeing his longsword still lodged through the stabbed soldier's spine, he noticed the Turk beneath trying anxiously to free himself.

Matching the frenzied approach of the oncoming soldier, Vlad rushed unarmed towards his enemy, he too yelling words of offense. Such fury confused his opponent enough to give him time to cower and swiftly collect a thick branch from the long grass. And just as his opponent's sword swung down at Vlad, he held the branch between outstretched hands so it met the enemy weapon. Before the soldier could grimace to feel his blade lodge deep in the soft wood, Vlad had slid with legs outstretched, his boots catching the man's ankles to take the Turk's feet from under him. He heard his opponent holler as he hit ground, but knew the soldier would soon try to defend himself. And so he raced to fall on the man, the branch held between his hands now used to crush the soldier's throat. Vlad swapped hands for feet and as he stood on the branch feeling the man's windpipe collapse, he pulled free the Turkish sword. He looked at it for a second, observing the darker tone of metal and the decoration of its handle. But then Vlad noticed the soldier (whom he had grounded earlier) had rolled his dead comrade aside and was scrambling to his feet. At seeing the dead soldier's body pivot against his impeded longsword, he strode through the mud to retrieve his weapon but looked upon the Turkish one already at hand. From one enraged swing, Vlad felt the tip of the foreign weapon plunge deep into the Turk's head; the area about his right ear erupting with blood, the soldier's face and shoulder soon coated blood red.

He placed his boot against the head of the agonised soldier, his weight pivoted to pull free the weapon. Deafened by the noisy battle surrounding him, Vlad could only feel the sickening crack of splintered bone as the tip of the curved blade was wretched from the soldier's cranium. After watching his enemy collapse, Vlad scrutinised the weapon again, but had never took such things as souvenirs. However he was now curious to how it had been made. He knew the Turks produced these curved swords to aide battle on horseback, but now their weapons were slightly heavier, more robust – composed of some bronzed coloured metal. And why decorate them so elaborately just for one purpose? Or was it like his longsword – a prized possession for a prince, a lord or boyar? He looked at his last kill with distain – surely that had been none of any?

Thinking of weaponry, Vlad again wondered to the whereabouts of his valued longsword; the one he had reclaimed from his dying father many months ago. Well in truth, it had been found by Henrik; his second-in-command and closest friend had brought it back with saddled possessions found from one of their scouts – one who after returning from his father's realm, had fallen from his horse after taking a barrage of enemy arrows. The unfortunate scout had hardly become adult, but was determined to prove himself, scouting north to return with news about his great father.

Vlad searched the edge of the woodland and the fields about him, observing the brutality of battle. Like a lot of the foreign soldiers he had slain, the scout had been just as young, but Vlad was baffled to why many did not resemble Turks.

As valuable seconds allowed him take pause, Vlad remembered being like the unfortunate scout – a boy always wanting to prove himself – but not to the Turks. He wanted to honour his father and uphold the Order of the Dragon, to preserve their Christian ways, to defend their land and the people in its realm… to defy the barbaric and callous beliefs of the Ottoman Empire. The endless battles he had fought and bloodshed he had seen had almost turned his head – his sanity an ever-constant worry to his beloved Jusztina. But those bastards were merciless – the Turks had been a torment since childhood. It was haunting for him and his brother (as boys) to have been bought up by such creed. And now he was revolted by them, found them disgusting – was determined to eradicate such vermin from all Wallachia. Maybe it was this tormented past that made him fight on so brave and strong – his father blackmailed into surrendering him and his brother (as young boys) to establish peace – his constant fight to keep Christian belief alive and honour his father. Or was it now, he had his own family to protect?

His mind ached from contesting thoughts, his heavily perspired body now cooling below his armour, beads of running sweat soaking his undergarments. But Vlad's mind reached beyond memories and turned to curiosity. How did Henrik manage to scavenge his father's sword from the young scout? Why did the enemy not pilfer his prized weapon beforehand? Strange that he had never questioned Henrik about it, as the Turk's should have known the handle engraving. But how speechless had he been to first hold it aloft and twist it in the sunlight.

And so he located his longsword, its cross-guard almost up against the stomach of its last execution, its blade jutting out from the dead Turk's spine. Vlad glanced up after retrieving his prized possession, and after searching for Henrik amongst his battling, fellow men, knew his past question would have to wait.

After slicing his way through many assailants with his father's trusty longsword, Vlad reached a ridge on the long-grass field to observe the battle below. Stepping up onto a low-lying branch of an aged chestnut tree, he pulled himself high to see at better height. He could not detect Henrik amongst the countless number of bouts that raged below, but found his mind drifting again.

Why was it that this beautiful and serene land had become host to such brutality, his loyal Wallachian men outnumbered and accosted by such merciless invaders, their foreign weapons increasingly strong and their faces younger, somewhat dissimilar to Turks? But the Ottoman Empire had been ever expanding; taking border settlements by strength, pushing not only north and west towards the Hungarian King, but also lands east and north along the coasts of the Black Sea?

It grieved him to remember the Turkish conquest of many cities along the River Danube; the fortresses and castles that once protected his precious, prosperous lands south and east, now seized, captured by the dirty hands of the Ottoman Empire. And now these bastards crawled over his fertile, bountiful farmland and river settlements, spreading their disease like locusts eating away at tender crops, leaving pastures and farmland infertile, killing and pilfering as they went. And as the Moldavian King, the Hungarian King, and all allied boyars dithered to help, it was up to him and his loyal men to prevent the son of Sultan Mehmet capturing anymore of Wallachia.

Vlad stepped back just in time to prevent a Turkish blade from slicing the arm that balanced him. Unsteady at first, he then lunged forward to notice the usual dirty face of a Turk grimace at finding his sickle-like sword lodged deep into the bark of the tree. Vlad took his advantage swiftly and wielded his longsword from behind, lifting it up into the air and down against his enemy. The Turk screamed as he stumbled back, realizing his right hand still held the wedged sword but was detached from his arm. And he stared in horror to see blood emptying his body from his wrist, the shock somehow overwhelming the agony. But then he recoiled to stumble against protruding roots of the tree; a thick, red liquid pumping out of his gaping wound and squirting about him before he fell.

Quickly relieved to see his enemy disabled, Vlad leapt forward to stand tall again upon the low-lying tree branch, his eyes searching the battlefield below. It was then that he noticed Henrik; his second-in-command struggling to eliminate several Turks. His friend needed help. But so did many others.

Vlad raced down the slope of the lush field, his feet sometimes slipping against the wet blades of long grass, but his precious longsword was poised for action, its weight balancing him as he ran. And he was just in time to reach Henrik – his friend oblivious of the danger behind – fighting only a Turk in front. Vlad yelled at the top of his lungs but Henrik barely heard his call. It was not until he had disposed of the Turk sufficiently that Henrik turned at recognising Vlad's voice. But still the second-in-command was unaware of the danger behind, and Vlad could see that soldiers were almost upon him.

It was the tip of Vlad's longsword that caught the Turkish weapon just in time, and although its tip stabbed into Henrik's shoulder-plated armour, the foreign blade did not pierce flesh. Feeling the clash of metal against his back, Henrik span around to see the weapons fall. Henrik stood aghast to first watch Vlad's longsword pull down the curved blade, but then regarded the scowling Turk who held it. Henrik sprang into action as though propelled by fear, his own longsword swinging from below his knee and up between the soldier's legs. As Henrik felt the longsword blade slice deep into the Turks groin, he observed his screaming opponent for a second before Vlad dashed across him. Puzzled at knowing the enemy was hurt, Henrik span around to see why Vlad had rushed past so hastily. For Henrik, it happened all too quick, but seeing the decapitated head fly over his shoulder, again he realized he owed his life to Vlad – not only his Lord and the Prince of Wallachia, but his long-time friend.

He had hardly raised an eyebrow to thank Vlad for his Lord's timeliness as another assailant sprang from behind. But this time the soldier bypassed Henrik to get to Vlad. As the Turk raced passed Henrik, wielding his sword ready to inflict damage, Henrik swung his longsword at the Turkish blade. But as both weapons clashed and swung to the ground, Henrik's longsword snapped in two. Within seconds the Turk's face changed from astonishment to a wicked grin, revealing that he had gained some lucky advantage. But as Henrik looked aghast from his broken weapon to establish the Turk's next move, the soldier just stood paralysed like some frozen statue. It was not until he watched Vlad's blade withdraw from the soldier's stomach that Henrik again realized how quick-witted Vlad had been.

'Behind you my Lord,' Henrik screamed. 'Watch out!'

Vlad turned whilst dislodging his longsword and caught his new assailant just in time. However, the body of the wounded Turk fell on Henrik and together they fell upon the long grass. Unarmed and with the flailing soldier on top of him, Henrik panicked to find some weapon to slay the aggrieved enemy. Pushing his opponent away, Henrik reached for his broken longsword, but found it out of reach. He glanced back at the Turk who crawled at his side, wondering if the soldier had some other weapon. But then, as the Turk pulled himself up, his head level with Henrik's chest, he noticed the tip of a longsword blade eject out of the Turk's throat and scrape Henrik's breast plate. Abruptly as blood squirted upon Henrik, he glanced at Vlad; his commander now levering his weapon to throw the enemy body aside.

Henrik wiped blood trails from his face to see an outstretched hand offering help. 'So how many times has my Lord saved me now?' Henrik gasped as Vlad pulled him to his feet. 'If it not be for such weak swords, we'd be cutting them down easy.'

'It not just be our weapons, my dear Henrik,' Vlad announced, his eyes directing his friends to observe the battle around them, 'but it be numbers. And many of these are young men, and ones indifferent to the usual foe.'

'What do you mean by that my Lord?'

'Foreign men, young men,' Vlad explained, his temper flaring. 'These are not soldiers sent by the Sultan, or marched across southern borders from the Ottoman Empire… these we fight here have bright eyes… lighter or darker skins… speak with a different tongue.'

Henrik watched Vlad clean the blade of his longsword against the cloth of a dead body and then point his weapon at the enemy soldier's face. Henrik stepped closer to look down Vlad's sword and observe his Lord's proclamation.

'Yes my Lord,' Henrik agreed, his lungs still gasping for air. 'I have noticed it in battles of late also, but kept quiet… tried not to arouse suspicion.'

'You think wisely my good man!' Vlad stated admiringly, patting Henrik on the shoulder. 'Our men battle hard enough and do not need such uncertainty clouding their minds.'

'But the numbers they battle my Lord,' Henrik scowled to find his weapon, returning his eyes to Vlad to show sincerity. 'Our men talk nothing more of how they are outnumbered, and so how do I convince them to battle on?'

'They know the consequence if battles are lost,' Vlad snubbed his nose away from his friend's eyes of concern to observe the battlefield. 'They fight like me… for their loved ones, families, land, their religion… their lives!'

'And with what,' Henrik shoved his broken sword onto his commander's chest-plate, 'if we have not the toughest of weapons and the Ottoman enemy increase, then what?' Henrik's voice tamed in ferocity as Vlad turned to reveal his annoyance. 'Neither of our neighbouring allies assure us of any assistance?'

'Then pick up that weapon and use it against the enemy,' Vlad scoffed, knocking Henrik's broken longsword from his chest-plate before pointing at the Turkish sickle next to the recently killed soldier. 'Until our craftsmen match the skills of our enemies… then use that!'

'I will not use a weapon forged by our filthy enemy,' Henrik stated adamantly. 'It does not go well with our… belief.'

'Then you be a stupid man, and a dead one at that,' Vlad chuckled at first but soon came serious. 'There be no victory on any battlefield if one be dead. It is our minds that keep us safe, not our arrogance.'

'But our weapons need to be as robust, my Lord.' Henrik grasped Vlad's hand and raised it to hold high his commander's longsword. 'We need more forged from the magic of your father!'

'We be working on that my comrade,' Vlad snatched away his hand to walk over to the dead soldier and retrieve the Turkish weapon. 'Up until then, we fight like the animals they be and beat them at their own game.' Vlad swapped his longsword for the sickle sword and after strolling over, pushed his prized weapon against Henrik's chest. 'Use mine if you be too arrogant to wield theirs!'

'But this be your Lord's weapon,' Henrik pulled it out from his chest to admire. 'And one used only by your father… it be engraved with emblems of the Order of the Dragon?'

'It may be forged for the Prince of Wallachia, but what be a weapon if not used for battle?' Vlad's hand clasped his friends to grip the sword tight. Henrik then followed Vlad's eyes as they opened wide with alarm. 'It was one that you saved from our enemy… and one you need to use it now!'

Henrik felt Vlad push him away as a sickle sword came between them. And after stabilising his balanced, Henrik took the opportunity to wield his Lord's nostalgic weapon at the Turk's back. However, he did not appreciate the fine metal of the precious weapon until he swung again and felt its weight cut through the soldier's neck like a knife through butter. Henrik ignored to watch the Turk's head bounce within the blades of long grass; he was too enthralled by the heavy but nimble longsword, swivelling his wrists to again hold it high and admire it against the low morning sunlight.

'We'd cut through these bastards, no matter how many, should all our men have these.'

'Get used to it my friend,' Vlad chuckled. 'Soon I will see that all our men take advantage of such weapons.' He stepped toward the soldier Henrik had just slain, and before retrieving another sickle sword from the dead man's hand, pointed towards the main fight. 'As I told you before my good friend, I am no leader and therefore no Prince without an army to defend me. And I fight with the same reason as they do… to keep our lands free of the Ottoman vermin.' Henrik watched Vlad swing a sickle sword in each hand so their blades clashed together over his head. 'And I'll use whatever comes to hand. I'll fight fire against fire if need be to match them at their own game.'

Henrik watched Vlad race forward, knowing his intention was to join the main battle. And so Henrik followed.

The second-in-command watched his master slice through Turkish soldiers with unmatchable strength, carving at their limbs with their own forged weapons, leaving Henrik to terminate the maimed and fallen. As they caught up with an outnumbered line of his men, Vlad dived and rolled like a ball, his newly discovered weapons light enough to slash at the enemy's heels. And with Henrik following immediately to cut the injured down, the Wallachian line of men advanced somewhat.

Vlad sprung from the long grass to stand tall and dispose of surrounding enemy soldiers, pausing to hear Henrik approve on approach.

'An eye for an eye,' Henrik barked. 'A tooth for a tooth as you wishes to say...'

But Henrik stopped before he could appraise Vlad. He was puzzled at why the line of Turks had suddenly retreated; not just backing away but running down the gradual slope. Maybe it was just to regroup – some tactic the Turkish army had invented to collate men from disbanded groups? But Vlad knew of no Turkish ploy.

Vlad stood at the front line with Henrik and his other men, all bewildered to see the enemy retreat. Many Wallachian men started jeering the enemy on their withdrawal, pointing their longswords to the sky whilst calling the Turks small, dirty cowards and other profanity. Others behind slowly caught up with their fellow men; their time taken by either slaying injured enemy soldiers or nursing fellow wounded.

Henrik looked at Vlad. His Lord was baffled as much as he was. Then he witnessed fellow men joining him from behind. His garrison had lost numbers, but not as many as he had first dreaded. He turned back to observe Vlad again and saw the terror in his eyes.

As the last line of retreating swordsmen parted, Henrik too stood in horror to see revealed a wall of archers slowly walking towards them with bows poised and arrows ready to fire.

TWO

After seeing the last of the Turkish swordsmen retreat behind a line of advancing archers, Vlad rushed toward Henrik. Knowing the enemy were quite close, he perceived that arrows fired would penetrate his men at chest height and so pulled his second-in-command to the ground. Vlad turned upon his back to shout at the top of his voice, commanding his men to take cover. But as enemy arrows took flight, he grimaced to see many of his Wallachian men still standing. From Vlad's order the nearest of his men had taken cover and those close behind crouched in fear, their faces baffled by the sudden action of their comrade's. However, most that followed or near the rear were still marching on foot, their eyes apprehensive and mouths agape, all wondering to why the enemy swordsmen had withdrawn?

Although somewhat hushed, Vlad heard an assemblage of arrows fly past and within seconds saw the result of their passing. It was the first of the standing that took the main assault. Although protected by shields, axes and swords, the nearest standing line of the Wallachian soldiers took face or chest damage. Many collapsed through injury, just their limbs impeded by arrows, but some fell from severe or fatal damage. And as those who had survived were helped by comrades nearby, Vlad anticipated another onslaught; the archers already lowering their bows to reload as they trudged on.

After the first attack most men cowered to the ground, aiding those injured but also sheltering behind those less fortunate. Many dug their swords and shields into the ground – a quick manoeuvre of self-defence. But with the line of archers advancing and now ready to fire again, any escape – even a run to the cover of the surrounding woodland – could end in injury, or death.

Vlad grimaced to watch another onslaught of arrows accost his men. Many were protected by their swift actions, but some fell; the rear soldiers finding their lower body impeded by arrows, their legs and feet ruptured and disabled. But now somewhat wise to the timely onslaught of arrows, many of Vlad's swordsmen advanced cautiously, sheltering nervously behind their shields or whatever was at hand.

Vlad tensed to watch another fray of arrows take flight and his mind pained with anxiety, or was it, anguish? He, Henrik and the nearest of his swordsmen were not close enough to render an attack upon the archers. And if they did, were fellow swordsmen hiding close behind, ready to spring out and defend them?

The only chance was to split the garrison. Whilst the archers reloaded, two groups would run for the cover of woodlands either side. He would take one group and Henrik the other. And once regrouped in the cover of trees, each group could wait for the archers to be near. As the slope down from either woodland would provide a swift advantage on foot, each army could pierce the line of archers from either side. And should they escape to the woodland, a few of Vlad's swordsmen could pick them off by surprise – jump them from the trees. It was an idea, but would it work?

Vlad watched another line of arrows fly past. It had to be done.

He ran to Henrik to tell of his plan, enticing nearby men to follow and listen, all the time knowing that they would be vulnerable once the archers had reloaded. And now being so near, the archers could pick off his men explicitly.

As soon as Vlad saw another onslaught of arrows fly past, he yelled to command his men to follow; as did Henrik his group. Each grounded but able man raced for the woodland nearest to them, leaving the rear part of Vlad's garrison to fend for themselves. The rear soldiers trudged on vigilantly, pulling the injured into the safety of the group as they went, picking up shields and armour from the dead or wounded for added defence. The archers marched toward the larger group of Vlad's men. He, hidden behind a wide tree trunk, anxiously watched the enemy's course of action. From afar, he could not see Henrik in the opposite woodland, but knew he'd be awaiting Vlad's attack.

Vlad grimaced to watch the archers test the distance to his soldiers, arrows now falling against shields held out as protection. But to grasp the best opportunity, he had to wait for the archers to be level. And as he had expected, after observing the line of archers draw level, swordsmen were following, scattered behind for both protection and defence. But a gap had developed between them, and it was this that provided Vlad's best opportunity. Another fray of arrows accosted the marching garrison, and although protected by a barrier of shields, some fell. Vlad gripped his sword anxiously, his jaws clenched and teeth grinding, his eyes wavering to count how many of his men were now poised on the edge of each woodland. Just a little more time he strained – await the next fly of arrows to hit ground.

And then came the opportunity; the gap between Turkish archer and swordsman was level between him and Henrik.

Vlad's swordsmen followed in the rage he exemplified, but as the slope hastened their approach, they silenced as to improve the surprise of attack. And with his heart pumping again from fury and exhilaration, he grinned to notice Henrik's group now charging the archers from the other side. Some held back the Turkish swordsmen with shield and axe, but most of each group attacked the rear of the archers, cutting through the line between them until Vlad could see a smirk of triumph on Henrik's face. But as Vlad recoiled to take thought and relief from exhaustion, he noticed enemy reinforcements gathering behind.

It was the long, straight branches of the pine trees that that gave him the first idea. And now seeing spears scattered about the battlefield (like the ones the Turks used to spike heads), he could see them as the best weapon against the sword – the short reach of the Turkish hand along with their circular blade would be no match for the thrust of such a long and spiked pole. After watching escaping archers flee to the ambush set for them in the nearby woodlands, Vlad picked up a spear, and after replacing his sword in its sheath, started to rush the gathering line of enemy soldiers.

Somewhat exhausted, Henrik stood tall to gather breath, but sniggered to watch enemy archers flee about him – Vlad's covert plan had worked! It was then that Henrik turned in surprise to observe his commander carrying a spear and marching toward an increasing line of enemy soldiers. After looking bemused at one another, Henrik and surrounding Wallachian men searched the bloodshed field to find any other similar spears. And within a minute Vlad was joined by Henrik and a line of Wallachian soldiers; his men marching alongside their Lord, all with comparable, makeshift weapons. And again, as they approached the enemy line with spears extended, Henrik realized Vlad was taking advantage of the disordered enemy – that his Lord had seen no Turkish leaders present. And even before Vlad yelled to run with spear outstretched, Henrik had followed suit, knowing his master's plan.

As Vlad, Henrik and a line of spear-fortified men pierced deep into the disorderly Turks, he was relieved to see that his rear garrison had caught up, his swordsmen cutting down any remaining archers. He grimaced to watch some of his men take injury either minor or fatal, but observing the battlefield as a whole, Vlad noticed the enemy depleting. And slowly, he was winning.

It was not until he heard the jeers from his men that Vlad stood tall to take breath. And instead of stabbing at the enemy with his makeshift spear, he used it to lean against to watch Turks flee. A sudden rush of energy burst through his veins as he sensed victory. And feeling his anxiety and anger both climaxes, he lifted his makeshift weapon to impale a lumbering Turk and release his kept emotion. Vlad shook his fist to the sky and ridiculed the Turks as small men and big cowards – a race of twisted foreigners following a jilted religion.

'This'll be one victory the Sultan will not be pleased with my Lord,' Henrik spun Vlad round by his shoulder to see anger and tears in his commander's eyes. 'They'll have picked off many through the trees too… I saw many flee that way, as you said.'

Vlad calmed from his overwhelming joy of success but felt exhaustion taking a toile on him.

'It'll be a stout victory that be sure, and one that'll be celebrated,' Vlad needed to take breath. 'But please my good man,' he too held onto Henrik's shoulder, 'check the horses and be sure none of the enemy has ruined our ride back.'

'I left a number of good swordsmen to defend them and keep them quiet my Lord,' Henrik gritted his teeth anxiously, but soon a grin revealed the white of his teeth. 'I'm sure our ride back will be unhindered after such a victory as this.'

'You may want to celebrate success early my good man.' Vlad started to trudge uphill where he saw axemen jeering success on the edge of woodland. 'It'll be good for them as they deserve it if not more… but let us ride to safety first.'

Henrik followed Vlad up the slope of long grass towards the woodland and stopped his master half way.

'It still doesn't make it any easier you know my Lord,' Henrik looked troublesome as he again pulled Vlad back by his shoulder. 'Every battle is getting harder as there are more to defeat. And as you said my Lord, many be different to the usual Turk?'

'There maybe more,' Vlad put a hand over Henrik's after removing his gauntlet, 'but we be taller and stronger than any of them.' He paused before a smile stretched across his face.

'But today we've battled in the sight of our Lord and He has blessed us with victory. For this we shall pray unto Him on our return… and in special celebration so we be again so fortunate in battle.'

'Our Lord has indeed blessed you with a gift,' Henrik paused after seeing his master puzzled by his comment.

'What do you mean Henrik?'

'That you have been gifted with a great mind, one that helps to do battle.' Henrik followed as his master paced on. 'That tactics you use never fail to amaze me.' He saw Vlad glance at him inquisitively but continued uphill to the woodland. 'To split the garrison and take the archers from the side and behind…'

'That's just knowing, how these idiots fight,' Vlad chuckled loud. 'My time with them as a young soldier is all that I need to draw on to plan battle.' He stopped Henrik on the edge of the woodland. 'Should they not choose to change tactics after all these years, then be it I will know their ways… help me to kill them… and kill them all I will.'

From horseback Vlad glanced behind to notice how weary his trailing soldiers were. But it was important to keep what horses they had to carry weaponry, food and water; only he and Henrik rode up front and alongside each other to navigate their way back home. But Poenari castle was at least another day's travel, even if they cut across country and camped only after nightfall.

Since the battle that early morning, they had travelled miles northwest and Vlad was feeling the sweet, heavy air of late summer slumber his mind and body. Maybe they should turn off the main route to follow the River Argeş north and bypass the city of Curtea-de-Argeş; a shortcut through gorges and woodland may well provide more cover. By avoiding major towns, he could prevent enemy scouts from knowing his whereabouts, or any publicity of his return home. Vlad took several deep breaths, anger stirring his thoughts. But this was his land, his country, so why should he? And although he again felt he had been out in the wilderness too long, he secretly admired the countryside. It was just that now his enemies denied him true governance of Wallachia, that somehow its beauty had been stained. And why now did he come across as such a hard-hearted leader, treating the men like cattle although he knew he'd be nothing without them. This bloody war was taking too much of his time. Maybe it had already taken its toile on him.

He glanced around again at the sullen faces of soldiers who had won an arduous battle; men like him who had loved ones, children and relatives – family and friends who could only pray for their safe return. And although thrilled by such a gallant victory, Vlad's thoughts turned somber to think of Jusztina and Mihnea. All he wanted to do was embrace his wife and son. It had been no more than a month since he had ridden out to battle, but knowing how fast his son was growing, it seemed like an eternity. But at least Mihnea was growing up fit and strong, and a Christian like him who maybe a king himself one day.

Vlad's thoughts were severed by a call from behind. Henrik too, riding alongside and half asleep, snapped into action. As they turned around together, both could see one soldier point to the roadside ahead. Although on horseback and having the advantage of height, both commanders thought nothing of the scene but regarded the objects as large, oval-shaped stones spaced some similar distance apart. But as they drew near, men from close behind ran toward to what now resembled heads.

Indeed, they were heads of injured men buried alive to die, their whole bodies weighted by the earth, only their mouths left above ground to gasp at air for a slow death. And these were Vlad's men, Wallachian soldiers captured by the Turks. Vlad knew the Turks took no captives, even if a reward was known; prisoners would only grow hungry and crave their thirst.

'A number of these are barely alive my Lord,' a man scouting the scene ahead turned to announce.

'Then pull them out!' Vlad commanded. 'These be men of our good Lord… We'll tend these soldiers back to health so that they may fight another day!'

'My Lord,' Henrik turned to ask, 'what about those more unfortunate?'

'Pull them out. Put them for proper burial,' Vlad instructed, but looked up at the sky to notice dusk was already upon them. 'We'll take camp soon. We'll check as far as they go and…' He paused to cough in spasms.

'Are you alright my Lord?' Henrik asked.

'Yes, my good man.' Vlad wiped the phlegm from his gauntlet onto his trouser, his lungs easing. 'It's just that all this… it disgusts me.'

'What do you mean my Lord?'

'Why should Turks bury our men in such a barbaric way?' Vlad outstretched both palms to show admission. 'We end our enemy pains in such a more deliberate but direct way?'

'Would you be sure of that, my Lord?' Henrik's nose twitched as he questioned Vlad, not knowing his master's reaction. 'Tools have been used to…'

'To interrogate yes,' Vlad interrupted, 'only when such methods can be useful and save the lives of such as these.' Vlad pointed to the men been dug out of their involuntary graves, but recalled his history to keep law and order. 'It be punishment that keep these men loyal and in good order, but it be justified and I feed them well… not like how those bastards of the Ottoman Empire treat all.'

'Yes, I guess that be true,' Henrik looked down in sympathy at one of their men been dragged to a cart after receiving water. 'Maybe it because we keep them strong and loyal, that they survive ordeals such as this?'

'And so, my good friend,' Vlad turned his head from the scene to face Henrik, 'would you be so bold as to tell why these bastards punish our men in such a way? Is it something of their religion, as I not know of any such method?'

'I not know to be sure my Lord,' Henrik admitted, 'but I hear from villagers about a superstition of the enemy, or maybe it is just to spite us or to ridicule your rule, but it be to make our people – their enemy – suffer more before death.'

'Excuse me for interrupting, my Grace,' a soldier intervened as he held the neck of Henrik's horse, 'I hear it be an old superstition where the earth prevents the soul from leaving the body and so not be able to haunt its murderer beyond death.'

'To me it be sounding like our enemy has indeed lost their plot,' Henrik scolded. 'What utter superstitious rubbish!'

'I know one thing be sure,' Vlad interjected, a determination in his voice after watching more men dragged from the roadside to be buried suitably, 'I will avenge their ways with such a more wicked atrocity… I will… I shall spike them high in the air and let their souls come haunt me… just let them try!'

'But my Lord,' Henrik stated, 'you be remembering me argue that, although bought up by them, you agreed not to be anything like them… that in your heart you not become like the enemy… and not to be as you put it… as such low vermin?'

'Yes, and I be Christian in faith above all.' Vlad nudged Henrik forcibly. 'It be a good thing I have thee to steady my mind – seeing too much of this bloodshed somewhat wavers me beyond approach.' Vlad winked an eye at Henrik before digging his heels into his horse's flanks to trot on. 'But should our Lord turn a blind eye, I shall avenge equal to this stupid superstition.'

THREE

Since taking up camp at the break of dawn, Vlad's garrison had marched north along valleys cradling the River Argeş and through forestry pathways leading to the foothills of the Făgăraş mountain range. He had wanted to keep inconspicuous and not alert any subversive occupants of Curtea-de-Argeş, but Vlad had required food and water plus medical supplies for the injured. So with a number of his best men, he had ventured covertly through the crowded city to gather supplies, asking himself to why he should have to roam warily through settlements in the beauty of his own land. Yes, taxes were high, but surely residence knew this was just – the constant war against the Ottoman Empire required monies – surely the people of his land understood this – how else could he pay soldiers to provide protection?

The halt of his horse took him away from his thoughts of Curtea-de-Argeş; Vlad now wondering to why soldiers up ahead had stopped to talk amongst themselves. After leaving the city mid-afternoon, Vlad again had become weary and so rode the garrison through Corbeni and Arefu at steady pace, knowing that they should reach the shelter of Poenari fortress before nightfall. And as the long shadows from the setting sun had disappeared to reveal a more prominent darkness, Vlad was annoyed to see his men stall just before dusk. Beyond a forest clearing, some distance ahead of the garrison, Vlad knew that leading soldiers should be able to see the walls of the fortress. So what was the delay?

Along with Henrik, Vlad galloped to the head of the stalled garrison to see what the delay was.

'My men,' Vlad announced, as he passed his soldiers, all lined in three, 'we should be making haste. Our fortress is no more than a mile away. It should be visible, high above the Argeş?' He slowed his horse to a trot as he reached the front of the garrison. 'Is the river impassable from heavy rains… can we not take the bridge?'

'No, my Lord,' one soldier shouted back, 'but we see a stranger at our door.' 'What does he mean?' Henrik questioned, catching up to be alongside Vlad.

'There be others at the gate,' the soldier added, 'a small garrison of about thirty… maybe forty men?'

'And they be not one of ours,' another soldier told. 'They not be any of our scouting parties, that'll be sure!'

'Be quiet,' Vlad commanded. 'We march on in silence and under cover until we reach the river. And then, if need be, we'll cross the river in secret.'

'My Lord,' Henrik asked as he troubled to steady his horse alongside, 'will we be able to identify them before having to cross the river?'

'I hope so,' Vlad spoke. 'I not pretend that my eyes are as good as yours Henrik, or that of any of these men.' Vlad paused before cantering his horse ahead to lead the garrison. 'I hear that ingenious instruments are being made in far lands that could help in such a task.'

From leaving the garrison in the cover of nearby woodland, Vlad and Henrik rode cautiously out along the shore of the river to capture a clear view of their visitors. Rightly so, with nightfall almost upon them, the gatekeeper asked for verification again and several fire torches were set alight to reveal their identity. It was when the firelight revealed the emblem draped from the leading horse that Vlad gasped in disbelief.

'In the name of God, and my father,' Vlad murmured, 'it cannot be?'

'Cannot be who, my Lord,' Henrik squinted, using his hand to shield his eyes from flickering moonlight reflected from the river. 'I cannot make out the man on the leading horse, apart that he be fair headed?'

'But you not recognize the emblem… the insignia below the leader's saddle?' Vlad prompted, but saw that Henrik became even more anxious. 'You not see that it be the same on the sword you found me… my father's sword… the crest of the Order of the Dragon?'

'Then that'll be a messenger with news of…' Henrik deduced, his face slowly changing from surprise to confusion. 'Your father… Vlad Dracul… but isn't he…?'

'Fair headed you say?' Vlad smirked as not hearing Henrik. 'It is not just a messenger!' Slowly his smile wilted as squinting eyes narrowed to see more clearly. 'I'll be crushed by Heaven and Earth should that be Radu… my brother!'

'I thought he had been tainted by Turks and so stop under their rule?'

'No, he be not,' Vlad declared softly. 'We were both taken by the Turks so that father keep peace… a sacrifice for peace, father bestow.' Vlad's voice grew strong from rising anger. 'I told you of our history – of what became of us and why we separated – that we both promised to rid ourselves of such filth!'

'And now *he* be free to bring news of your father?' Henrik probed delicately. 'How am I to know that,' Vlad ridiculed, trying to hide the fear of being told the truth and how to deal with his father's death should rumors be true. 'I not see Radu since I escaped the dirty hands of our enemy.'

'But now, he be free also?'

'It must be so,' Vlad did best to hide mixed emotions, 'and must have gathered belongings to father… raised a garrison… maybe that be only some of it?'

'But Hungarian scouts rumored your father to have been assassinated,' Henrik professed softly and carefully, 'along with your brother Mircea, who had been buried alive… subjugated by rival nobles in Târgoviste.'

'I refuse to believe that,' Vlad snapped. 'How could simple nobles… boyars of our country take away their sovereign king and a prominent prince?'

'But you know the dubious power of our own boyars,' Henrik quizzed, 'not just in Poenari, but the settlements we've passed these weeks gone by.'

'I will entertain my brother and hear the tales he has to tell,' Vlad exclaimed pointing his index finger, 'but until I get answers from Târgoviste myself, I shall believe that my father be still alive… and so my eldest brother!'

'But how can you go on to believe as such, if they died years…?'

'He was only ill with fever…' Vlad interrupted angrily, 'the curse in battling this Ottoman Empire.' Vlad whipped back his horse's reins before darting away. 'If my father be dead, it will be recorded somewhere… for he was like his father, Mircea the Old, a great Wallachian voivode… a King!'

Vlad stopped his horse not far from the old slab bridge that spanned the valley escarpments on which the fortress stood, annoyed to see a man pounding the outer wall gate with the butt of his longsword. Noticing Henrik draw alongside, Vlad pondered on recognizing his younger brother; was this truly Radu the Fair? However, Vlad slowly identified a few men in the garrison, elderly soldiers who had fought alongside his father. Vlad's wavering thoughts were interrupted by Henrik.

'Is it him, my Lord?'

'I cannot be telling,' Vlad admitted and actioned his horse to trot on. 'We must get the garrison home before nightfall, so there be only one way to tell. I will see them for myself.'

'Then I'll head back to fetch the garrison.'

'It is Radu, I be sure… a little older so having less a pretty face.' Vlad disclosed, but his mind strained to think of the past and spoke aloud. 'My boy is nearly five and has never seen his brother.' Vlad rode on after seeing Henrik turn back. 'How has it come that defending this realm has taken up so much time, could my good Lord answer that?'

As Vlad slowly trotted towards his visitors, questions again came to mind. Maybe, like Henrik proposed, Radu was here to confirm his ill father's death and the untimely demise of his elder brother.

Yet what did Henrik know of *his* family? Yes, he was his closest friend and second-in-command, but like himself,

Henrik had been subjugated to the disorientation of warfare. Maybe optimism had become something Henrik lacked? After experiencing so many years of bloodshed, and having no loving wife or child to comfort in, maybe his friend *was* stupefied. However, Vlad could not question the loyalty of his man-at-arms, but what of his brother – someone he had not seen for years? Was Radu still of Orthodox Christianity, or had he been succumbed to the conviction of the Ottoman Empire? Optimism again, Vlad thought; positive news to eradicate all rumors about his murdered father and brother?

Vlad rode close to within sight of his gatekeeper. He could now see clear his aggravated brother. Yes, Radu had aged somewhat since their days in captivity, but after seeing him remove his helmet, he still looked the untainted, childlike blonde, whose hair now blew long from a stiff night breeze. By appearance he was still the same man – the fair-haired younger brother who had suffered years with him under Ottoman rule – the Turks teaching them how to fight in hope that they acquiesce to their demented values. But unlike Vlad, had his brother's heart changed? Although perturbed again by many mixed emotion, Vlad thought again of optimism, and to this he galloped forward to greet, what could be, his only remaining brother.

It was a tactic he had learned from the Turks; dismounting his horse as it galloped to reach the garrison, but held onto the saddle as if flying alongside. Finally, as he reached Radu, Vlad flung from his horse and caught the ground on foot; running with reins in hand until his weight slowed the horse to stop.

'It has been some years past since I gazed upon that mop of fair hair,' Vlad announced loudly, a chuckle in his voice.

Radu turned from thumping the butt of his longsword handle against the fortified wooden gate to glance over his horse's mane.

'Why dear brother, there you are,' Radu conveyed in a suave dialect that Vlad thought rather eccentric, 'my eldest and most ugly brother… it be what, how many a year since our eyes met?'

Vlad strode forward, but paused to stare pensively at the coat-of-arms that draped over the rear of Radu's horse. Pulled by holding tight the reins of his own horse, Vlad stepped back to study Radu, who after dismounting, was standing with arms outstretched. 'Sorry little brother, I am but surprised by such a visit,' Vlad sighted his father's

insignia now blowing hard on flagged spears pointing overhead. 'We had no delivery of visit or any word by scout?'

'Then a surprise be even more welcoming,' Radu took Vlad in his arms and both patted each other's back hard before separating. 'But you embrace me like an old woman. Have all years of being some Prince made you soft?'

'No, it be you that be soft.' Vlad tested the rigidity of Radu's shoulders and body strength, almost pushing him back against his heels. 'You may well be handsome to fair women, but you not make a soldier in my garrison… for you have no clout!'

'Not all kings or princes need be strong in heart and body,' Radu ridiculed, a strange patois still to his voice, 'but the mind be the most powerful asset – for was it not you who taught me that?'

'Yes, I guess it was,' Vlad pinched the bridge of his nose and massaged the lids of his eyes between thumb and forefinger. For some reason – probably the excitement – he felt nauseous again. 'Pardon me for my pause, but we only just return from battle. It be nearly a month since we slept deep in our own beds. And the enemy grows more.' Vlad hesitated to look down the line of Radu's men; armored soldiers on foot holding shields and sword, but a garrison of not more than fifty at the most. 'It be a long way to come for you also, so how did *you* avoid the enemy?'

'We be taking cover most of the time,' Radu turned his nose high as if royalty. 'And we be having admiral guides to this part of the country. We avoid battle… not just plough into it!'

'I am not the cause of this battle, but defend our realm,' Vlad angered. 'But please young brother,' Vlad restrained feelings of negativity, 'let us dine and talk in comfort for sure we be both weary from travel.' Vlad glanced behind to see Henrik leading his garrison towards them and so needed to enquire quickly.

'But please dear brother, I must ask of the truth concerning father… and Mircea, the eldest?'

'So, I gather you have not been told,' Radu declared slowly as he looked down at his feet. 'It grieves to be the one to tell that father died some year back after suffering an aging fever.' Radu could see by his glistening eyes that Vlad was anxious. 'It was something he caught after battle, he being too old to fight on principle, but you know how stubborn the old mule…'

'And Mircea, he was buried alive?' Vlad interrupted before his garrison arrived. 'Was it our enemy's doing… they buried him as they do the injured?'

'No,' Radu said quietly, 'you may know it a Turkish custom to bury persons alive, but neither died by the hands of the Ottoman Empire. I too have heard stories through war struck lands such as those speaking Hungarian tongue, and the tales come deceived, sometimes perverse.'

Vlad took Radu by his shoulders and shook him, 'It was not the Turkish Sultan who murdered our brother?'

'No, the soldiers of the Ottoman Empire had nothing to do with either death.'

'But our father died because of this bloody war.' Vlad released his brother before turning his face away in disgust.

'Maybe so,' Radu lowered his head to study the muddied earth leading up to the fortress gate, 'but father died by the hands of unruly boyars in Târgoviste, who because of his frailty, murdered him in his sleep.' Radu glanced at Vlad. 'You know not any of this?'

'Only to rumors I have heard from scouts or by travel.'

'Then rumors you hear be true.' Radu coughed before steadying his horse. 'But it should hearten you to know, if only be in resolution, that it was I who implored father to be buried at his keep, and this is from where I have travelled.'

'If this be the truth,' Vlad declared, 'our family may have not been murdered by a Turkish blade, but the war they rage be the reason for such of their death.' Vlad gritted his teeth in anger as Henrik dismounted to join him. 'It be one thing that I do not trust a Turk, but for the Hungarian king to allow his nobles to do such depravity, is unjust.' He stepped close to Radu, enough to feel his brother's breath on him. 'If it be true that father be dead, I will not give up the throne of Wallachia to anyone… come Turk, Hungarian… be it any foreigner!'

'Do not upset yourself so older brother,' Radu patted Vlad's shoulder somewhat affectionately. 'I hear that the King of Moldavia, Stephen the Great, is willing to agree an allegiance and that he should arrange meetings in the eyes of his daughter… as I believe Jusztina is now your wife?'

'Yes, my brother,' Vlad snapped out from his stupor, 'and you must meet her… and our son, Mihnea.' Vlad stepped back to shout instruction for the gate to be opened.

At first there was a lingering quiet as the brothers glanced at one another, but eventually the heavy gate groaned against its hinges as the doors opened inward.

'Things be different now my brother,' Radu told as he mounted his horse to look down at Vlad. 'Maybe we can both redeem our good father's name.'

'It be not just his name I redeem,' Vlad affirmed as he too remounted. 'The Order of the Dragon must be upheld, if only for Wallachia alone.' Vlad looked anxiously at the fire torches alight and to the dark, surrounding wilderness, from where enemy eyes could see. 'We must hasten to be inside; a great supper waits to quench my empty stomach.'

'I hear you had this place built stone by stone for a more resilient defence,' Radu rambled on as he and his garrison followed Vlad through the main gate and past its thick outer wall. 'It looks no stronger than any other keep, let alone a fortress or castle?'

'There be yet many defences to put in place,' Vlad spoke resolutely, examining the high battlements and the arch of the inner wall as he approached it. 'The exertion of this constant war has kept our ideas on paper, but soon they be put in place. And the fortitude of this keep will be something the Turks will underestimate.'

'You must explain your plans my dear brother, so we may offer help.' 'I must first be told of our father's demise, and that of poor Mircea.'

'I am not sure how long we may be able to stay, so you must take advantage of our presence.' Radu dismissed Vlad's request, his wide eyes inspecting the inner walls of the fortress. 'As our father's realm has become somewhat vulnerable, the old boyars agree an exchange between them and the Sultan.'

'On God's good earth,' Vlad angered, 'what possible good exchange could keep you from the mercy of our enemy?'

'An agreement was made to send numbers of adolescence, young and healthy men, as a tribute to keep piece with Sultan Mehmet.'

'And father's boyars,' Vlad came so irate that his voice screeched, 'such old and wise men of his realm agreed to such a despicable plan?'

'It be the only way to keep the enemy from our gate.'

'Father be rising from his grave to oppose such an act,' Vlad coughed from his extent of anger, 'and the ghosts of our men who have laid down their lives to defend our Christianity.' He stared at Radu with stern eyes. 'And you let this be agreed?'

'There be it no choice, dear brother,' Radu again concerned himself with scrutinising the outlay of the inner keep. 'Our young men deplete at such an agreement, but what are we to do?' Finally Vlad caught Radu stare at him inquisitively. 'Maybe my good brother's great tactics in battle may put us to some advantage?'

'All I will suggest is that you put our good Christian men to do battle against our enemy and not to sell as trade for some despicable peace treaty.' Suddenly Vlad felt sick to his stomach; it was not that he had scarcely eaten for days, but envisaging the many strange eyes that had stared at him on the battlefield, that he had probably killed good Christian men… ones deluded by Ottoman rule.

He heard Radu praise him of having a strategic mind and how he could save men back home, but Vlad's body came rigid with anger; to think what depravity had been imposed at his father's keep since his death. And then there was his brother; was it because Mircea fought against this agreement, that he too, was murdered? Vlad himself was far from being a kind gentleman, but he knew to uphold law and order, discipline and justice, were crucial. Vlad pondered on his past to uphold the Christian faith, but heard Radu ridicule the inner keep and the scarcity of soldiers.

'It be because of stupid agreements imposed, as the ones you describe, that leave us outnumbered,' Vlad announced slowly to empathise his displeasure. 'But little brother, let me take all those back from father's keep to fight alongside me here at Poenari.'

'I do not believe that would be possible,' Radu again lifted his nose up against his brother. 'They would not agree to such.' Radu could see that his words had angered his elder brother and so continued with a more solemn tone. 'Besides they be not enough room to bed such numbers here, so where…?'

'They be lands kept safe by this keep and the fortress be deep as it is wide.' Vlad interrupted, but paused to see firelight glint in Radu's blue eyes. 'There are miles beneath this fortress dear brother, and already its depths are being used to forge new weaponry and propose tactics that will put us to some advantage.'

'What advantage be enough to pit you against such an increasing enemy?'

'Patience dear brother,' Vlad smiled, his mind thinking of material, not men. 'I shall show you what our army will *have* to crush this Ottoman rule.'

'That be so,' Radu derided cynically, 'and will you crush the enemy before all young men are sacrificed back home?'

'We will discuss such matters inside,' Vlad replied with resentment in his voice, but tried best to again be positive. 'But firstly dear brother, you must dine with my wife and son and be guest to the hospitality of our nobles.'

After noticing the outer gate closed and with both garrisons inside, Vlad banged a beat on the outer courtyard gate, announcing that they be opened to welcome soldiers of Wallachia.

It had been several hours into early evening before Vlad had organised hospitality for his visitors. All but Radu had been taken to the inner courtyard to replenish their strength with rations of food and water, but for some reason Radu insisted that his men camp separate. Although somewhat disturbed by Radu's request, Vlad granted that his brother's men set up barracks in the south of the courtyard, and so rest not far from their small chapel and outbuilding collection of ornamentals and scripture.

After embracing his wife and son with much awaited affection, Vlad had taken a short nap before joining his brother to dine with Henrik and many others in Poenari's great hall. Half a dozen of these men consisted of boyars, nobles and a Christian cleric; others were commanders to Wallachia's depleting army.

Vlad had hardly taken a sip of wine or a bite of grilled pheasant, but sat back into his deep, dark-oak chair, to admire all the lavish food upon the table. On seeing his wife and son approach the enormous, oval table – shapely carved from great tree trunks of the horse chestnut – he placed down his goblet of wine to go and greet them. Grimacing to the pain in his side, Vlad heaved himself up from his throne-like seat to introduce his wife Jusztina and son, Mihnea.

Staring nervously at all the men deep in conversation around the table, Mihnea walked awkwardly behind his mother, his small body almost dragged by his mother's hand. But then the boy's eyes gleamed at noticing the large, freshly prepared feast;

his nostrils opening wide to savour the smell that filled the room.

'Dear brother,' Vlad announced after coughing aloud, his arm reaching around his wife's shoulder, the other pushing Mihnea into view, 'this be my dearest wife Jusztina, one noble daughter of the Moldavian king, and this will be my first son, Mihnea.'

'You expect to have many more,' a distant voice mocked, 'yet you be away for weeks long?'

'Well now he be back,' another voice declared from around the table, 'no doubt he be making up lost time!'

'Shut all your foul mouths in front of my beloved wife,' Vlad ordered. 'With word today from my brother here, it maybe be that Jusztina be soon your queen.'

'How be it so?' voices questioned, but Vlad waved them to be silent as he noticed Radu question tamely his son.

'And how old be this dearest boy... one with the name, Mihnea?'

'Answer my son,' Vlad beckoned, kneeling to Mihnea on one knee, 'this man be my brother Radu, and so be your uncle.'

'I am Mihnea,' the shy boy shrieked, 'and I be five last month.'

'But you not walk astute on your own?' Radu declared. 'When I was your age, I was running about all corners of the castle.'

'He be walking alone soon as he be growing strong every day,' Jusztina intervened reservedly, 'but have some strange limp to his left leg… we be not sure but hope this disappears as he matures.' Jusztina glanced timidly at Radu. 'It being the first, his was a difficult birth you see.'

'Let it be hoped the poor boy will grow out of such debility,' Radu turned to look inquisitively at Vlad, who was now back upon two feet. 'As the Prince of Wallachia is so known for being a tempest in battle, no doubt he would wish his son to follow suit.'

'Maybe not all Christians are gifted with such handsome looks and healthy body, or maybe that of the soul.' Vlad looked pensively at his younger brother. 'I believe it be something that deterred our capturers from torturing you.' Vlad paused to recollect, his index finger probing his mouth. 'Or was it that you cunningly used your pretty guise to appease the Sultan?' Vlad could tell by the glower in his brother's eyes that he had touched some secret nerve and so changed his line of discussion. 'Our son here was to be named Mircea, but Jusztina did not want it so.' Vlad again paused to regard Radu. 'But it be a pity, since now if we can only remember our eldest brother by memory and not by endorsing his name.'

'My dear Vlad,' Jusztina intervened coyly, 'it be a good thing that we did, as in my country it be regarded as unlucky to name one after another's death.'

'Well, we need nothing less than that of bad luck to strike us anymore, do we?' Vlad turned to see Radu seat himself and look upon other guests. 'But please my dear, take yourself and our son enough to eat from the table, in that you may dine else...'

'I take it that we both are not invited,' Jusztina griped and looked mockingly down at her son. 'It be looking that your father only wants us to be an exhibition to his...' 'We have much to discuss my dear,' Vlad interrupted, his hands open as a peace gesture before one patted his son's head. 'I need to ask my brother things of family, but at first we need to discuss war and battle.' He watched Jusztina turn his son's face toward the door, and with her back to him, heard his wife protest about *them* being his family.

'You know this talk be important my dear. There is much to be learned.'

Jusztina stepped away, shunting Mihnea towards the door and supporting her son as he limped. 'Just don't be hours as you need to rest.' With wild eyes, she glanced back at him. ''I know you do, I can tell.'

Indeed it had been hours – almost into the third hour to be precise – and still Vlad conversed with his guests from his wooden throne-like chair. Eating enough had made him quite drowsy, never mind just finishing a second goblet of wine. But Vlad needed to learn family news and came engrossed in hearing about battles fought. Radu had eaten, but told of no longer drinking wine, disclosing to how liquor clouded one's mind. Seeing boyars sneeringly look at one another after hearing Radu's declaration, the young man shook his long, blonde hair like a disconcerted lion and returned to nibble on the remnants of his food. With many eyes regarding him circumspectly, Radu hid himself in the pleasure of eating and decided to complement his brother for his hospitality.

Radu continued by explaining more of their father's death and to what had become of their brother, describing that the war not only raged between them and the Turks, but of how it unsettled differences between other countries and realms. After seeing his metal plate now empty, Radu anxiously swilled down all with a blend of fruit juices – a special concoction that Jusztina had made from a Moldavian recipe.

'I must complement your wife in both cases,' Radu announced to purposely watch Vlad frown, 'as she be making a beautiful extract of fruits… as beautiful as herself.' Vlad was getting used to his brother turn his nose up when visibly deriding people, an act that was becoming increasingly annoying. 'But I believe it to have been an arranged marriage, one to keep harmony between you and the Moldavian king?' He paused again to peek sneakily at Vlad. 'To have both gained such a beautiful wife and son… and to inherit such an illustrious title… my brother has done well for himself.' Radu again glanced over to witness Vlad's reaction before outstretching his arms as he reclined into his chair. 'To have all this to fight for and being the one true Prince of Wallachia, it be a blessing now you have such wealth, especially after we lose both father and elder brother?'

'What be it as your point?' a voice questioned.

'Sorry, you must take me as being awfully rude,' Radu answered, directing his reply to the nobleman across the table – one to which, although they had been introduced just hours previous, he could not remember, 'but I don't recall your name, let alone your status or profession?'

'This be Lucian Dumitru,' Vlad explained again. 'He be our highest boyar and council to both garrison and church. He be a learned man of more than any. He oversees our literature and finances.'

'Argh, like your second in command,' Radu conjectured inadvertently.

'Yes, our Henrik Vasile commands weapons and garrison,' Vlad gestured an open palm towards Henrik. 'And be my most noble friend.'

'What be it your point?' Lucian repeated, wanting to know why this strange young man would question Vlad's inheritance and his authority over the realm. 'You bring word of our departed king and subsequent murder of your brother, but be it you have other news?' The old councillor took breath, his old, frail fingers wiping the white bristles of the beard surrounding his mouth. 'I know that our armies defend difficult the boundaries on the southern realm of Wallachia… even those east to the great lake,' Lucian's eyes glared at Radu from under darker eyebrows. 'But does Stephen the Great – our allies from Moldavia – not defend lands north of the Transylvanian Alps… the Hungarian boundaries, including Bukovina?'

'I not know of that arrangement,' Radu starred at his empty metal plate. 'Maybe such contracts died with my father… your king?'

'And that be why the Ottoman Empire set you free,' Lucian queried, 'because past contracts die with their architect?'

'It be an arrangement of sorts,' Radu coughed and muttered, 'but I was free from Ottoman rule a long time before our poorly departed king was murdered in Târgoviste.'

'You were freed,' Lucian probed, 'or did you find your own method of escape?'

'I escaped the Turks by stealth my good man, and be it me that discovered the dismissal truth about our king and our eldest brother!' Radu gestured to him and Vlad. 'I have already…'

'You said you'd be finished hours ago!' a voice interrupted, shouting from the entrance of the great hall. 'You said we make time together as you be gone for so long!' Jusztina paced angrily up to the edge of the large wooden table. 'As I have placed him to bed, you will not see your son now until break of morning.'

'Argh, my dearest Jusztina,' Radu intervened as Vlad stood to apologize. 'I must complement you not just on your fruit extract, but on your timely interlude so that I return to my garrison before they retire… as we have much to sort out.'

'Surely my husband can talk all of politics and war tomorrow,' Jusztina turned her angry eyes from Vlad to focus on Radu. 'You may be his brother who he not see for…' Jusztina paused, her temper shaking her auburn locks that now looked sandy light in the shimmering candlelight. 'But I not see him for a month long now, and he be not kissing his son goodnight.'

'Then we must all retire,' Vlad stood behind his throne-like chair, grimacing to how his wife stood with arms and legs folded, a great expectancy on her face. 'Time has indeed flown as fast as plagues.' He approached Jusztina but hesitated to roll his arm around her waist. 'Henrik, Lucian… my dear council… as my good wife reminds me and it be true, I not spend enough and precious time with her but can talk all this tomorrow.' Vlad took a goblet and filled it half full of Jusztina's fruit extract. 'I drink in toast to my good wife and health in marriage, and that she bring such beauty and acumen to our realm.' Vlad slurped the last of the fruit speciality, but stood unmoved as Jusztina tried to wrench him from his guests. 'Dear Lucian could you give my brother a tour of Poenari?'

'What now, my Lord,' the councillor quizzed disapprovingly, 'at this hour when it be dark, and be truly time to retire?'

'Yes, I do agree with your council,' Radu intervened, his body somewhat stiff as he rose from his chair, 'old Lucian here would do best to show me the décor of this great fortress come morning light.' He circled the great table to approach Vlad. 'Besides, like you I propose, we both be tired after such our journeys.'

'Then be it so,' Vlad agreed. 'Lucian,' Vlad announced, 'please see that a room is prepared for my brother and that all that is uneaten from our banquet be served amongst my brother's garrison… this be a gesture of goodwill, to assert these men help to fight beside us in battles to come.'

'That be an honourable gesture indeed, dear brother,' Radu stepped up to pat his brother on the shoulder and Vlad observed him wink. 'But they need full bellies just to get them to march, let alone fight!'

'Come tomorrow brother, I will talk amongst your garrison to hear their tales of battle, and show you all the new secrets to forge weaponry in the depths of Poenari.'

'You may be the Prince of Wallachia,' Radu scoffed, his face and curly blonde locks now close, but several inches below

Vlad's, 'but my soldiers… my garrison, be only answering to me.' Radu smirked, but Vlad could not interpret whether it was in jest or whether it composed some stern agenda. 'But I tell them you send all what you have left here as a gesture of goodwill, even if we not stay for long.'

Cautiously Vlad opened the entrance to the bedchamber and with the heavy, wooden door standing ajar, peered warily through. After carefully releasing the hoop-shaped, metal handle, he examined the room inside, trying best to identify shadows cast from candlelight. It was then that he saw a figure cross the room.

Beside a black oak cabinet and with a matching, low dressing-table below her, he watched Jusztina slip herself into a flimsy garment before standing to massage ointment onto her limbs. Slowly and silently he entered and crept towards her, and anticipating her thoughts elsewhere, placed down the goblet of wine. And he confirmed his prediction – her body shuddered to his touch upon her shoulder, her eyes wide and startled as she turned to face him.

'What you go do that for?' In tense reaction, Jusztina pulled the flimsy, robe-like garment tight around her. 'Make me near jump out of my skin!'

'Well, why don't you remove this light attire and we be making up lost time,' Vlad proposed, his fingers sliding along his wife's smooth shoulders to penetrate under the seam of the garment. 'Such a gorgeous banquet has somewhat revived me.'

'It be too late for that now,' Jusztina snarled, her body moving craftily to the dressing-table to retrieve a large, oval brush. 'I have washed and oiled fresh my body and have my hair to address.' She sat down on a low stool, the brush weaving back and forth through sandy-coloured hair that glimmered in the candlelight. 'Besides you have been drinking wine again, and maybe have had too much.'

Vlad stood above and arched over Jusztina, his fingers trying to penetrate an opening about the chest of her garment, but finally had to settle on cupping her breasts. He could feel their weight within his palms and would have subjected himself to the excitement if he had not noticed her sharp eyes glancing at him through her hand-mirror.

'You act as if a virgin juvenile,' Jusztina judged, angling the mirror to observe Vlad's face behind her, 'teasing himself with toys never played with before.'

'It be such a long time… it be hard to remember,' Vlad muttered, his initial excitement now somewhat oppressed. 'These days of endless war, I see only the beauty of nature… not like to what you can give me… the feel of the body… my skin against yours… our hearts beating as one.'

'You talk of heart dear husband,' Jusztina spun swiftly on the stool, her hands now free to push away her husband's groping. 'You have changed in some ways, but least I know to where *your* heart does lie… amongst other things.' Jusztina smiled mischievously before urgency overwhelmed her face, 'But what of Radu? You told me that your younger brother was condemned to suffer a long time under Ottoman rule, or that he had been influenced to stay somehow.' She faced Vlad with full attention, her eyes searching his. 'So why take up this interest in family now?'

'I not be sure,' Vlad confessed; one set of fingers now cupping the curvature of his wife's cheek, as the other stroked her hair. 'Maybe it is because of losing father and Mircea together… it must come as such a shock.'

'But he delivers this news as fast as lightening, and shows no remorse,' she rolled her eyes and exhaled hard. 'Not that you show any either… maybe it be…'

'Just because I do not shed any tears my dear Jusztina, it does not mean feelings are not in my heart,' Vlad interrupted. 'It just means I have learned to contain them.'

'And he does too… show no emotion by containment… just shakes those blonde locks and sticks out that arrogant chin of his.' She paused momentarily. 'But tries to convey *his* change of heart.' Jusztina looked upon the sparsely decorated floor, a tone of anger catching her voice. 'To think that he may have witnessed such crimes and yet he acts the way he does.'

'What's it you mean my dear, by acts?'

'He shows no remorse in all this doing, even plays to your reaction. To me he pretends that it has affected him, although it may be different.' She looked back up at Vlad to make sure she had his attention. 'Maybe he is jealous of what you will inherit, or that you could now become king?' She eased herself from her stool to wonder over to the wooden crib that had been enlarged specially to accommodate Mihnea's disability. 'Your brother is both young and well handsome, so why his interests only be for land and money, or is it he be not blessed to have children?' Jusztina leaned over the crib and kissed her sleeping son on his forehead. 'Maybe it be jealousy that he hides... as you know, I can sense these things.' She looked affectionately upon her son before noticing Vlad stand close. 'He is asleep, your son, but kiss him all the same, this is one blessing we share, and that you return from battle this day.'

Jusztina watched Vlad lean over the crib and touch his lips against his son's forehead, but frowned to watch her husband withdraw in pain. 'What is it my love, what's wrong?'

Vlad retreated to take comfort on the edge of the bed, his face grimacing as he pulled at his leather waistcoat and heavy shirting. Jusztina drifted over quickly, her light garment making her look ghostly in such a swift action. As she reached her husband, Vlad was still struggling to remove his leather garments and shirting. Jusztina wrenched at his leather waistcoat, hearing Vlad curse as she strained both arms through the openings. And, although she now pulled his arms through somewhat cautiously, he cursed again. Then with his chest and arms naked, she could see why.

Vlad had taken heavy bruising across his chest and shoulders and small lacerations had congealed along parts of each arm. But it was when he leaned back to unbuckle belting from around his waist, that Jusztina noticed blood ooze from a wound about his left side. And standing back to scrutinise more his body, she could see deep bruising run down along his spine.

'Undress my dear; I will attend your wounds.' Jusztina implored, trying desperately to find some sort of bandaging within drawers of furniture. 'Why such a prince, or now possible *king*, should not live in a more creditable establishment with such better wealth, I fail to comprehend.' She searched more provisions, but could only find handkerchiefs. 'Castle Bran is much more an admirable place, or somewhere north of Sighişoara or Bistrita, would be more honourable.'

'My good wife, should you remember the troubles I went to build this place… we have no better safekeeping,' Vlad paused to grimace against removing the heavy garments about his waist. 'This fortress at Poenari was built as a great mountain retreat against the enemy. And sitting between Wallachia and Transylvania trade lines, it allows great scrutiny.' Again, Vlad winced, but was determined to deliver his point. 'But most of all, it being perched on a crag high above the deepest of gorges, it gives the best lookout along the Argeş valley. An enemy garrison can be spotted from miles distant.'

'It not be good enough to stop such hurting.' Jusztina paused to stare at Vlad. 'Lucian agrees that witch-hazel be good to sooth such bruising, but he hates to potions of such conjuring.'

'What be his problem?' Vlad retorted. 'They not be conjured by sorcery. Such medicines are made in ways much like to how our weaponry is forged from different metals.'

'I'd like you to convince dear Lucian of such, he being highest minister and all.' 'But I must agree with you about Castle Bran.' Vlad differed to his wife's original conversation.

'Oh yes, but why?'

'It hold good scrutiny along gorges south and trade through Braşov.' Vlad winced again to movement. 'Be easier to keep eye on travelling merchants, especially those...'

'Come my dear, you have more important things to attend to.' Jusztina urged Vlad to lie against the bed, his elbow propping him up in defiance. 'I can only find frail handkerchiefs to dress it now, but come morning I'd find proper dressing.'

'My good woman, it be only a flesh wound. I have survived worse.'

'Such a gash is hard to heal,' Jusztina insisted, kneeling close to examine his wound. 'And be continually bleeding to invite infection.'

'Then I hold it in place whilst you put that good ointment on me.'

'But I should have no witch-hazel, as Lucian forbids such potions of sorcery.' 'Then use other oils,' he contorted, 'maybe they be soothing also.'

'But they just be tender to make smooth the skin?'

'They worked to sooth last time,' Vlad scowled in discomfort. 'Help me sleep, they did.'

Without dispute Jusztina soon returned with a collection of vials and confessed, 'Oh dear husband, it be somehow that I have left some witch-hazel... some that dear Lucian would not know of. And should I mix such with my ointments, he will not know and you be sleeping well... maybe healed come morning.'

'But what of my wound... is that to be left until morning?'

'I'll see to that first,' Jusztina grumbled, patting her potion-sodden handkerchief along the slash of his wound.

'That hurts, woman!'

'Argh,' Jusztina sniggered, 'you fight bravely to kill many a man, but a little ointment?' She forced his hand to hold firm her makeshift bandage. 'But let's see to your bruises brave warrior.'

Jusztina had not long slid her delicate fingers up and down his spine and circled her palms around his shoulders, when Vlad felt aroused. Her soothing touch made silky by the oily potion and the strange aroma drifting nearby, made his tired body dip into some reserved energy tank. Maybe it was the wine, the good food he had gorged on earlier, or most probably the compassion and company he had missed from his wife whilst battling out in the fields for nearly a month.

Eventually Vlad could not withstand the eroticism any longer; he felt twinges of arousal between his buttocks, his organ stiffening awkwardly between his thighs. And so he turned to pull Jusztina eagerly around to face him, her legs splayed over his waist, her feet dangling the edge of the bed.

'My dearest wife, your love raises me above all my pains so that we be together again this day.' He looked longingly into her excited eyes. 'After all the bloodshed I see, the loss of good soldiers in battle, and exhaust myself in hatred for thy enemy, it be you that delivers me on.' He cupped her hands together as she lost a vial to the floor. 'I can sleep tomorrow long and heavy, so tonight make me good to know that you are mine.' As Vlad took one of her hands to touch his erection, the other propping up her back, he leaned forward and powerfully embraced her before kissing vigorously her neck and bosom.

'My Lord, with vigour, do not treat me so,' Jusztina pulled away to disapprove, 'but treat me unlike some battle scene, and take me kind and gentle.' She glanced down to acknowledge to what she had felt between her nibble fingers. And Vlad's erection was growing in her palm as her other hand cupped his testicles; her probing action pulling loose his undergarments. 'Shall I do my special treat to help excite my good Prince?'

As Vlad recognised the mischievous glint in his wife's eyes, Jusztina shifted back and lowered her head to his groin. As he knew of her intention, he shifted back toward the centre of the bed and grasped at her golden hair. Soon he could feel the hot, glossy touch of her mouth wrap itself around his to-near-full-extend erection, and as he felt her move up and down, he felt juices escape and run over his testicles.

As blood raced to satisfy his erection, Vlad felt his mind go faint, knowing a premature ejaculation was close. But he did not want to release such tension so soon; he wanted to savour the moment after missing his wife over many long nights alone. Wishing to stroke her tender, unblemished skin, Vlad pulled Jusztina away from her treat and up towards him. As he caressed quickly her supple waist and stomach, to eventually fondle her breasts from under her robe, he saw her wipe saliva away from her mouth as she stared questionably at him.

'Let me treat you my dearest Jusztina,' Vlad murmured, his voice croaking. 'I am wanting this to last and be special for you.' As he scooped his forefinger to slip away the flimsy garment from his wife's shoulder, Jusztina honoured his intention and so let the robe fall altogether. But after he winked an eye, Jusztina was left perplexed to see Vlad get up from the bed and step across the bedchamber. Confused, she slid her slim legs together, and huddled to watch him retrieve a goblet from a cabinet, one she had not noticed before.

As he returned back to sit beside her, she was just about to protest, when she felt a chill upon her one breast. At first it was the cold of the metal, but as the goblet tilted to nuzzle her breast, she felt the cold of the red wine accentuate her nipple. And before she could react to such an unusual gesture, Vlad had removed the goblet to watch rivulets of red wine run down his wife's body, but caught them with his tongue before they disappeared between her legs. And before she could relish the feel of it against her one breast, Vlad had dipped her other, and was now circling his tongue about each, now protruding nipple, alternately sucking away at the sweet liquid.

'My Lord,' Jusztina questioned excitedly, 'what brings on this?' Vlad paused momentarily as his eyes shone with excitement.

'It be better to taste good wine from your sweet body, than taste blood from the battlefield.' He looked strange but longingly into her eyes. 'It make better my mind and soul that I share my afflictions this way; that I remember the red of sweet wine upon your body and not of blood split in battle.' He turned away as if ashamed, but returned to strengthen his gaze upon her. 'In only you can I confide such afflictions of warfare, and pray every day that I return to such beauty.'

'Make love to me then my dearest Vlad,' Jusztina lowered his head so his tongue could continue playing. 'And enrich me with all your manly ways, but go gently on such a loving soul as I.'

Vlad teased her more as he tried best to suppress his aggression, but grasped her sturdily to move her upon the bed. As she succumbed to amplified hostility, she knew again he was releasing tension; bad recollections and affliction from the battlefield.

'Please my Lord,' Jusztina again implored, 'I am but a delicate bird, a small loving creature held tight within your grasp.'

Vlad manoeuvred Jusztina with less vigour, but forced her to sit on her knees and take him from behind. As she felt his forearm force back her throat, she winced to feel his erection probing her wetness. And then, as she felt the bristles of his chin rub her shoulder, his erection slid successfully within her an inch or two. At first she controlled such overwhelming enthusiasm, exhaling comments to make her husband be slow and deliberate, but he was again groping and pulling belligerently.

Her pleas to take slow such a sexual act came out in breaths of undisguisable disagreement; her lungs now starved of air by his quickening motion. With such exhilaration, she was out of breath to object to her husband's ferocity, but knowing Vlad would not truly hurt her, she relied on his known compassion.

As juices ran during her climax, Jusztina's breaths came low and hard; her husband still entering her forcibly, sometimes coming free and steered by the slippery wet to her anus.

Without wanting to masturbate again, she twisted to prevent him entering her wrong and guided him inside her vagina, trying to cease his erection and slow him down. But Vlad did not slow down and at this she sensed him climaxing. So she lowered herself, slowly pulling her legs together, making him lie on his side and enter her more tightly. As predicted, this proved hard for her lover's thrust and made him slow in rhythm. But with his breaths wild against her back and his gasps at air ecstatic, she knew soon her husband would ejaculate. And she would have spoken a lie if she had not enjoyed another climax during his final moment.

For minutes they lay together, Vlad snuggling Jusztina from behind, hearing nothing but the smouldering logs crack within the fire. And as their sweated bodies cooled from exertions released, both felt a cold breeze send them to shiver. At first the cold did not affect Vlad; he huddled close to warm Jusztina, his chest and stomach pressed against her back. But with the fortress windows exposing the dark night and feeling the return of autumn winds, Vlad felt a shiver run down his spine. Maybe it was his bruising, or that the ointment Jusztina had applied was working. Nevertheless, Vlad felt he needed warmth, and somehow he knew, so did his wife.

Naked, Vlad strode from the comfort of his wife, to place further logs upon the fire and poke at it to gather flame. As he smiled to see it flare back into life, he turned to see Jusztina watching him from the bed. He knew from her expression and inquisitive eyes, that although he was cut and bruised, she was admiring his muscular body. Maybe it was more to how the increasing firelight flickered against his body, but now he felt the warmth gave him more vitality. And on returning to Jusztina, he proved again to how much he loved her.

FOUR

He had traipsed through woodland countless times before, and even after nightfall had liked the still of nature; but somehow this was different. As he trampled bracken and heard twigs snap beneath his gingerly place boots, he felt apprehensive to the darkness surrounding him. It was as though someone or something was watching him. And the usual sounds of the night forest had somehow become silenced; no screech of an owl, no animals scurrying through the undergrowth to safety – not even the tap of branch on branch or the rustle of leaves above.

At first it was a sudden breeze that chilled his bones, but then somewhere beyond the dark of night, a distant cry made him shudder. Nervously he paused for a moment to decipher from where the sound had come, but then, on hearing it again, turned to tread towards it. On hearing the cries once more, he paused again to establish its direction, but came perturbed by the unusual silence. Determinedly, whilst leaning against a sturdy tree truck, he pulled his sword slowly from its sheath. But as the noise of withdrawing his sword ceased and he held it strong before him, he could hear birds squawking. And searching the trees above, he detected countless ravens lining their branches in the shadow of the near-full moon. And strangely, their black eyes seemed to scrutinize his every move.

Disconcerted, he ran, trampling carelessly through undergrowth and bracken, his face scratched by twigs and foliage, but trying desperately to reach the cries ahead. Perturbed to see his deep breaths exhale against such a usual cold night, he strengthened his determination at knowing he was close. But with fear, he suddenly stopped; as he now recognised the source… they were cries from his son.

Identifying that Mihnea desperately need help, Vlad pounced into action and ran unwaveringly towards his son. But as he reached a small clearing and leaned to rest against the bark of a sycamore, he froze in terror to watch his son crawl through fresh fallen leaves that glistened from a ground frost. Sprawled out upon the cold woodland floor, Mihnea pulled himself towards his father using only his hands, his legs somehow paralysed behind as he dragged his feet.

Mihnea called in pain; distressed to why he could not get up and walk as normal. And so Vlad shot eagerly forward, reassuring his son to how he would carry him to safety. But as Vlad neared his son, he found his feet sinking in mud. At first it was nothing but what covered his toes, but soon it reached the ankle of his boots. And for some reason, although he had trod through deeper marsh, he found himself immobile, his legs quivering through effort to lift forward his feet. He glanced up from cursing his feet as his son called out in sudden pain. And Vlad soon found out why.

A scythe like blade had swung deep into the back of Mihnea's left thigh and started to drag him backward. Vlad was past his point of anger and was so enraged not to be able to move. In desperation he replaced his sword to its sheath before clutching a nearby branch; one he hoped would reach his son's grasp. And although, under his father's direction, Mihnea had grasped the branch end, its weathered bark had stripped away his grip as he was again drawn backward.

Vlad stared in hatred at the weapon dragging back his son, but then turned his anger to the Turkish soldier he thought had caused harm. Frantically he tried to escape the mud that entrapped his feet and free his son, but could only try to identify the culprit.

With overwhelming concern, Vlad could only observe a dark figure whose hand now clasped around the ankle of his son's uninjured leg. His son cried out again in both pain and terror, but all Vlad could do was observe the dark entities – hands from dark, ghostly figures – reaching to grab at his son and drag him through the undergrowth and into the depths of the dark forest.

*　　*　　*

Distraught by the horror in his dream, Vlad awoke; his body trembling and perspiring with sweat. For a while, as his skin cooled giving a discomforting shiver, Vlad's heart pounded, his neck pulsating to race blood to his head. Increasingly, as he swept the visions aside and could hear his son weeping, he realized that he had been subjected to a terrible nightmare.

Still agitated by the visions in his dream, Vlad turned to notice Jusztina asleep; her back towards him, her golden hair somewhat emaciated. And then, after propping himself upon an elbow, he turned his attention towards his son's crib. For some reason, Mihnea was weeping and called out intermittently. Maybe this is why I dreamed of such, Vlad deliberated, my son's disturbed resting. But why should a boy of his aging cry to such like a baby?

Decisively Vlad pulled back the bedclothes to see to his son, but found a soft hand grip his arm and soft lips kiss his shoulder.

'By the motions of your sleep and your sweating my dear, I take it you have had a bad dream?'

Vlad turned to observe his wife directly, 'Yes Jusztina, my sleep be agitated by our son's dismay and my mind be having…'

'Do not trouble your rest my Lord,' Jusztina interrupted with a hint of contempt, 'I felt your discomforts before Mihnea woke me, but he often cries himself to sleep. And so I left him.' She lifted herself up to turn and face him, her eyes reminiscent. 'I will see to our son whilst you take rest. As my Lord, you must be tired from your exhaustions of battle, and of that from last night.'

From the edge of the bed, Jusztina walked over to contemplate Mihnea's distress. Watching him curiously, she retrieved a light robe draped over a chair to cover her from the morning cold.

'Why does he make such cries like a baby,' Vlad questioned, 'he be a boy now?' 'And why do you dream such nightmares that make you kick me in my sleep?'

Jusztina replied grinning. 'Wake me many a time you do!'

'That I cannot help my dear woman,' Vlad scoffed in return, his eyes turning away toward the window as he thought about his survival outside. 'It be some hindrance from battle… Henrik tells that such bloodshed has affliction upon him too.'

'The battlefield and this bloody war is all you see,' Jusztina mocked as she lifted Mihnea to calm him in her arms. 'You not notice such things as your son's ill fortune and troubled wellbeing.'

'But what can I be doing to resolve such disability?'

'It not just be his leg I be saying, but what of the love his father should give.' Jusztina lowered her voice after seeing Vlad pained. 'Surely you can give him the encouragement he needs, be it though you never had such from your father.'

'I remember much not from my father, but it does not mean I did not love him as such.' Vlad paused, his thoughts elsewhere,

'And now we hear of both my father and brother betrayed… somehow murdered.'

Seeing Vlad glum, Jusztina changed the conversation. 'Maybe your son does have the same as you, as you used to rock yourself and bang your head against walls to get to sleep, did you not?' She continued after seeing him admit her accusation. 'Maybe your son suffers too from such bad afflictions?'

'Yes I be having such as a boy,' Vlad admitted tentatively, 'but the suchlike I had just, are because of war… yet they be so vivid!'

'Maybe it be such warfare as you say my Lord,' Jusztina hobbled over with Mihnea in her arms to look at the extinguished fire, 'or maybe you and your son here do share more than you know.'

'I only wish he could stand tall and strong as I do,' Vlad muttered, thinking Jusztina had not heard him, but glanced up to see her eyes glaring at him.

There was an uncomfortable moment of silence, but watching Jusztina dress and do everything for Mihnea, Vlad had to react.

'You treat that boy as he be still a baby and not teach him to dress himself or learn the things Lucian told to get him fit and strong.'

'Lucian not see the dismay his stupid twists and stretches put on our son!'

'But my dearest Jusztina,' Vlad again scoffed his words, 'our most judicial boyar find new ways that prove to be affective... not the bewitched crafts handed down by the old wives or hermits found in your country.'

'Do not scoff at such an old and wise craft.' Jusztina shook her head and looked longingly at her son. 'It be not just my country that has such people.' Annoyed, she placed Mihnea down to watch him walk awkwardly to the door. 'You make such a talk in a morning when your son be dressed and ready for breakfast. And you have guests. But first you should rest before I attend your dressing.' She winked an eye after seeing their son open the door and go through quite admirably on his own. 'After my Lord's most thrilling exertions last night, I shall provide a large luncheon before he entertains our guests.'

'You should let our servants do the work and not apply yourself so much.'

'But it keep me busy as you be gone for so long in battle. We never be sure if you come back, but can only pray morning and night for your safe return.' Jusztina noticed Mihnea peer at Vlad from around the door, before looking back at her. 'Little Mihnea, we miss him so much, do we not?' Jusztina smiled after seeing her son nod in agreement. 'Now rest and I be up later to address that wound... maybe kiss it better.'

Jusztina moved swiftly to the door, a heavier robe now draped about her and tied at the waist. But before she could join Mihnea and turn him around to walk out the door, she heard Vlad pronounce.

'What funny creatures be women?' He paused to see his wife stop and frown. 'The woman prevents her husband talking battle all night, and although injured, she use all his energy to spend private time with him... but now insists he rests?'

'But I not know if it be the last time we make love,' Jusztina scoffed as she joined her son to hold his hand beside the door. 'I not know what injury you may come back with... if back at all.' Again there was a moment of unease, before she fretted, 'How is your wound, has it stopped its bleeds?'

'It aches but does not red the bandage any longer.'

'Then that be good a sign.' She signalled Mihnea to go to the breakfast table downstairs before readdressing Vlad. 'I will awake you later, redress your wound and prepare a hearty luncheon. After which, you should keep your promise to your younger brother, and show your ways to forge stronger metal for hardier weapons.'

'Yes, should I remember our discussions last night, and then that be true.' Vlad closed his eyes and pressed the bridge of his nose with thumb and forefinger. 'Yes indeed, as I have not seen him since our indifference with the Turks, I did agree to show Radu the bowels of our fortress... to where my dungeon furnaces are to melt our enemy weapons to establish their composition. I also promised to show him methods from that of the Hungarian king, in which to forge more robust weaponry.'

'Well my dear, after such rest, you may spend all day with your brother.' Jusztina smirked to whisper, 'As long as you make love to me again like last night. But you can leave out the wine… it left my body sticky this morning.'

'Maybe women are easier to satisfy than I first thought,' Vlad chortled.

'Maybe, if we had the luxury of an elegant place like that of Castle Bran and not this cold, drafty fortress, then we be making love in warm and long, comfortable beds.'

'Dearest wife,' Vlad stated emphatically, 'this fortress was purposely built for defense. And it was my duty first and foremost to provide for your safety, whether the Moldavian king wanted me to honour this or not.'

'I know of this my dear,' Jusztina spoke softly as she came over to sit on the edge of the bed to glance at the extinguished fire again. 'I know how much you love me and that I do you also, but are you not at least a bit inquisitive to where Radu's loyalties lie, as he did spend more time under Ottoman rule than you did as a boy?'

'I recall my good wife, that you questioned me on this very same subject last night.' Vlad shuffled to sit up in bed, his wound still giving some grief. 'So why you ask again?'

'It just be, he comes now, at a time when battle seems so frequent and severe. And yet he travelled over such distance of land, unharmed?'

'And it be strange to how you question such the same as Lucian did at dining last night,' Vlad pondered. 'As without me arriving, and although he had father's coat-of-arms, the gatekeeper was instructed not to let anyone in.' He hesitated to deliberate. 'Also, Lucian interrogated him about travelling unharmed through territory he had little knowledge and to why we should entrust his news about my father and brother.

'And what was your brother's reply?'

'Radu consistently told of using the cover of trees on high ground, and camping without fire... moving by stealth, I believe he called it.'

'Well, I cannot believe such.' Jusztina stepped over to the fire to poke and turn the charred logs to hopefully relight it, but her attempts were in vain. 'Pardon me that he be your brother and much your history I do not know, but I think him pompous and vindictive.' She stabbed at the fire with the metal poker once more before turning to express her honesty. 'I appeal to you not to entrust him as I have...'

'Not those feelings again,' Vlad interrupted to scorn. 'We talked of this last night and I told you somethings about us.'

'And you believe his word over mine, is that it?'

'Did I not explain last night to how we were persecuted as children… how we were bought up under Turkish rule as part of some allegiance set by our father… that we were given to the elder Sultan as honoree sacrifices to keep peace between the old order and Ottoman Empire?' He saw Jusztina hunched and contemplative, and so continued. 'In reaching manhood, our arguments and differences increased, and so we went separate ways. I did not like to how Radu neglected our father's teachings and discipline. To this I conjured an escape as Radu would not agree to such, but kept his silence to my intent.' Vlad paused again to contemplate. 'I still would not take my brother's side to such, but pray that he has changed his beliefs to honour father through Christianity. It may be that he regrets his past, and the news about both father and my older brother has been much a shock to him.' Vlad saw that his wife looked bemused. 'Simply my dear, maybe Radu wants conciliation about his past… maybe he has questions of family now that he has lost them… as will Mihnea ask things about us in years to come… like to why we married as part of an arrangement?'

After seeing Jusztina pensive, Vlad wriggled to ease his aching side. An awkward minute of silence passed between them before Jusztina declared her defiance.

'Sorry my Lord, but I see your brother as an arrogant provocateur. He comes here to confirm death in your family but shows no remorse whilst doing so. And using this bloody war as some excuse, he insists that foreign boyars plotted and murdered your father, likewise your brother.' Justina paused to deliberate. 'Yes, to that, it could be true, I have no doubt, but it be his conduct on the whole matter that disturbs me.' She glanced at Vlad from starring into the fire, and seeing him pensive, put resolution to her stance on the matter. 'My Lord and dearest husband, this Radu may well be your brother, but he never be part of close family to me, or as a brother in law by marriage.'

'First of all, dear wife, whether you like it or not, Radu be my brother and by law of marriage, be yours too.' Vlad knew his voiced disproval to her opinion had clearly aggravated her, but doggedly continued. 'But in reflection to his story concerning my father and elder brother, this could well be possible. As you have witnessed, imposing higher taxes to fight an increasing enemy, has pressured both Wallachian and foreign boyars to gather such wealth. But you know also, that although many keep safe in the walls of our keep and our lands, these persons revolt against such levies.'

'I do not think such a man, whether he be young or somewhat grieved by loss of family, be able to change.' Jusztina was dedicated to her disapproval of Radu.

'I can all but try and give him time to repent,' Vlad encouraged as he slid back into the bed for more comfort. 'Remember that Radu is my blood, and I hope he redeems

Orthodox Christianity… that maybe, one day he will fight alongside me on the battlefield as a true brother?'

'I doubt this, my Lord,' Jusztina murmured ruefully.

'Then we give him time to refute our doubts,' Vlad announced emphatically. 'Such like a trial period, as Henrik would train a new recruit, and maybe Radu will prove his loyalty to my father and the Order of the Dragon.'

'I doubt he will follow as such,' Jusztina said pacing towards Vlad, who was now mostly hidden beneath the heavy bedclothes. 'He may appeal as attractive to some women with those deep blue eyes and locks of wavy fair hair, but he be having the most shifty and untrustworthy look.'

'You not know his past,' Vlad dejected. 'Boyars to the Sultan had a common interest in a man so young and fair, and having such unusually light skin.'

'The filthy Turks abused him?'

'I only heard tales of such, but never saw any of such with my own eyes.' Jusztina hesitated before making her opinion resolute.

'Then maybe he does have some nervous disposition.' She glanced back at him in resolve. 'But that does not change my feeling that he has something to hide.'

'Feelings again my dear?'

'Yes, feelings husband,' Jusztina stated energetically, 'like how you can choose to ignore the fact that with all but yourself gone as family, your dear young brother could be wanting the throne of Wallachia for himself!'

'He would never make a prince or king.'

'And that be good, as I would never be his queen,' Jusztina said defiantly. 'Although he have fair skin and hair, he be like a Turk. And I would rather be eaten away by wild animals or savage fishes of the river, than feel such filthy hands on me.'

'But why compare Radu to our enemy,' Vlad questioned as he tried to find comfort again, 'we be brothers of the same blood, and blood be the life?'

From the upper chambers of Poenari castle, Vlad had described much of its layout and had even paused to show Radu the impressive vantage points observed through the narrow windows. But after admiring many a hawk-eyed view and progressing through lower tiers of the keep, Vlad stopped abruptly before descending the circular stone stairway of a west facing turret.

Bumping into his brother from his sudden stop, Radu noticed Vlad exhale his breath into balls of mist. Baffled by his taller brother's halt, Radu stepped forward to peer around him, his eyes searching Vlad's face before feeling an upsurge of cold air.

'Young brother, can you feel that cold sting your eyes?'

'Yes, it be like icy wind,' Radu agreed, his breath also producing vapor. 'Be chilling as much as death itself.'

'Can you hear the groans and whisper of death also?'

'Yes, it be weird,' Radu leaned forward, his snooty face troubled, and then turned his head sideways to hear more acutely the sounds. 'But does death haunt such a place?'

'It be nothing to fear dear brother, as I be only jesting,' Vlad chortled. 'Jusztina being somewhat gullible to such superstition, thought the same also.' Vlad stared at Radu intensely, his eyes unusually wide. 'That until a simple explanation was found… by our Lucian Dumitru of all people.'

'Which was…?' Radu asked eagerly, feeling the breeze chill his bronzed face.

'With the door of the dungeons open below us, this chilling air is sucked up from the bowels of the keep to the higher tiers of the fortress.'

'And that groaning, those ghastly voices,' Radu shuddered to hear echo from below, 'where do they come from?'

'They simply be the voices of my men at work in our dungeons.' Vlad saw Radu stare at him, his blue eyes glistening with confusion. 'Lucian tells that the sounds they make and the work they do, get distorted as it travels up from furnaces below.'

'You have furnaces in this keep?'

'But of course, young brother, this be Poenari,' Vlad poised to observe Radu as he descended the first few steps into the chilling updraft. 'I presume that there be much to be learned after being detained by our enemy for such a long time.'

At first Radu did not know how to respond to such cynicism, but eventually replied, 'I now not be under Ottoman rule and live a free man, but as you know, we learn much from our enemies.'

'That be true,' Vlad said raising an eyebrow, 'and so we be melting Turkish weapons to find their metal composition.'

'And have you been successful?'

It was as though Vlad had not heard him, or had chosen not to, but Radu griped to follow his elder brother down against the icy breeze, their hefty boots clomping upon the stone of the descending, spiral stairway until they reached a large, wood and reinforced door. As it stood ajar, Radu could feel the icy draft force itself through the gap and on past him. But as he shouldered the door wide to step into a wide cavern, Radu could only chill to a breeze emanating from nearby passageways that he assumed were natural caves. He glanced around after moving from the cold draft that had caused him to shiver, listening to Vlad describe the place.

'Mostly we dig out only what already give passage, but open the places ahead as it have solid rock foundation. Mining down here we must be so careful, as it would hollow out the mountain upon which Poenari stands.' Vlad took breath and then steeped ahead, pointing as he led. 'Ahead and through that large passage I will take you to show you what we forge.'

'What of these passageways,' Radu grasped Vlad by the arm to ask, 'where do such caves lead?'

'Only the left passage do we know lead to the old well on which this fortress was built, but the others, well they can lead a man to starvation…' Vlad paused to also discredit the old well. 'But it can also be that the old well be the same.'

'An old well,' Radu enquired, 'by what do you mean by that?'

'As the old well was known to retain water from swells from the river Argeș, this fortress was built on top of it. But it is now believed that the underground streams that once supplied water have since caved in, and so water not reach the well bottom.'

'Then there be passage from this well to the river?'

'If so, I hear of no man surviving such a deadly antic, not unless they be following my instruction.' Vlad sniggered, but realized he was near to disclosing his great secret. 'Come, less of that… let me show you the marvel of our underground workshop.'

Again, Radu followed Vlad with overwhelming interest, his eyes excited to enter a wide expanse of cavern from which he now felt warmth. He side-stepped his elder brother to wonder at the metallurgy performed before him, studying in turn, each of three great furnaces that circling him. But as he heard Vlad question strongly a nearby sentry, he listened intently.

'To why have you not put blockade against the entrance?'

'Why my Lord,' the stocky guard explained, 'the other squire was to do it on his way up.'

'And how was he to push the metal plate across the other side of the door after closing?'

'I would presume he was to use the bolt on the side of the stairs.'

'That bolt be rusted and stiff, you should know that!' Vlad composed his anger to go on. 'You must bar the door all times and only open to the sound of three fast thumps, you hear?' He saw the guard nod and take a nervy gulp. 'Make sure all know of this in future; the open door sends icy drafts up into the keep, so I know when it is open!'

'But what if we do not hear such knocking,' the guard asked fretfully, opening out his hands to indicate the workshop, 'with all this noise?'

'You will hear me should you stand in guard on the other side,' Vlad replied, his voice croaking somewhat with annoyance. 'Just be sure that the door be secure always. We not want all to see our secrets down here!' He gave the sentry a sharp glare before guiding Radu to the center of the manmade, fortified cavern.

Leading Radu down some steps contrived from stone in the cavern floor, Vlad described to how each furnace could all manufacture similar weapons, but of late he had designated each to separate experiments. The larger, central furnace was used to melt Turkish sickle-shaped swords as he had found them light but wholly durable through battle. The others simply continued his manufacture of experimental weaponry; sword and spear weaponry such as longsword, broadsword, gisarme, trident, pikes and mace; helmets such as skull-cap or basinet; experimentations with armor and chainmail, as well as different shapes and weight of axe.

Whilst escorting Radu around each furnace and workshops between, Vlad described the difficulties they had endured to establish the metal composition of enemy weaponry. But with metallic experts from Hungary and Moldavia, along with his fine Wallachian craftsmen, he had concluded that ores extracted further south and east – from mines of the Ottoman Empire – had more iron in their composition. Vlad had therefore experimented in smelting steel around an iron rod base and found it, not only more robust after doused in oiled waters, but with a hardwood handle, it was less reverberant from shock. However, his experiments proved inadequate in training bouts, as he confessed that wooden handles tended to slip grip upon the iron rod. He had therefore entwined hemp tight around the handle with gluing agents. After again testing this in training, he found it not only light and robust, but easy to twist and swing.

'Argh, here be one,' Vlad announced, picking up one of his experimental swords. 'This be a longsword as you see, but you will feel the difference to that of which you swung earlier.' He handed his experimental weapon to Radu, who at first tested its weight. 'This have a robust iron shaft but hardened steel forged about it. As once the softer metal hardens about the iron, it is embroiled in mixed oils and cooled in a mineral composite.' He watched Radu wield the sword and observed an impressed expression on his brother's unsullied face. 'They be like women,' Vlad described with a chuckle. 'They be light, nimble and swift, but strong and hard in argument and attack.' Vlad recognized his brother's amusement, but then saw a frown come over his face.

'But surely such a mixture of metals be awkward to forge together?'

'Argh, but that be where my craftsmen be noble to our enemy,' Vlad steered his younger brother over to another workshop where casting was performed. 'The granites that hold the mix of molten metals are flexible, but once in place, hold firm the iron rod base until somewhat cool enough to broil.' Vlad placed an example rod in place as he described how molten metal was poured into the cast. 'Once set upon the rod, as the metal hardens, it is shaped and sharpened until good to polish.'

'Have you then concocted a special mixture – a special ratio of differing metals – some composite that be superior to that of the Ottoman Empire?'

'I believe I may,' Vlad replied with a smirk on his face. 'And what be the formulae?'

'Well that be the secret. And one only my experts here share.' Vlad noticed an eager jealousy come over Radu's boyish face. 'A sorcerer or bewitched woman does not reveal their secret potion… or maids tell of their mother's secret recipe.' Vlad stood hovering over his smaller brother, before he backed away somewhat.

'And you make other weaponry using such methods,' Radu questioned, his curiosity getting the better of him, 'other implements apart from swords, that is?'

'Of course, my young brother; have you learned nothing in your detention with our enemy?' Vlad grinned again, but this time more widely. 'Remember the blade be the most effective instrument against our enemy.'

'Being much nobler of course, I prefer the arrow myself,' Radu muttered before continuing, his blue eyes glimmering from the firelight of the surrounding furnaces. 'But that be it… there be no other secret to these hardened blades but that of a central rod and that secret proportion of smelted metals forged about it?'

'Of course, my brother, but we still experiment, both with metals, broiling oils, mineral cooling and lighter handles.' Vlad paused to think a while before continuing. 'Henrik is of Hungarian descent and in his ancestry they too experimented with hardwood handles. How do you reckon they conjured the beasts of war, like that of the flail, bludgeon, cudgel and mace?'

'It be not the weapons you use that take advantage in this war.'

'No, I agree; it be the soldiers wielding them.' Vlad held one arm around his small brother's shoulder and squeezed tight. 'I mean not to test your intelligence of such matters young brother, but want you to fight alongside me.' Releasing Radu, Vlad shrugged his shoulders and outspread his hands. 'I'll even have my craftsmen make you up a cross-bow… one made special as to your liking.'

'Indeed, your newly forged weaponry could be advantageous against that of the Ottoman Empire, but I speak principally about enemy numbers.' Radu glanced slyly at Vlad, thinking he had not seen him. 'Since father's death, much land have been lost to enemies from both sides… discrepancies north and west against the Germans of Transylvania and supposed allegiances with the Moldavian King. That is discounting the Ottoman Empire.'

'Yes, dear brother, again you remind me that my lands be squashed from all sides,' Vlad stipulated tetchily. 'That it is indeed hard to determine tactics to prevent warfare from all the different lands that surround us; that only the Moldavian King has ever come to our aide.' Vlad paused again to think for a second. 'But I be making extra weaponry in order that you return back many a garrison from father's kingdom. And before you return, I shall recruit young and healthy men from many local villages that surround this keep, so Henrik may train them to fight strong. And from then, we be not just stout and able to defend this realm, but also conquer back that which has been taken from us!'

'I be lying if I was not impressed with what you achieve here,' Radu admitted, 'but as I must reiterate, it be the sheer number of enemy soldiers that be the problem.'

'Yes, and if for some insane reason I was to surrender young Wallachian, Transylvanian or Hungarian men as tributes to the Sultan, surely the Ottoman Empire would outnumber all our lands through fear, not honour!' Vlad paused to contain his anger, and pulling out his father's sword as an example, indicated, 'I will endeavor to make blades for my men like this… ones that be lighter and tougher than their circular blades and long enough to cut down twice, or thrice as many Turks!' Vlad strode ahead and Radu had to keep a fast pace to keep up with him, eventually grabbing his tall brother by the arm to stop him.

'I know that be father's sword and again I be impressed with all you do here,' Radu emphasized, 'but you must face facts!'

'And they be?'

'Turkish armies are increasing double or three-fold. So even with all your new weaponry and armor, would it not be better to agree some arrangement, than to send men to the slaughter–?'

'There be of no such thing,' Vlad interrupted angrily, 'not as long as I be alive!'

'But I have seen Turkish garrisons reach north of this keep,' Radu stated, 'armies more than twice of any Hungarian west or Moldavian east.'

'As these foreigners be small and meek, then tempered chainmail and leathers will protect my men. And with our new weaponry, each soldier will cut down many before he be defeated in battle.' Vlad laughed to repress his anger. 'Why these Turks be small enough to squash under foot. Only Sultan Mehmet be almost equal to your height dear brother.'

'I believe you only met the Sultan once when we were captive,' Radu paused to recollect. 'Or would that be his senior?'

'Come, it not be important,' Vlad declared, turning to walk over and consult a craftsman. 'This be my brother Radu. See that he get a crossbow made to his liking. And in my absence, please see this fulfillment of weapons be granted to his garrison. Use the weapons of experiment if need be.'

'Yes, my Lord,' the craftsman agreed, but turned back to hear Radu contest.

'So, my garrison is be used as one of your experiments are they… like ravens against a wolf pack?'

'They be better than the weapons with which you came!' Vlad retorted. But then, pondering over what Jusztina had mentioned earlier, he towered over his small brother to ask, 'Tell me little brother, how just did your small garrison get you over such distance… so swift and unharmed?'

'Why my brother,' Radu's eyes blinked agitatedly, his mind acute, 'as you should know by our time with the Ottoman Empire, the Turks do not venture much hillside, and by cover of forest, such a small number did not attract attention.'

'Or maybe you engaged some mysterious good fortune?' Vlad changed his spate of scorn to lead Radu back up to the ground floor of the keep, where he stopped in his stride to face his younger brother and declare, 'Maybe if Henrik trains young men from our farmlands and villages – men that want to be fed, paid well, and learn how to fight – we will not need to accrue allies from other lands, as many cannot be trusted.'

'All I be saying, and I know you oppose such,' Radu said calmly, 'is that the Turks be taking Transylvanian lands by many a number. And with the ignorance of Matthias Corvinus, the Ottoman Empire encroach Hungarian territory also.' Radu looked sternly at Vlad, his eyes testing his. 'Maybe one day the Hungarian king will need to grant some truce with the Sultan.'

'I know the king would never agree to such. Matthias Corvinus has taken his allegiance with us, not some unscrupulous, untrustworthy bastard. But I admit the king be a difficult man in keeping his word, so we may have to recruit allies north and east of the Danube… maybe more distance lands across the Black Seas to the cold lands of the Tsar.'

'With what I be knowing,' Radu condemned, 'as the Ottoman Empire increase their numbers north, you may not have the time to approve anything with anyone.'

'Corvinus was stupid in never realizing to how important the lands along the Danube were, and so never gave his support. It be important we withhold cities bordering such an important river, as it give entry from shores reaching the edges of southern Hungary to the coasts of the Black Seas. This be the reason why the city of Constantinople had been a great standpoint.' Vlad turned to walk away in disgust, his face contorted. 'And without any aide from Corvinus, it was lost.'

As both brothers reached a wide lobby where several corridors converged, Radu took again Vlad's arm to stop him and ask.

'I take from your accounts, that without such of the king's support, you have not the capability to take back such cities as Constantinople?'

'It be my truth to admit that defending this realm and those lands that surround our keep are becoming increasingly difficult.' Vlad progressively felt glum, but looked up at rays of light filtering through narrow windows above as he paced slowly towards the entrance of a decorative parlor. Maybe the good Lord will spare such an honorable Christian from such adversity; that maybe this Prince of Wallachia will one day become a king of this land.' Vlad spoke out loud as if alone, but knew Radu followed. 'May I pray that the Lord spare me from such premature death? And should I depart my time on earth, that my spirit be endorsed in the heavens.' Vlad paused at the parlor entrance after hearing his brother mutter a question.

'Could you tell me brother; about what are the numbers of garrison in this keep? Are there timely patrols about Poenari?' Radu poked Vlad's chest with two aggravating fingers, this eyes staring up with purpose. 'Have you a constant lookout to detect any oncoming army?'

'Yes, lookouts are constant in the turrets and watchtowers but be somewhat blind to the river, but cliffs being so tall that side, well…' Vlad paused to look down at Radu's annoying little fingers, but continued once he had removed them. 'They change at dusk and dawn always on schedule unless of course –'

'Has one of you gentlemen seen my vanity mirror,' Jusztina interrupted on exiting the parlor, her face somewhat flushed with exhaustion. 'I be wanting it and mislaid it so?' 'No, my dear,' Vlad responded somewhat stunned by her intrusion, 'I not see it

since you used it last, in our bedchamber.' He looked at Radu with raised eyebrows. 'Have you seen my dear wife's mirror?'

'No, no I have not.' Radu said boldly. 'Did you not have it when I was admiring the views across river from the upstairs chambers?'

'Yes, but then I bought Mihnea down to play,' Jusztina replied, her eyes gleaming with light tears of frustration.

'Then maybe he be having it?' Radu professed.

'No, I ask already,' Jusztina contested, before leaving in a fluster. 'He have not and knows not to play with such things.'

Both brothers turned their heads to watch Jusztina disappear quickly around the corner, obviously to ascend the great, stone stairway to check her bed chambers.

'She's been somewhat peculiar since you arrived,' Vlad said. 'I be open to admit that she does not like you much.'

'And usually women are all but fervent with me,' Radu stated, a grin expanding across his face.

As the two brothers continued across the expanse of the great hall to approach the large, wooden banqueting table, Vlad enquired to Radu's previous questioning.

'Why do you ask of our guards?'

'I be inquisitive that's all,' Radu said striding ahead, his head drooped to admire the polished stone floor of the great hall. 'Some of my garrison be wanting to be safe whilst in their beds.'

'Your men be safe here whilst I be at rule; that I promise you!' Vlad defined, and pointing to his boyars who were seated about the great wooden table, stated, 'You may confer any problems you have with any of my nobles here!'

'I must expose my concerns to you all, as I have to my elder brother.' Radu stood in front of the great table, leaning upon it with fists clenched tight, his knuckles bearing white. 'Since our father's demise, I have sent out many a scout to find out truths of what happened and in listening to your own scouts, I can only surmise as such…' He paused before continuing, eyeing all boyars from left and right. 'You cannot be expecting aide from other countries who are too prevalent in their own skirmishes, and with the garrison numbers I see here depleted, you must put aside your virtues and make tough decisions that may save all that you hold dear.'

'What it be that you try to suggest?' old reliable Lucian challenged as Vlad knew he would.

'I know for facts reported to me before my entering this keep, that nations such as Albania, are signing a truce with Sultan Mehmet to prevent the murder of thousands; which in turn they give a small number of young, orphaned or peasant land workers away. These in turn will have food and are well –'

'Why, you expect us, after all what we have endured, to even consider such?' Lucian contested.

'It be an outrage for such an imposter to convey as much,' another boyar wildly contested, but glanced quickly at Vlad, 'even if you be a brother to our Lord!'

'Then the Ottoman Empire gather more young men to fight and oppose you,' Radu spoke calmly.

'We fight our enemies only with our own kind and do not ask of others to do our dirty work!' Vlad interjected.

'So, your marriage to Jusztina dear brother, this was not to forge some allegiance with the Moldavian king?'

'No, it be to stop the Turk's spreading north and east.' Vlad felt his blood boiling. 'It be only a ploy to discourage the Ottoman Empire; that a combined army would prevent the advance of such like.' Vlad took a deep breath to take composure, but had to oppose Radu's take of discourse. 'Why take this view young brother? Why do you question that we cannot be victorious on our own behalf?'

Radu looked up from the table to peer at Vlad.

'Earlier I took conversation with your wife my dear brother, and although fervent against my reasoning, she agreed that you may need to renegotiate with Stephen the Great so that his Moldavian army can come again to your aide. Or maybe you could set new allegiance with other bordering nations.'

'Our marriage still endorses the Moldavian king's commitment to provide aide… his word at our wedding was entrusted.'

'But I hear from your council, of all past battles, and never once has the Moldavian king intervened. Surely all victories have not just been due to tactics and strategy … or to the great new weaponry you exemplify?'

'No, it be that we entrust our Prince to fight to the death with us; all Christian men alongside our Lord in the battlefield!' a boyar spoke.

'I say again, I be impressed with all such commitment and the craftsman of such weaponry,' Radu reasoned, 'but as the Turks be increasing in such number as I have witnessed from scout reports and my own travels, then they outnumber this keep at least three to your one!'

'All of us here would rather be enslaved, or better executed, than forge some alliance with such filth!' Vlad enraged.

'My brother, I speak only of facts and surmise that in but a year, the Ottoman Empire will outnumber this realm and quash it to surrender.'

'You speak as if some foreign delegate, sent here to warn us and make us surrender to some enemy allegiance,' Lucian declared.

'I be but a brother to your Lord and Prince, but understand things different to he.' Radu paused to swallow and again observe all the pensive eyes that stared at him across the large, oval table. 'Would it not be better to surrender a few peasant farming children than to have this keep rampaged and many a man slaughtered?'

'The Turks should fight fair with us and gain victory by honour, not squander others to do the Sultan's biddings!'

'But it be a fact of happening my dear brother,' Radu replied again calmly. 'It be how they have increased in number... you admit yourself to men not of their nature... men not dark of skin!'

'The Sultan and his soldiers should fight eye-to-eye and tooth-for-a-tooth to gain victory, not pilferage from others.' Vlad stepped forward and slammed his fist against the table, making some of his boyars shudder. 'But if Sultan Mehmet wants to scavenge young men from the lands, then we do the same and so play him at his own game! We will train young stonemasons, carpenters, ironmongers, farm boys and peasants... recruit all like to fight with a sword! Henrik can teach best his men to make them be willing to die for Wallachia... not some foreign land!'

'I still impose on you dear brother, that in a year or so, both resources of men and monies in Wallachia will not be enough!'

'What be of this negativity,' Vlad condemned passionately, 'I be sick of such attitude. If we then don't have such numbers in recruiting the poor and starving from our lands, then I see that the enemy be purged and looted so their armies be starved and ours fed… that we poison their drink water if need be!'

'And how you be recruiting enough to do such tasks?'

'Bring garrisons from father's realm and that be some start, dear –'

'My Lord,' Henrik shouted to interrupt, somewhat out of breath, 'the east wall reports a garrison of Turkish soldiers moving south!'

'Do they turn to approach the keep and take the gorge south?'

'Not sure my Lord,' Henrik ogled all the boyars about the great table, some now standing with fear gleaming from their eyes. 'They be distant and mainly on foot, only a few horsemen on last count.'

'Then we take every caution and alert all guard and garrison.' Vlad turned to face Radu. 'You may wish to inform your garrison, but they be safe in the courtyard barracks.' He paused but waved on certain boyars to go about their business. 'But at first you may find it an interest to follow me and Henrik, to observe that of our new defenses.'

Radu stepped back in raising an eyebrow, but had to pursue quick to keep up with Vlad and Henrik's pace.

At first they strode along the high curtain wall that stretched the height of the exterior keep between bastions; Vlad instructing archers to maintain arrow-slits, pike-men and slingers to stand on raised terraces poised with spear or rock, men to maneuver slender cannons into booths – their nozzles shadowed within the darkness of small, square openings. And as they ascended steps to walk high above the arched, main gate, Vlad poised to command more instruction.

'Observe here my brother,' Vlad announced in a deep, proud voice as he pointed at portals in the brickwork. 'We make no waste of the broiling oils and tar used from production in our dungeon workshop.' Vlad smiled as he saw Radu observe soldiers open barrels of oil waste and pour them into troughs, some drowning wood-meshed stones into the thick liquid before loading nearby catapults. 'See hear where the liquid can be set free?' Vlad pointed to a small sluice gate, Radu's eyes following the conduit until it disappeared through the brickwork above the gate. 'Ignited, the oils pour but sprinkle anything below the main gate and areas wide.' Vlad paused to see his brother's face contort to recollect. 'And such installations defend our battlements and turrets.'

'This be what I saw on entry to Poenari,' Radu conveyed. 'Spills upon the earth when we first requested access to this keep.'

'Yes, we have tested it many a time to ensure ferocity and range.' Vlad waved Radu on as he advanced to the stairway of the eastern turret, but his young brother was, for some reason, poised by thought. 'Come we must establish exactly our threat.'

Radu followed best, but found himself fatigued as he joined his elder brother at the highest bastion and lookout of the eastern tower.

'It be not the clearest of days and I must admit my eyes not be as sharp as they once were.'

'Where they be?' Radu enquired, squinting at the distant pines and evergreens that lay beyond the autumnal treetops of nearby sycamores and silver birch. 'I not locate them.'

'There, between those two tall trees, you can make out helmets and blades from horsemen at the tail of their garrison.' Henrik pointed as he joined the brothers and overheard their conversation. 'It be strange as they not turn west to join the path south of our keep, but meander south-easterly.'

'Maybe they make camp as it be sunset within a few hours?' Vlad questioned his second-in-command.

'Maybe, it could be so.' Henrik answered slowly, but gave more speculation. 'Maybe they be trying to squash our scouts and armies outside this keep first… to squander young men to recruit as your brother describe?'

'Then if that be it, I will raise a scouting party,' Vlad said imperiously. 'We need to know our enemy plan and beat them before it be resolute!'

'Am I to saddle alongside you my Lord?'

'Yes Henrik,' Vlad confirmed, placing a hand on his shoulder, 'I may need you to disperse our garrison so that we become a two spread of attack.'

'Or better if one leads them astray as the other does follow.' Henrik envisaged; a chuckle to his voice. 'Maybe scatter them like lost chickens, eh?'

'Make sure the keep be following my orders of defense before I join you at the main gate.'

'But Lord, should we not use the rear gate to be cautious?'

'We have not the time Henrik.' Vlad fretted, but paused to grimace at the thought of loading armor against his injured side. 'We will ride light as it be just to establish their intention. Without my command, we do not battle unless they attack, do you understand?' 'Yes, my Lord,' Henrik answered assertively. 'Then I gather ten score men and meet you at the gate sharp!'

FIVE

After mounting his light-armoured horse just inside the main gate, Vlad glanced around to observe the nearest of his ten score garrison. Maybe this number was extreme for a scouting party, but should they need to divide or endure combat, he needed to be confident in enough. But if Turkish garrisons merged to attack Poenari, would he have enough men to defeat such an assault? Although much of his army had depleted this past year, surely he had enough military to protect the keep – especially with men now trained to work such defences. His thoughts were interrupted by Henrik who came beside him, his horse jolting after riding from the rear of the garrison to get ready all troops.

'There is not much daylight left my Lord,' Henrik gestured, his eyes scouring the sky. 'With heavy clouds gathering by such a brisk wind, I suggest we have but a couple hours.' He looked eagerly at Vlad to await his response.

'It be to our favour if we scout beyond dusk,' Vlad replied boldly, but also regarded the sky. 'We have the advantage of knowing our lands and so can outwit these bastards.' Snuggling deep into his saddle, he was just about to ask Henrik if all soldiers were ready, when a voice yelled from above.

'My brother,' Radu called from a parapet that extended from the gatehouse, 'you may have enough to scout those we saw, but what if you endure battle?'

'We be at haste dear brother, as they travel fast,' Vlad shouted back. 'The enemy may pilferage our villages so hurry. Whatever it be, we be outsmarting such as this be our land, and I be knowing much to outwit such predictable vermin.'

'I could follow up with my men,' Radu conveyed determinedly. 'They be now well fed and good for battle!'

'No, my brother,' Vlad replied, his stallion jolting its reins as Henrik's horse too clawed its hooves nervously against the stone laid floor. 'There be enough here to maintain our new defences, and others to protect the township outside the keep.'

Vlad glanced up to notice the gatekeeper signal to whether he was ready, and after a quick nod from Henrik, the heavy, main gate was slowly opened.

'I follow should you get into trouble,' Radu shouted, but his voice was drowned by the sound of hooves and then the clatter of troops marching forward. 'I will check from the watchtower!'

'Stay here and protect Jusztina!' Vlad cried after faintly hearing his brother.

From a barbican lookout high above the gatehouse, Radu watched the five-wide march of Vlad's garrison disappear into the distance. But as Mount Cetatea steeped high above its valleys below, he lost track of the soldiers as they had to descend single file. And as the sound of hooves and marching feet faded, he now heard the main gate shut and the portcullis being lowered.

Impatiently Radu rushed to observe Vlad's army high from a bastion of the eastern tower, but after sighting the last soldier gone, he returned to the highest bedchamber to look out beyond the autumn treetops and into distant pinewood forests.

'Why Radu, my dear husband's brother,' Jusztina asked inquisitively, but showed some restraint, 'what it be that you are doing?' With his back toward her, Jusztina did not recognise her vanity mirror in his hands, but questioned his use of candlelight. 'Why light a candle so early... it be over an hour before dusk?'

'I was trying to observe my brother through the trees, but not all leaves be fallen yet.' He saw her grey eyes glimmer expectantly at him and so continued. 'Well, whilst observing, I noticed something shimmer in the darkest corner...' He crouched to point below tables enshrouded by racks of drying linen. 'And with regard to your concerns earlier, and by this candlelight, I recognised of what you had lost...' Somewhat tentatively, Radu revealed Jusztina's vanity mirror from his side, but then gazed admiringly into it. 'It have good depth to show such a handsome face...' Seeing Jusztina somewhat unimpressed, he handed it out to her but enquired. 'Could it be that I keep it for a while... for my own vanities that is.' He glared earnestly at her again, but she detected his shifty eyes waver. 'I shall return it to you by tomorrow, if it be alright?'

'Why it be mine,' Jusztina argued, 'so I be wanting it back!'

'But surely just for this evening?' Radu insisted, but seeing her eyes stare inquisitively at the candle, he blew out its flame before placing it down on a nearby table.

'I thought of it lost, but now I know it just misplaced, I'd like it back!'

'But surely, as your husband beckoned,' Radu said sneeringly, holding her mirror at some distance whilst his other hand guided her out the room, 'we have more important matters to attend to.'

'Such as?' Jusztina gawked at him, not liking his forcefulness.

'Why your husband insisted that I ensure your safety...' And pushing her toward her bedchamber, he added, 'and as there be many of his garrison out scouting, there could be an attempt to attack this keep.'

'But you have enough men to assist, have you not?'

'I believe it necessary for my garrison to follow and support my brother,' Radu held her by one wrist to guide her into her bedchamber. 'As your husband expressed before leaving, enough be here to maintain his new defence. And such defence be robust and effective.'

'Then I be safe in this keep, as always.' Jusztina recoiled to escape Radu's clasp but felt him grip her wrist tight. 'Why you be hurting me so,' Jusztina whined, glancing back into her bedchamber as he pushed her. 'Why you be like this?'

'You want your mirror back don't you?' Radu glanced about the room and released her, but clutched her mirror to his chest. 'So take order from your dear husband and keep safe and be quiet in here!'

'But I want my mirror you rogue,' Jusztina wheezed as she lunged forward to seize her mirror, but Radu held it firm. And using his other hand, turned her by her own force, to send her sprawled across the floor. 'Why toy with me like this?'

'As to your husband's request my dear,' Radu sniggered as he withdrew from the room, his blue eyes glaring unkindly at her, 'I be taking care of you and so make it be that you cannot leave the safety of your room.' He snatched the key from the inside lock to slam shut the door. 'Dearest Jusztina, I merely be taking care of *you*... and your beautiful mirror.'

Before she could get to her feet and test the door, Jusztina heard the key turn in the lock outside. Several times she pulled and twisted the doorknob, but found the door locked tight. She whinged and slammed her fist against the door several times, but all she could hear from the other side was faint sniggering.

'I be afraid dear Lucian, for her own safety, I have shut Jusztina in her bedchamber, as she be fretting about my brother leaving so soon and…'

'I must protest against your action Radu Bey,' Lucian interrupted, turning to face his small, fair-haired stranger. The elder boyar leaned against the large banqueting table, his large but frail hands sprayed upon the polished oak surface to support his aged body. 'Miss Jusztina be getting very distraught these days, and we be thinking she may be again bearing child.' Lucian noted how Radu's face contorted as if to sneer objection. 'And it must be that she can look over Mihnea. We have limited women within this keep, and not many do her mistress trust.'

'Then you should oversee that someone she trusts be taking care of her and her son.' Radu stepped around the table and as Lucian stood tall to face him, he stabbed his little fingers at the elder's chest. 'As we my noble friend, have another duty.'

'Such as?' Lucian stepped back to free himself of Radu's aggravating fingers.

'Well, as I also be fretting and anxious to my brother's welfare, it be wise that you guide me to follow my brother, and so my garrison be put to good assistance.'

'But what about the numbers to defend this keep?'

'Vlad told me in confidence that enough are here to maintain such new defence. And I heard him speak with Henrik; that indeed he did not take all troops, only those well rested from his last battle.'

'It means nothing in what you say,' Lucian turned away in protest, 'our Prince of Wallachia is well learned and experienced in combat, and be most victorious in battle, whatever be the odds!'

'But what if we denied a chance to assist and… I hate to state this, but my brother was defeated?' Radu pulled Lucian around by the shoulder to show the concern on his face. 'Where would this leave us? I could not defend this realm as I have an obligation to bury right my father and return to Sighişoara. And I swore allegiance to Transylvanian boyars to help defend their lands… a last wish uttered by my father.'

'But I understand, from scouts and foreign word,' Lucian turned away again in denial, 'you were not there to hear any last words from Vlad the Dragon, the first true Voivode of Wallachia.'

'No with regret, father's death came before my arrival… I had to hear his wishes repeated by a second hand.' Radu stared at the ground as if recalling despondent memories. 'I missed my chance there and then, but will not want such again… especially now, for I only have one brother!'

'But I must object that such action would be irrational, and against the wishes of his lordship.' Lucian looked for once ashamed at Radu to admit, 'And I am, as you may deduce, not the knight and instrument of battle as I once was.'

'Then ride with me and be glorious just once more,' Radu beckoned, his arms extended long for his hands to grasp Lucian's shoulders. 'Although he be smart and strong, it may be our day to save my brother.' Lucian looked away but took sight of the shimmering blue eyes which glowered up at him. 'It may be your last chance… our last chance to prove ourselves worthy for the next Wallachian king!'

'It be true that your words move me young Radu,' Lucian announced whilst making his way slowly out of the main hall, 'but I be afraid, as I do not know you well, that a little trust be absent.'

'Lord Lucian,' a shrill of a voice broadcast from the doorway as they saw little Mihnea appear, 'my mother be locked in her chamber and have no key!'

Lucian regarded the little boy's flustered face before turning back to face Radu. Suddenly he felt plagued by mixed emotions: him wanting to ride with Radu and again prove his worth to Vlad; but why had Radu been so unjust with his brother's wife, one who could soon be queen? He turned his face away from the stranger to comfort Vlad's son, but Radu was already by his side and secretly offering him the key to Jusztina's bedchamber.

'Be finding someone to take care of her mistress, will you not?' Radu whispered to Lucian as he too viewed the anxiety on Mihnea's face. 'For we have a duty to honour our Lord and Prince, do we not?'

'My honour begins by releasing our future queen from your stupid excuse of protection.' Lucian paced quickly to pick up Mihnea in his arms and hug him. 'And make sure her son be comforted and not strained by such action.'

'My Lord, by now we must be many miles south of our keep,' Henrik groaned as he trotted his horse alongside Vlad's, 'and yet, although they be in sight, in cover of this forest we do not attack?'

'Patience my friend,' Vlad replied. 'We can cut them off at any time. But first I must observe their movement.'

'Then why be so quiet?' Henrik paused on noticing the sharp glare his commander gave. 'I know you well my lord and never see you so pensive?'

'I must admit my good friend,' Vlad slowed his horse to converse quieter. 'These bastards we follow circle east our keep and then go south, their route uncommon.'

'Could it be that they have another plan,' Henrik surmised, 'other than to attack our keep?'

'I do not think they intend to attack Poenari my friend. So at least my wife and son be safe.'

'How can you be sure?' Henrik was bemused.

'They approached our keep miles back, but now lead us to meander east. This be highly irregular for Ottoman soldiers.' Vlad saw Henrik even more perplexed and so explained. 'You forget that I, and my young brother Radu – one other as last of the Draculesti – were brought up by Ottoman tutors – *Effendi* – that we, against my father's wish, were first imprisoned, but later learned much about Turkish life, including their methods of conflict and tactics to engage in battle. These be lessons you never forget, especially when half-starved and persecuted. Their efforts to convert us however, were made difficult, but within a year we could recite their Holy Qur'an. This book refutes to convert religious belief, yet we were required to denounce our true religion and reject Christianity against our very own will.'

After sensing Vlad's anger grow fervent, Henrik altered his discourse to mention the safety of the keep.

'To your word then my lord; I be sure that such a small enemy would never penetrate our keep… and it being so near dusk, we can fortify the gates well beyond nightfall.'

'Patience again my friend,' Vlad said holding up one hand to stop all. 'But again dear Henrik, you open your big mouth to speak so soon.' Vlad's eyes gleamed at Henrik

in frustration. 'As we trail only the tail of our enemy as we meander, we not notice the front half gone.'

'Is that not but some enemy tactic my lord?'

'No, not unless they be taking surrounding towns or villages… maybe squander our common people to pilferage their resources... to rape particular settlements and convert them to strongholds to link and surround us.' Henrik was about to make another suggestion but knew not to interrupt Vlad as he thought aloud. 'It could be that the front garrison have split to meet a larger army or that our route back be cut off.'

'Should we double back then, my lord?'

'Yes, I'm afraid so my friend.' After amassing such curiosity, Vlad grimaced in dismissing his chance to engage the enemy. 'We continue to scout, but have Ilie and Ion circle back with the rear half to clear our way home.

'Yes, my lord.'

Vlad pulled on the reins of his stallion and the dark russet beast neighed heavy before setting a steady canter; men behind following on foot, their eyes squinting curious to why Henrik rode back along the lines of marching men.

As the rear half of the garrison turned to double back and Henrik rode back along the troops to lead again at the front, he saw several of his men fretful.

'What it be that you look at soldier?' Henrik slowed his horse to ask. 'We see people in the trees my lord.'

Another soldier added whilst pointing, 'Eyes in the darkening shadows!'

'Keep your wits about you men,' Henrik announced, glaring wide-eyed at them. 'They be just thieves and brigands, so as an army, we be untouchable.'

'But my lord; why the rear half go back?'

'Don't worry, we follow shortly after I speak with our Prince,' Henrik announced but then whispered to himself, 'I hope we do soon… before nightfall.'

All eyes looked expectantly at Henrik, but soon he rode on his horse.

'How long must we go on my Lord,' Henrik interrupted Vlad's inquisitiveness as he joined him up front. 'The men get jittery to be halved by number and venture further from home.' Henrik glanced at the darkening sky and the shadows within the woodland. 'They say there be eyes watching us.'

'Brigands most likely,' Vlad interjected, somewhat disinterested.

'Yes my lord, that be what I mention and that they not…' Henrik paused to notice flickering light between wavering tree branches. 'But something else be there my lord… and we have lost the enemy's trail.'

'No dear Henrik,' Vlad crouched to pry at the flickering light through the shadowy woodland. 'I think they play but a game with us.'

Vlad galloped on and so Henrik followed, but at first glanced back in concern to see his men confused.

'Follow us as fast as you can,' Henrik announced before his horse shot forward. 'And form circle in clearings ahead... I shall return with our Prince!'

A score or so of men from the front of the Vlad's battalion followed swiftly on foot, but many not archers or light swordsmen failed to keep up. Instead, these heavier armoured pike men, longsword and shield bearers, raced through the woodland until a large clearing came in sight.

As one senior officer took charge and barked out orders for all remaining men to form circle, his voice was silenced by a short scabbard blade that sliced his throat. As Wallachian soldiers looked in horror to watch their acting chief fall, many others were being slain from beyond the shadows of trees. Recognising their turban helmets and shape of armour, along with their kilij swords, Wallachian soldiers dispersed in panic to try and join comrades already kneeling with shields to form a circle. But many, as they and raced into the clearing to help fortify their defence, were cut down either by arrow or sword.

Although panicked, Vlad's soldiers soon realized that they were set in ambush and fought tough against the enemy assault; the determination to join their fellow men within their hasty protection, their incentive. But Turks came from all angles, their pikes and spears now piercing the formation of shields before they could close access left for others.

A dozen archers had made the shielded centre and reeled arrows back out to the enemy, but many protective swordsmen had already been injured or slain. And without their usual heavy armour, the makeshift defence was soon breached; many Wallachian soldiers breaking away from the fight to race back to the garrison already heading back.

Vlad, Henrik and two score soldiers, who had raced to keep up, had heard skirmishes back within the woodland and so rested to contemplate.

'It's a trap my Lord,' Henrik growled. 'Some sort of ambush helped by your incessant curiosity!' Henrik tried best to steady his anger, as he did so his horse. 'And because of you, we leave the main group… and be defenceless!'

'It not be a large group, remember?' Vlad snarled.

'But they kill us by having advantage,' Henrik snapped back, spittle now drooling his light brown beard. 'They be the ones in the trees!'

'You fool; these bastards do not jump from trees!' Vlad glanced all around him. 'But it be an ambush, you be right!'

'Then my Lord, there be an enemy tactic you not know.' Henrik tried best to humour their situation, but saw Vlad's green eyes glower at him again.

'We take route back to gather what men still fight,' Vlad announced, and waving on the remainder of his garrison after his stare left Henrik, he proclaimed, 'We collect all injured and make haste our keep!'

Vlad and Henrik turned their horses to set route back to Poenari, trotting slow enough for soldiers to run steady ahead and make haste through the woodland. Dodging many low-lying branches, Vlad and Henrik found it difficult to decipher whether they were heading back in the right direction. Also, it was nearing dusk and the claws of darkness were clutching at Henrik; why did they not head back earlier, get back before nightfall?

As they traipsed cautiously the trail of what they conceived was the remains of the other garrison's footfall, Vlad's remaining soldiers came to a small clearing where all stopped abruptly. Not only did they shudder on hearing distant cries, but halted on seeing dead bodies strewn about the clearing, comrades lying slaughtered in undergrowth, their eyes glazed and fixed to stare at the ever darkening shadows. And then a nearby shrill pierced the quiet.

It was a Wallachian soldier – a light swordsman. But before he could run to the sanctuary of the group, an arrow pierced his back and he stumbled to fall against Vlad's stallion. As the soldier cried out and tried eagerly to grasp the horse, the beast suddenly jolted and reared before bolting.

In the first few seconds Vlad was jerked back and almost left his saddle, but holding stiff the reins and digging his heels into the stallion's flanks, he held on as the beast galloped on frantically. Seeing his commander in trouble, Henrik followed, and like Vlad, had to quickly avoid low-lying branches as he sped to pursue. As men raced to follow their commanders, they could only best follow the deep hoof marks embedded within the woodland earth.

Through dense woodland Henrik spotted his commander about fifty paces ahead. Nearing an embankment, as his horse dawdled, Henrik noticed Vlad taking control of his steed, but then something else startled the beast.

As Vlad kicked away at Turks who shot out from the shadows, Henrik noticed one man jump from the embankment to land on the horse's rear, a dagger flashing above his turban helmet. Luckily the first few strikes of the Turk's scabbard hit only the back-plate of Vlad's armour, before the horse bolted again.

Vlad tensed, trying best to shake off his enemy, but the Turk now held one hand onto the rear saddle, his other wielding the scabbard high, again ready to strike. But the prince now controlled his stallion and used his gallop to his advantage; crouching forward not only to dodge the attacks from behind, but to evade low-lying branches of trees he rode under.

Approaching one thick, overhanging branch, instead of avoiding it, Vlad rode swiftly towards it, pulling the grasping

Turk up with him as he stood tall in his stirrups. And then, just before darting underneath the branch, Vlad plunged his chest against his stallion's mane, leaving the Turk perched high.

With wrath to inflict damage to who he knew was the Prince of Wallachia, the Turk did not notice Vlad's helmet fly from his head. But like it, he too hit the sturdy oak branch; the assailant flying from Vlad's horse, his nose and jaw broken, his face mangled from the sudden impact before his crumpled body hit the floor.

Vlad glanced around to see that his tactic had worked. He grinned to see his enemy dismounted from his stallion's croup, glad now that his enemy was sprawled somewhere behind in the muddied earth. But then his horse jolted suddenly and stepped back, kicking out its forelegs as it reared. Vlad held on but felt the beast shudder to lances and pikes that pierced the leather and light armour about its neck and shoulders. Again the stallion trudged back, its front hooves kicking away turban helmets from enemy soldiers who stood close. But as all he could do was hold on, Vlad grimaced to see enemy spearheads stab again at his trusty steed, the beast petrified and exhausting.

In one, last desperate attempt to escape the assault, the stallion twisted and reared again, ready to bolt. But as the beast met another lance that pierced its leather flank, it wavered sideways, it legs a quiver before Vlad was thrown. It was all that Vlad could remember… that and the thick oak branch that hit his forehead.

Henrik pulled forward his horse as soon as he dismounted, squinting through trees and undergrowth that he hoped would conceal him. He glanced back, disconcerted that none of his garrison had kept up, but smirked to notice his horse quietly nibble leaves from nearby saplings. He pulled down tight on the horse's bridle, hoping his ride would also go unsighted by the enemy, but then looked back at hearing voices.

They were Turkish soldiers, and unfortunately Henrik had a limited understanding of such quick dialogue. But as they poked their spears at Vlad's body, he recognised their word for *beheading* and the Sultan's name *Mehmet*. And although the Wallachian prince was not dead – simply knocked unconscious – Henrik worried that soon he could be.

Suddenly a more dominant voice blurted out foreign words above all others, and being dressed in finer armoury, Henrik professed that this was their glorified leader. The commander came bounding towards Vlad's lifeless body, his arms flinging men out the way. Although recognising certain words, Henrik came confused to the commander's intent.

'He's to be taken back alive for Sultan Mehmet,' a voice announced startling Henrik. A secondary commander slumped down beside him as others from his garrison caught up to follow suit, 'although that bastard wants the glory of murdering our prince for himself!'

'Did you *all* follow me here?'

'No,' the secondary commander replied. 'We got caught up in scuffles, but most of us here evaded the enemy by hiding in the oncoming dusk.' He paused for a moment to glance around, Henrik searching his eyes for certainty before they again met his. 'Many fled after sighting our garrison's reed torches from afar and so...'

'So,' Henrik interrupted, somewhat impatient, 'how many of you are there?' 'Not enough to deal with this lot.'

'But our prince is to be captured,' Henrik stressed, his eyes counting the number of men joining him, 'unless that bastard takes his head first!'

'Nothing but a score followed me,' the soldier explained, 'so we have no more than what you see here my lord.'

Henrik turned from noting the anxiety in the soldier's eyes – that and the tiredness that darkened them – to see two Turks begin to drag Vlad's body, a man at each foot.

'We must all try and rescue our prince. Our land be never the same if we do not.' 'But you see here my lord,' the soldier expressed, his hands gestured towards his comrades, 'we may have enough to take on those here, but what if more of the enemy–' 'It be a chance we must take,' Henrik blurted out, his horse coming agitated by his restraint on the reins. 'Our land be nothing without Christendom ... the Dragon Order must prevail!'

It was the agitated snorting of Henrik's horse that revealed their hiding, and in that moment, even the secondary commander knew that they had no choice but to assail the enemy with all that they had.

Almost instantaneously, all Wallachian's shot forward from their hiding place, whether it was behind trees or nestled in the undergrowth. Some almost tripped against the bramble, their rage consumed by what may be the last fight for their kingdom. Many took Turks by surprise, using the cover of the shadowy woodland to add to the confusion, but enemy numbers were still equal after many had been slain. And with limited weapons, only a circle of shields now defended them from the Turkish pikes and spears that surrounded them. Henrik searched for an escape route, but found him and less than a score of his men encircled by pressing spearheads.

Suddenly, as they were gathered – shepherded like a flock of frightened sheep – a laugh animated above the snarling and shouts of abuse; it was the Turkish commander.

And although Henrik did not understand his enemy's words, his secondary commander was still alive to interpret.

'Like trapped lambs waiting to be slaughtered by the almighty wolf,' the sneering foreign tongue blurted as he paced towards Vlad's still body, 'and so tell me any of you Wallachian scum, how you be saving your prince from our most honourable Sultan?' He knelt down and grasped Vlad's dark hair, lifting his flimsy head to turn his face for identification. 'Yes, this be truly the Prince of Wallachia… the son of the original Dragon, and so,' the commander smirked, 'whether I return with just his head or not, surely our almighty Sultan shall honour me.' The commander glowered as he withdrew a short but sharp dagger. 'It not matter if I do it, or our most honourable Sultan… he will have his head mounted on a spike sooner or later.'

As the Turkish commander's eyes gleamed at ogling his weapon – the sharp blade pressed against Vlad's twisted throat – Henrik tensed and blinked nervously; the intermittent darkness behind his eyelids filled by fleeting memories like a jumpy, cinematic film. Was this it for him and his master – not just the Prince of Wallachia, but a long and devoted friend? Under a breath Henrik whispered a prayer; that the Almighty should save such an advocate for Christendom – a ruler so earnest of his place in the Heavens after trouncing so many against Christianity. And then Henrik opened his eyes. Had all hell broke loose, or was it that his prayers had been answered?

At first he stared straight at Vlad, and then his commander's assailant. But the Turkish commander sank from his knees to suddenly flop over Vlad's body, his hand reaching to nurse his injured scalp before dropping. And then Henrik noticed the small, hooded figure behind, its fingerless, gloved hands throwing aside the branch it had just used as a weapon. Within seconds it was accompanied by another, but enormous, hooded figure.

Henrik glanced round to see his men perplexed at watching many dark, hooded figures now jumping from trees to assail the Turks; the swift surprise of their scabbard blades massacring many a Turkish soldier. Bewildered, but seeing more of the enemy appear, Henrik bawled.

'Take arm soldiers of Wallachia, it not be their fight alone,' he yelled, but then noticed several Turks race to their commander's aid. Or was it to finally murder Vlad? 'To my side men, we fight for Christendom and country!'

Henrik sped forward with just above a score of men, his sword cutting down several enemy soldiers before he could near his master. But the tall, hooded figure had kicked aside the Turkish commander to grasp Vlad; the other, smaller figure directing the giant through undergrowth and toward a fallen beech tree, where it pointed at space beneath. As the huge figure pulled Vlad through the bracken to hide him as instructed, the smaller figure stopped, its hands pushing back its hood and long hair to reveal its face.

Although enshrouded by darkness, Henrik stood mesmerised to see a pretty, round face, with tight crimson lips, pouting self-assuredly. And the gypsy girl's dark eyes exhibited an unusual wisdom, or were it the strange, mystical background from such a vagrant? He had hardly time to admire such wild beauty, as a couple of Turks were crawling through the bushes behind to locate their commander.

At sighting the unveiled gypsy, two enemy soldiers advanced towards her and so Henrik raced to her aid. Although standing tall at just over five-and-a-half foot, the gypsy girl stood her ground – a small, curved scabbard now drawn and ready for defence. The girl scowled at him, perturbed at his advance, knowing that they shared a conjoint enemy. Oblivious of her assailants, Henrik knew she was unaware of the danger, but would his sprint be in time to save her?

As the first Turk strode fast towards the girl, his curved blade raised above his head, Henrik lunged to strike his longsword at the assailant, severing the offender's outstretched arm from his right shoulder. As the enemy faltered in losing his limb, Henrik swung his sword to strike through the soldier's chest. But within seconds, as the girl glanced to acknowledge Henrik's heroic act, the other Turk was almost upon her.

Embedded in the leather and armour of the now writhing Turk, Henrik struggled to free his sword, and for a second considered whether to warn the gypsy of her other assailant. The girl spun round, the Turk almost nose to nose with her. But in hesitating to gawk at her soft skin and hazel eyes, she had valuable seconds to step back before Henrik's sword cut down upon the soldier's turban helmet. As the force of the blade splintered the soldier's cranium, the girl stood petrified. And then she noticed blood stream in rivulets down the Turk's face before he collapsed.

Henrik had never seen such a change in a woman's face. From a look of ultimate horror, to an innocent, almost timid smile, as in that moment she glimmered to thank him. 'That be close my lady,' Henrik said, his eyes again drawn to her natural beauty.

'They be having your pretty, little head too if...'

But within a fleeting moment, after she turned to locate her huge accomplice, she smiled back at him, the dimples in her cheeks more profound as she replaced her hood. He had hardly captured the wild but innocent beauty of her face, before she ran to join her accomplice under the fallen tree.

He glanced round. Other Turks were now searching for their leader. Or were they persevered in capturing the Prince of Wallachia?

For a while at least Henrik thought Vlad was safe; dragged but hidden under a fallen tree by some strange gypsies. But were these vagabonds as honourable as he could hope? Surely so, he contemplated – they shared the same enemy – the Turks? However this was not the time to deliberate, but to do battle. And so Henrik joined his Wallachian comrades in eliminating as many of the enemy as deemed possible. But now, after the surprise from the gypsy attack had worn off, they fully experienced the brunt of the Ottoman Empire.

Henrik winced to see more Turks approach. But enemy soldiers ran straight past him to frantically drag their unconscious leader to his feet and thrust him upon the rear of a horse. As the beast sped off with many injured following, Henrik gathered that another garrison must have arrived. But was it friend or foe?

Fighting bravely but with such lack of energy left, Henrik grimaced to watch more of his men get butchered as they gradually came outnumbered. Although helped by their hooded, vagabond friends, Henrik saw that in the skirmish that he and a few other Wallachian soldiers were now the only armoured resistance.

'They outnumber us my Lord, both us and these vagabonds,' Henrik turned to see a comrade alongside. 'I watched them hide our prince too, but soon it may all be in vain!' 'We can all but pray for a miracle from the Almighty!' Henrik replied, but pondered to consider on whether his earlier prayer was all that would be answered. 'I be sure this not be our day to–'

As if Henrik had placed a curse upon the soldier, he saw the tip of a kilij sword appear though the armoured shoulder of his comrade. As the man stood petrified, the enemy blade retreated; blood now beginning to pour from his wound as he began to waver. Henrik swung his sword into action but paused to watch his comrade drop, finally seeing the Turk grinning in the shadows. In a spurt of mad rage, Henrik drove his sword at the Turk, swinging with all his might.

Exhausted from discharging the last of his frenzied strength, Henrik turned to his injured colleague after beheading the

Turkish assailant. He fell upon weary knees as if they too had been drained of strength, encircling his arm around the fallen soldier's neck to cradle him as knowing he was still alive.

'Fret no longer my friend,' Henrik glanced at his injured comrade, but peered up to locate Vlad's hiding place. 'I make sure we fight another…'

It was then, as Henrik thought both he and his friend were doomed, that enemy soldiers fled from cutting down the last of his garrison and the vagabonds who stayed to fight. Although there were but a few injured soldiers and a score of gypsies left, Henrik rested back on his haunches to frown at the enemy's sudden dispersal.

But then, through the shadows of the woodland, appeared a number of horsemen, who stopped in the dim of the forest clearing for pike-men to encircle them as protection. Through bleary eyes but attentive ears, it was then that Henrik identified the croaking laughter of Lord Lucian. And alongside him on a white horse, was a smaller man, his head crowned by long-flowing, fair-coloured hair.

'You scare them off with nothing but your unsullied face and golden locks Radu Bey,' Lucian Dumitru chuckled, but paused to wonder on what could be the real reason, as it surely was not the number or supremacy of their garrison. 'But I guess we be just in time.' The elderly man pointed eagerly to Henrik, who now was squinting to make out a positive identification of the boyar. 'Yes, Radu you be right, but are we in time to save our prince… your brother?'

Radu stopped from laughing at Lucian; his face now alarmed at counting how many bodies lay slaughtered about him. And then he saw several gypsies appear from behind trees or scurrying through the woodland. It was then, after he turned from spotting Henrik, that Radu squinted to make out a small, hooded figure that seemed to rise from the woodland floor. And then, like some cloaked colossus from the shadows, another figure appeared, trudging slowly to follow the small one into the woodland clearing. And on the giant's shoulder was draped a body that Radu squinted to identify as Vlad.

'What have you done to my brother?' Radu barked before dismounting. 'Vicious vagabonds, what have you done?'

Quickly Radu strode toward the large, vagabond figure but stopped as pike-men hesitated to part their defence. Was it the fact that this huge, bearded gypsy stood so tall over Radu – standing over six-and-a-half feet high – or was it to watch the giant rest awkwardly his brother to the floor?

'What have you done to my brother, you dirty, great rogue?' But the giant stood silent and impassive, only his feet scraping to take a couple of steps back. 'Speak you bastard! Why have you killed my brother?' Radu's mind sped into overdrive. 'Sell him to the Turks would you… try deals for money!' But the huge gypsy stood silent. 'Speak you bastard, before my men slaughter you all like these.' Radu pointed to the many bodies that had been slain.

'He cannot speak,' a sweet but angered voice erupted. 'And we do not take money from enemies… or *you* come that…' The small, hooded figure came to stand beside the giant. 'Unless you dead and not need such.'

Radu stood up from kneeling to examine Vlad's unconscious body.

'Luckily my brother still be alive but,' Radu mused, his eyes narrowing to think; that unblemished face now disclosing a mischievous look that glared at the two gypsies in turn. 'Lucian my dear man,' his glare now turning to the shadow of the boyar mounted on his horse, 'it be my belief that these vagabonds were to sell my brother's head to the Sultan, so what could the punishment be, but death?'

'It not true,' the small gypsy figure protested, stepping nearer but still hooded, 'it be that we save this man… *your* brother… before enemies remove his head!'

'That be a lie!' Radu bawled and signalled for his troops to take action. 'Seize them in that they take punishment!'

As soldiers grappled with the giant, he simply pushed them away and tried to stop two seizing each of the small gypsy's arms. In the struggle Radu noticed the hood fall from the smaller one's head to expose a girl's sweet but angry face.

'Why a pretty face, for such a vagabond!' Radu stepped nearer to the girl, his sharp, little dagger poised in defiance. 'It be a pity to punish and maim such a pretty little one.' He gestured a soldier to hand him a reed torch, its flame fresh and vibrant. 'But punishment you will take for your intent to my brother... burn that prettiness away should I?' As he detected how the flames reflected the fear in the girl's dark eyes, he saw her break free one hand and reach for her hidden scabbard, but she was quickly restrained. 'Resistance be useless!' Radu stood tall and circled a spot to speak aloud, one hand holding out the flaming reed torch to expose those deceased about his feet. 'Take a good look about you.' He saw many gypsies pause to withdraw concealed weapons or lower those at hand. 'You vagabonds have all but perished already... taken up the wrong deal with the enemy no doubt.' Suddenly Radu faced the gypsy girl and shouted, 'Tried to put a greater price on my brother's head did you?'

'We not need money,' the girl enraged. 'We live but simple from the land!' Radu stood poised with anger, but took admiration for her defiance and beauty. 'Beside this,' the gypsy girl continued, 'we enemy of the Turk and they the one who to try murder your brother.'

'I think not vagrant girl,' Radu retorted, again full of contempt. 'You gypsy type... the vagabond scum that live off our lands, take legions with whoever they please.'

'Then why we kill enemies… they that would take head of your brother?'

'You ask too much a higher price of course,' Radu responded derisively, his patience soon ending. 'This deal went sour and scum like you be expendable.'

The girl's face contorted; it obvious to Radu that a vagrant would not understand such a word. Or was it from her short and sharp dialogue, that she too, was a foreigner?

'It matter not,' Radu bawled. 'I want lands rid of this scum before morning and–'

But then Radu stopped to see Henrik race toward him, the encircling pike-men hesitant after recognising their chief commander in the torch light.

'If it not be for these vagabonds and *my* men, your brother would not be alive.' Henrik stopped to take breathe, his hands resting on his knees as his eyes scorned Radu. 'They hid your brother from the enemy as we fought… *all* of us!'

'It not make sense but that these vagrants tried to strike a deal for my brother's head!' Radu moved close to the gypsy girl, his grin wide. 'Or could they be informants for the Ottoman Empire?' He paused before stating aloud, 'Such scum cannot be trusted!' 'We not scum as you lie,' the gypsy girl retorted, 'but simple folk who travel much from the north and east and coasts of great Black Sea.' She glanced at Henrik, knowing he and his fallen comrade were her only defence. 'We save your brother and hide. We take sides with no one, and the Turk be our enemy… kill many our people!'

'You are nothing but vagabonds!' Knowing her in restraint, Radu moved closer to the girl, his face but inches away. Speaking slowly to exaggerate his disdain, he said, 'And scums like you, even one so pretty, have no right to reap our lands.'

'I not know what sides you on,' the gypsy girl exasperated, 'but hope your brother not like you… see without mud in his eye!' Following her words, the gypsy girl spat at Radu's face.

Almost instantaneously, and in one sweep, Radu wiped the girl's spittle from his cheek and hit her across the face.

Brusquely the giant figure lurched in Radu's direction, but pike-men pinned him to stop before he could come as the girl's aide.

'You will *all* be executed,' Radu bawled, glaring at the girl and then up at the nearby giant. 'Pretty girl or giant, hang all these vagabonds!'

'No, no…' Henrik wailed as he approached Radu and clasped his wrist that held the reed torch. 'You should be indebted to *us* that fought here… all of *you* grateful that these people fought with Wallachian soldiers to save our prince!'

But Radu snatched away his hand to raise the torch again near the girl's face.

'But they be untrustworthy and have you cursed to believe such.' Radu smirked at the gypsy girl who wriggled against the men who held strong her wrists. 'And this one, although all pretty, is probably one who casts such a curse.' He poked the reed torch close enough to singe the girl's exposed hair. 'Maybe they should burn for their punishments!' Somewhat nervous at how the giant motioned to protect the girl, Radu stepped back to see the girl glare at the towering gypsy and mutter strange words. 'You see… she be cursing us!'

'I simply tell him to ignore such a bigot,' the girl intervened sharply, 'so he not rip your head from its neck!'

'Please all, in the least,' Henrik shouted above all the din, 'give these travellers fair trials… hear their story to pass judgement?'

'But there be only their word… and yours of course,' Radu belittled.

'And that of my comrade!' Henrik pointed to a body that lay still in the shadows. 'But he be dead soon also and so be of no–'

'But justice is what keeps us from the barbaric ways of the Ottoman Empire,' Henrik interrupted fervently, turning to Lucian for council. 'Compassion is what keeps Christendom so righteous!'

'It be correct to honour our prince's council,' Lucian shouted from his horse. 'That such matters be dealt with back at Poenari. And as it be getting dark with still such an enemy out there, we should return directly.'

'But what will such prove, other than we safeguard such brigands?' Radu strode contemptuously to Lucian's horse. 'These vagrants do nothing but curse and bring the plague with them!'

'I give final word on behalf of our prince's council and state that we do judgement back in the safety of our castle!' Lucian anticipated Radu's protest, and so overruled him. 'We do judgement before an assembly at Poenari. And it be to our prince's wishes that we deliberate such matters when he be conscious.'

'The truth will be told and judgement given,' Henrik intervened to stand tall against Radu and look up at Lucian. 'Myself, and my comrade, will tell evidence to honour the bravery of these people.'

'May I remind you dear Henrik,' Radu derided before mounting his horse, 'that you are nothing but a soldier and hold no royalty upon council.'

'I am highest council to that in absence of the Prince of Wallachia, and so,' Lucian commanded, 'I command that we take this matter back at Poenari and do judgement when our prince feels fit.' Lucian scowled at Vlad still unconscious and lying dirt-ridden on the woodland floor. 'Retrieve our prince and make sure we tend careful him as we take him back to Poenari.' Lucian's pointing hand now was held to silence both Radu and Henrik who were squabbling. 'Give carriage to our prince and have them nurse his health.' Lucian glared down at both the second commander and Vlad's brother. 'Now we make haste back to Poenari… to the safety of our beds!'

Henrik turned in disgust from the seated council to instead admire the firelight that flickered against the banqueting hall roof. It was his method to keep calm but resolute about the incident, especially now that Radu was contesting the authority of many of their leaders. As Vlad was still unconscious and so unaware of what had happened, Henrik regarded Radu with disdain – hearing him argue with such a late gathered council – the arrogant, little man spitting venom like some provoked snake. And now Henrik heard him question the authority of young boyars seated about the great, oval table; that they had no statute or nobility to represent his brother.

'I must protest on your–'

'Restrain your anger Henrik Vasile,' a boyar interrupted, 'we can answer not only this man's questions, but defend our honour to his brother.'

Henrik stood apprehensive for a minute, but then sat to hear a boyar elaborate on the history of the castle and their devotion to Vlad.

'It was our fathers…'

'And father's fathers,' another added, all around the table now regarding him after his interruption.

'It was our fathers,' the first continued, 'that helped your brother rebuild this keep… and build well the walls, being how difficult it be as shaped to top a mountain. It was the generation before them that helped your once young brother escape a siege from the Turks as they ravaged the nearby village of Arefu.'

'What be this to feed those vagrants chained outside?' Radu snapped.

'It was but simple farmers – land workers like those travellers – and craftsmen such as stonemasons, lumbermen, cobbler or blacksmith, who assembled to oppose the unrelenting ravages and pilfering fingers of the Ottoman Empire. It be to them we give praise. As following your brother's wish, they constructed the very building here to what we sit in, protected by thick wall and steep escarpment.'

'And to walls later built that surround Poenari… whose that protect all township alike,' another voice added. 'Our past fathers even nurtured the slopes of this mountain for lumber and built viewpoints to protect the women as they fished the river Argeş… outlooks erected high to keep view of the gorge and give warn to the sight of the enemy.'

'His past deeds be noble and I know my brother be clever,' Radu intervened after placing down the goblet from which he guzzled the last remains. 'But I can assure you that should these vagabonds stay, they shall bring nothing but misfortune, be it dishonour or plague.'

'But the last strain of plague vanished from these regions many a year back?'

'But that girl,' Radu wiped his face in contempt of her spite, 'she told that her people had travelled some distance from the north and east, and so it be likely they still carry the plague and spread it upon us.'

'Yes, but we have them confined to the outer courtyard.' A voice reassured.

'But like leprosy,' a troubled boyar interjected, 'they could pass on such to the very hand that feeds them?'

'I shall feed them myself, be it necessary,' Henrik announced to quash their fears. 'Or at least a few of us could show some compassion to their keepings.'

'You be but cursed by such a pretty face,' Radu muttered cynically.

'And so Radu Bey,' Henrik asked after distinguishing more mockery, 'you want to punish this girl to an extreme, just because she spat at your face?'

'I know the women to be a witch, a female disciple of the...' Suddenly Radu stopped. Was it that he stumped to question his religion – that imposed onto him after childhood against being born into Christianity?

From around the banqueting hall, mutterings and whispers echoed the word

strigoi from which Radu questioned.

'What are your council muttering Henrik?' Radu glared at the commander, but Lucian's voice spoke.

'As you not be from these parts, many still be quite superstitious, and the word be describing as you said… a witch, a *strigoi*… a woman who can curse man and move like some winged demon in the shadow of night.'

'But these be nothing but travellers… simple gypsies,' Henrik derided, 'we pass them like country brigands or town thieves but such do not oppose us as we be an army.' He paused to think for a moment and then put it on himself to commit. 'If it be necessary, I take full responsibility on them until our prince and council give judgement.'

'I guess it be easy for such a pretty face to bewitch such a fool,' Radu whispered but knew Henrik had heard. But to his disappointment, the commander did not react, but tapped Lucian on the shoulder.

'So, with you my friend as high council, and with my statement to pass as evidence,' Henrik pressed on Lucian's shoulders but his eyes pried Radu, 'and with evidence too from the soldier who saw also well their deed, we consult an assembly tomorrow in front of our prince?'

As Lucian agreed whilst making his way out he banqueting hall, Henrik noticed Radu scowl at him.

'Where you go with just bread and water, boy?'

'To feed thinly the vagabonds my Lord,' the minor explained to Henrik. 'They be direct instructions from Lord Lucian, although that brother of our prince disprove.'

'See to it they also get meat and broth,' Henrik told, but saw the boy hesitate and look up to a battlement high above the outer courtyard. Sighting the golden crown of Radu's head at such an angle, Henrik overruled. 'You take instruction from me boy, and feed them as *I* say, or you be cleaning out soldier quarters for days.' He saw the minor dither, his young, sharp eyes revealing a troubled mind.

'We have nothing but cold and dry foods at this hour my lord?'

'Then cook meats and boil broth...' But before Henrik could continue, the boy retreated to the direction of the kitchens, his head turning back as if still in question.

'Wait!' Henrik called and the boy stopped as if frozen like a statue. 'Let me take what you have.' The commander snatched the jug and half loaf from the tray he carried and beckoned him on. 'Go tell the kitchens my instruction, and if they be questioning as such this late hour, they be answering to me, Henrik Vasile, second commander in the line of combat with that of our prince!'

Henrik chuckled to himself as he wandered over to find his injured comrade. It was not that he was humored by how quick the boy scarpered, but more for overruling that fair-haired and pompous brother of Vlad.

'Are you alright my brother?'

Supporting his head with a rolled tunic, Henrik noticed the soldier's eyes waver and so poured a little water from the jug to wet his lips. Tasting the fresh, cold liquid, the soldier aroused a little more and so Henrik probed to interrogate.

'Soldier, are you alright?' He trickled more water into his now parted lips. 'I must but know my friend; did you see what happened to our prince tonight?'

The soldier nodded as his hoarse voice gradually became more coherent.

'I saw the same as you my lord.' The soldier coughed against gulping too much water. 'He was knocked from his horse, we were surrounded… their commander was about to take his head, and then…' Henrik shook him slightly, knowing he could black out any second. 'They came from the trees like ravens, dark with shiny blades, but they slaughtered the enemy…'

'And what about the girl?'

'What girl, my lord?' the soldier queried and frowned.

'And the giant… the huge gypsy… did you see them save our prince?'

'A small hooded gypsy hit their commander with a branch, then both dragged our prince to the fallen tree, but that's before we got surrounded again… outnumbered although we fight together, we and those vagabonds.'

'Yes, we *all* fought together to eradicate those bastards… and many of those poor vagabonds died too. That be what that pompous…' But Henrik's sentence tailed off as he watched his comrade fall in and out of consciousness. 'I have bread as well as water for you to gain strength before morning. And soon there be…' But this time the soldier's head dropped to one side.

At least Henrik knew, after seeing his comrade's wounds treated, that he had a good chance to see morning, and once nursed back to full health, this soldier could give evidence to support Henrik's statement.

SIX

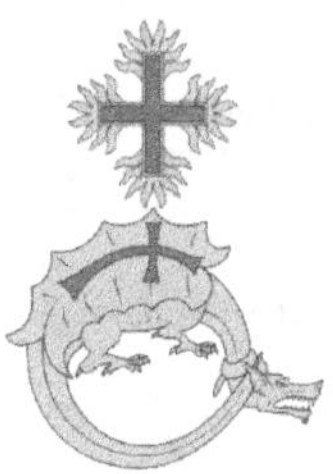

On hearing a distant commotion, Lucian stepped quickly across the courtyard onto its centre, where he noticed an ever-growing crowd gather around the scaffolding of the newly built well. After months of excavation to reach a source of water – likely an underground stream from the river Argeş – Lucian knew stonemasons had not finished its encircling wall and so assembled a wooden stage to safeguard construction. But someone was standing on top of the platform and protesting to amass more a crowd.

Although obstructed by a somewhat resilient mob, Lucian pressed closer to identify the small man shaking his clenched fist in the air. With his long flaxen hair waving in the morning breeze, Lucian could see Radu shouting his objection to safeguarding the gypsies within the walls of the keep. And as he pushed his way through people, Henrik could now hear Vlad's brother deride the strangers, calling them filth and vermin that sided with their enemy. Then on reaching the well, he looked straight up at the little man; a stranger himself not long ago, but one now ridiculing the vagabonds and referring to the gypsy girl as some witch… a *strigoi*!

Lucian turned to observe Radu's gathering audience and came quite alarmed at the malice expressed from so many, especially when he told that if the gypsy girl was not burned as a witch, she would no doubt curse their township. He continued to incite that these vagabonds were travellers who had come from foreign lands and warned that they could carry disease or plague.

Lucian wrestled with Radu's leg to dispute after seeing the line of gypsies chained by wrist and foot, but Vlad's little brother sneered at him from his artificial height to accentuate that if these travellers were to nestle in the confines of the keep, all could be at risk of pestilence. Lucian tried to shout above the frantic crowd; to tell how the matter should not be disputed in public but judged by council through an orderly session. But Radu ignored the elder boyar to incite how the witch – as he called the gypsy girl – with her vagabond mob, had helped the enemy ambush his brother and his army. An angry voice from the crowd disputed that Vlad was too clever a warrior to get ambushed and fortified to how much they trusted in their prince. So, opening out his hands in gesture, Radu calmed to agree that his brother was indeed a noble leader and that his people should trust him implicitly, but changed his discourse to stipulate that the gypsies allied with the enemy so they could sell his brother's head to the Sultan.

With hands held high to attract attention, Lucian faced the gabbling audience to state that in fact the girl and her gypsy giant had actually saved Vlad from the enemy, but their prince was not aware of this as he had been knocked unconscious. But Radu belittled the elder man, to tell that *his* was some fantastic story – one conjured up by some traumatized soldier.

It was Henrik that now stood beside Lucian in defiance; to explain how incredibly the two gypsies had saved Vlad from being beheaded. But Radu crouched over the edge of the wooden construct to declare that Henrik only supported the injured soldier's story as he took pity on the gypsies. And then he gestured to the crowd that their second-in-command had become besotted by the gypsy girl, and as being a witch, she had cast some type of spell on him. Radu stood tall to address the crowd in full voice and tell how he had consulted his brother to speak on behalf of their prince. But Lucian immediately objected, stating that their prince had not been consulted and that they must all follow the order of council, as it was law.

Radu glowered at Lucian and Henrik, thinking his promoted height made him somehow superior, and so again lectured the crowd; articulating to how the gypsies consorted with the enemy but rebelled as they did not receive the high price for his brother's head. Henrik pulled Lucian aside from his bickering and snarled his protest to Radu's lack of authority, but Radu simply pointed at the girl to reiterate; as being a witch, the gypsy should be burned before she can curse anyone else. Radu grinned to watch Henrik squirm as he turned to see the crowd grow wild and bark out orders to finally eradicate witchcraft.

In all the disorder, Lucian again screeched his disproval of having the gypsies chained like prisoners, but in retaliation Radu questioned the boyar's disloyalty to his people. The small man pointed once again at the line of chained gypsies to emphasize that they should not be housing such vagabonds, never mind feeding them. But suddenly, as the crowd parted, Radu turned his attention to someone who approached them.

'What this fool be up to enticing such a crowd?' Jusztina shrieked as she paced through the parting assemblage, her eyes glowering at Radu already with scorn. But then her eyes followed the direction of his arm as Radu discredited the so-called witch and her gypsy mob. 'So why has punishment not been given?' Jusztina queried as she eyed the gypsy girl's dirty but pretty face. 'Do we not burn witches for public display in order to eradicate such evils?'

'Such laws be old and somewhat condemned my lady,' Lucian projected. 'We have more present methods that can determine–'

'The truth to be told my lady,' Henrik interjected somewhat fervently, 'of which your husband's brother not detail, is that these vagabonds… gypsies as they claim to be, actually helped to save your husband from being beheaded.'

'But the girl he said was a witch… a *strigoi* as they call in these lands.' Jusztina never once turned to acknowledge either Vlad's men or his brother aloft; her glare fixated only on the gypsy girl, a jealousy boiling inside as she watched her wild but pretty face scowl as she tried to remove a rag stuffed in her mouth. 'With eyes as dark as the devil's, she's undoubtedly a witch. And she must be burned as be the old law, or she put a curse upon us!'

'I must object–'

'We object, as I tell again my lady,' Henrik interrupted Lucian. 'If it was not for those gypsies chained like prisoners, your husband… our most honourable prince, would be dead!'

'I not care what be your story, whether it be truth or lie,' Jusztina again eyed the gypsy girl up and down as she bit onto her lower lip. 'Our people, whether they be Moldavian like me, from the northern lands of Transylvania or be Wallachian like yourselves… civilians here have suffered enough bloodshed, political turmoil, plagues and disease… need not have some witch put a curse upon us.'

'With all respect that is due my lady,' Henrik told, his eyes nervously watching the line of prisoners, 'you have just arrived and do not know quite well all the story.' He paused to observe her actually look him in the eye. 'These people be nothing but gypsies from lands afar… and I believe they have no plague or carry any disease… they be just travellers living from the land. But fight good against our enemy!'

'I hear quite well the story and this once believe Radu Bey… that the girl must burn as a witch and all others imprisoned as being imposters to this land.'

'Again with all due respect my lady,' Henrik choked to elaborate as yells echoed about the crowd to burn the witch. 'You married our prince to counter allegiance between lands… so why not show our understanding to these as fellow Christians?'

'And as Christians will we be immune to plague,' Jusztina glowered at the gypsy girl again, 'or blessed enough to be protected from witchcrafts?'

'Witchcraft in these parts is all but extinct and so the old ways of execution are somewhat outdated,' Lucian held Jusztina by the arm to state. 'And justice can be done different to old Christian belief… by having tests conducted.'

'But what about disease and plague?' Jusztina again eyed the line of chained and dirt-ridden prisoners.

'That too can be tested,' Lucian proclaimed, 'as we have medicines and learn much these…'

But voices protracted from the attentive crowd to question the elder boyar; stating that if the gypsies were Hungarian, such foreigners were known to still carry the plague across the western borders. And as many others bunched forward to express their concerns, Jusztina suddenly realized to how exposed she was to such spirited unrest. But then a frail, but determined voice, shouted over the din.

'These people not be Hungarian or have allegiance with the Ottoman Empire,' Henrik's injured comrade leaned upon his commander's shoulder to shout support for his story, 'but be in fact the few remaining gypsies left after our fight which saved us from ambush!' As the crowd bunched awkwardly about the soldier, his words came faded by the jeering mass. 'These people be fellow Christians from lands north and east… ones that simply live from what our Lord provides in the earth… they be little different to us but…' Gradually the soldier was jostled enough to prevent him from speaking and with concern for his injury, retreated to safety behind his commander.

'Good citizens, you may hear *their* story,' Radu hushed the crowd to assert from his elevated standpoint, 'but how could these vagabonds survive such a long and perilous journey from north of the Black Sea?' He raised a clenched fist to point an index finger. 'I tell you how… they had an allegiance with the enemy to survive such… but of course asked too a high price for my brother's head!'

The gypsy girl shook her head side-to-side violently until the gagging rag could be dislodged from her mouth.

'We be just gypsies that try settle in peace upon your lands.' The girl continued after kicking away the rag, 'I be no witch and he no monster… just travellers from shore of Black Sea.' She paused to hear the mob jeer her declaration, but shouted out in defiance after observing such an angry crowd. 'We travel miles by foot from your shore and have fight a lot these Turks… and many our kind injure or die.' Again her voice came overwhelmed by bawling ridicule. 'We fight good, we fight brave, but you treat us as this? We fight to save your prince and you treat us like this!'

The gypsy girl noticed someone point and question her giant friend; to why he did not speak to defend her story. So after spitting out dirt from the rag that had dried her mouth, she announced angrily that indeed the man was of a different tongue to her, but could not answer anyhow, as his was cut out after refusing to be a slave for the Turks. She tried to describe to how she had saved him from bleeding to death, but the crowd yelled evermore as they began to taunt the gypsies by pulling on their chains. The girl looked up at her jostled giant friend as many gypsies' legs were pulled from underneath them. It was then that she noticed a different fear in his eyes, one that was certainly rare.

'Ah, you be awake my lord,' Henrik said peering through the door to see Vlad sat hunched over the bed, 'sorry to interrupt, but we have problems.'

'Then do not dawdle my friend,' Vlad replied but grimaced to turn his head, his one hand now massaging the back of his neck, 'come in and tell.'

'Your brother Radu Bey is protesting against a group of gypsies he have in chains and declare we should burn one of their females as being a witch… a *strigoi*.' Henrik could see Vlad somewhat pensive to move as he began to dress into light armour. 'But these people helped us my Lord… they helped save your life!'

'Did they?' Vlad stood up and pained to stretch. 'So where they be now?'

'You can observe from your bedchamber window,' Henrik instructed. 'You should see them down and across the courtyard, quite near the new well.'

Squinting against the morning sun which now rose above treetops, Henrik joined Vlad at his window to witness the unrest in the crowd below.

'You say these people helped save us… from the ambush last night?'

'Yes my Lord, but your brother want all executed, especially the young girl. He be wanting her burned as a witch.' Noting Vlad's expression, he, like Henrik, was impressed by the prettiness in the tainted gypsy girl. 'They all fought brave last night and it be a pity that such a young and pretty girl should be punished in such a grotesque way.'

'Has the cardinal given approval to such an order?' 'Not yet my Lord.'

'And Lucian Dumitru, what say he?'

'Lucian contests the old way of burning witches. He describes it somewhat brutal and archaic.' Henrik took Vlad's shoulder to turn him away from observing the crowd below and to take notice of the sincerity in his eyes. 'But Radu have already convinced many in that public crowd. And soon he will probably have many boyars inciting such unjustifiable punishment.'

'But they know,' Vlad contested, 'whether boyar be citizen or guest, they know it be law that only I, or my council, can grant execution.'

'This be what I tell your brother, but he be obstinate and not listen to the truth!' 'Has Lucian arranged council session?'

'I not be sure my Lord as I came directly once the crowd got somewhat fervent.' 'Look at them down there; like rats gathered in a cellar by that stupid brother of

mine,' Vlad coaxed Henrik to stand in front to observe more. 'But such a crowd be craving the amusement of punishment as they be subjected to oppression for too long… the enemy has prolonged its offence for many a year now.' But then Vlad brushed aside Henrik as he saw more of the girl. 'You are indeed right about the girl… and her accomplice be a certain asset to any army.' Vlad paused to scowl at Henrik, his face with question. 'What did you mean earlier… my brother not listen to the truth?'

Henrik told the story of which he could not convince Radu; as when they had been ambushed yesterday and Vlad knocked unconscious, the Turkish leader would have cut off his head to impress his Sultan if it was not for the gypsy girl who whacked a branch against his head. And as gypsies jumped from trees to take the Turkish soldiers by surprise, she and her giant friend dragged him to safety beneath a fallen tree. Vlad questioned to why the Turks did not have the numbers to overpower them. In response Henrik stated it was the sudden surprise of the gypsy attack that gave his men precious time before Radu's garrison arrived and the remaining Turks escaped to rescue their also unconscious leader. Henrik went on to describe to how the gypsies fought with a ruthless tactic of stab and retreat, an effective strategy in woodland but one Vlad disapproved to work on the wider field of battle.

Vlad questioned Henrik further to why would a band of brigands – in their case, gypsies – attack an armoured Turkish garrison? Henrik answered by recalling to how the gypsy girl told that the Turks were their enemy too, but as Radu interfered, she did not explain her reason in full.

Vlad paused again to observe more from the window, but then chuckled to himself as he described wishing to have been awake just to witness the gypsy girl knock the Turkish leader out. In mentioning the girl, his eyes caught sight of her chained to her giant accomplice and admitted that she had some dark and strange attraction to her but could not see fully her face because of her veil. Henrik indicated to that is why many think her a witch. Both men paused to observe more again from the window until Henrik braved to forward his suggestion.

'My Lord, would you not think it better to recruit these gypsies as they prove strong and eager to fight?' Henrik saw some disapproval from his prince. 'We require *all* able men, whether they be from this township or from settlements further afield, but after the ambush last night and after nursing our injured, our number be reduced somewhat.'

'These vagabonds be difficult to train, even by your standards my friend.' Vlad saw Henrik take notice of the girl and stare at her longingly. 'But what of the girl… is it because you be attracted to such a wild but tender looking animal?'

'Many think her a witch and maybe I have my doubts. She be a wild vagrant… a stranger from shores north of the Black Sea. But she has beauty unlike any witch… not that I have ever bestowed one.'

'You be quite right my friend,' Vlad interrupted him with spoken thoughts. 'But what I need to know is, how does such a vagabond beauty outwit Turkish armies and travel such distance?'

'She has her giant as protection my Lord.'

'No my friend, it be not just that. She must have knowledge of the terrain along the Danube or through gorges north and east from here.' Henrik went to offer a suggestion, but paused knowing Vlad was thinking aloud again. 'Maybe she be knowing unhindered routes to Moldavia… or maybe new and important trade routes through the Carpathians?' Suddenly Henrik came perplexed by Vlad's change of discourse, as it went back to his story. 'Did any others witness the bravery of these gypsies last night?'

'Only one man… my second commander, but he be injured as many who witnessed their bravery perished in the skirmish,' Henrik explained, his eyes recalling the death and brutality. 'But he be a man of good character and give nothing but full loyalty to you. He tried to speak up and support my story down in that courtyard, but was silenced.' Henrik turned Vlad by his shoulders to face him. 'Could we make sure he be heard at council session as it be the truth?' He saw Vlad nod and took it to be an agreement before striding for the door.

'Henrik Vasile,' Vlad asked to pause his friend's departure, 'what be the religion of these gypsies?'

'I would presume them to be Christian, but if the girl and her Tatar friend be from more the north and east of Moldavia, I believe they be Russian Orthodox.'

'But that be likened to Christianity, would it not?'

'Yes, I believe so my Lord, as the land of the Tatars battle hard the Ottoman Empire. Like us, they choose not to let them roam their lands.' Henrik scratched his head. 'But it be all not what I know, but what I hear.' A puzzled smile came across Henrik's face that made Vlad smile in turn.

'I shall not draw attention to myself, but shall spare the gypsy girl and her Christian friends. Should they prove good with our Lord and adhere to the Order of the Dragon, then they shall prevail.'

Vlad strode across the dusty courtyard after locating its centre of attention, but was obstructed by Henrik supporting a soldier.

'My lord,' Henrik announced, determinedly blocking Vlad's path, 'this be my second commander and the one who saw all that happened in our ambush last night.'

Vlad looked at both in turn but settled his eyes on the injured soldier.

'Comrade, you can validate Lord Vasile's account of last night's ambush?' Vlad lifted the head of the lethargic soldier with one hand and with the other pointed to the line of shackled gypsies. 'That *that* gypsy girl and her giant companion saved me from being beheaded by our enemy, and all others that be chained fought alongside you?'

'Yes my lord, that be some account of last night as…' the soldier coughed, his eyes flickering but stared resolute. 'That be right, as it be the truth my lord.'

'So you would support Lord Vasile's account of battle before our council?' Vlad noticed the soldier nod if only feebly.

'He needs more rest my lord, but he has sworn to give oath,' Henrik moved him aside before announcing, 'I make sure he be ready for council session and accompany...'

The crowd, although somewhat more depleted and dispersed from his previous window observation, was fervent with screams and shouting, and so Vlad strode on to investigate.

He came onto a sight he could have never imagined; his wife Jusztina wrestling and scratching at the gypsy, voicing obscenities that condemned the girl's way of life.

'Why do you persecute this woman?' Vlad grasped both Jusztina's wrists after she knocked the gypsy girl's headscarf from her head. 'They may be gypsies... even ruthless, dirty vagabonds... whatever you may want to condemn them as, but they not be our enemy like the Ottoman Empire!' He pulled his wife close to stare in her eyes.

'She will bring a bad omen upon our keep and so the plague will return.' Jusztina writhed but her effort was quashed by Vlad's strong grip. 'She be a *strigoi!* She bring a curse on us if we not get rid of her!'

'Dear wife,' Vlad commanded as he lifted her somewhat, 'it be wars and battle that we need to deal with, not tales of superstition!'

Jusztina was again about to argue her concerns, but felt Vlad's grip ease as he stood to watch the gypsy girl rise from the floor to replace her headscarf. His glimpse of her bedraggled but thick, long dark hair took him by surprise, as he first saw up close her pretty, round face. And even from some distance, her charming, little smile captivated him. But it was her large hazel eyes, enshrouded by long, black eye lashes that for a moment mesmerised him.

Jusztina glared at Vlad before following his eyes to see the girl look sheepishly at him, her smile somewhat mischievous by the impressed dimples in her cheeks. And then on noticing his fixation upon the girl, Jusztina writhed again, but this time avid with jealousy. With him still holding firm her wrist, Jusztina condemned her husband for being spellbound by such a witch and expressed that he should flout her pretty looks.

After ridiculing the gypsy, Jusztina pulled wildly on Vlad's grip until his eyes fixed only on hers. It was then that she scorned him; stating that a lord and Prince of Wallachia should not be tainted by such low-life. And after hearing Henrik's ploy to let them go, she told Vlad not to tame his rigour of law and order to appease the gypsies.

Vlad pulled Jusztina round and as her heels scrapped awkwardly through the dirt, he heard her bark out orders to have the girl burned as a witch. Vlad told her to be quiet, but Jusztina stamped her feet in defiance, reiterating her husband's past words describing such vagabonds and beggars as useless to humanity… that they live off the work and sweat of others… that such indolence be the lowest of thievery!

Vlad held his temper but swivelled his wife around vigorously by her wrist to eventually face her up close. He ordered her not to cause protest and question his authority, especially in front of all that stared from a now, amplified crowd. He released her wrist and as she rubbed it in dismay, she heard him order her to take refuge in their bedchamber and look over Mihnea instead of showing concern in such matters – decisions to which his council would give ruling.

In final and stubborn protest, Jusztina again stamped her feet as she stated that the girl should be punished. Suddenly with spite, she turned and strode over to the gypsy and after picking up the dirt-ridden rag from the floor, tried to stuff it back in the girl's mouth. But before she could hold the fidgeting girl's jaw, her neighbouring gypsy giant stepped forward, wrenching his chained hands forward to oppose Jusztina's act.

In surprise Jusztina sprang back, but after her initial scare, she ridiculed the gypsy girl and her giant bodyguard; stating that the scrawny girl had the ideal man to protect her – one so large, but as she had heard, one who cannot answer back, even without rags gagging his mouth.

Vlad strode forward to intervene and again after grasping his wife by one wrist, pulled her away from the line of gypsies. Again controlling his anger – that his wife had defied his previous order – he stated ardently that it was his policy and ruling to give an eye-for-an-eye, a tooth-for-a-tooth, and so reaffirmed to how his council would hear all evidence before passing *any* judgement. Jusztina calmed somewhat as Vlad let go of her wrist, but as she again rubbed it hard, she heard Henrik reiterate to how without the gypsy's help, all Wallachian soldiers, including her husband, would have been killed in the ambush last night. Jusztina was again about to protest but hushed after gawping at her husband, who again ordered her to leave.

Shortly after Jusztina had retreated grumpily back to her abode, Vlad and Henrik noticed commotion as the line of chained gypsies were now being pulled and jostled. Quickly Vlad told Henrik to collect two nearby guards so all four could force their way through the crowd. As they went, Vlad ordered other soldiers to disperse the crowd and provide protection, but one soldier pointed, spluttering his description to how Radu had ordered them to move on the prisoners. Vlad strode past the guard; his green eyes glowering at the soldier, his voice demanding that he take orders from only him. The soldier stood petrified – frozen like some stone victim of Medusa – realizing his allegiance should only be that to his prince, as he had heard stories to those who had not being so loyal.

With help from his guards, Vlad eventually dispersed the crowd to notice Radu trying to pull all gypsies away by use of their chains. In confronting his young brother, Radu informed

Vlad to how many boyars in the council wanted the gypsies imprisoned in solitary confinement as a precaution to the plague and to prevent the girl casting spells of witchcraft upon them. With angry dissent, Vlad ridiculed his brother and chuckled to profess that he was a superstitious fool like his wife, and ordered the prisoners be freed.

As Radu protested in holding firm the gypsy girl's wrists – trying best to avoid the spit that flew his way – Vlad approached to instruct the matter be conducted in an orderly way, without humiliation or public disorder. But still Radu held tight the gypsy girl, even though her interconnecting chains had been released. The girl kicked out at Radu, but as he joked to how such a wild animal she was, Vlad towered above his brother to state that as Christians they deserved justice, and that in the sight of God they should not corrupt themselves to that like their enemies.

Distraught that his brother overruled him, Radu tossed the now free but cuffed girl to the ground, stating that she belonged in the dirt like the scum she was. Vlad stood tall to glare down at his brother and soon Radu recognised his elder brother's rage. But it was Lucian who eventually stood between them; intervening to confirm that a council session had been scheduled after luncheon so Vlad would be fully informed about last night's ambush come nightfall.

Vlad turned to the guards who surrounded him and ordered that they escort his young brother back to his accommodation. Radu protested but came overwhelmed by the many armed bodies that began to shepherd him on across the dusty courtyard. Lucian began to assert particulars regarding the council session, but saw Vlad pull the gypsy girl to her feet and ask her name. The girl shook herself from lingering dirt and stepped back a few paces before looking bashful at the Prince of Wallachia.

'Your peoples call me Tariana,' she said, wiping her face and clearing her throat of dirt, 'but in my lands north and east, I be named at birth Tatyana.'

'So you not be from Wallachia?' Vlad asked, noticing how the giant peered down to study him.

'No,' Tariana explained as a guard pulled the chains through her cuffs, 'Me, Sorin, and few others, were taken in by travellers on your lands east and along coast… we be like them… farm and cultivate the land.'

'Like many my lord, they fail to pay taxes,' Lucian interrupted and sustained to intervene, 'so we should not continue to provide salvation or protection.' Pointing a finger northward, he went on to interject, 'It be the same as Hungarian merchants who travel our towns, imposing extortionate purchases on our citizens but pay no tax.'

'This be different,' Vlad juddered to hear Henrik shout, 'with all that happened last night they surely deserve some reprieve.'

Henrik glared at the girl and warmed to see her smile back at him.

'My good friend,' Vlad turned his attention to Henrik, 'just make sure all these people are released and have food and water before trial.'

Again Tariana smiled at Henrik as he released her wrist cuffs, but grimaced to the pain where they had dug into her skin and bone. Henrik knelt to unlock her ankle cuffs and flushed red to take sight of an exposed thigh; a lot of Tariana's lower dress now threadbare with a slit torn down one side. Although rubbing at her wrists gave her discomfort, she smiled thinly down at Henrik. As she could now feel her ankles free, she stepped a few paces to speak to Vlad, but strangely kept her distance.

'My lord,' Tariana copied to address Vlad, 'I not know of your standing, but to what the man say, you must see we have no income to pay taxes but live kindly from your land.' Tariana contorted again to feel pain about her ankles. 'From last night, it be clear we share the same enemy.' She messed with her headscarf but found it dirt ridden. 'Although we possess little… the enemy raid and take and kill many our peoples without remorse or reason…' She glanced aside, her eyes swelling of tears. 'And so that why we hate them… these Turks.'

Vlad could not quite comprehend her short, sharp dialect, but knew she was not of Turkish origin or from lands south like Turkish Bulgaria. In addition, she had an unusually pale complexion that was beautified by an unblemished skin tone. But it was her dark hazel eyes that were captivating; enshrouded by naturally thick eyes lashes, her eyes sparkled like black jewels until flickering sunlight moved across them, and then he noticed the shade of brown in each iris. For seconds Vlad was captivated as the rays from the sun penetrated her dark hair to reveal hidden streaks of auburn and made her face glow like some angel. But was she indeed angelic, this wild, gypsy vagabond he had spared from punishment?

As he stepped close, she moved back a pace before Vlad was close enough to look down at this petite, attractive girl, standing now to the height of his shoulder. Her gown of faded greens and blue was girdled tight at her waist, with what he could make out as some type of waistcoat overtop. And although this garment was shoddy and unlaced, its tautness accentuated her shapely figure and squashed voluptuous breasts.

At first Tariana felt a strange allure to this man, but suddenly pulled away from his charm to notice how his emerald eyes now gawped over her body before glancing back into her eyes. And then Vlad smiled with all the charm he could administer.

'Forgive me for staring at you as such,' Vlad rolled his eyes and parted his hair from his eyes, 'but you not be like Wallachian women or those like that of my wife.'

'She like me as much as I do the Turks.' Tariana puckered.

'That be true by looks upon things, and you be right as we share hate for the same enemy, but tell me,' Vlad inched closer to the now solemn looking gypsy, 'why attack them last night if they not provoke you as their enemy?'

'Turks be everyone's enemy… here and where I come from… everywhere.' The gypsy looked sad at her feet as she messed again with her headscarf, which to Vlad's disappointment hid again a lot of her face. 'They kill many my peoples… both my parents and nearly my brother during many a scouting raid to my land… far colder lands north and east, beyond the coast of the great sea.'

'It be the Black Sea coast east of Silistria,' Vlad said, but then continued to think aloud. 'Or it be Chilia more north and east as you describe.'

'Yes that be it, but we travel from miles north and east of that.' Tariana scowled to realize how long it had been since her travels started. 'We travel the coast until meeting many of your peoples, and we went with them along river to next big place.'

'Braila, the city on the river Danube?'

'I not sure, but I stay away from city. Sorin want go north to mountain where less the enemy. But I want the warm of south so we…' She glanced at the giant gypsy she called Sorin to obviously try and find the right word. 'So we compromise… compromise and go west between mountains north and south the plains.'

'You must tell of your travels,' Vlad cut short to ask but his curiosity was more to why they first took refuge in his country. 'But tell, why you travel so far to be in Wallachia?'

'We much like your peoples and them who travel with thee.' Tariana pointed out particular gypsies in a line of bewildered vagabonds, including the giant one called Sorin. 'They be same as us in their religion and not take offence with our ways. Beside you be having not so harsh winters here and though your soil not rich and black as my father's lands, more the weather be kind to grow crop.'

'Was lands you cultivate along the river much like your fatherlands?'

'No, like I say, we come from north and east and it be more harsh a winter.'

'And *he* came from your fatherland also?' Vlad asked, pointing at the giant gypsy. 'No he escape from more north… lands of ice and snow.'

'I heard of this,' Vlad declared, moving close to study the giant man better, 'it be called the land of the Tatars.' He heard the giant grunt and use his hands as if some sort of communication. 'What he be trying to say?'

'He just listens and obeys,' Tariana slapped the giant's hands away and scowled at him, issuing short signage displays of much the same. 'But he knows what be right and wrong.'

'Why does he protect you so?' 'It be a long story.'

'And we not have the time to talk openly here!' Henrik interrupted, but Vlad hushed him away.

'Properly disperse this crowd my good man.' Vlad ordered Henrik before ushering the girl along with the giant called Sorin following. 'And get ready food and water so they shall feast at luncheon the same as we.' He turned back to Tariana to repeat his question to which she had stopped to answer whilst glancing up at her friendly giant with light-hearted affection.

'I escaped Turk raid with brother as they kill both my parents.' Tariana paused to console herself, and as Sorin knew her story, the giant clasped sympathetically her shoulder with one of his large, strong hands. 'We ran for miles but came separated. My brother get captured but Sorin and his travellers from the north escape to free him, but for his defiance they cut out his tongue. They left him to bleed as would not chance the man again to be their slave. Many of his people were taken, some escaped along with my brother, but I stay to stitch best his tongue so not bleed to his death.'

Vlad had been listening attentively to understand Tariana's words and follow her story, and although he had learned Turkish through his youth – besides the many other languages that surrounded Wallachia – he found it difficult to decipher her native country. It was obviously a country he had not heard of, but was to the north and east of Moldavia, but not as far as the land of the Tatars.

The petite, gypsy girl went on to describe how, as she was small but had to look over her little brother, she had grown strong at heart and with determined spirit. But Vlad came lost in her narrative about her past as she fully removed her headscarf to reveal her gorgeous long, dark hair that glinted with shades of auburn in the rays of sunlight that now glinted over the mountain treetops. The sweated deep auburn curls that stuck to her forehead and ears did not deter Vlad from becoming totally entranced. As she shook her head before continuing her story about searching for her brother, he noticed how her little, snub nose was cute against her wide, hazel eyes and her pretty round face. And as she described passionately her past, he watched how her crimson lips parted and glistened to wetness as her small tongue ran between them. And he noticed too – which was unusual in gypsies – that beyond her parting lips lay the most perfect set of white-shining teeth. But as she lowered and bundled up her headscarf, it was something else that took his eye from her pretty face and long, wavy hair.

Falling around her neck, to stop just above her ample cleavage, dropped a strange and large, silvery charm which lay suspended on a black rope necklace.

'What be that?' Vlad again jumped to hear Henrik ask from behind.

'I asked you to disperse the crowd!' Vlad interjected as Henrik came close to point at the girl's jewellery.

'They be doing so,' Henrik responded avidly. 'The guards have it at hand!'

'Then be away and see to meals for these peasants.' He turned to face the gypsy girl, his eyes full of curiosity. 'Tell me, why do you wear such a large and funny-looking thing?'

Tariana to that point thought Vlad a stalwart but righteous man, but catching the last word of his sentence to Henrik, took her aback. And so when he approached near to ask about her necklaced charm, she backed off to flap away the dirt from her headscarf. But persistently Vlad approached to enquire to why she wore such a large and bulky item. 'It be from old silver dug many year ago in my lands and crafted by the fathers of

my father.' She revolved it beneath her chin to glance at it with affection. 'It be most precious thing I have so none will take… it value be to how you mean… sentimental?'

'It look like some tuning-fork!' Henrik chuckled to interrupt.

'Go about your duties my good man.' Vlad ordered his commanding chief before turning his attention back to Tariana, 'Food and water for all those who fought against our common enemy.' A wink from an eye made Tariana ease and smile more gently as Vlad agreed. 'He be right though, it do look like some tuning-fork.' He noticed how the gypsy frowned to describe her object. 'It be an object our musicians use to tune their instruments.'

Tariana stood perplexed; as having only heard the most rudimentary gypsy tunes from the most basic of instruments, she knew nothing of more prestigious musical instruments and their more composite tunes.

'I not know of what you speak, but this be my sacred protection against creatures of the night as I have a virtuous heart.'

'You be just as superstitious as my foolish wife,' Vlad chuckled. 'And many that live outside and within this keep.' But Vlad stopped suddenly to wonder upon her last word. 'What be it you mean, have a virtuous heart?' He gazed into Tariana's dark eyes as they looked up at him curiously. 'What become of someone with an evil heart?'

'I not know as it I keep safe.' Tariana frowned and stood agitated before continuing. 'But my father's father told of it being a curse on the bearer if should their soul be corrupt.' Again she paused, her nerves somewhat overwhelming her speech. 'He told that a corrupt soul could make them a slave of the Dark One.'

'Such powers do not exist, do they my young gypsy friend?' Henrik burst in their conversation to ridicule. 'The people of your homeland must be as superstitious as many of the fools here.' He pulled at his beard as he looked at Vlad close. 'But maybe Radu was right about this girl being a witch.' Tariana felt a different vibe coming from her original friend Henrik and so came confused to his change of temperament. 'It be obvious their intentions be good, but what come of her should they stay?'

'I'll be the judge of that,' Vlad muttered. 'Or at least it be our council!'

Suddenly Tariana stepped towards Vlad to hit her tuning-fork against his armoured breastplate.

'You may not hear it, but silently it keep away the hunting creatures of the night.' 'Like wolves and bears,' Henrik asked cynically, 'they have acute hearing?'

'But I heard nothing, let me try.' Vlad went to take the gypsy's old silver charm to try it himself, but found his fingers slapped away.

'I tell you,' she snapped defiantly, 'it be the only thing I be having left for me and remember my parents and those before!'

'Indeed sounds like some tale of witchcraft,' Henrik suggested with sarcasm.

'Our customs be different to that of your lands here,' Tariana interjected. 'But if gypsy people of your lands get along with our way, why be it *you* cannot?'

'Then if a so corrupted soul was to get hold and use your charm,' Henrik snapped to ask, 'then would it still work?'

'As I said, and the curse be told by my father's father,' Tariana spoke slow and strong. 'An evil heart would attract the same evil as a virtuous heart provides sacred protection.'

Vlad looked at Henrik full of scepticism, but then turned to face again the gypsy he felt mesmerised by.

'Forgive us in our understanding, as we not know of your ways as you come a long way.' Vlad touched her shoulder to emphasise his sincerity, but saw her giant friend step forward. 'But for tonight, and until I hear council by morning, you stay to the accommodation I provide.' Again he winked secretly at the petite gypsy girl before removing his hand that roughed kindly her hair. 'Adhere to our ruling and avoid trouble with our peoples within this keep and you be safe in your beds.'

'That one be taking up two abreast my lord,' Henrik joked, pointing to the giant as he did best to separate the girl from Vlad.

'He may take two spaces for his bed,' Vlad humoured, 'but could crush many more Turks for his keep!'

As Sorin the Tatar could still hear fine, Vlad noticed how his comment made him smile. But as Vlad turned to give order to his guards, he felt a hand take his and restrict his pace.

'My lord,' Tariana called, 'but where are we to stay?'

'You and your friends can camp on the outer eastern flank of the castle courtyard.' He turned to Henrik and several guards to instruct. 'Where we be having no use for the soldier's quarters as they now be unoccupied.'

'We should not take room of your soldier keep, but sleep under stars,' Tariana told, pulling on Vlad's hand.

'You are welcome to such, even if you usually make the earth your bed.' Vlad now recognised Tariana's frown, and it told him that she did not understand. 'They be the residence of the many soldiers we once had here, but after last night's ambush and many battles previous, they be empty, so you be welcome to such.'

'My lord,' the gypsy girl pulled again on Vlad's hand, 'we haves many a gypsy friend camp by the river!'

'Your friends must fend for themselves as they be under no protection of the walls of this keep.' He turned to release Tariana's soft hand. 'And you must not attempt to escape until I hear council and give verdict come morning.'

'But I want we share food and water with friends who be hungry?'

'Only those with my permission can leave this keep at night, whether it be scout or pilgrim.' Vlad again noticed how sad Tariana looked to fail her friends, but he knew the importance of security, whether it be of gatekeeper, night-watchman or guard.

'You may have escort to visit them come morning,' Vlad gestured with a smile, but grimaced to add, 'should you be reprieved of punishment.'

SEVEN

As she was led through the halls and passageways of Poenari, Tariana had never seen such stonework and architecture, and so stopped to gawk at the pictures, tapestries and draperies decorating the walls of the keep. Passing rooms either side she peeked at lonesome items of furniture, some decorated in vibrant coloured material, but most were bare, exposing their naturally dark, wooden structure.

She had paused to scrutinise animal rugs, beast hide and skins scattering the dark oak floors and then looked aloft to ponder at paintings and embroideries that had somehow captured this glorified Prince of Wallachia. But to her the man now leading the way was just some lord of the land; a warrior who had agreed for her and her people to settle upon land just outside his keep. But what was it he wanted in return?

This lord and prince had come to her that morning with the verdict of their council; his face flushed and energetic, his eyes wide with excitement to tell the good news. But as she had been restless all night by the revolt against her yesterday,

Tariana did not at first respond to the decision asserting their reprieve.

Nonetheless she had smiled with him and contained her joy to quietly celebrate with Sorin and her other gypsy friends later. She thought to sneak a bottle of the old wine back from those camped in woodland outside the keep, but as they did not know the news, considered it best to keep her revelries secret and dine with them later. But to be granted a visit to those outside, Tariana knew she had to be virtuous and keep her word to honour this lord's order of security. And circumstantially she was terribly curious to this man's request as he had described to how much he had argued for their reprieve. But as he had told, she owed much gratitude to Henrik (and his surviving comrade witness) who had provided evidence under oath to the council that morning.

She noticed this Prince of Wallachia turn and regard her curiously, and after seeing him wave her on, glanced behind to find guards waiting impatiently. She strode forward as if knowing to where to go, but Vlad's hand stopped her as she reached a turret of the keep. As his hand clasped her shoulder she shivered, but it was not to his touch. As she glanced down at a steep, stone stairway that circled into darkness, she felt cold air freeze her face and numb her naked legs. Scared, she shivered uncontrollably, and looked upon Vlad's face.

'Forgive me my young gypsy,' he smiled knowing to why she felt discomfort, 'but the chill here be drawn from yonder stairs as be opened the confines of our secret artillery.' He drew close taking her one hand with his, his green eyes glancing to examine each of hers in turn. 'Sorry but I took it that you, so called Tariana, had been introduced to who I am?'

'I know who you be,' Tariana said timidly. 'They say you be a most noble lord of this lands… the Prince of Wallachia.'

'Yes my dear girl, I be that in title,' Vlad chuckled. 'But please, for us to be better acquainted, please know me as Vlad.'

At that he smiled before leading her down against the chilling breeze and into the darkness of the stairwell. She could for a moment feel nothing but the warmth of his strong but gentle hand as she lost her footing in the dim of the stairwell. Several times it was her push against Vlad's tight grip that kept her from falling, but once a following guard had to steady her.

As they approached a narrow corridor at the foot of the stairs, Tariana could see how the draught that swept through the opening of a tall, armoured door almost extinguished the flame of a lonesome reed torch. Eagerly she was thrust through the opening as Vlad pulled strong on her arm; his strength almost wrenching her elbow out of its socket. And as she rubbed her aching elbow after he released his grip, she shuddered to hear the door slam and be bolted behind her.

'You will soon be led into the bowels of this keep that we know as Poenari,' Vlad stated, his one hand outstretched before him to point the way, 'the only safe way out being that stairwell, as this quarried cavern be my secret artillery.' He led the way, and pretending to be fearless Tariana followed in silence. 'But it not be plans for battle or the crafting of weapons I could ask from such a gypsy girl.'

'Then what be it I am asked to do to honour the freedom of my gypsy people?' 'From what you have told, I gather that you have travelled much over these past

months,' Vlad probed as he constantly led Tariana through rooms he had a month back shown his brother. 'And though you may not have the mind to endorse battle plans upon my lands, you can inform us of enemy strongholds and so help to secure safe trade routes.' He held out his hand to encourage her to stand beside him and look upon a great stone table, but she frowned at his invite with hands clasped together behind her back. 'Or at least declare to where you have seen our enemies north and east and along our shores?'

Slowly as his eyes scrutinised her, she moved forward to observe drawings and maps scattered about the table top.

'This be Poenari and this your route you describe coming west from Braila.' Vlad pointed out their location and swept his hand past etched names of towns and cities that Tariana could only frown upon. 'We have mapped many my land north and west, but south and east be difficult as many scouts avoid Dobruja and Moldavia, and the east coasts from where you say you came.' He watched her lean over to view better the etched maps and move some about, but could see from her face she did not understand much.

'I not know wordings as not read or write,' Tariana stated awkwardly.

'Excuse me then my lord,' Henrik interrupted after secretly listening from behind, 'but how am I to draw up maps to avoid enemy camps and establish new trade routes if–'

Vlad raised his hand to silence Henrik before speaking.

'Have faith in our gypsy friend,' he said, pondering on a way to simplify his discourse. 'But describe to us on how you travel… what did you see on your way here?'

'We not follow road or river using town or city,' Tariana explained, her hands now gesturing the snaking of a river or the peak of mountains. 'But we track river, lake or mountain by cover of tree or rock… although it be slow for wagon and mule, it be safe.' She paused to look Vlad in the eye. 'I remember much as pictures… have visions in dreams and such… have second sight should you call it that!'

'And she not be a witch?' Henrik whispered sarcastically, but eagerly continued, realizing he did not want to upset his beautiful gypsy friend. 'But surely if she *can* recall these routes and give enemy sightings, she cannot project them on a map?'

'There be a way,' Vlad exclaimed with determination and held up one of the maps to point to towns and name them.

'This be Chilia and west along the big river we name Danube be the city Braila. You may have come this way and seen many sights.' On an empty piece of parchment Vlad drew landmarks that he knew were associated with the towns or that lay between them along the river, and although somewhat crude, Tariana identified a few by pointing at them.

'Did you see enemy camps or garrisons on foot between these towns?'

'Yes, some be travelling along river near here,' Tariana pointed to a bend in the river she recognised, 'but most be still and camping above shoreline.'

'And where would that be on here?'

'I not sure, but remember one big camp outside the town you draw.' 'Was it daylight or night?'

'This be getting us nowhere my lord!' Henrik interrupted as he overlooked the gypsy's shoulder.

'Ignore him my dear,' Vlad instructed and then stared at Henrik. 'But listen to what I ask my good man, as you be doing the same to draw up maps from her travels.' He pointed to the map to continue his interrogation. 'When you were here, you were travelling at what time?'

'I not understand.'

'When you sighted the big enemy camp not far from here, was it morning… sun low and east, was it overhead, or low and west?'

'It be just before we camp at dusk and the sun set on river.'

'The sun set on the river flowing up or down?

'Where the fresh water flows from source… flows towards us.'

Vlad pointed and marked crude etchings on the parchment before presenting it to Henrik.

'See my good man,' Vlad grinned, 'if you can do all but the same, over time and using many sightings from our gypsy friends, we can draw up maps to avoid confrontation.'

'But as I know you my lord,' Henrik interjected, 'do we not engage in battle to decrease our enemy?'

'Yes, but that be to *our* decision and when it be *our* advantage,' Vlad reassured with a hand upon his chest, 'but I want our scouting and trade routes effective. And for that we must ensure the route is secure, have minimal but adequate protection, so our precious merchandise not get ransacked or stolen.'

'So you want me to work with Tariana here and interpret her *visions*…?'

'Let us call it… *experience*,' Vlad exclaimed winking at the gypsy girl. 'And we can ask others from her group to provide *their* experience.'

'Except the big man,' Henrik smirked, 'the Tatar from the north!' Tariana scowled at Henrik and he knew he had annoyed her with his remark. 'Well it be only the truth that he cannot speak!'

'But it not stop him talk to me!' Tariana stated with conviction.

'Please let us not fight amongst ourselves,' Vlad intervened, 'our enemy be out there and we be ever the few if we argue.' He turned to take Tariana by her shoulder and describe his plans, but first wanted to hear her story in brief. 'Tell me from as far as this map stretch from where you have travelled.' He glanced at Henrik with earnestness and instructed, 'Please do not interrupt, but interpret and etch such as she may describe on this map as we not know much south or east.'

In a tetchy and rather melodramatic account, both Vlad and Henrik listened with measured patience to Tariana's story; of how she and her younger brother had escaped the Turks after their parents were killed, and then helped by a group of travellers from the cold north, to which Sorin was the last survivor. And with reference to maps that Vlad provided, how their group of amalgamated Ukrainian gypsies and Tatars survived along the coast of the Black Sea before reaching the River Danube (of which Vlad explained to be the border between Moldavia and Dobruja). Here they barely survived the persecution of the Ottoman Empire and so joined Romanian gypsies travelling inland, boiling water from the river but coming starved of food. As not being able to settle and grow crops of their own, they had to pilfer what they could on the outskirts of farmlands and towns. As she described avoiding the many Turkish settlements she had sighted throughout her journey, Henrik did best to record what he could, but Tariana came overwhelmed with emotion to recall her and her brother's perilous journey through mountains and gorges after many gypsies had got slaughtered because they chose to traipse the open road or river shoreline. And by the time they reached the outskirts of Chilila, many were starved and so desperate to camp near the plentiful settlements surrounding the city.

It was because they risked camping so close to Chilila that the Turks raided them and took all they had, including children old enough to travel on foot. And although terrorised to watch their loved ones get taken, Romanian gypsies had interpreted the Turkish soldier's instruction; that the Sultan wanted their young captured alive. Shortly after Tariana described of how Sorin had prevented many abductions, she broke into tears to exclaim that her young brother must have been taken.

Vlad could not watch Tariana grieve uncomforted, and so consoled her with open arms. It was the first time in years he had embraced another woman and so stepped back after feeling a strange desire take hold of him. And as she peered slowly up at him, her hazel eyes gleamed like dark jewels, as if emanating a strange mystical energy. Had Vlad been wrong to not think her some witch? Had he become besotted by her as Henrik had clearly become? No, although pretty like some wild rose, he denounced her as just some gypsy girl that held nothing but useful information from her travels.

But then, as Vlad took another step back, Tariana stared at him with conviction. Somehow, from her glistening, dark eyes, Vlad acknowledged her pain and suffering; moreover, the want to have her little brother back. But determined to put resolve to his mapping and focus on generating safe trade routes, Vlad ushered Tariana aside in hope to lessen her grief. At first she looked dreamy, but as he repeated to interrogate her about sighting the Turkish enemy on her travels from Chilila, she sniffed and pouted before describing how the remainder of her group snaked their way through Transylvania, traipsing the southern scarps of the Carpathian Mountains to avoid battles along the borderlands with Moldavia.

Henrik intervened to argue that with many weeks passed Tariana's information could now be obsolete, but Vlad told of how the Turks established routes into foreign lands by conquering one stronghold before moving on to another. And to guarantee a quick retreat, they would defend that which they previously captured.

Henrik observed to what he had etched, and by analysis projected that the enemy had been restrained by Moldavians north and Hungarians west, so it was indeed these encounters that moved the enemy south and east into Wallachia.

Timidly interrupting Henrik, Tariana told of how some of her gypsies interpreted enemy discourse to determine the fate of their young. She disclosed to how the enemy was to move far as they could west and then turn their attack north. This was why she travelled at height along the escarpments and woodland at the base of mountains. And travelling light, they could pass and avoid heavy armoured artilleries below them, most of which followed the clear and solid ground along rivers.

Vlad disputed that traipsing through woodland at such height was laborious, but agreed it would be stealthier, if as the gypsies were (and as he had seen them) lighter on their feet.

Tariana continued to describe of how many a time her group spotted the enemy in valleys below. She spoke of how such large garrisons needed wide and clear routes to travel, and of how soft woodland or silted river shorelines hindered their travel. On one such route, she sniggered to describe how many enemy soldiers tripped and fell with such burden as they ushered mules and oxen. She went on to chortle at the enemy's attempts to cross a wide but shallow river, but was silenced by Vlad, who was curious to her use of the word *burden*? Tariana scrunched up her little nose in puzzlement before describing best the artillery weapons of the enemy, but

Vlad came confused to her description of *heavy barrels of steal resting upon wagons.*

It was Henrik who disturbed a long silence between the prince and the gypsy. He had heard of such horse-drawn cannons from Hungarian soldiers but thought it myth. He asked Tariana to describe their size and evidently came worried to where she had spotted them. Etching roughly Tariana's location at the time, Henrik described the stories he had heard about such cannons known as *Ballista*; of how a few blasts of its cannon balls could break through the hardest of stone and breach the defence of the toughest castle. But he also told of how many men were required to manoeuvre such a weighed instrument of war and agreed with Tariana for the need of many a man and animal.

Smugly Tariana indicated that the mountainous area that they were on would certainly make things difficult to move such burden, but Henrik told that these cannons did not need to be so close, only that they were aligned to be accurate.

Suddenly Vlad interrupted both Henrik and Tariana, who were glaring at each other, both silently contemplating to what they had discussed. He too had heard of such weapons used to siege Constantinople many years ago, and knew now the reason why many young and able men were being abducted. Like Tariana's brother, this despicable enemy were using children as slaves, or worst still; they were fostering them to fight against their Christian fathers.

Vlad circled with disgust on his face and questioned openly to how his brother Radu could have known that Turks were taking young men to recruit. Both Tariana and Henrik poised to watch in silence, but only the soldier knew Vlad well enough to know he was thinking aloud. Vlad stopped to stare at both, and although seeing Henrik restrain the gypsy, he glared beyond them, again openly surmising to how the enemy must have started this wicked business whilst his brother was still in captivity.

With kept rage Vlad grasped Tariana by her arm and pulled her to view a map. As she did not recognise the location to where he pointed, Vlad constantly interrogated her to the position she saw the last stronghold. Raising his voice Vlad shook Tariana, and it was not until he calmed to see the hurt in her eyes that he glanced down at his hand clutching her wrist. Reflecting on his frenzied temper, suddenly Vlad released her and apologised, watching the gypsy again rub her wrist in pain. He turned after scouring the map and mouthed illegible words, obviously frustrated at the news of how close the enemy could be with such weaponry. But then he stopped to watch Tariana finger the horseshoe of the Carpathians and follow a line between Braşov and Braila. As she scrolled her finger along the parchment, her now timid voice described seeing one large cannon being transported with difficultly along a river south.

Henrik shifted Tariana aside to see and voiced his concern that her sightings could be wrong. And if her observations were indeed correct, they would now be somewhat obsolete. He glowered at his prince and projected that even by all what they could amalgamate, they could not determine the Turk's next plan. Henrik paused to see Vlad raise a hand to silence him, and then saw his prince observe a pained Tariana.

Vlad moved close to tower over the gypsy and seeing her pensive changed his approach. With a soft voice he apologised and asked her to reflect on how she had lost her parents and then her brother.

At first Tariana just stared up at him, her eyes glazed and distant, but then she moved to scrutinize the furthest north-easterly point of one of the maps. After clearing her throat of apprehension, she began to recall her parent's constant struggle to live upon a land not only ruled by cruel kings north, but their clash with the Ottoman Empire south. It was after her parents had viciously been slaughtered by Turks moving north, that she escaped with her brother to move down the coast and find refuge in other lands. It was on these travels her group met Sorin and his comrades from the colder lands north and east. At first they differed from their objectives, but sharing a similar religious background and a common hate for the same enemy, they progressed south of Moldavia to traipse along the coast. She revealed (pointing to the furthest point north-east on a map) that it must have been close to the border to where her brother got abducted.

Without thinking, Henrik interrupted the gypsy to state that she had pained herself to describe such before, but again with a raised hand, Vlad silenced him. With a nod from the prince, Tariana continued to express her anguish against the enemy; reciting to how, although Sorin and many fought back, she lost sight of her brother and so assumed him taken. She stepped to circle the table, studying the maps upon it with tearful eyes, but came back to regard Vlad close. With an unwavering vigour to her voice, Tariana conveyed her hate for the Turks. For the first time since Radu had treated her so unkind, Vlad and Henrik saw a wild fire erupt in her as she conveyed her dislike at the enemy kidnapping children. And she spat at the floor to show her objection to the enemy treating children so horrible – bringing them up half-starved to fight against their own kind – children cruelly converted to not know their true origin, their true religion – not to know even their true father! She slammed the table with her little fist and as tears ran from her hazel eyes, she confessed to how she prayed for her brother every night.

As again she was overwhelmed with anger but sad emotion, Vlad cushioned her in his arms to admit that he would rather die than see his Mihnea be taken. He too confessed he would not know how to confine his anger should such a terrible thing happen.

Tariana glanced up at Vlad with dark, swollen eyes to tell of how many a time during her travels she had heard about young boys been taken whilst girls were raped; that after so many years these young men would have no idea to who they really are, to who they should really be, whether that be farm boy, gypsy or squire. Suddenly her head dropped as she again mentioned her brother and told of the many boys taken years ago when they were both very young. Forcibly she removed herself from Vlad's embrace and stepped over to observe once again the maps. As tears began to eject more freely, she blubbered about how her brother could be one day fighting and pilfering against his own kind.

Henrik stepped forward to try and console the gypsy himself, but told of how a man comes to know his indifference as he grows older, of how a man questions his past to seek resolve. But again drying away her tears, Tariana contested Henrik's words to question of how a man can know such if taken as a child. And with an enemy having such a terrible reputation, surely most abducted adolescents would have no other choice but to keep silent in order to put food in their bellies.

Vlad turned from his thoughts to watch Henrik approach Tariana, and before his friend could voice more a disagreement with the gypsy, Vlad raised his hands to intervene. Towering in between to separate the two, Vlad stared to calm Henrik, but turned to Tariana with a voice of assurance. With green eyes glowering and a stern face, Vlad told of how he would never let his son be taken by the enemy as it would be against decades of conflict to uphold the Order of the Dragon. The gypsy frowned at him, and so seeing her bewildered, he explained in brief his ancestor's history and of how his father had to make an allegiance with the Ottoman Empire to keep peace; of how he and Radu sustained years of internment to honour a truce agreement.

Tariana spoke slowly and softly but voiced her concern that Radu was not like Vlad; that she had found her dislike for his brother as soon as they met. She grumbled on to question his brother's time with the enemy, and overhearing her, Vlad agreed that Radu had indeed endured many more years under Turkish rule than he. Again Tariana mumbled her apprehension about Radu; stating that his arrogance must come from years of much torment and that maybe the enemy had changed him for good. But turning away, Vlad denied that Radu had changed. Yes it was true that his brother seemed somewhat pompous and hard-hearted, but surely his allegiance was to him, his father and the Order of the Dragon.

Tariana stepped past Henrik (who was now regarding the maps and etchings he had drawn) to approach Vlad and see him close. As he quickly glanced to notice her dark but sympathetic eyes, he heard her again question his brother's fidelity. Vlad started to grunt his objection, but then heard Tariana tell of a vision she had had whilst sleeping out in the courtyard; of how Radu tricked Vlad's son, and with many screaming boys kidnapped, dragged them into pits to work as slaves. She went on to explain more her dream, but Vlad turned to push her aside whilst verbally scorning her vision. Tariana poised to stare at Vlad, and although disliking his sudden aggression towards her, stepped cautiously to notice his eyes lost in thought.

Although recalling the strange repetitive dreams he had been having himself, Vlad sensed the gypsy girl gawping at him. For a long moment he could not turn and face Tariana as he was considering whether he had indeed saved a witch from persecution.

EIGHT

'Why is it my husband is not to go scouting with you?'

Startled, Radu looked round to see Jusztina frowning at him, and in his panic felt her vanity mirror slip from his fingers and fall from his seat.

'It be…' Radu peered down and grimaced to see the mirror now cracked. 'He be weapon forging I suspect.' He placed his foot on top of the mirror and manoeuvred it into hiding, but Jusztina noticed it as she moved further into the room. 'Henrik is to test these vagabonds of their knowledge and I am to learn the landscape of this mountainous region.' He was about to explain more about securing trade routes when Jusztina suddenly squealed with excitement.

'There it be,' she shrieked, edging forward to squat and retrieve her again, mislaid possession. 'Why it be cracked,' she screeched as she stood tall to examine it, but then glowered at Radu who seemed unimpressed by her dismay. Instead she noticed how he kept peeking out of the bedchamber window. 'Have you broken this you fiend?' She pushed her cracked vanity mirror almost against his nose. 'It was missing again from my room yesterday!'

'Calm yourself woman,' Radu sneered, 'it be nothing expensive!'

'It be to me, brother by law,' Jusztina protested, rolling the mirror in her grasp whilst lunging in front of his face. 'I so not have much for a future queen and probably not get much after either!'

'If I confessed would it make it any better,' Radu said cynically, trying to usher Jusztina from the window. But she stood unmoved to notice a light glimmer in the distance, somewhere she pinpointed near Curtea-de-Argeş. 'Indeed I took it again from your room and without asking… I be such a rogue, but a vain one may I add.' He saw her again take sight of a distant flickering light and so whisked her away. 'To tell you the truth, there be something in my eye that annoy me terribly and so I endeavored to remove it. Such a thing can be so annoying, do you not agree?' Restraining her by her shoulders and grinning wide, he knew she could no longer see outside the window. 'And yes it be the devil in me to drop it, but I will replace it, I promise.'

'How can *you* replace such a thing?'

'Why, I bet I can get you another from this scouting trip.' As he spoke, Radu shepherded Jusztina again into the passageway and down on towards her own bedchamber. 'It be obvious that it will not be like that one, but it may be bigger and better... something to admire oneself on their wedding night.'

'I be married already,' Jusztina stated, again annoyed by Radu's urgency to escort her back to her room. 'And it be your brother who be my husband and who be in charge here!'

'Not for this scouting trip he be not!'

'I must confess that I be grateful to have Vlad for myself whilst you be gone,' Justina smirked, 'but why is it that you go and not him?'

'As I said previous,' Radu rolled his eyes and stuck his nose aloft. 'Henrik is to show me this part of the country whilst he tests the scouting of these vagabonds, including that dumb giant. As they have traipsed not far the borders of your birth country, it be vital they secure safe passage for merchandise between my brother and what be his name?'

'My relative, the King of Moldavia… Stephen the Great!'

'Yes that be him,' Radu interjected and then cleared his throat to continue. 'Vlad be knowing, and so I have gathered, that trade with Hungary diminishes as their king…'

'King Matthias Corvinus,' Jusztina affirmed as she entered her bedchamber.

'Yes, well him indeed,' Radu again cleared his throat as he followed her. 'Well many in Wallachia, as well as Bukovina, have much disagreement with this Corvinus, and so my brother plans to make more allegiance and trade with *your* country. But to do that, we must at first establish safe passage before we can ensure the carriage of goods. Your brother confessed to me his problem… the guarantee of such goods, whether the merchandise be the fine weapons he forge here or the simple crops he grow in farmsteads protected below us.'

'But why be it my husband not go if it be so critical?'

'He be away for so long and be needed to oversee his new developments being forged in the bowels of this keep.' Radu paused to look upon Jusztina with a glint of supremacy in his eyes. 'He is to see to it in person that I get the specified crossbow made from my own drawing.' He sniffed loudly as a pride overwhelmed him. 'Hopefully I'll get such an exquisite weapon before I leave.' He observed Jusztina contemplating what to do with her broken vanity mirror. 'Do not worry my dear, I be sure to get you something that will suffice, even if it be foreign.'

'I not be wanting anything stole from the enemy!'

'And why not,' Radu contested, 'some of their lady's instruments of vanity are nothing but the finest… and be worth much as decorated in gold and jewels.'

'I not want anything from the Ottoman Empire,' she said adamantly, 'even if it be a lady's best vanity case… as it probably be stained in blood!'

'Again, calm yourself my dear,' Radu gazed upon Jusztina with a stern face. 'I hear you may have another nephew on his way so do not fret.'

'Or niece.' Jusztina muttered as she sat down.

'You sit and rest my dear and make precious time with your husband as we go and scout these lands my brother own.' As he went to close the door, Jusztina again saw that awful grin on Radu's face. 'I might just find you something you cannot refuse!'

'He not listen master Henrik,' Tariana shouted in frustration, her voice croaking as she grasped the reins of his horse and scowled, 'we should make between those valleys to scout towards the risen sun.'

'Lord Radu,' Henrik called as he whisked the reins from Tariana's grip to speed forward, 'we be following the guidance of young Tariana and her gypsies and so should not continue south.' He stopped to canter beside Radu's grey mare and awaited his answer, but there was a long pause.

'What be the problem Henrik?' Radu asked cynically.

'You not hear me?' Henrik asked in annoyance and so repeated, 'The gypsy girl says we should now head east and traipse that valley.'

'I heard her.'

'And so you obviously heard me!'

'Yes, but there be a change of plan you see,' Radu looked down his nose at Henrik and squinted. 'As agreed with my brother, it be first that we head for Târgoviste.'

'Our prince never mention any sort of deviation to me. He be stating that we follow the guidance of–'

'We have special business to attend to in Târgoviste,' Radu interjected sharply. 'It be something my brother ask before we turn in the direction of Moldavia. Once we establish a safe trade route, I be heading back and meet my garrison in Braşov.'

'Braşov,' Henrik cross-examined, 'your men be heading there?'

'Indeed, they would have left shortly after us.' Radu peered at Henrik to reveal part of the plan. 'The fact is that my brother be in desperate need of soldiers and so my men leave this morning. When finished in this venture, I join them in Braşov and head for Sighişoara to allot more infantry.'

'But I was told by my prince…?'

'Like I said,' Radu stated smugly, 'there be a change of plan.'

Henrik was perplexed to the authority he could bestow. Apart from training and ordering his men to battle, he had always gone by Vlad's instruction. But now his pompous brother was either lying or indeed he had some endeavor that Vlad wanted kept secret. But Vlad had always been open with him; unless it was some family matter on which he should not intrude. He dropped back to ponder on whether to intervene when he felt his arm being tugged.

'Master Henrik, my friend be worried,' Tariana shouted as she strode quickly to keep up alongside his horse. 'Sorin tell me by sign that we must move out of sight… move off road and climb to track slope of mountain.'

'To avoid detection of our enemy you mean?'

'Yes here, the enemy can spot us… track us to where we go.'

Tariana slowed to walking pace as she watched Henrik again gallop his horse towards the leading Radu.

'It be the gypsies that lead this scout,' Henrik announced resolutely, 'and they be worried that the enemy will sight us easy by road.'

'It not be far and it be best we make haste by road… Soon we shall traipse the valley so be under cover.' Radu then snapped, 'It be urgent business I have to do for my brother so follow suit!'

'With all due respect my Lord, none here be told of such a change of plan and the girl be afraid of us entering such a large town.'

'But they will only see you as Wallachian soldiers and me some merchant.' Radu contested, his arrogance making Henrik's blood boil. 'Nothing wrong with Wallachian soldiers visiting a Wallachian town now is there?'

'And them?' Henrik nodded in the direction of Tariana and her giant accomplice. 'Then why we be having these vagabonds… these gypsies your brother instructed that we use as scouts?'

'Why they be used later,' Radu derided as he trotted faster ahead, his voice muffled somewhat by a fortified gallop. 'They be used when my brother's business be done in Târgoviste. They find us a safe trade route to Moldavia after that.'

'But they be off track,' Henrik disputed. 'The girl stated that they could only track the route they took.'

'I repeat to you Henrik,' Radu galloped ahead and needed to shout to be heard, 'my brother's business in Târgoviste takes precedence above all!' As Henrik followed (envious of Radu's new crossbow fixed to the rear of his saddle), he waved on his men to pursue. But the last he could hear from Radu was his instruction, 'Quick then, we traipse that hill and make for Târgoviste!'

The three remaining horsemen of the garrison sped to follow Radu, but Henrik glanced back to his men on foot, noticing them and the gypsies struggle to climb the slope. Determinedly, Henrik and his two fellow riders left behind their comrades on foot in order to keep the speeding Radu in sight. But by now Henrik could only spot him intermittently through the trees and so instructed his two other horsemen to pursue some distance either side of him.

Henrik glanced left and right, ensuring he could observe his fellow riders, but sighting Radu ahead was getting increasingly difficult. And the slope was increasing with ever thickening woodland. As he edged towards the rider on his left, Henrik instructed him to hold back for the others and so went on to the other rider, dodging low branches whilst he guided his horse between trees and thicket. The other rider was also instructed to follow, but at pace to await men on foot as Henrik galloped ahead.

After charging his horse in Radu's direction, he soon came clear of the forest and found himself high on a precipice of an escarpment. Although somewhat obscured still by morning mist, from a cliff edge Henrik could see the large town of Târgoviste, its outskirts patterned by farmsteads and harvested land. But suddenly Henrik's admiration for the autumn scenery was disturbed by a voice.

'My lord, I not see the brother of our prince anywhere along this ravine,' a horseman affirmed as he came into sight. 'Unless he be in hiding, I not see him double back.' The horseman searched the long line of trees and then glanced nervously at the cliff edge. 'He cannot have gone that way, but I not see him anywhere?'

They turned to sight the other horsemen come into view along the edge of the woodland, his head shaking to reveal that his pursuit had also failed.

Minutes later, as the two horsemen gathered with Henrik to question Radu's whereabouts, a number of the fittest but exhausted pike men and archers appeared. And then some swordsmen stooped to catch their breath in the shadow of the last trees.

Unexpectedly from within the woodland came deathly screams and wails of agony. Although fearful to investigate, Henrik's soldiers retreated back between the trees and dispersed into the woodland shadows. To what they found was shocking.

Turkish soldiers were appearing from the gloom of the undergrowth as if rising from hidden graves to ambush the main bulk of Henrik's garrison. As they raced around in dilemma, many were slaughtered in the confusion. And those who evaded the onslaught, to escape back up the slope to the edge of the woodland, were met by a line of Turkish pike men who Henrik and his horsemen could see assemble along the edge of the escarpment.

Henrik directed the two horsemen to follow and with longswords in hand swept at the line of enemy pike men before they disappeared into the cover of trees. But with only the three, and arrows now assailing them from emerging enemy archers, their influence came ineffective. Bemused, Henrik suddenly found himself alone in wielding his sword at any Turkish helmet he could reach.

Following the rear of Henrik's garrison, Tariana, Sorin and their group of a dozen other gypsies were soon to be horrified by the conflict in the scrub of the woodland. As they watched Wallachian soldiers bravely fight, many were overwhelmed before they could even raise their weapon, whether it was longsword, pike or bow. And with them also vulnerable to attack, Tariana's gypsies rifled any soldier they could find (whether injured or dead, friend or foe) for weaponry to protect themselves. Sorin had found two Turkish sickle swords of which he hacked back against the enemy, and other gypsies began to ransack what they could. But Tariana's heart sank as she reached for her precious scabbard to realize how it had been confiscated. As soldiers from higher ground ran down towards her, all she could do was dodge them and hide between trees, hoping Sorin would cut them down as her short height paid some advantage.

Tariana pulled away her headscarf, taking the veil from her face to observe the bloody warfare about her in more detail. It was then that she noticed one of Henrik's horsemen come into sight, his horse trudging through the undergrowth, exhausted but unscathed. Unfortunately not the same could be said of the steed's rider, who with his remaining energy, hung on to the beast's mane after several arrows had pierced the rear of his breastplate. As the horse came to an abrupt halt nearby, Tariana grimaced to watch the rider fall and fall awkwardly to the ground.

Determinedly the gypsy girl raced to grasp hold of the horse by its reins and glancing down saw the man's eyes flicker with life. She knelt down to understand the words that spluttered with blood from his mouth.

'We cut some down… top of the hill… many as we could, along the ravine,' the horseman gargled, 'but Henrik battled on… we not see him as we…'

Abruptly an enemy sword cut into the injured horseman's chest with such force that it removed the last of the man's life. Tariana glanced up to see a Turk pulling on his sword in order to retrieve it from being lodged in the horseman's sternum. Once free, he glowered at the horse and then at Tariana, but she pulled the beast towards her, grasping a whip coiled from the saddle about its flank.

The Turk lunged forward to steal the horse but felt a whip slash across his face and its end snap at the air. He stopped to check his face and pulled away his hand, bewildered that it was not covered with blood. Paused in his dilemma, Tariana recoiled the whip to send it to wrap around the soldier's legs. She puckered to feel how easy it was to pull the man off balance and send him flat on his back and into the undergrowth.

Noticing how quickly the Turk got up to glare at her, she searched for another weapon, but found neither dagger nor sword as she pulled away the horse. Fortunately (and reliable as always), Sorin bounced close into action to save Tariana from further conflict; one of his sickle swords now lodged in the soldier's throat to pin him firm against the trunk of a tree.

But by now several other enemy soldiers were trudging through the scrub to get at the horse, their weapons wielded high above their heads in contempt. After noticing a dropped pike, Tariana clapped her hands together to get Sorin's attention and pointed at the weapon not far from his feet. With a sweep of hand gestures, Sorin acknowledged Tariana's idea and so ran to retrieve the pike. And as planned, Tariana lured the soldiers, enticing them by trotting with the horse as Sorin ran at them; the pike eventually surged across them to fling them off balance. And it worked, until all but one rose up, their eyes glowering with anger.

Paused by their predicament, both Sorin and Tariana searched each other's faces, each considering their options as a voice called from behind. Galloping down the slope and finding it difficult to halt his frightened horse, the other of Henrik's horsemen warned of more Turks coming down the slope after many of his men had been slaughtered. As he approached he told of how he considered the whole escapade to be an ambush set up by Radu, who he foretold was untrustworthy from the start. As he pointed to the increasing movement about them, the horseman offered an injured soldier a ride and told all to escape to tell Vlad the bad news.

Tariana asked to what become of Henrik, but the horseman shrugged, only to look sad at the ground and tell of how his commander fought brave at the top of the hill. She went to shout other questions but felt the strong arm of Sorin lift her and place her on the horse as he grabbed the creature's reins and sped the animal towards the other. It was indeed an urgency that who was left could escape with their lives, as enemy eyes now stared at them from all dim corners of the woodland.

Nervous at knowing how near enemy soldiers were, the horseman struggled to pull an injured comrade up on the rear of his horse, and as a few other Wallachian soldiers and remaining gypsies started to follow on foot, their eyes glanced round to comprehend where the enemy were.

As Sorin rushed towards the horseman (now accompanied with his injured comrade), he caught sight of him point at his fellow horseman on the ground. Looking down from being mounted on the horse, Tariana saw Sorin cut his hand across his throat to confirm the horseman's comrade dead.

Tariana clicked her fingers and leaned over to touch Sorin on the shoulder, her hands eventually indicating that they should quickly go, as against so many, they has no chance.

With arrows starting to assail them, Sorin pushed and Tariana pulled another injured soldier up to ride along with her. And with more survivors from Henrik's scouting party following on foot, the depleted group escaped north and in the direction of Poenari.

NINE

'Open the gates! Let we in!' Tariana glowered up at the eyes that stared down from the battlements of the outer wall, their faces scared at hearing Sorin thump the sides of his fists on the large, oak doors. 'The enemy be not far behind and many be under threat.'

Sorin retreated from his pounding so he too could observe the frightened faces that glared down at them. And by now many from the fields and farmsteads were joining the remainders of Henrik's scouting group in fear of what was told: that the enemy had followed them to the river and were but miles away.

Again Sorin went to hammer on the doors to enter the keep, but Tariana whistled from the saddle of her horse for him to come to her; she had recognised Vlad's green eyes and long brown hair as he appeared above the barbican. And like the guardsmen who stared down with him, he stood in amazement to see Henrik's garrison back so soon. But then she noticed how Vlad's eyes searched all that remained of them and grimace at how many were injured. His eyes then noticed the frightened people who ran to join them and beg for their prince's protection; field and farmstead workers, along with groups of gypsies that had previously camped along the shoreline.

Tariana raced her horse through the gates as soon as they opened; her, injured accomplice rider nearly falling from the rear of the horse as she pulled hard on the reins. She saw Vlad run towards her and so jumped from the saddle, amazed at how sprightly she could still ride as well as dismount.

As she ran towards him, Vlad paused to search for Henrik and many other faces he should recognise, but it was then that he saw the expression on Tariana's face and so gazed upon the crowd hurrying through the gates. He noticed how injured soldiers had taken ride on farm wagons or were being supported by either farmstead worker or gypsy. And then he noticed the giant gypsy named Sorin carry in an injured soldier to safety before lifting another from a wagon. As Tariana came close, she knew by his expression that Vlad was speechless but wanted to know all.

'I warn you my Lord,' Tariana spoke out of breath. 'Did I not tell master Vlad that his so brother not be trusted?'

'By what do you mean by that?' Vlad responded with both anger for her scorn and at the sight of all injured. 'Where be Radu?'

'You so be brother took off… giving story that we head south… but it be as soldier call… an ambush.' She paused to turn and watch Sorin take the injured soldier from the horse, but again stared back at Vlad with dark, angry eyes. 'We save many who we can, but many die as result.' She glanced around again to observe those now been placed for treatment, but heard Vlad enquire about his second-in-command.

'And Henrik,' Vlad's voice croaked to ask, 'where he be?'

'You need to ask him!' Tariana pointed to the remaining horseman. 'But he say he be lost in battle… fought brave he said but there be no sign of him as we leave quick to escape.'

Vlad paused to contemplate Henrik dead, but could not believe such; his friend had been proven a hard and prudent warrior.

Gazing at how vagabonds now walked freely amongst soldier and farmworker, Vlad watched Sorin before staring at Tariana to wonder if this was indeed some witch-stricken ploy. As Tariana and Sorin appeared unscathed, had he been cursed by letting these gypsies into his keep? Had Jusztina been right to disapprove of these people, or was his wife still set in her old, conceited way? He gritted his teeth in thinking of how such vagabonds could squander his keep, but then saw how carefully the gypsy giant placed an injured Wallachian soldier down so a young gypsy woman could tend to him. Vlad's thoughts were disturbed by Tariana who stood close to look up at him.

'Lord and master Vlad,' Tariana said, as the flames of lit reed torches reflected in her dark, hazel eyes now that dusk descended on them, 'my sense to your brother be proved right… he be not trusted from my first meeting him.'

'It be probably as he was to burn you as a witch,' Vlad interjected, 'of *which* you be not, I hope?' Vlad managed a smile as he again came overwhelmed by her raw beauty. 'I not know what side my brother be taking after all years of persecution, but must converse with my men to know what happened.' His effort to neglect his dismay came squandered as he thought of Henrik. 'But we must look for him!'

'Master Henrik?' Tariana surmised with a frown.

'Yes, and many others which may still be out there, injured but alive and needing our help.'

'But it be dark soon,' Tariana responded sharp, 'and we know what happened last time in a night attack.'

'That be then and this be now,' Vlad retorted angrily, 'and I be knocked unconscious.' He held strong the lapel of his doublet to secretly gape at the gypsy girl. 'So many be lost under trust and so my brother escape with his garrison… surely it be not that he take side with the enemy… after all we planned and did?' He watched Tariana hand signal Sorin but turned away in disbelief at Radu's pretense. 'Maybe he come back with more infantry from Braşov?' Silently cursing himself, Vlad saw the giant gypsy lift up an injured soldier and carry him towards him. 'I even made sure my craftsmen forge him a strong bow to his liking... surely he be honouring that?' He watched as Sorin placed the soldier in front of him as Tariana instructed.

'You tell your Lord what you tell to me on horse!'

'It be true my Lord,' the soldier held his pained chest as he gazed awkwardly up at Vlad. 'It be that your flaxen brother take haste towards Târgoviste and we follow but loose him through steep woodland. And then as we see Lord Vasile and his horsemen confer at clearing at top of hill, the enemy attacks us...' Vlad moved forward to stoop and steady the man by holding his shoulder. 'We regain breath on edge of woodland and see Turks appear like dead rising from their graves... attack us from all angles they did... rose from out of the earth like evil corpses... and began to slaughter us as we ran down to escape.'

'But surely this not be a plan by my brother,' Vlad stood back with hands held wide, 'it be some sort of coincidence?'

'I must not say this my lord, but guess that my time be short...' the soldier glanced up at Vlad to stare at him hard. 'But it be that I trust more these gypsies than I do that golden brother of yours.' He squinted as Vlad raised a hand to him but paused to hear him go on. 'My chest had been spiked and my arm slit, but that giant of a man pulled me to safety after taking on many the enemy with scythes of their own.' The man gasped to laugh, but had to spit blood from his mouth. 'And that gypsy girl… kept them at length with our horseman's whip as we gathered to escape.'

'If it be not for these gypsies, along with our archers and swordsmen that fought strong,' the remaining horseman approached to add, his arms pointing at the injured that were being place about them, 'half you see here, would not be alive now.'

'And the others,' Vlad interjected somberly, 'Henrik included?'

'I fought with Lord Vasile at the top of some escarpment,' the horseman knelt beside his injured comrade after seeing him nauseated, and then looked up. 'We carved at the rear of enemy spearmen who pushed our men back down through the woodland but it was useless.' The horseman paused through thought of guilt. 'We hacked at the enemy, but as our horses and legs came sliced by spears, I retreated… we retreated.'

'And Henrik,' Vlad grabbed strong the horseman's shoulder, nearly toppling him off balance as he enquired, 'did Lord Vasile escape?'

'Not with us my Lord,' the horseman confessed shaking his head. 'Then we must depart and search for survivors at once!'

'But to stand any chance against the numbers that followed us back, another garrison would take more than can defend this keep?'

'Especially now many here be weak or injured,' another soldier added. 'And we have not your brother's garrison?'

'They be wiser than you think,' Tariana interjected with sarcasm, 'men of your brother go before be asked questions.'

Vlad glared at each around him with controlled anger.

'I recon they not talk anyways,' a soldier reflected, 'be my guess that their wives and kids be at peril if they did.'

'You talk such with them?' Vlad directed at the soldier who spoke.

'No, but you get a sense of these things,' he stuttered whilst glancing at each of them, 'it be the way they avoid such talk of family… and friends.'

'But you have no evidence that my brother arranged such an ambush!'

'He not need such,' Tariana interjected moving close, 'it be obvious it be all arranged!'

'And how gypsy girl,' Vlad hovered above Tariana to parade his authority, 'my brother be confined to walls of this keep until he left *before* his men?' He stooped to snarl in her face, but saw Sorin enclose to tower above him. 'You be nothing but as *he* said… a peasant and vagabond… a foreign gypsy with nothing but knowledge of scouted lands… and now that be useless!'

Tariana backed away and grasped Sorin's cuff to follow suite, but the horseman approached to exclaim.

'My Lord, these people fight as hard as any Wallachian and many be dead if they did not.' He saw Vlad squint at him as a reed torch reflected in his green eyes. 'But many be tired or injured, hungry and so weak. We can switch guardsmen for swordsmen but we still be at a disadvantage.'

'And how that be?'

'They followed us back and know many be injured,' the horseman looked at the many receiving treatment. 'Should we leave the injured to defend here we –'

'They not know how many we have to protect this keep!' Vlad snapped. 'But it be that Lord Radu saw all in here,' Tariana explained coyly.

Again Vlad exposed his anger, but could not lash out at the gypsy girl although he knew him a Lord and Prince, and her some foreign vagabond.

'We must at least try,' Vlad clenched a fist to thump his leg in frustration. 'Lord Vasile and many other Wallachian men be out there and need our help!'

'But by now they could be…' the horseman coughed.

'Then we be knowing and grant them a Christian burial!' Vlad turned to exclaim to all crowded round, 'How can I not be a true voivode and Prince of Wallachia if I not honour the men who fight for me… to honour my father and uphold the Order of the Dragon… to keep our Christianity strong against that depraved religion of our enemy!'

'We could take all horses and ride with God's speed,' one soldier muttered, 'and have a search party back before they know it!'

'That's be the spirit,' Vlad encouraged, this clenched fist now punching the air. 'But they will see our many hoof tracks in the earth,' the horseman interjected. 'And we not have many horses,' a soldier interjected. 'The enemy be too close to sneak past… or should they see us leave?'

'With the able and rested we should have enough men to ride as garrison. It must be a chance we take and so I will lead.' Vlad stepped to separate the crowd but turned to face all with concern in his eyes. 'As the enemy be so close as you state, let us pray to God the enemy not see our horses leave or the fresh tracks that prove so. Poenari may have my new lines of defense, but knowing we be at a disadvantage to manage such, they may attack this keep.' Vlad paused to consider the time to arrange his venture. 'We leave whilst darkness be some advantage.'

'But many need at least some hours to rest,' Tariana exclaimed. 'Sorin and I will go and show way, but need some rest!'

'But time be precious,' Vlad claimed. 'Men may be dying as we speak?'

As Vlad started to walk through the crowd, a big hand rested on his shoulder to stop him. He glanced up at the big Russian, now noticing a scar stretch from his eyebrow down through his cheek; his eye slightly closed from his misfortune during some combat long ago. Vlad took a step back and took fright to his height and strength, but now noticed him grunt as he signed with his other hand in the direction of Tariana.

'What does he want?' Vlad contested. 'What does he stop me for?'

'He tells of an idea that may make the enemy think we have received more soldiers…' Tariana glanced back to read from Sorin's hand gestures as he grunted. 'We have horses come but we will have left.'

'And how can that be?' the horseman contested before Vlad could.

'He say that gypsy cobbler could add fake shoes to hooves of horse, so as they leave, it look as they come.'

Apart from the last of Sorin's grunting whilst he hand signaled, there was silence. 'It would at least cover our tracks if we followed the river,' the horseman exclaimed, 'maybe fool the enemy into thinking we *have* received other soldiers… such as a garrison from the home land of Lady Szilagyi?'

'Yes, it may prove wise,' Vlad thought out load, before disclosing discussion with his brother. 'He did ask if Corvinus might send reinforcements… but that was if we had safe trade routes with Moldavia.' He glanced at the giant gypsy before directing his question to Tariana. 'How long would it take… to fix these reversed shoes to about a fifty… maybe one hundred horses?'

'We have not that many horses my Lord!' the horseman interrupted.

'We do if we use those from farmsteads and those of our gypsy friends that have entered this keep for protection.'

'My friends from along river shoreline will provide horses,' Tariana interjected, 'provided his Lord provide shelter and protection to them as you have we?'

Vlad nodded but had another question.

'How long will all this take?' He looked at the giant Tatar again, but realized only Tariana could speak for him. 'It be urgent that we save as many my men as possible… and that we find Lord Vasile.'

'We be able to leave…' Tariana waited to interpret Sorin's grunts and sign language. 'At dawn… maybe an hour sooner.'

'Make it a couple of hours before dawn so we can be well on our way before light.' He paused to wink at Tariana, but his brief wit came shadowed at whether Henrik was still alive. 'At daybreak, when they see our tracks, they should think we have gained reinforcements overnight.' He too thought still about trusting these foreign gypsies as he had agreed now to take more of these travellers. 'We go two hours before daybreak with as many of these faked hooved horses we can… with as many able of my men to show us the way.'

'We show you way!' Tariana ratified as she pointed at herself and then Sorin.

'Then you better get what sleep you can before we leave.' Again Vlad winked at the gypsy girl but stood back in astonishment to see his wife approach.

'I hear from soldiers to what happened.' Vlad stared at Jusztina in silence, but noticed how his wife glared scornfully at Tariana. 'I distrusted that brother of yours and I guess…' It was hard for Jusztina to confess that she thought the same about Radu as some gypsy vagabond girl. 'I should have told you things he did beforehand.'

'Like what?' Vlad tried to usher his wife away from the staring eyes of the crowd he had just talked with. 'Did he try and force himself upon you or something?'

'No my Vlad, he did not.' She grinned a little to divulge, 'He be too pompous and changed for that!'

'By what do you mean… changed?'

'I deduce that he be abused as a handsome boy... when he was young and kept by such a depraved enemy that is?'

'I think not.' Vlad neglected and deferred the subject back to what Jusztina had stated initially, 'What things should you have told... beforehand?'

'Remember to how I told you that I lost my mirror?'

'To do your hair and face...' Vlad concluded, 'your vanity mirror?'

'Yes, well I caught *him* with it, or at least he admitted to using it...' She paused in remembering it broken. 'And it was cracked when I found it in his room... but he had accidentally dropped it, the pompous fool admitted!'

'Excuse me my dear, but with Henrik missing and all, what relevance has this?'

'Well it did not occur to me at first as he be escorting me back to my room...' Again Vlad came inpatient to her pause and so pressed her cheek for her to look up at him. 'Well I be sure Radu did drop it... because I caught him using it.'

'And...?' Vlad rolled his eyes.

'Oh, not for his own vanity, but...' Again she paused, but this time to glare at the gypsy girl. 'But see I remember spotting flashes of light that be visible from his window and did not think of –'

'Flashes of light… from where?'

'They be in the direction some distance north, somewhere near Curtea-de-Argeş.' 'And you not tell of this before I left?' Vlad scorned angrily.

'I thought it not important as you be so occupied to instruct Henrik's scout and present that unduly weapon to your so good brother.'

'Yes, my so great brother.' Vlad could still not accept that Radu could betray him, even with new evidence now disclosed by his wife. 'Surely he not side with the enemy.'

'Radu was using my mirror to contact the enemy?' Jusztina assumed. 'But who be it he know?'

'It not matter now, but as I put my trust in him, so it be my fault.' Vlad said slowly and deep, his eyes glazed with anger. 'He must have signaled his departure and prepared his men safe passage.'

'And signaled to arrange poor Henrik's ambush?'

'Yes my dear,' Vlad looked upon her with contempt, 'that's exactly what my so good brother must have done.'

TEN

'Save as many as you can,' Vlad instructed, 'we may need to use them again.' 'Many be bent or rusted my Lord, so will be melted down once back at our keep.'

The horseman glanced back at the gypsy farrier at work before facing Vlad again. 'But some be good enough to replace horseshoes already worn.'

'So how soon can we have our horses' hooved as normal?'

'I not be sure my Lord,' the horseman stated, 'as you see the gypsy cobbler is at hand, but to him the gypsy girl gives order.'

'Not any more she will not. Get ready the horses as soon as you can.' Vlad strode past but suddenly paused to ask, 'So where be the gypsy girl and her giant friend?'

'They be looking over that ravine my Lord.' The horseman circled to gather shoed horses by their reins. 'They trail the route we took, but be anxious.'

'I guess I would too.'

Vlad reached the top of the hill to find Tariana standing with the Russian Tatar, the two observing the landscape from the edge of the ravine. At such a distance he could not hear the girl but could see the giant communicating with his special sign-language. And seeing Sorin nod and converse in silence gave Vlad a strategic idea.

'It be beautiful if not drenched in such bloodshed of war,' Vlad announced to the two gypsies as he approached and observed the view. 'It be partly the reason we Wallachian's fight so strong for our country.'

'It be beautiful that be true Lord Vlad, like both Sorin and I have different lands which we much admire,' Tariana turned to look at him as did the Russian, 'but like your lands it come invaded by the enemy and we be cast out.' Tariana turned back to note the valley below. 'But now we move on as soon sun shall rise and we be seen by the enemy.'

'If our horses be ready that is?'

'They be ready,' Tariana replied.

'Where be it the enemy chase you back to,' Vlad pointed to the valley below. 'Was it that road snaking beneath us?'

'No,' Tariana answered, 'that be the road your brother be determine to follow before we set foot up that hill as he set off very sudden.' Tariana pointed at an escarpment carpeted in trees, out at the murky morning countryside. 'He told that the town he agreed to visit for you was but miles that way.'

'That be Târgoviste,' Vlad leaned over the edge of the escarpment to see better the road snaking the valley below. 'But Radu never mentioned any venture to the city… especially on my behalf.'

'Then it be true, he lie,' Tariana walked to stand by Vlad and look straight up into his eyes. 'He make all of thing up to ambush Master Henrik… so he be no true brother if man do such!' Tariana pointed to where deciduous trees came replaced by hardier pinewoods that lined the foot of the highland above. 'We track forest where winter tree give cover but see through ones where leaves fall.' She paused to wipe her little, snub nose. 'We look out for enemy but hide our tracks by fallen leaf.' She looked about her to notice how the daylight had intensified. 'We move now and save those that be alive before sun break shadow… before enemy move camp.'

Vlad raised an eyebrow in admiration to a simple gypsy girl who deemed to exhibit war strategy and military tactics, but thought back to how she and her travellers had survived years of enemy's oppression. He also contemplated to how such people lived from the land and never achieved to create or build anything, other than what tools and shelter they needed. Maybe these foreign travellers were different to the thieves and rogue vagabonds who stole and lived off the hard work of others.

'We must go now…' Vlad's thoughts were broken by Tariana shouting, 'Lord Vlad, we must go!'

Traipsing mainly singled-filed, with horses alongside, the group trailed the gypsy giant Sorin, with Tariana in conversation with a couple of Vlad's men helping to track the area to where they had been ambushed. It was when they approached a woodland clearing that the leaders halted and so others bunched as they stopped. Vlad was the only one on horseback, and although Tariana had contested that he would be exposed, Vlad insisted on observing the way from the height of his saddle. With a short burst of a gallop, Vlad raced his horse and dismounted to where he could only at first see Sorin.

'What be the problem,' Vlad asked anxiously, 'do we spot the enemy?'

'Quite the contrary my Lord,' a soldier said looking at the undergrowth and woodland earth covered with dead bodies; both that of their fellow soldiers and that of the enemy, 'looks like we be too late to save anyone.'

'Surely not my man,' Vlad pulled on his horse to see all grimacing at the fresh dead bodies strewn across the woodland earth. Swallowing hard he croaked to announce, 'we reuse their belongings and bury our dead… let the enemy rot.'

'We so do not have time!' Tariana contested.

'I am voivode of these men and these soldiers died for our Wallachia, so we bury them.' Vlad saw the gypsy girl stare wild. 'We give an earthly Christian burial for all.'

'So how do we find Master Henrik before sun take shadows?'

'Half of this garrison will remain to honour our dead, but we ride on to find Henrik and others… hoping they still be alive.'

As he spoke Vlad noticed from such gradient the road snaking the base of the valley below. And sporadic things lined each edge of the road, but from such distance he could not make out what they were. Suddenly it dawned on him that he had seen such horror before.

As half of the garrison descended to lower woodland, Vlad grimaced to realize he had seen this awful sight before: Wallachian soldiers buried with only their head and shoulders above ground – their dying souls trapped below the earth so not to haunt their perpetrators – as defined by irregular customs he had heard about the enemy. But knowing much about the Ottoman Empire, this was some new kind of warning aimed at Wallachia, or more probably, himself.

He rode silent to ignore Tariana's plea for him to dismount and not approach the road below, her advising that it could be but a trap. But Vlad sat upright and resolute in his saddle, even to hear men describe how enemy soldiers ambushed them by rising out of hidden graves like livid corpses in the very woodland they traipsed. Now and then they came upon a corpse and if it was one of theirs, he had them take the body for burial.

Again Tariana ran alongside Vlad's horse, pleading that he keep under cover, but as he approached the road, he could make out his buried soldiers, some faces he had seen not long ago.

'I want all these raised and given a Christian burial,' Vlad instructed, his nose raised high to imitate his brother, 'as no doubt they all be dead by now.'

'But we be open to more attack?' Tariana disputed, with others now in agreement with her.

'What I say is done,' Vlad shouted angrily, his rage again squashed by restraint. 'These men deserve not to rot this way!' He pulled up his horse to look down at a buried soldier's face. 'I know not why our enemy bury us alive this way, but I will see to it I expose them for *all* their ill deeds and punishments… hang them high for the slowest of death if need be!'

Suddenly shouts started to echo back as men that followed pulled to exhume their dead comrades – some buried soldiers said as still being alive.

'Then give them water,' Vlad commanded, turning his horse sideways to see, 'and take them back quick by horse to the others!'

'I not yet see Master Henrik,' Tariana's voice spoke quiet but enough for Vlad to hear. 'He be not here as yet I see.'

'Then check all that's here,' Vlad stared harshly down at her. 'Check the woodland to where all happened… search the edge from that ravine!'

As Vlad circled his horse to count the number of soldiers exhumed to be alive, Sorin ran ahead with other gypsies to search more of the countryside.

And as horses took immediately back the survivors – all others straddled across the saddle of mules – Vlad grimaced to watch his men have to pull their comrades from the earth and check them. With all but a few further up the road and those slain in the adjacent woodland; he had not had any notification on Henrik.

Vlad trotted his horse towards Tariana, who he noticed squinting at the rising sunlight to see Sorin and others search ahead. She looked up at the sharp fall from the ravine, the rock face now observant from a turn in the road.

'I know much about the Ottoman Empire and their tactics of battle, but I not know why they bury us alive as such.' Vlad saw Tariana go to respond, but continued. 'You know the stories I be told… of how the earth traps our souls as so we not haunt them beyond death… so what come of those already dead… is it not just some torture, some display of arrogance… an evil cruelty?'

'I only know what my gypsy friends tell Lord Vlad.' Tariana turned from watching Sorin disappear, and after a glimpse at Vlad, came concerned with their exposure now the rising sun flickered between tree branches. 'Again we must be quick and hide in the scrub until all be taken.'

'I never see all this before.' Vlad came enshrouded by solemn memories. 'We learned a lot, me and Radu you see… when we were young and bound by my father's agreement with the Ottoman Empire. It kept peace and indeed we had not to be harmed. But now I must realize that Radu was subjected to more than I… and his change to their way was more prolonged than mine… I was left aggressive and desolate from their religion, but the Sultan took him as a *fanciable subject* I think it was described.'

'None the least Lord Vlad,' Tariana stepped close to take the reins of his horse to steady the beast, 'he be your brother but betray your trust.'

'Yes, but he still be of my flesh and blood?'

'That may be so, but he still be corrupt enough to betray.' Tariana paused to cringe. 'Like my brother… these the enemy take him.' Tariana looked to the floor, her eyes tearful. 'Or maybe he be better off dead than be changed to their ways.'

'I be stupid as to what I have done,' Vlad cursed his gullibility, 'inviting him in as still a Christian and telling of all our plans… knowing our numbers in Poenari… and my weapons to defend the keep.' He paused again to thump his thigh. 'God forgive me for being so trusting… but he be still my brother.'

'And what else has your dishonest Radu learned whilst under such invite?' Tariana glanced up timidly.

'Maybe he overheard my plans with Henrik… asking for support of the Moldavian king as by honour to my marriage with Jusztina… reinforcements to my army in exchange for specialist weaponry forged in the bowels of Poenari… and of course what riches I can accrue, not there be many?' He paused to think. 'But surely the Moldavian king will be sympathetic and honour our commitment to eradicate the filth of this enemy and their barbaric methods… send more warriors.'

'We have also taken so much from this enemy.' Tariana spoke as she led Vlad's horse to see a fresh living survivor be pulled from what was to be his grave. 'But we have herbs and tonics that be helpful. We get well these men of yours… ones that survive this day and the next… should we take protection in your keep?'

Vlad eyed Tariana pensively. Should he still think of her as some witch, and was this a ploy by her gypsy clan to take advantage of his keep? He could hear the gypsy girl moan and speak of her detest of their common enemy, going on to ask him to trust her more than his brother. But was he himself becoming clouded by the deceitful act of his brother? Who could he trust?

Suddenly they were stopped by Sorin, who outrunning an injured soldier, got to them with eyes open wide with impatience. As he struggled to sign and groaned loud to his excitement, Vlad insisted to what all his palaver was about.

'He has found another soldier,' Tariana said, but watched Vlad stare glum. 'And he has news to where Henrik be!'

Eleven

'Are they still alive?' asked Vlad, 'How many?'

'There is a number of them my Lord who we pulled out of the earth,' the young soldier said, guiding them briskly on. 'They must have been buried by the enemy after falling over the ridge.' He paused to wait for the rest of the group to catch up before turning a corner. 'Many we check be dead, but a few...' The young soldier pointed to a gypsy girl and another young soldier attending an injured swordsman just below the precipice of the escarpment. 'But he be alive and say he knows what happened to Lord Vasile.'

'My good soldier,' Vlad asked stridently as he approached, 'you be a swordsman to Lord Vasile and know what happened to him?'

The soldier acknowledged Vlad and nodded, his eyes wavering as he blinked constantly. Vlad could see that the man was rife with pain and delirious, but still his curiosity compelled him to ask.

'Where be Lord Vasile... what happened?'

'He fought brave as ever,' the swordsman struggled to explain. 'We got accosted by an ambush… after tracing your brother as he set off…'

'Yes, but where be Henrik?' Vlad insisted. 'Where did you last see him alive?' 'He told long ago never to die in such ways as you find me…' The soldier paused

to swallow water that a gypsy girl put against his lips. 'Rather die sudden in battle than be tortured so.' Vlad was becoming impatient but let the swordsman babble on. 'It be a miracle that you find me, but I be ready to meet the Almighty have he take me this day.'

'Do not talk such doubt, but tell to what happened to Lord Vasile?' Vlad knelt down and gritted his teeth to repeat, 'Did he die in battle or be taken by the enemy?'

'He… he…' the swordsman stared at Vlad but looked blankly at his face. 'Lord Vasile would not let them do to him that they do to me… he and his horse got spiked… must have been near death as he rode over the ravine… the same happened to us, but we slid down to escape those pikes and arrows and…' The swordsman's words came garbled, but lifted his arm to point afar. 'He be slung high like our Lord Jesus Christ… but it be a sudden death, as he had wished.'

'So where is he?' Vlad asked in agitation.

'Look to the dead trees… at the foot of the…' Suddenly the swordsman's eyes wavered as he passed out.

After traipsing the base of the ravine for about five minutes, Vlad, Sorin and Tariana passed a clump of fallen rocks to view more of the escarpment, of which now towered above them. Following soldiers had stopped to pull another near-to-death soldier from his premature grave, but eventually caught up to stare at that which paused to shock Vlad and the two gypsies.

With its lifeless truck and branches hit by falling rocks, the dead tree was broken and pivoted at an angle, somehow anchored precariously in the earth by its remaining, unbroken roots. Amongst boulders that scattered about it, were the crushed remains of Henrik's horse. But it was not only the horse's blood that blotted rocks beneath the tree.

Henrik's body lay thrown amongst broken branches within the tree, some height above his crushed horse. Although his twisted body was caught amongst numerous dead branches, it was a main splintered branch that staked him through his heart and held him there. His paled face, with eyes glazed and wide, was frozen in the terror of his abrupt death. With much blood clotted in pools below and a river of dried blood extending from the splintered branch to the trunk, it was obvious that Vlad knew his good friend and commander-in-chief was dead. And although in their religion, suicide was considered a great sin, this had been his friend's choice to escape the enemy's wicked portrayal of torture.

'Help me take down Lord Vasile's body,' Vlad turned to soldiers to instruct, but saw the giant Russian stride ahead to do the task. 'We must honour his death and cremate as it be his wish.' Vlad strode with men following to retrieve Henrik's body. 'We must bury all our dead within the walls of our keep. It be our Christian duty to do so.'

As Sorin balanced Henrik's dead body over one shoulder and progressed back to the main group, Vlad walked with Tariana, occasionally glancing at her with suspicion.

'You look at me with cruel eye Master Vlad,' Tariana suggested frowning, 'but it is not me that you should distrust.' She leaped ahead to block his path and stood gazing up at him. 'I know something be wrong about your brother well before Lord Vasile's horrible death.' She glanced down at her feet in sorrow. 'I liked Master Henrik, as I know he like me…' She looked up to reiterate. 'It was not that I found him a man of my liking that is but he…'

'How did you know my brother was…?' Vlad tried to recall her words. 'That there was something wrong about him?

'When I argue with Master Henrik about your brother going south to that city…' 'Târgoviste,' Vlad interjected.

'Yes, well it be off the path as we plan to follow… not what be agreed.'

'Yes, but I guess Henrik put trust in Radu through me,' Vlad glanced down at Tariana as he set a stride around her, 'so why be suspicious all along?'

'I hate your brother as to how he treat me… and my people,' she said trying to keep up with his stride, 'but I had bad dream about him when I caught what sleep I could.' She saw him look at her skeptically before continuing. 'My visions be always so vivid when prove right… and this be off no exemption.'

'Exception, you mean exception,' Vlad smirked, but below his masked grin was the reflection to his own dreams and how vivid they had been. 'And we all know that dreams do not foretell such as the future.' Vlad sincerely hoped that the one he had about his son was certainly not some prophesy. But was this girl indeed some clairvoyant or a witch as he had first suspected? 'It be stupid to think so…' Vlad tensed with anger to Henrik's death, but sniggered to ridicule the gypsy girl and recall his friend's thoughts on the matter. ''I know what Henrik would have said to you about your *so-called* dreams.'

'Yes but if he had listened to such, he may well still be alive?'

'I very much doubt it as you waste my time on the matter, so we must–'

'Lord Vlad, my most noble prince,' a soldier interrupted, 'we find yet another soldier, but he wants to be left… alone to…'

'He be buried like the others?' Vlad saw the soldier nod, so gave instruction. 'Raise him up and I will speak with him.'

Vlad stepped close to where two soldiers were digging out the man to pull him free and saw the man wriggle in pain but stop to stare at him.

'You will come with us good soldier and live to fight another day!'

'My Lord… noble Prince of Wallachia…' the soldier spluttered out fresh blood over what had already congealed on his chin, 'do honour to me and let me die not this way, but to your blade.'

'To do that I would dishonour the Order of the Dragon… To murder an innocent Christian, especially one which has fought for our salvation, would be regarded as a great sin.'

'But my pain be so…' the soldier squealed as they heaved him out of the earth, 'I pray that our Lord will take me this day, as I see and hear Him call to me.' They laid him down beside the hole of his would-be-grave and gave him water, but spat it out to cough. 'Please my Lord, this water be wasted on me as my time on earth be gone.'

'Talk no more and drink,' Vlad squatted upon his haunches, 'We take you back… and like so many, they can fight as Christian soldiers again.'

'But I must tell… as I feel my time short my Lord.' The soldier struggled to sit up and focus upon Vlad's face.

'I be listening to you soldier, but you must be strong. Soon we will make it back to the protection of our keep.' He paused as he saw Tariana stand beside him, the gypsy giant behind her. 'In the eyes of our Lord we must fight and be great warriors against this our unholy enemy. The Lord will see that we are given the life to be strong and fight against our enemy another day… so come back you must…'

'Please my Lord,' the soldier spluttered blood again, 'I have but no family now, but always wanted a daughter. I know many wish to grow and have brave a son but…' He spluttered again. 'My only provision be this about my neck.' He revealed a stained, wooden crucifix of which he extended up to show Vlad. 'It be great that some child bear it in my absence as I cannot…'

Vlad went to give the man a ladle of water as soon the young gypsy girl returned with a fresh pail, but watched his eyes twitch before staring in a fixed glaze. He had witnessed too many men die before him and knew when a dying man took his last breath. Slowly Vlad closed the soldier's eyes with thumb and forefinger before stating aloud.

'Why be it that our enemy punish us this way?' He glanced up to see Tariana's glum face look down upon the soldier. 'This idea that they punish our soldiers to death, and do so, so that their dying soul cannot rise to haunt and avenge them… where has that ever been an evil of the Ottoman Empire?' He knelt forward to take the crucifix from the soldier's clenched hand, and hearing the cord snap from behind his neck, took a long breath in defiance, glancing sadly upon the dead soldier's face. 'I promise I will avenge this man's death and many others, including that of my friend Henrik.' He paused to see that Tariana was actually listening to him as he thought aloud. 'I will avenge this way of tortured death by tenfold… a score… by hundreds!' He crouched back to reach up and offer the wooden crucifix to Tariana. 'I want you to grant the wish of this dying soldier and…'

'I hear already all that he wished Master Vlad,' Tariana revealed. 'I will see that his wish be granted.'

TWELVE

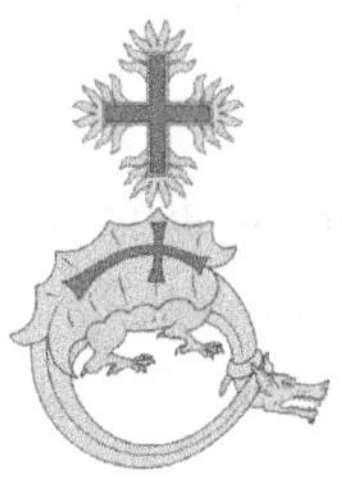

Holding a reed torch at arm's length, Vlad stared into its flame, his aching and tearful eyes strangely not blinking. His thoughts were a jumble of memories both recent and old: times when he and Henrik had rejoiced at the completion of Poenari and danced like jesters in the rain after having had far too much wine, all through to the countless times he and his friend had come close to death during battle.

Henrik had never been one to plan or think war strategy, but when it came to hand-to-hand combat and the need of someone to watch your back, the Hungarian renegade was your man. Now his deathly pale face was gaunt but at peace, his limp body now becoming stiff with rigor mortis, soon to be cremated as to his wish and that of this Hungarian ancestry. With his favourite sword held between folded arms and his shield covering his legs, Henrik was to be burned but not forgotten. Raised high on blocks of stone, the Hungarian awaited cremation by means of oiled twigs and branches to which his body rested flat upon. With everyone silent – hypnotised by the roaring flame of Vlad's reed torch – they paused to witness the cremation of Lord Henrik Vasile; a lonely, unmarried man but a loyal commander who fought for his principles to the bitter end.

'I speak here and now, not as your lord and prince, but just as a man to describe the loyalty and devotion of this our Lord Henrik Vasile... a once young and distraught Hungarian soldier, but who after many years came second-in-command to the Prince of Wallachia.' Vlad's voice croaked to a dryness that overcame it and so had to clear his throat before continuing aloud. 'But I claim this man as being the most loyal friend and subject, and so announce words to honour his dedication and determination to eradicate our enemy, the Ottoman Empire...' As Vlad took to climb a number of steps temporary set for the funeral, he lowered the reed torch and pushed it into the nest of oiled twigs and branches. 'I therefore spread this flame to bring ashes to Lord Henrik Vasile's body so that they later be spread upon the flowing waters of the River Argeş, as be it his wish.' Vlad paused, his eyes tearful again by the heat of the sudden flame, or was it a sudden rush of sentiment. 'We will gather and be silent to watch the body of Lord Henrik Vasile disappear. But later we shall toast a drink to remember a man of such great kindness and to honour such a brave warrior.'

Apart from the roar of flame and the snap of burning wood, the crowded inner courtyard lay silent; only the howl of a distant wolf turned heads to scrutinise the darkness of the night outside the walls of the keep. Vlad turned from the horror of the burning corpse to stop himself wrench at the smell of smouldering flesh. Yet he had liked camp roasts whilst travelling through the glorious countryside of Wallachia, swilling down the tough gristle of wild boar or pig with wine. Yes, but this was different. And so after some minutes, he moved the temporary steps around to face the crowd and be some distance from the heat and smell.

'Citizens of Poenari, and those on this our lands, be it this day that I swear more of my vengeance to that of our enemy, the Ottoman Empire… that Lord Vasile may have committed sin in the eyes of our Lord – to fall to death by his own accord – but this I be sure was to escape the evil ways of our enemy… that they for no reason, but of immoral belief, bury our injured soldiers to die a slow and agonising death.' Vlad paused to point his father's sword to the night sky, his wide and watery eyes reflecting bright green against vibrant flames. 'And for this our enemy shall suffer tenfold or score… that their dead will consider themselves the fortunate ones as they will only be pilfered and left to rot. But those injured or be caught alive shall suffer in a barbaric fashion as they do unto us… they shall be staked and left to die as was our Lord Vasile, or impaled so that they be kept alive to long their suffering. And they shall be crucified like our Lord Jesus Christ, but left to rot and be shown to our enemy as example of our wrath. Let no enemy soul be granted the Kingdom of Heaven and let them have the flesh of their body torn away by raven or crow.' Vlad paused to hear cheers erupt from an emotive crowd. 'We may continue to be intimidated and persecuted by this Ottoman Empire, but let us as Lords, boyars, soldiers, farmer or gypsy, take on whatever number they beseech upon us.' He held his father's sword by the blade to reveal the crest of the Order of Dragon upon its hilt. 'All good citizens here, and to those you may tell, if you fight alongside me or wish to do so, you are welcomed to the protection of this keep.'

'But what about women and children… the beggars and poor?' Tariana asked, but glanced around nervous to the silence that followed.

Vlad leaned forward, elevated by his small, wooden podium to glare at his new gypsy friend.

'It be not just that we keep the enemy outside this keep, but prevent them from pilfering our people and their lands, for without craftsman or farmer, our soldiers grow hungry or be defenceless. Whether you be tailor, cobbler, stonemason, carpenter or work a farmstead, these be skills to make our lands plentiful and prosperous.' Vlad lowered his sword to wag a finger. 'But for those who are found upon my lands that sponge from the hard labour of others or steal their worth, they will be impaled or staked high as example to their corrupt ways.' Vlad glanced back to the burning remains of his friend, before facing the crowd to continue. 'It shall also be put in writing and passed by council, that any wife proven guilty of dishonouring her husband, shall be burned alive like the old law states it is done for sorcery or witchcraft.' Vlad blinked the tears from his eyes and stood proud before descending the little wooden staircase. 'We will deliver laws and order here and to that we shall spread terror into the heart of our enemy and cast them out of our lands.'

As Vlad strode briskly across the courtyard, Tariana skipped her step to catch up with him, her face scowled with concern.

'Master Vlad,' Tariana crouched to walk and take Vlad's stare away from the floor, 'why be so angry and harsh against your peoples?'

'Have you not just witnessed the cremation of my friend?' Vlad stopped to point angrily at the fire still burning upon the construction of stones. 'And many were killed or suffered torture... ambushed and murdered because I believed in a brother who I thought would one day fight alongside me... but instead... instead I be gullible and let things ease, as I did for you... but you and...' He looked over at the giant gypsy standing not far away. 'Well you have proven a worth against the enemy. But he... my own brother, took me as a fool.'

'But peoples here not flout you,' Tariana interjected, 'they live under your rule.' 'Yes and so they must know the rule.' Vlad glanced at the vexed but nervous

crowd before directing his words to Tariana. 'Without strict laws and order, the power of fear that steers them becomes degraded… as an army would be powerless if not fed and armed.'

'I wish not to annoy Master Vlad,' Tariana said shyly, 'and speak only as simple gypsy girl… but to soldier I have seen, you have not much of army left.'

'Then I will recruit,' he shouted angrily, of which made Tariana cringe. 'Train men off the lands or from our borders. Anyone who will stand with me against the Ottoman Empire!' He glared at Tariana before observing the dispersing crowd. 'Why, you have many a gypsy that slaughtered the Turk that night?'

'But they not be soldiers Master Vlad.' Tariana eyed the ground. 'They be harsh and sharp as to their upbringing, and murder like do assassin, but be only men who live from the lands like farmer or shepherd… try to survive, as all we gypsies do.'

'Well likes I said,' Tariana sensed Vlad had mellowed somewhat. 'As long as peoples on my land be productive – if only growing crops – then my army will not go hungry.' Tariana could have sworn she had seen Vlad wink at her. 'With countryside gypsies and peoples from townships combined, maybe I will train a new great army?'

'But I thought,' Tariana hesitated to look over at the still roaring fire. 'I thought it was Master Henrik that trained your soldier?'

'Then maybe it be time that I do so… do such to honour my friend?'

'And what become of those frail or injured… not able to fight as soldier? Will those such as beggars or plagued be burned if shelter on your lands?'

'Many injured soldiers cannot fight until strong again,' Vlad exemplified, 'but they still have determination to fight… or contribute to this keep.' He paused to stare hard at Tariana. 'But vermin found to live lazy from the sweat of others and not offer to prosper this our land, or help to defend it, will be impaled and strung high as example to law and to keep order.'

'I not know you long Master Vlad, so test not to what I say.' Tariana grasped strong Vlad's arm to hold him beside the new well – a site to where all had seen Radu protest against her – but she hesitated to ask questions as they may cause offence. 'I see change in you, and be from what your brother do, I understand.' Tariana waited until his gaze fixed on her. 'But I saw before compassion in your eyes… to me and my people, but now green eyes turn red… have evil in them.'

'It be called vengeance dear gypsy girl.' Vlad took pause to take deeper breaths. 'What should you expect after me losing…?' He thumbed back at Henrik's smouldering corpse. 'And I must train weak and feeble men… ones to who have never held axe or spear?'

'I know many a woodman, farmer or gypsy, who fight strong if given food and shelter… to better their life of poverty.' Releasing Vlad's arm, Tariana glanced down the well as she sat on its circular stone wall. 'You said yourself that my gypsy did well in night attack.'

'But I hear that be due to the surprise and cover of trees,' Vlad condemned. 'And many Turks fled as they recognised my tainted brother… as they must have agreed to some allegiance with him!'

'I only follow to try and help, as many a gypsy suffer too.' Tariana glowered at Vlad, her eyes like dark jewels, each shining with pin reflections of light. 'But if want, I take all gypsy from camp… leave and hope there be no bad spirit between—'

'A Lord of this land does not compromise such to a gypsy,' Vlad interrupted, 'never mind being the Prince of Wallachia!'

'I not know wording of com…pro…mise, but see by face that you come same as brother… have greed in heart and no love… or compassion.' Tariana noticed her words had troubled Vlad enough for him to turn and walk, but construed he was hardening his skin to hide deep emotion. But then she realized he had Jusztina… and of course Mihnea. He still had family, whereas she had lost all of hers. And so she changed her questioning. 'Master Vlad I be sorry, as simple gypsy girl I go as please and not live by rule… only live from nature and care for land.' She observed him turn as he stood poised to walk. 'We can only get best our situation and so I be curious…' She pointed to the well and waited for Vlad to show interest. 'Do you brother know secret passage from river to old well… the one like this but in cavern below keep?'

Vlad approached Tariana and at first stood to contemplate her question, but then sat beside her, he too looking down into the dark of the well.

'Radu had many a tour of this keep and may have gathered many of our plans during all our council.' She noticed how grim his face had become, obviously recalling all knowledge Radu could have gained in order to infiltrate him. 'I cannot remember telling of any access to the river, but if I did so, he like any other, would perish trying so.'

'Any other?'

'I know much about this keep that many do not.' Vlad glanced over at the now fading fire. 'Even once young Henrik, who helped put brick upon brick, learned nothing of safe passage to the river. It however, could prove a useful escape route.'

'Escape route,' Tariana prompted. 'So there be some way from bottom of well to river?'

'I know of a way if not caved in, but it be treacherous as one needs to follow a number of successive passageways. To what I know, only one route will prevent any man from hunger and death.'

'But number of men, enough of the enemy, could find way to bottom of well?'

'Maybe so,' Vlad grimaced to admit, 'but each man would need to individually assail the slimy wet walls of such a high well.'

'But if in escape, this problem be same unless you use rope?'

'There are, but not in this well, bricks that stick out at certain points,' Vlad described, pointing down the well whilst motioning his forefinger in circles. 'They descend at certain points, but be hard to see at first, unless you look for them or know that they be there.' Again Tariana could be sure she noticed Vlad wink at her. 'But descending a well must be easier than climbing, do you not agree… even if it be slippery in both cases.'

'But a rope with hook thrown up would–'

'Be thrown back down along with hefty bricks to knock off any of such enemy,' Vlad interjected.

'If you happen to be there.' Tariana whispered.

'Besides, and I be positive about it,' Vlad ignored Tariana's comment. 'Radu not know about such secret stepping and should they notice them, Turks be so stupid and small to climb such.'

'But was it you, or Sorin, that stated you should never undertake your enemies?' 'Underestimate,' Vlad chuckled. 'You mean to say underestimate.' But then

scowled to ask what she meant. 'By so, what do you mean by that?'

'Just as I tell before,' she reacted. 'I may be just a simple gypsy girl who be gifted by visions, but can see in my mind, a rope with sturdy hook can bring many a Turk soldier.'

'And like I say, they be hit back down as be easy targets before they can beseech the weapons forgery.' Vlad grinned wide. 'Pour burning oils on such stupid Turks.'

'If you happen to be there.' Tariana whispered again before raising her voice to proclaim, 'Would it not be best to seal the old well up, as you have the new one here for water?'

'But like I said,' Vlad proposed his old plan, 'it be used to evade assault should they breech this keep by gate.'

'But you say that a journey through such caves and caverns be dangerous?'

'It would be if you do not know the way.' Again Tariana saw Vlad wink at her and felt somewhat disconcerted as he now gazed wide-eyed at her. 'I now know why Henrik took a fancy to you, even if you be a gypsy.'

'Master Henrik be unmarried and like a lot he see… not just me,' Tariana looked bashfully down into the darkness of the well, before attempting to change discourse. 'But you not answer question… why not fill in well?'

'You have a strange but endearing beauty for a gypsy girl,' Vlad admitted, fascinated to how seductive she looked with flickering flames lighting her shadowed face and long dark hair. 'Have you never been married nor had a man in your life?'

'This have nothing to do as plan on escape.'

'So ignore me as a lord or prince, but ask only as a man… well have you… ever married?'

'I never have such feeling for man rich or poor.' Tariana turned away to stare down into the darkness of the well again. 'I wish only to survive and rich man do never take gypsy girl as bride.'

'Surely there has been some man in your life,' evidently he winked again.

'There be only two man in my life, but I be alone now.' She saw how Vlad looked confused and so elaborated. 'There be only my brother and father I have care for.'

'And you not be sure if…?' He paused as he did not want to upset Tariana's sweet beauty in the firelight.

'No, I must find my brother,' she whimpered, 'and hope you can help.'

'Maybe we can help each other?' Vlad stood up from his seat on the wall of the well. 'But at first I think you deserve this.' He took a decorative scarab from a pocket and displayed it to her. 'It belonged to Henrik, and as we took the one you had…?' He saw her eye it with interest and hesitate to take it. 'You and your gypsy friends did save me in that night attack and without Henrik, well Radu could have had you burned and others…?' He watched her roll it in her hands, her eyes wide with excitement. 'But if you and all others you can get serve me in eradicating our enemy, you have a guarantee of safety within these walls.'

'And farmers or gypsy like outside this keep?' Tariana glanced up at him.

'As I defined in my speech earlier, in hope that many will spread the word… all people of whatever background, if they serve the Prince of Wallachia, then they be welcome and safeguarded by soldiers of this keep.'

'But admit Master Vlad,' Tariana was again hesitant to state, 'many a soldier you do not have?'

'Then you shall find me men… farmer or gypsy, woodman or cobbler.' He glanced down at her. 'So that then I can train them and raise armies to avenge the death of Henrik Vasile.'

THIRTEEN

Vlad walked gingerly through the grounds of the outside courtyard, trying best not to disturb any guards or arouse suspicion. He had passed by the army barracks and seen many asleep, both his men and gypsies who were still recovering from long term injuries. He had spotted the large Russian, but where was the gypsy girl, Tariana?

On the east side of the keep, Vlad had offered all gypsies shelter throughout the army barracks as he had been training those eager to fight and provided privacy to vagabond girls to whom could nurse those still injured. As he stepped through the dark, thoughts ran quickly through his mind; recalling the difficulties he had had in training such vagabonds, and considered that although these men's hearts were resolute to fight the enemy, their physique or aptitude was not. Still, he had kept his patience and recruited some of his boyars to assist and train many, but deeply missed Henrik, as he knew his friend had such a natural skill to embolden men.

He took pause to stop and search the grounds, rubbing his eyes from his earlier slumber and thinking back to Mihnea and his son's disturbing restlessness. Watching his sentries change guard on night duty, he almost forgot to why he can come outside to find the girl. But then, as one of his sentries strode away to place a flaming reed torch into a stone receptacle, he noticed a figure slumbered on makeshift bedding below the wall.

As he stepped gently towards the sleeping figure, he had deduced to who it was before he came close. Although she had her back towards him, Vlad knew it was the gypsy girl by her long and bedraggled, dark hair. And he pondered on how such dark and clammy hair could glimmer such a beautiful auburn in the firelight. Cautiously he took a couple of steps nearer to admire the glint in her soft, natural curls, but stopped suddenly to see her body flinch and hear her murmur something aloud. He poised to crouch nearer, but could not make out her muttering.

Again he saw her twitch as she gasped loudly at the air, almost sniggering at her sharp intakes of which were similar to Jusztina's snoring. Of course his wife had arguably denied that such a lady would do such a thing, but this thought made him chuckle even more. He contemplated to why the gypsy girl would refuse the sanctity and shelter of the barracks to sleep outside, but then as Vlad looked up, he paused to admire the clarity of the autumn night; as indeed without any cloud coverage, he noticed how the stars sparkled with no appearance of the moon.

Suddenly he heard movement and glanced down to see Tariana roll over, her hair entangled between blankets and swept wildly over her eyes and face, but through it he could see and admire her simple but beautiful features. With her appearance peaceful and her delicate skin bronzed in the flickering glow of firelight, he knew now why Henrik had liked her so, and considered her now not a witch, but more that of an angel.

For a long moment he crouched beside her, listening to only the wind and how it rustled branches of distant trees, admiring her beautiful face until it came troubled and her hazel eyes shot open, her breath short.

Frightened not just of him but of something she had dreamed, she recoiled in her blankets and stared questioningly up at him.

'Why you be there?' Tariana asked, her body all a quiver. 'Why you stand over me so?'

'I came to asks questions in secret, but saw you asleep,' Vlad pulled his hair back from over his eyes and long about his neck. 'I did not want to wake you but…' He paused to consider his words, 'you looked so peaceful but then disturbed.'

'What you mean?'

'You were asleep and muttering words… but nothing I could understand.' He awaited her response but noticed her just staring inquisitively at him. 'You sleep outside but I provide shelter inside?'

'I sleep better the fresh air,' she responded, curling her knees up to find comfort, 'be closer to the nature and feel its power.' She noticed Vlad frown. 'I should not confess as you think me a witch…' She saw that his face had come somewhat more sympathetic. 'But I suffer from bad dreams that many a time become visions to the future… different in meaning but foretell things going to happen.'

'I know what Henrik would say about that,' Vlad chuckled but saw her serious. 'Do you believe that nature have such powers?'

'I do not,' Vlad rejected, 'but see only the power of wind, that of rain and sea… and that of fire.'

'Well that what be nature,' she explained and pulled out the 'tuning-fork' charm she had in her grasp beneath her bedding. 'It be like this… it be a portent to harvest good, protect and fend off evil.'

'I be sorry to say my gypsy friend,' Vlad prescribed sombrely, 'but such powers, if be any, most likely be conjured by witchcrafts and alike… some dark practice that has brought plagues and disease that have ravaged the lands for many a year.'

'Then it be that you think me a witch like your brother?'

'I do not think the same,' Vlad stated assertively and then had to admit, 'as you have a beauty unlike any witch.'

'And then I can trust you should I disclose my past?'

'I will listen and my mouth stay closed,' Vlad winked, but asked curiously, 'but why you camp outside when I provide shelter, and why do you twitch so?'

'But I feel, I be like you,' she told, hiding her charm beneath her blankets whilst her other hand pointed to the sky, 'like to be with nature… look at stars at night… feel wind on face.' She paused to frown. 'You say you like your country and its look of lands when we…' She grimaced to recollect the ambush Radu had put upon them later that mission and so wanted to know if she could trust him explicitly. 'I tell you of my dreams that foretell future if you keep quiet my gift?'

At first Vlad raised his eyebrows but nodded and approached to reassure. 'You can trust in me, as would I trust Henrik, and as he would me.'

'I not know I twitch so, but it be from my dreaming.' She stared at the ground in pause, but then looked up to study him as she explained. 'I be gifted with what my parent call 'second sight'… it be given to me by them and they be gifted with it by their parent.' She eyed him curiously before continuing. 'I not like to reveal such as people think I be a witch… as they not understand.' She shifted to sit cross-legged, her blankets enshrouding her. 'You not still think me a witch, do you?'

Vlad nodded to neglect the possibility but came curious to her charm. 'Is this dreaming of yours anyway connected to that charm of yours?'

'I not think of that before, but it could be so?' Tariana revealed again the charm from between her bosom and revolved it in her hand to study it. 'But it too was given to me by my parent from their parent.'

'Then what was your dream about should you have such a gift of prophecy?' 'You not be trying to trick me as to prove me a witch?'

'No my friend I be not,' Vlad chuckled, 'besides… witches be old hags who be barren to men and not beautiful as…'

'You think me beautiful Master Vlad?' Tariana blushed somewhat. 'Is that be why you ask if I be married?'

Vlad turned his stare away from those deep, dark, gleaming eyes, the flickering firelight enhancing the beauty of her long eyelashes.

'It be improper of a lord to comment on such like,' Vlad almost disappeared from her view but stopped in the shadows. 'I be married to Jusztina, and we be with son who be our most Christian treasure.'

'Every child should have both father and mother to love and bring up them so.' She looked gravely to the shadowed earth about her. 'And not be taken as orphan slaves.' 'And for that child to be worthy to God, He forbids any spouse to betray their

partner.' Vlad turned to Tariana, but the gypsy could see only the shadow of his face in the darkness. 'That be why I inflict new law to preserve the sanctity of marriage.' But then Tariana noticed how Vlad gawped at her in the half-light.

'If such a lord was not married,' Tariana stammered somewhat, 'you would have time for such a gifted gypsy girl?'

'Your knowing of my feelings be not important as I be married.' 'I tell meaning of dream if you tell of finding me attractive.'

Knowing he had been aroused by the gypsy girl but angered that she had ignored his testimony of marriage, Vlad began to walk away. 'All you women be deceitful creatures of nature, whether you be beautiful or not... rich or poor.' Slowly he disappeared into the dark of night.

'My dream gave me vision of crying orphans captured and being drowned on the shore of the great sea I passed long ago.' She paused before continuing to declare, 'And one of these was not my brother but your son.'

'How can you know of my son?' Vlad stepped back into the light of the flickering reed torch so she could see how angry his face was. 'You never have seen him!'

'I just felt it as it was in the dream… the vision.'

'Jusztina and I would die before any enemy hand could harm Mihnea!' He approached to stoop with annoyance. 'How can such be if you not know my son?'

'I just tell truth of what I felt,' Tariana recoiled seeing Vlad so maddened. 'It be you who insist I tell of what my dream… vision –'

'Then it be wrong!' Vlad interrupted. 'Mihnea be kept safe with Jusztina by his side, and it be I that keep them safe… in the walls of *this* keep!'

'I just tell as you asked Master Vlad,' Tariana muttered. 'It be what I felt and dreamed.'

Tariana looked up at the troubled prince, identifying his dedication to his wife and son, and came silent herself to think of her only possible relative – her brother that was snatched by their mutual enemy.

At the end of a minute of haunting silence, she pondered on the question he had originally came to ask, but seeing Vlad so displeasured, was apprehensive to enquire. But then the brave animal instinct inside her spluttered to ask.

'Master Vlad, what be the question to come to ask… that before you ask about my dream?'

'It not matter now.'

'I know it anger you, but do you not believe in visions that foretell future and that people be gifted with such?' Tariana shifted uncomfortable in her cocoon of blanketing, afraid to remark, 'Does God not bless people with gifts as do you have skills in battle?'

'What you mean by such words?'

'Only to what Master Henrik told.' Tariana awaited a response, but Vlad stood cold and still. 'He said you have God's blessing to save Christianity from the Ottoman Empire… that you have great courage and ability to envisage battle so that you should win.'

'Henrik should never have revealed such to a simple gypsy girl, but I expect it be because he found you so pretty.' Vlad approached and seemed angry at first but calmed to explain. 'And I know Henrik had nothing but admiration for his prince, but he should have also known that such a talent is only gained from years of training, learning the tactics of enemy battle through many years of bloodshed. And being captive years as a child –'

'But it be also true that you dream like the visions as I be having,' Tariana interjected as she wriggled to find comfort in her make-shift bed, turning her body to lie with her back to Vlad. She glanced up at the flaming red torch as she announced, 'Such terrible nightmares.'

'You must foresee that indeed I have many a disturbing dream,' Vlad disclosed as he took a couple of steps towards her. 'But it not surprise me as Jusztina reminds me of the disturbing bloodshed I encounter to keep the Turks beyond this keep.'

'And do she say that you twitch in the bedding also?'

There was a long pause that eventually made Tariana look over her shoulder at Vlad. She could see that he was thinking and was about to turn back when he announced his original intention.

'I came here to see you and ask...' Vlad paused briefly. 'I came to ask if you and a number of your gypsies – ones who be strong and can fight – if they would accompany me and my soldiers to scout again trade routes east and then north to Moldavia.' Vlad circled as he thought aloud. 'It would be that we make way to Braşov to where we can take camp whilst I send word to Stephen the Great of Moldavia – a relative of Jusztina – to ask for more infantry. I must admit that your gypsy friends be difficult to train but their numbers be vital. I not be a critic, as your people have much heart to rid us of the enemy, but...' Vlad caught her again glance at him over her shoulder. 'It be again, much a perilous journey.'

'Many my gypsy want to stay and fight… learn much skills you offer,' Tariana explained. 'Many old and child want stay as be protected here, but some, as be myself and Sorin want to venture west… be free from all this… we fight enough –'

'And your brother,' Vlad interjected, 'if the enemy have him… you want to run and desert him?' He stepped close so his voice came clear. 'I know you want ratification.'

'What be rat… if…?'

'You need closure…' Vlad explained with more empathy. 'If your brother still be alive, you have more a chance with my army… *our* armies… to rescue him!'

'And there be no more the danger of changing route all whiles?'

'No, as you remember it be Radu that did this, and I need closure too…' Vlad stood tall, feeling himself cold and rigid. 'My brother betrayed me for some reason.'

'I will go and rescue my brother, pray he still be alive, but…' Tariana paused to contemplate. 'We travel to my terms.'

'I am Prince of Wallachia and my men answer only to their Lord,' Vlad smirked, a gleam coming from his green eyes. 'But this time I listen to you and then they follow their leader.'

'And I trust you keep secret my gift?'

'If only you not predict our loss in battle.'

'We make good partners… a great, as you say… add…vic…ery.' 'I think you mean… adversary'

'Yes, should my dreams foretell our future; we can change our ways… but…' Tariana pouted to think before stating. 'But if you be having bad dreams that envisage our future, then you not need my gift.' A cunning smile stretched across her face as she cleared long hair from obscuring her stare. 'But I be scout as I know where to go as I have come such ways.'

FOURTEEN

Standing on a precipice that jutted out of the northern face of a steep escarpment, Radu squinted into the distance to ensure he could observe all in the snaking gorge below. Like his brother, he had come to admire the Wallachian countryside, and from such height the autumn colour of deciduous trees compared to misty evergreens, was magnificent. Apart from the bristling wind that numbed his face and hands, the scene was still and surreal, as if admiring some gallery painting. But his quiet moment came suddenly disturbed by a foreign voice that asked irritable questions.

'Why we camp up here in this cold wind?' the Sultan asked, one hand holding onto his turban as if it would blow off. 'I see days getting short in these lands and so soon you have winter.'

'Our winter be months away yet,' Radu mocked, sniggering at the Turkish leader in detecting him shiver. 'You should know this climate by now Sultan... as you have battled many a time in Wallachia and as far north and west as Hungary!' Radu glanced back to his observations and so his voice came distorted by the cold wind that blew about the mountainside. 'Did you not battle and take lands as far north as the Tatars?'

'Yes, but we camp in cover of such winds, as their shores and river lands be flat.' The Sultan sniffed as he poked Radu's shoulder. 'My soldiers are restless as camping at such height be difficult!' He waited until he finally got Radu's attention. 'Again I ask… why camp up here to be exposed to such wind and cold?'

'As I explained previous, if should you listen,' Radu moved away from the edge to speak out of the bristling wind. 'As Jusztina is some relation to the Moldavian king – the one known as Stephen the Great – I heard talk about recruiting some of his troops.'

'And so why await here and not in cover of valleys below?'

'As would an eagle, we can only make observations from such height. And it be important that your soldiers stay out of sight.' Radu pulled the Sultan to one side to shelter from the wind and glanced at makeshift camps packed about him. 'You see, the Prince of Wallachia must pass through the gorge below as there be no other way to deliver heavy weaponry and merchandise east and north to Moldavia. If he transports such in payment to honour the Moldavian king, then he can take no other path.' Sweeping back his long, fair hair, Radu paused to think aloud. 'Unless he has a route he not mention?' But then he glowered at the Sultan to announce, 'Besides we must hide your army as my brother have eyes like that of a hawk.'

'That be true,' Sultan Mehmet agreed. 'That brother of yours be clever in battle and so cunning to evade many my plan in the past.' But the Turkish leader held strong his posture and after looking down his nose at his unusual consociate, gave his reassurance, 'I will have your brother's head one day, should you like it or not!'

Radu ignored the Sultan's impudence to feel a strange admiration for the brother he had betrayed.

'But Sultan, even with an army such as yours and after taking so many recruits from other lands, you have not his head so I may take the throne. Your attempts of taking his keep have always failed miserably.' Although the Turkish leader stood several inches above him, Radu pushed the Sultan aside to point at the valley below. 'If you want to capture my brother – to do *whatever* you want with him – you must take my word and seize him outside Poenari… and this cumbersome transport of goods, when it comes…'

'If it comes?' the Sultan interrupted.

'When he comes,' Radu insisted, 'it will be your best chance to ambush him outside the protection of his keep… as you know Poenari be defended well.' He again disclosed the strategy of his plan. 'He will be loaded down with carts within the enclosure of the gorge and so be vulnerable. And it being the only passage east to Brâila and north to Moldavia, well...'

'I must agree about his keep,' Sultan Mehmet grimaced to admit, 'it have the best of a natural defense as it sit high on that mountain and be difficult to assail.' His bronzed face contorted as his large, arched nose screwed up as he continued to explain, 'The turrets be high and narrow so that their archers can pick out men charging or climbing... he have not only small short-range cannons but catapults fireballs... a wide gulley surrounds one side of the castle that exposes any attempts to... oh, and the bastard has a new defense that took out my men when they had reached to axe down the gatehouse...' the Sultan prodded Radu to keep his attention. 'Surrounding the gatehouse and walls about its entrance he has sprinklers that spurt out burning oil and tar!'

'Yes I saw the likes of such,' Radu sneered to assert, 'if you remember I be once a guest there!'

'Then tell me Radu Bey,' the Sultan demanded, his dark brown eyes now glimmering as the rising sun broke through the mist and low-lying clouds, 'to how your brother escaped from many my garrisons that tracked him to the river?' He paused to recall many fierce battles that blooded the River Argeş. 'Somehow, as if protected by some magic spell, this brother of yours evaded us until we climbed the riverbanks to assail Poenari... and then suddenly his bastard men picked us off from behind as others took out our horsemen by rolling fireballs!'

'It be probably something simple to even you could grasp,' Radu scoffed, his tittering angering the Sultan and so the Turkish leader demanded explanation.

'What it be that you know and should tell?'

'More than *you* should ever know, dear Sultan,' Radu sneered, 'as that be part of my plan.'

'Which is?'

'I be outsmarting my brother once and for all.' Radu stared wild at the Sultan. 'I shall outwit him before he can return and defend Poenari.'

'But he did such many a time to my men, and I be great in battle.'

'Obviously not enough,' Radu mocked as he flicked back his hair and took the reins of his horse, 'it be *he* who be superior, if he outsmarts you every time!'

'And this plan of yours...?' Sultan Mehmet disregarded Radu's cynicism. 'As I explained previous, I be taking a garrison with me when...'

'My leader, our great Sultan,' a voice barked out as Mehmet's second-in-command approached, 'we sight the Prince of Wallachia... he be leading carts through the valley below!'

Radu noticed the Sultan glance back at him on hearing the news and so Radu declared, 'As you see my dear Sultan, I be prepared more than anyone.'

As Radu winked before mounting his horse, he noticed the Sultan's agitation. 'Then what do you plan to do with one of my regiments?'

'Like I said previous,' Radu smirked, 'my plan will take my brother's keep and make me heir of the Wallachian throne.'

'But I must know all should we work together?'

'I disclosed it earlier, and you confirmed my doubts with that story you just told!' Radu rolled his eyes after seeing the Sultan confused. 'There be some secret way into Poenari from the river. That must be how my brother evaded you and attacked later from behind. I overheard him and his wife tell about some cave that he described difficult to find and follow its caverns to his keep. Apparently only he and certain men keep it secret, as well as his wife of course. But I reckon my plan will succeed.' Radu trotted over to the Sultan and looked down his nose at him as he steadied his horse. 'You see, I overheard that the entrance be covered by a waterfall and that the caverns be marked in a way to traipse the right tunnels. That be how no other man knowing such would live to tell the tale.' However, he again recognized the Sultan's bewilderment. 'Sultan, I will lead a garrison to scare Vlad into thinking we will attack from the rear, but it be just a ploy to push them fast into your ambush.' Radu sniffed strong at the brisk air to contemplate. 'And whilst my brother be busy as you squander his merchandise, I shall search the river for this cave and take Poenari for myself.'

'But it could take days to search the river for such a cave?'

'Then you had best make sure you ambush well my brother!'

'Master Vlad, I told you not to travel so open!' Tariana twisted on horseback to search the woodland slopes of the gorge behind.

'Do not worry, I spotted them about ten minutes ago,' Vlad disclosed as the gypsy girl rode alongside him. 'We can deal with them about this next corner.'

'But they not spot us if you take my advice... stick to mountain slope and have cover of tree. We be but a mountain distant from big city!'

'That be impractical.' Vlad glanced at her to distinguish another word that she did not quite understand. 'This burden we carry must travel on hard and level ground so it travels fast and be less cumbersome.' Again Tariana looked perplexed to Vlad's last word, but he went on to disclose his plan. 'I will soon split this garrison... the majority will stay with the carts and make haste to Brâila, but some archers and swordsmen – me included – will stay behind to protect our rear.'

'And I, Sorin, and my gypsies?'

'I need you to take what horses you have and ride fast around the slopes. If you tell true and can sight the city of Brâila from the mountain, then you can observe and escort safe our carts.'

'So we stay with you until…?'

'Let our garrison take the snake end of this gorge, and then we await them.'

As his posse raced on, Vlad rode to the front of the garrison and then returned to the rear, telling of his plan as he went. And then, in the cover of the woodland, as soon as they traipsed the last turn, Vlad and others he had instructed, hastened to lie in wait with eyes wide and weapons ready.

Standing nervous but exhilarated behind the trunk of a sturdy tree, Vlad glanced back, but could not see that the enemy was now following. He looked about him to see many of his men also poised behind trees or kneeling in bracken, some archers hiding in the undergrowth. Vlad searched the woodland between himself and the distancing wagons to see Tariana apprehensive and awaiting his command. He winked at her, and although he noticed a smirk, her expression remained with that of concern. And her face remained stern as he indicated for her and her gypsies to ride on.

Ten minutes ago, he had sighted the enemy again, and indeed they had been nearing the rear, but why did they hesitate to attack? From his experience, by now a Turkish army would have attacked in cover of such a wooded, snaky gorge, and yet they hesitate. He glanced back to see that the wagons had completely disappeared from view before noticing many of his men staring anxiously at him. He returned again to search the woodland behind, but came perplexed to the enemy's failure to approach. Was this some new tactic Turks were now using against him, or was it some idea construed by that betrayal of a brother? Whatever was happening, he suspected something wrong and felt he had to act. Although apprehensive, he smiled inwardly to remember the premonitions Tariana had described.

Vlad emerged from his hiding place and signaled to his men, ordering them to make haste up the slopes of the woodland to the heights of the forestry that circled the base of the mountain. This had indeed been the same instruction he had gave Tariana and her gypsies. With two on horseback and lighter-loaded archers racing on foot to follow, it took them a good hour to catch up with Tariana's gypsies. But by the time he had reached them, he could see them grimacing from their distant observations.

Catching his breath, Vlad approached Tariana to ask questions, but hesitated after seeing her take no notice of him. At similar height on horseback, quietly he followed her line of sight as many of his men joined the gypsies, all now taking a sharp intake of breath. But this was not because they were out of breath from exertion.

Far away, in the valley below, Vlad could see garrisons of Turkish soldiers approaching the posse of wagons; his defending soldiers oblivious to the three separate enemy regiments approaching from the front and sides. It was not just that the attack would be a total surprise, but each enemy garrison outnumbered his posse. And as they would soon be traipsing on open grasslands alongside the river, they travelled slow and mired with such heavy burden.

'They have little chance,' Tariana said, after observing Sorin signing his concern. 'The river may slow them but…'

'Then we must reach them before they get accosted!' Vlad glanced at Tariana, his sparkling green eyes wide with readiness.

'They be outnumbered my lord,' a voice shouted, 'three to one!'

'Then we cut down three of them, before we lose one Wallachian!' Vlad scowled at the crowd now surrounding him, but then raised his sword aloft to announce, 'Follow your prince and fight for Wallachia… protect what be ours and our comrades that defend that which be ours!' As his horse reared and snorted in the late morning air, Vlad pointed his sword and bellowed, 'For the Order of the Dragon!'

All followed, Wallachian soldiers and gypsies alike, but obviously it was those on horseback who reached the posse first. But by then the battle was already rampant, and as sickles clashed against longswords and shields, Vlad could see many of his men had already been slain. He assumed that this attack was from the garrison that met them head on, and so grimaced to ponder on where the other enemy garrisons were. But there was no time to devise tactics, enemy soldiers were already ransacking the wagons or trying to drive them away.

Bellowing out orders, Vlad instructed his men to attack in three groups; he would take a main central group and others, mainly archers, would circle towards the left and right. But now he realized how much he missed Henrik as his friend would predict his strategy and determine his battle plan. He knew his men were committed to their prince, but many still carried injuries and the majority of gypsies had not been trained sufficiently.

With his heart pounding and saddle bouncing beneath his inner thighs, Vlad stood upright in his stirrups as he sped towards the nearest wagon. And with the momentum of springing from his horse, he cut down the first Turk and swung to slice at others. As some of his men joined to reinforce his actions, they cleared the wagon of enemy soldiers, but others were now climbing to replace their slain comrades. Vlad took quick to get the horses going but for a long, first minute the wagon refused to budge.

Arriving shortly after Vlad's men had rode down the valley to attack, Tariana and Sorin took to do the same, and with other gypsies following, mounted several wagons to escort them away. But Turks repeatedly charged at them and jumped to seize each wagon, their daggers and sickle swords ready. Many a time the gypsies would simply kick at the enemy soldiers beneath their feet and hope the delay would give them enough time to move the merchandise. Sorin quite enjoyed kicking his hefty boots at such small men, his grunts a vocal attempt to deride the enemy and show his contempt to what they had done to him.

Suddenly the wagon on which Sorin stood jolted and began to speed forward, the large horses finding some footing in the hard earth. And pulling on their reins, Tariana guided the horses, frequently having to lean back to adjust her balance. Sorin glanced round to see gypsies stabbing frantically at any Turk attempting to mount the wagon, and as it jostled on, the giant Russian grimaced at the enemy numbers racing towards them. Stabbing and kicking at the enemy, Sorin went to warn Tariana, and after seeing him point, the gypsy girl turned the wagon to race towards the shallow river.

As Tariana led the first wagon away, Vlad organized garrisons to slow the enemy advance; archers would shoot from either side until the bulk of each enemy advance was too close to them. And then it was up to him and his swordsmen to resist the attack. Several times Vlad's tactic proved successful, but more of the enemy approached, garrisons somewhat controlled in their marching. These were those Vlad had seen from the top of the valley; garrisons that had trailed the sides of his posse, awaiting orders.

Vlad searched the landscape, his thoughts and tactics hindered by Turkish swordsmen who found an opportunity to try and slay the Prince of Wallachia, but Vlad was far stronger and more experienced. He cut his way through the battlefield, ordering his men to retreat and protect what wagons the gypsies had rescued; most which were now following Tariana in haste.

But Vlad grimaced to watch the gypsy girl enter the river with other wagons following. He knew her intention was to slow down enemy soldiers on foot, but there was also one flaw; if the wagons did not keep momentum, if the wheels buckled, broke or got stuck in mud, then his merchandise would be stranded like wrecked treasure ships at sea. And so he bellowed out orders for the wagons to turn back and race fast along the hard and flat shoreline, but all were too far distant. Although he instructed his men to defend themselves beside the river, instead they followed him as he rode to speak to Tariana.

'You must turn these wagons back to shore or they get stuck in the river,' Vlad instructed Tariana, but saw her eyes wide and face firm with determination. 'We be exposed as enemy archers arrive!'

'We be strong and fast once we reach other side,' the gypsy girl yelled, 'I know secret way to big city… you get more men… re…if…force…ments?'

'You mean *reinforcements*,' Vlad corrected. 'But Brâila have little…'

All at once the wagon stopped and nearly threw Tariana from her stance as the horses' attempts to pull were stalled. And then as hooves dug into the riverbed, the water just below the knees of each beast, their strength buckled one wheel so it twisted.

Vlad jumped from his horse, and with comrades helping, tried to free the wheel. But even with the giant Russian helping to lift the wagon up as they did so, the wagon would not budge. And then suddenly, as Vlad noticed enemy archers marching towards them, the wheel splintered and broke.

'It will not move now,' Vlad shouted as he saw another wagon get snared upon rocks on the riverbed. 'My heavy merchandise gets stuck here. But we must move it, before they fire arrows upon us!' He glanced at the giant who simply stared at Tariana.

'We take what we can carry,' Tariana announced as she reached to the front of the wagon to release the horses. 'Saddle up all we can and ride fast to city. Escape north around mountain.'

'But then we must leave some behind,' Vlad complained, watching other wagons struggle through the river. 'We will have not enough to rally purchase for infantry!'

'Better some than nothing,' Tariana turned loose the horses whilst gypsies helped load them with all they could. 'Which be most important?'

'All of it,' Vlad cringed. 'It be difficult to transport, never mind hide in…'

Suddenly Vlad's mind ached as he envisioned blood flowing through the streets of Brâila, or was it Braşov? He shook his head to rid himself of the pain, but then considered what his strange vision was trying to tell him. 'No, we ride for Braşov… it be nearest to get reinforcements and hide what we salvage!'

'But my lord,' a soldier sheltering against the wagon told, 'Braşov have no reinforcements… it be nothing now but foreign merchants.' He saw all staring at him, but was resolute to speak his mind. 'I see trouble in Braşov should you go, I sense that it be another place of ambush!'

'You sense such do you soldier?' Vlad spoke cynically as was his anxiety. 'Maybe you have a second sight like that of our gypsy girl there!' Vlad saw the soldier stare back in bewilderment, but then noticed enemy archers now poised at the riverside. 'But you be right about some ambush soldier… that bastard of a brother must have suspected my maneuver… probably spied on me back in Poenari.' And then on speaking of his keep, Vlad froze. Maybe this strange vision – like his dreams, and what Tariana had told – was some warning. But it was not Brâila or Braşov that flowed with blood, but his very keep.

Suddenly an arrow whistled past Vlad's head before embedding itself not far from his hand upon the wagon. He looked back to the riverside and as many of his remaining men raced for cover behind trapped or moving wagons, he watched archers reload. Some of his archers fired back, but most men were now scavenging what merchandise they could take. As they ducked against another flight of enemy arrows, Vlad heard the big Russian grunt and watched him pull out an arrow that had penetrated his arm.

'Master Vlad,' Tariana pleaded as she raced to attend to Sorin's wound, 'we must take now what we can… escape with what we can to mountain!'

'We must take it all, especially the special forged weaponry… if it gets in the hands of…'

'But it be suicide to stop a minute more,' Tariana interjected, tearing the end of her makeshift bandage to tie it tightly around Sorin's arm. 'We take to shore what we can… ride best to mountains… escape quick this enemy!'

With Tariana leading, Sorin followed her with the other horse also loaded full. But as they trudged through the knee-high water, Turks were in pursuit. For enemy soldiers who managed to attack them near shore, Sorin simply pushed them into the river. But once Tariana had to defend herself with Henrik's old scarab, before she could ride her weighted horse unchallenged.

Reaching the shoreline, Tariana spun round to see Sorin not far behind and drop the sack of what he carried. He signaled for her to take his horse and then turned to trudge back through the river to reach the wagon again. She called for her giant comrade to stop, but noticed Vlad struggling to load all he could upon his horse as the beast was frantic.

Vlad had managed to toss sacks of his specially forged weaponry upon the saddle, but came approached by one ambitious Turk. By trying to reach for his sword, the heavy weight of a loaded sack took him off balance and made him fall awkward upon his back. As he scrambled to grasp his longsword, he saw the Turk now standing over him, the soldier's dark eyes wild with his opportunity to kill him. But for seconds the Turk stood frozen, his curved blade raised above his head, ready to carve down at Vlad. And without his usual heavy armor, the Prince of Wallachia would be dead in seconds.

It was not until he saw the metal tip of a newly forged longsword appear from the Turk's stomach that he realized someone had stabbed the soldier from behind. Suddenly the blooded tip of the sword withdrew and the Turk stumbled about the wagon before falling into the river. As Vlad slid back to pivot upon his elbows, he saw Sorin glaring at the newly forged weapon, an interest in it more than the man he had saved. But then the Russian glanced down at him and smiled before offering Vlad a hand up.

Whilst dodging zealous Turks, Vlad and Sorin raced for shore, carrying heavy sacks. As he trudged through the river, Vlad commanded his men to retreat, but to first release all horses from their wagons and retrieve what they could. Out of several, only one wagon made shore, and as Sorin guided it towards the mountains, soldiers and gypsies piled on what they had salvaged. As Vlad watched gypsies also load rescued horses, he saw that Tariana had unloaded his.

'We can ride your horse together,' Tariana suggested with a grin, 'now the wagon be full.'

'I always ride alone,' Vlad specified, but came absorbed by the gypsy girl's smile. 'But to guide you to big city…'

'Forget Brâila, and forget Braşov,' Vlad spoke adamantly, his eyes sincere. 'I need you, and your gypsies, to circle us back through the wilderness and back to Poenari!'

'Back to your keep,' Tariana frowned, 'but why?'

'I guess I had a sense of what you say you have,' he replied jokingly, but again came serious before mounting his horse. 'Something tells me Poenari be under threat.'

He reached down to take Tariana's hand and pulled her up to sit on his saddle in front.

'I thought you said you only ride alone,' the gypsy girl enquired, finding him firm

to snuggle against.

'We need all other horses to rescue what we have,' Vlad glanced at the back of her dark and wild hair. 'Like you said, you will guide us safe passage around mountain and through cover of woodland.

'I will do my best Master Vlad,' Tariana said, looking tearful as she glanced round at him. 'But I have failed otherwise.'

She thought that Vlad was not listening to her, only staring angrily at the Turk's now ravaging the wagons. But then he glared down at her to say.

'It be a pity you could not envisage this ambush and we might be...' He stopped to tally the number of his soldiers that remained, but then looked at Tariana as she spoke quiet to admit.

'I fail in another task for Master Vlad.' She looked dejected as she could hear the chanting and jeering from the river. 'Maybe Master Vlad and this gypsy not be such a good ad... ver...sary together?'

'It be not your fault,' he reassured, but smiled in an unjust way. 'At least those enemy soldiers and their Sultan be too stupid to know how to use longswords, let alone reproduce them.'

Tariana smiled inwardly, trying to hide her feelings of dejection, but tried to think positively as she pointed to the sack of newly forged daggers that hung over the horse's rear flank.

'At least we save some.'

Vlad glanced from watching the remainder of his posse escape quick to the cover of woodland to look at her with mixed emotions.

'Yes, some,' he mumbled, 'but not all.'

Fifteen

Radu mused as he leaned against the trunk of a sturdy tree. Inside he was anxious about so many things. He squinted to search the distant walls of Poenari, the morning air fresh at dawn, but yet there was no sunlight to reveal clearly any activity about the keep. But from his experience, he knew Jusztina always rose at daybreak, even if it was just to check on Mihnea. But would she still be in her bedchamber when he…?

From high ground on the opposite side of the gorge to the castle, he scrutinised the battlements, awaiting the change of guard that he had observed so many mornings, knowing for long periods how security was overlooked on this side. It was not the distance across the River Argeş he feared, but the long drop onto the rocky riverbed, knowing the shallow water would never cushion his fall. And then, if he reached that far, there were the rocky crags that were the foundations for that side of the keep. He knew it would take several minutes to reach the turret window, and being suspended high for that long, totally depended on anchoring a secure fix to some furniture or brickwork in Jusztina's bedchamber.

Again he checked his newly forged crossbow and the specially made metal bolt attached to the thin but fortified rope coiled like a snake beside his feet. He had always been an excellent archer, but this would test his skill to the extreme. He could not see clearly the narrow, tall window of Jusztina's bedchamber, let alone shoot the arrow accurately through it. But gradually sunlight was brightening the eastern horizon and dense mists at dawn were lifting.

Replicating his earlier practice, Radu pulled back the taut string of the crossbow and placed the metal bolt, ensuring that the attached rope was free and loose. He tried to relax as this would help his shot take aim, but found that he was quite tense. With a click and a vibrant whistle the elongated bolt shot into the air but hit the turret wall several feet below the window. A little more elevation he thought, but knew he would first have to painstakingly drag back the bolt using the attached rope. After recovering the bolt, again he tried but failed. And this time when he recovered it, he found the head dented and its little grip hooks degraded by dragging it across the riverbed. But at least the anchoring mechanism was not damaged. Nonetheless, how many times could he shoot before the steel spikes would not release?

After taking in a large breath and slowly exhaling, Radu shot the arrow to gratefully see it pass through the window and into the room. Slowly he pulled on the rope until it came taut – the grip hooks caught against something – and then he jolted a thin cord alongside to release the attached mechanism. Inside Jusztina's chamber, three steels spikes were released from the bolt, and as planned they would act as anchors against something sturdy, such as the legs of her bed.

As he pulled gently on the main rope, the attached mechanism dragged along the floor until one of its hooks snared against a leg of Justina's vanity table. At first Radu felt the rope tighten and then sag as it knocked things over. But pulling carefully and slow, he felt it had caught against something. Pulling strong on the rope, he contemplated whether it would stay fixed, as he had never tried such before. The main question was… would it work?

Pondering on this thought, he fixed the end of the rope about the trunk of the sturdy tree and anxiously ensured the knot was tight. With crossbow hanging from his shoulder, Radu launched himself upon the rope and at first thought it would snap, but anchored with legs crossed, he pulled himself along, each hand in turn, his back pointing downward. Clearly, although he was small and light, the rope took some strain, and so he whisked himself along as fast as he could. But there were times he had to stop; the rope went slack as the vanity table moved toward the window until it stopped. He hung there for precious seconds, gazing apprehensively at the river below; it obviously not deep enough to save him if…?

He was beyond half way when again the rope shifted and his body lowered. As he held firm the rope, he noticed how he would need to climb more of an incline to reach the window. It looked so near, but he felt so far… the anchoring mechanism could jolt or snap at any time. Yes, indeed it had been tested, but he did not know what it was fixed against or how secure it was. Being light and nimble, again he shifted swiftly along the rope and was soon within arm's reach of the tall and narrow window. But as he grasped for the window ledge, he felt the rope jolt and sensed the mechanism break. Feeling his weight jerk and the rope sag, Radu knew within an instant to bounce his feet against the turret wall and leap with hands outstretched.

As the rope flew past and the broken bolt fell, Radu scrambled to get his other hand to join the one which had miraculously clasped the window ledge. But the stone was cold and wet, and his fingers were slowly losing their grip. Clutching on for dear life, he swung his other arm to take hold of his crossbow, and just in time held the weapon's stock handle to swing it and anchor one of its bow stave onto the inner window ledge. Using his weapon as a pulley, he lurched himself at the open window and his small, slim body squeezed through the gap.

Turning over across the bedchamber floor, he dropped the crossbow as he felt his leg break something and his head hit something else, rendering him quite faint. He looked around; his eyes blurred but determined to focus. As his sight cleared and he shifted to sit up, Radu recognised Jusztina's bedchamber. A number of things from her vanity table had been toppled and were smashed upon the floor, but it was the spike from the broken bolt imbedded into the table's leg, that he gawped upon. And then he noticed her small vanity mirror; the one he had *borrowed*. But now it had numerous cracks. It was this he must have felt fall from his pocket and break. But Radu had no time to contemplate such; he had a job to do, as they would be waiting.

Sneaking through the corridors of Poenari within shadows of early light, Radu knew places to hide when guards and noblemen strutted past, and soon made his way down to the dungeon door; the only entrance to the keep from where Vlad forged all his new weaponry. And in the cavern opposite his brother's secret workshop, was the old well.

He tried to move the rusty bolt that once secured it from that side, but realized this was no longer used; the main sliding latch was what secured the metal door, and that was on the other side. Flicking back his fair hair, Radu grasped what he had to do to get it opened, so he banged loudly upon the door three times and waited with his crossbow poised.

After pulling back the latch and opening the heavy door, the guard suddenly realized that the Prince of Wallachia had not returned from a scout, or at least he had not been told his master had. But in his dilemma, the last thing he saw was Radu

Bey grinning at him, before the arrow pierced his forehead and streams of blood ran into his eyes and over his nose. He called out and was soon joined by another guard, giving Radu no time to reload an arrow. But the small man was ready and quick, and pushed the dying guard into the other, retrieving a dagger from his hip as he went. Fumbling to steady his falling comrade, the guard did not notice Radu until the last minute, and then it was too late. Radu drove the dagger up into the bottom jaw of the guard, preventing him from calling out in pain. And then he swung his crossbow at the injured guard to knock him out of his way.

On hearing no pause to the continuous clanging of metalwork from the distant workshop, Radu sensed that no one else had heard the guard call out, but waited impatiently for a minute to check. It was the other passageway that he wanted; the entrance that lead to the cavern of the old well, and from there he could hear voices. So after reloading his crossbow and retrieving his dagger, he stepped cautiously through the passageway, hearing the voices come louder as he approached the opening to the cavern.

Radu glanced round a corner to see two guards, one sitting on the dilapidated brick wall of the old well and the other hesitant to look down into its depths. Listening to their conversation, he deduced that one had heard voices, but the other guard mocked and ridiculed him, saying that his comrade was frightened and stupid. The guard sitting told of nothing down the well but darkness and cold, yet the other edged forward to point and argue about noticing firelight.

Radu stepped stealthily towards the two guards, knowing he had to get some advantage of distance. His arrow could take out the one standing, but he had to be close behind the other to slit his throat. As his eyes concentrated on watching them, Radu's foot kicked something and the guards looked round.

Immediately Radu raised his crossbow and fired an arrow through the throat of the guard standing as the other glanced round in horror. Sitting there in shock, Radu had time to rush at the guard with his dagger and thrust it in his jaw before pushing him into the well. Quickly he glanced down, hearing the guard's muffled scream before all went quiet. And then as he noticed firelight glimmer at the bottom of the well, he heard the exchange between foreign voices.

Seeing the faint flicker of firelight at the bottom of the well, Radu unfolded a small backpack that had been tight around his shoulders. As he pulled out a compact rope ladder, he contemplated on whether it would be long enough. Guess there was only one way to find out.

So after nailing its ends into the crumbling cement between brickwork, Radu set free the rope ladder to watch it swiftly unwind into the depths of the well. He then dropped a coin into the well as this was his signal. But then he thought this stupid; even if the awaiting Turks did not spot the rope ladder, they would have seen the mangled body of the dead guard at the bottom.

As the first Turk climbed over the wall of the well to moan about the ladder being short, Radu ignored him, but questioned to where his dagger was. The soldier shook his head as he helped pull others out. So Radu shouted down for them to bring up his weapon, as no doubt he would need it.

Jusztina stepped back into her bedchamber, pondering to why Mihnea had troubled sleep at the same time nearly every morning. She had again got up to calm him from his nightmares, and although her thoughts were also for her absent husband, she now thought that she could have some rest,.

It did not occur to her that her vanity table was pushed up against the window, until she noticed all perfumes, powders and vials toppled or shattered on the floor. She knelt down to inspect a strange metal spike embedded into the leg of the table, but then noticed something more familiar. It was her handheld vanity mirror – the one Radu had taken – but now it was even more cracked as it lay amongst other things scattered about the floor.

She picked it up to deliberate whether he had returned it long before his betrayal, but this had been the first time she had seen it since he *borrowed* it. She frowned at the strange metal spike and puzzled at the table's position, gradually coming to the conclusion that her husband's brother must have climbed through her bedchamber window. But glancing down with unease, the window was at least thirty; maybe forty times her height from ground, and the walls surely impossible to climb. And then there was the rocky crags and river, so how could he… and why?

A shiver shot up her spine as Jusztina remembered Radu using the mirror before; it obvious to her now on how he had been signalling to the enemy. But why would he assail Poenari from her bedchamber window alone?

Suddenly, after envisaging what Radu could be planning, Jusztina's body came rigid with a cold feeling of dread. Surely she had to act and do something? But then there was Mihnea; should she wake him and take him for protection, or should she check first? If she alarmed the guards on duty, would they think her naïve, or could the evidence of the strange metal spike convince them? But how could the enemy find their way through such deadly caverns from the river… had Radu learned of her husband's secret? There was only one way to make sure, she would have to look for herself first.

Jusztina scuttled through corridors with light feet until she stopped at the top of the stony staircase that spiralled down the turret to Vlad's dungeon workshop. Pausing to look down into the gloom of the stairway, it was not the cold of a breeze that made her shiver, but she knew such an updraft came from the door being open. And no one would dare leave the door open, even if her husband was absent. Vlad had explicit instructions to always have it bolted shut. But now, with nearly all of his men out scouting with him, the door was evidently open. Should she close it? Would she be strong enough to move such a heavy rusted door? Again there was only one way to find out?

As she crept warily to descend the spiral staircase, she realized how the morning light never reached such depths and so had to step careful through the gloom, holding herself against the cold, dank walls until she reached the bottom. It was then through the gap of the heavy metal door that she heard voices. And they were not of a Wallachian dialect, but of Turkish origin.

She squinted to peek through the gap, the draft powerful against her face as she tried to push the door a little more open. Suddenly with a groan the hinges of the door screeched loud enough for busy voices to hear. And then in a daunting quiet, Jusztina could see Radu standing with a Turkish leader, their eyes staring to distinguish her face between the heavy door and its hefty stone frame. For long seconds, the only sound she could hear was distant Turkish soldiers, guiding others from the old well to distribute weaponry.

Clearly it was Radu who recognised Jusztina, and with a snarl he revealed her identity to the Turk beside him. It was then that she knew they would be after her, and so before they turned to sprint for the door, she was pulling with all her might to close it.

She had managed to heave the door closed, but could hear their voices and footsteps near. The main bolting mechanism – the large strip of metal – she knew was on the other side, so frantically she placed a beam of timber at an angle to prevent them from opening the door. And frenzied to wonder if it would hold, she found a similar beam to start hitting at the old rusted bolt. At first the old locking mechanism was rusted firm, but frenzied to hear voices on the opposite side, she whacked the timber against the bolt until it moved slightly.

Jusztina could now hear fists pounding on the other side of the door, but hit the bolt with all her might to see the timber push the bolt a little through into its clasp. The door was now reverberating from the enemy pounding its other side, and so Jusztina backed away in terror to watch the angled beam reverberate loose against the earth. As she raced up the stairway to warn others, she did not notice the timber beam fall, and that now the rusted bolt was banging to loosen its clasp. Jusztina's priority was to protect Mihnea by hiding him away somewhere safe.

With Mihnea still half asleep, Jusztina dragged him from his small bed to whisk him into a corridor where she frantically tried to warn two guards to what was happening. But the two men stood in bewilderment as they watched her retreat to the end of the corridor and desperately poke a stick at a trapdoor in the ceiling. With her son struggling in her arms, she flustered at loosing urgent time, knowing that the rusted bolt would not last for long. She shouted at the guards to warn others, but all they did was offer help with unlatching the trapdoor above her. As she cursed them for arguing whilst prodding determinedly with her stick, finally the latch snapped loose and the trapdoor in the ceiling fell down to swing close above her head.

Without hesitation she lifted her drowsy son and commanded him to hide in the secret refuge. Although persistent in her instruction, her son was slow to put down the knotted rope. And when she finally sprang upon it to climb, the rope unfortunately snapped and soon she found herself sprawled across the floor. With Mihnea crying and screeching down words for his mother, she again stood resolute to launch herself to grasp at the frame of the trapdoor, but fell again as her frail energy and tiredness overwhelmed her.

It was then as one guard approached her, that she saw Turks appear. Quickly she prodded at the swinging trapdoor as she told her son to hide. And once seeing it shut, glared down the corridor at the guards turned now to face their enemy. And it was Radu that she now recognised, his wild eyes staring past the guards and directly at her. Had he seen where she had hid her son, or would he be safe?

Noticing more Turks appear to stand and glare at them, Jusztina ran down the corridor, knowing that the guards would not hold back their assailants for long. As they battled for long, precious seconds, the guards gave Jusztina time to sprint through to her bedchamber; the only room she knew was secure in such urgency. With tears streaming down her cheeks and her eyes blurred, she banged the door shut and fumbled about to lock the door. And there was the extra bolt above her.

But what had she done in such haste? Unlike many bedchambers in Poenari, there was no escape from this room. And unless the Turks oversaw her chamber, she would be captured, raped and murdered, or kept as Radu's hostage to bribe her husband, if indeed Vlad was still alive? But this was the very room that Radu had entered to let Turks into the keep from the dungeon. Surely he would know to where she would hide, and be confined until they broke down the door.

Jusztina grabbed ink and paper to scribe her last words in defiance against the enemy, hoping that her husband would forgive such a sin against Christianity; she would rather have the fish of the river Argeş nibble at her dead flesh than have filthy Turkish hands fondle and rape her. And her determination to commit such sin in the eyes of the Lord was fueled by that betraying brother-by-law; he was truly the culprit to this their end of days, having wormed his way back into their lives and to defy them after all their kindness. Heroically, she would not let them wreak havoc against her, but rather await her beloved Vlad in Heaven.

But there was one, deeper oppression she had to close her mind off to. What would become of Mihnea? Maybe, just maybe, Radu had not seen her hide him, and Vlad would return to rescue their beloved son from his secret hiding place.

But as she sat to write nervously at her displaced vanity table, her heart jumped and her pen wavered at hearing fists pound at her bedchamber door.

'Master Vlad, we must rest,' Tariana shouted, but the Prince of Wallachia and his remaining garrison ignored her to march on along the shore of the River Argeş. She turned to her giant friend with wide eyes. 'Sorin, why do he not listen? We all be tired and need to make camp to rest!'

Sorin paused to signal that he agreed, but pointed to all other gypsies that trudged on to follow, gesturing that many were weary but wanted sanctuary. Tariana gritted her teeth and ran with exhausted legs to stop Vlad who was leading. She pulled him back by anchoring her hand inside his armor.

'Master Vlad, we must rest,' she implored. 'None of we be any good if not rest, even if just a while?'

'We must keep on, otherwise we lose time,' Vlad scowled. 'I not sight the enemy behind, but fear they be pursuing us!'

'But please master Vlad, just a while to catch our breaths,' Tariana pleaded, glancing back to point at many of her gypsies, who were exhausted, 'even if it just be a little time to have food and water?'

Vlad scanned the lines of his men plodding along the shoreline, noting that they too were exhausted. He gazed back to notice the sincerity in the gypsy girl's dark eyes and again sensed her heartfelt passion.

'Alright, we rest for a few minutes, eat little and drink fresh from the river,' Vlad agreed. 'But we must make Poenari before nightfall.'

'Why you be so eager to return to your keep?' Tariana asked, glancing back at Vlad after observing both soldiers and gypsies take rest. 'I know my people be wanting safety inside the walls of your castle, but we could camp overnight… we gypsies take refuge wherever we be.'

'Do you remember my friend, the conversation we had about our dreams and such like?' Vlad shuffled close so his voice could not be overheard. 'At first I thought your visions nothing but a vivid imagination, and I must confess I thought they be connected to… to your way of life.'

'What you mean?'

'You being a gypsy you see,' Vlad was troubled so much that he could not be dishonest and staring into Tariana's dark glistening eyes, so expressed his true thoughts. 'And gypsy women are often looked upon as witches… not that you be…'

'No I be not,' Tariana interjected adamantly, 'but be gifted in some way.'

'Well, I understand such now,' he said agitatedly, 'and must confess that I too had such a strange vision. But it be when I was fearful upon the battlefield. And as emotion and strain came the better of me, I had a vision like you.'

'A vision like the ones I told?'

'Yes, it be like I see all around me and then I view other things.' 'What other things?'

'It was a vision of blood flowing from the very walls of Poenari… and as dark ghosts float about the battlements, I hear them laugh and chant before hearing my son scream… as he did in the other dreams I had. It was chilling and…'

Tariana reached up to place the palm of her hand against his soiled and blooded cheek, her eyes narrowing, but sympathetic. And then she realized to what his vision could all mean.

'You think that this mean your son be taken from your castle?'

'I not think, but feel such.' Vlad's anger overwhelmed his emotion to sob.

'But he be safe inside such high walls and by such defense… and be in the care of Jusztina?'

'But most my men be here, and now *they* be depleted,' Vlad stressed. 'Maybe the trick with the horseshoes was not enough. Maybe the enemy knows now how desperate I need reinforcements.'

'I think you, like all we, be tired… beat by fight and marching.' She removed her hand but gazed at him compassionately. 'Maybe we all need a good rest.'

'But we be so close, I be sure of it,' Vlad stated as Tariana escorted him to sit on a boulder and searched the contents of her bag. 'I sent a scout ahead to determine our location. He should meet back within the hour.'

'If we be close then we go take refuge,' Tariana agreed, offering Vlad a laden of water along with a slice of her seasoned bread. 'But it not be hard for us gypsies to make camp in woods nearby.'

'I would rather be at home,' Vlad stated, gulping a mouthful of water, 'knowing my son and…'

Suddenly a voice shouted from afar; the scout had returned early after noticing the light from fires high above them and further upstream. As Vlad and Tariana stared anxiously at one another, together they both swallowed hard.

Vlad was up in a second and handed Tariana back the laden and slice of bread. Although many were still eating or drinking water, with his urgency Vlad's garrison took haste to follow. And so Tariana and her gypsies followed too.

As Tariana caught up with Vlad taking lead with his scout, she heard the young man describe seeing fires at a distance that were high up on the mountainside. But unlike the naivety of such a young soldier, she had shuddered cold at knowing that this was indeed the location of Poenari. And as Vlad paused to take breath, she glimpsed to recognize that he feared the same.

The scout ran ahead, pointing to the location of the fires ablaze high upon the mountainside, but the shadows of dusk were only an hour away. Yet it was by early evening shadows cast upon the river that the scout noticed something white floating down stream. Quickly he ran towards it and waded into the river, but stopped abruptly before the water reached his knees. Standing aghast, he could not at first put sound to his voice, but then shouted to Vlad to make haste.

Vlad sprinted to wade into the river, but then stopped suddenly to stand alongside his scout companion, his heart pounding and legs all aquiver. He could not believe his eyes.

Held against the current flowing down river by her white dress snagged on a fallen branch, Jusztina's body lay half submerged in the water. As Vlad took nervous steps to approach, he at first recognized the dress she had worn most mornings to attend to Mihnea. He grimaced at first to notice her twisted head and dislocated arms, before approaching slow to distinguish her pale and swollen face. Although she was battered from journeying down river, Vlad recognized her frozen stare just before his own eyes blurred with tears.

He waded further into the depths of the river, his heart pounding against his chest and ears flooded by a strange silence. At first as he reached her, he could not wrench her body free, the current strong against his unsteady footing. But suddenly the snagged dress tore and came free, almost taking Vlad down river as he clenched his wife in his arms. As he turned away from glaring at her clouded eyes, he found his strength again; enough to haul her body back to shore. And by the time he collapsed upon his knees to place Jusztina's body down, many approaching soldiers quietened from venting their anger at seeing Poenari alight. And like Tariana, all that saw Vlad uncontrollably sob, could do nothing but grieve in silence for his loss.

Nervously it was Tariana that approached Vlad first, but as he pushed her away and cursed everything and everyone, he noticed a crumpled piece of paper clasped tight in his wife's hand. Relinquishing his intense grief and emotion, Vlad's eyes released more tears as he tried desperately to unravel Jusztina's rigid fingers. He almost grimaced at hurting her as he forced open her fingers to pull out the note, but inside he knew she had been dead for some time.

Although the fresh ink had been blotted by river water, Vlad wiped away his tears to read best the note he could.

Dearest Vlad,

I write in haste as the enemy be at my door and pound against its lock. It be that betraying brother that lead them here after learning secret passage from the very river I shall now drown. I commit this sin against our beloved Christianity as I will not surrender and have foreign hands take pleasure against me.

I put our son in hiding in hope you find him and crush our enemy to deny your brother the throne.

I shall not regret my sin in the eyes of our Lord, but hope that He forgives me so that I may one day join my beloved husband in Heaven.

Jusztina

Although his eyes were blurred by tears, Vlad read the note over and over until he felt Tariana touch his shoulder. Timidly the gypsy girl reached out a hand and asked if she could see. Vlad did not even question Tariana's ability to read, he was too upset in gazing at his dead wife's staring, but lifeless eyes. And as Tariana nervously picked the note from Vlad's fingertips, she glanced down to see him close Jusztina's eyelids with his fingertips.

Holding Jusztina tightly in his arms, it was then that Vlad sobbed and muttered incomprehensible words. As she had always been limited in her ability to read or write, Tariana called over an elderly gypsy man who she asked to read out loud the note. But before the man could finish, Vlad snatched the note from him and grabbed Jusztina's body to take refuge away from the shoreline.

'Master Vlad, you know I cannot read much,' Tariana said timidly as she approached Vlad who was slumped over his dead wife's body. 'I only want to know how and why this –'

'It be because of you that I be cursed,' Vlad spoke venomously, but could not look Tariana straight in the eye. 'Trusting you and your people has bought nothing but death and despair.' He stroked his wife's hair affectionately and cleared her mouth of dirt. 'Since knowing you, many my men be dead… my best friend and comrade… and now my dearest wife.' He paused again as his voice came choked with emotion. 'And now I not know what become of my only son.'

'We only do as you command,' Tariana said resolutely. 'We saved you from night attack and stay to destroy our same enemy.'

'But now all but my son be gone,' Vlad said animatedly, caressing Jusztina's hair. 'And he too could now be dead, or worse an orphan for that foreign army!'

'The note tell of him in hiding,' Tariana spoke optimistically, although she knew nothing of where this was. 'It only be right to check.'

'You not understand do you gypsy girl,' Vlad said derisively, 'with my keep ablaze, it be evident that they take siege of it… and all within be…'

'And how they get in to do such?'

'That be that bastard of a brother!' Vlad took to stare at her and disclose his anger. 'He learned the secret of those passageways from the waterfall. He must have heard us talk as she did not disclose…' He looked down to stare at Jusztina's broken body, but not able to distinguish if her lacerations were just from the river. 'But how did he get through the…' Vlad began to sob again.

'Well we can do the same, can we not?' Tariana said openly, her face serious. 'Take these tunnels by surprise to get back your son… your keep?'

'They be too many guarding the ways,' Vlad interjected after placing Jusztina's body down. 'And I have not the number in garrison.'

'You should at least try,' Tariana stepped close to Vlad and squatted to talk eye to eye. 'If it were my young brother… I'd risk all I have to get him back.'

'It be difficult to assail the old well,' Vlad said thinking aloud. 'And I have not traipsed those caverns for the longest time.'

'Well the enemy did it,' she disclosed openly. 'And is it not your worth to take back what be yours… and find your son?'

Vlad glared at her for many seconds before standing, his subdued personality changing unusually quick to a fearful vengeance that Tariana had not seen.

'Yes you be right,' Vlad agreed, his determination returning; fortitude comprised from many things, but mainly revenge for his wife's death. 'I should not blame you for this, as many of you die too. I take only my fit most men but maybe some of your gypsies?'

'Yes Master Vlad, but I and Sorin will take care your wife until she be buried.' She glanced over to locate Sorin and then looked assertively back at Vlad. 'We will hide her under this waterfall you speak of... keep her safe while we make camp.'

'That giant gypsy friend of yours could come in handy.'

'Not if they be low or narrow passageways to get to your keep.'

Vlad etched a smile before commanding his remaining garrison to gather. He instructed that he would need a group of his best men to scout his keep; check to what they were up against and rescue his son. As he spoke powerfully about taking back Poenari, Tariana encouraged those gypsies who could fight like assassins to put themselves forward also.

As a handful of gypsies followed Tariana, they stopped beside Vlad to hear him bellow another commanding speech to take vengeance against their enemy and plot to take back their keep. She came almost to tears herself as he spoke of revenge for his wife and to rescue his son. But as she glanced over to Jusztina's body, she could not help but think that this man was losing authority; not just for reduced soldiers or people, but power in his heart. She realized now to how much this Prince of Wallachia had been tested and all that he had lost. And if he could not take back his castle and find his son, what would come of him?

It was an hour before nightfall as they made camp in woods alongside the river, and as Vlad showed Tariana the hidden tunnel that lead to underground caverns from the waterfall, he laid Jusztina down in hiding. Gypsy scouts found several enemy soldiers placed about and inside the entrance, but like assassins they picked them off quietly. And by the time his scouting group was ready; all had eaten well and were supplied with ample reserves of water. However, Vlad could waste time no longer. He was eager to avenge his enemy and commanded his group to follow with reed torches held low as not to arouse suspicion.

Vlad passed Sorin at the mouth of the cave; the giant holding back willow branches that drooped to conceal the entrance. He paused to stare at the giant as he knew he could be valuable, but realized how impassable some tunnels could be. Sorin signed a gesture that Vlad had learned meant good luck and nodded to the giant before moving on. But then he felt his arm being pulled back and turned to face Tariana.

'Master Vlad, let my gypsies go ahead,' she requested, jabbing high Henrik's dagger. 'They see like night animals in the dark and hear the enemy to kill with surprise.'

'But I must lead,' Vlad shunned. 'They know not the correct paths to take.'

'Then correct them if you must, but let them clear the way. Let them avenge the enemy also… and be like silent assassins'

'Very well, but it be I who commands.'

'Yes, Master Vlad,' Tariana said holding strong his arm. 'And take care my Lord; we need you back to be Prince… I want you back to be Prince.'

Sixteen

Tariana approached Vlad cautiously. She was anxious to know more about his mission to find his son, but was afraid to ask. Those who had returned from searching the keep had told of their mission, but Tariana wanted to know why Vlad had failed to find Mihnea. She kept glancing up at him, but his glistening green eyes were fixated on Jusztina's body lying on a wood pyre ready to float downstream.

With it being dusk, the oncoming shadows made Vlad's face glow red against the torch flame in Tariana's hand. Finally she stood to block his sight of his wife, her curiosity getting the better of her.

'Master Vlad, I hear from others…' She paused in noticing how solemn he looked. 'They said you search secret place but not find your son.'

'No I did not,' he responded quietly. 'We searched the hiding place… killed the enemy by stealth.' He stared back at his pale wife's body, smelling her perfume and looking over her skin preserved by ointments. 'We searched all we could, but the enemy have the keep by number. We be lucky to escape and secure that entrance.' He pointed to the distant waterfall.

'You will not try again?'

'He not be where she...' Vlad looked grimly back again at Jusztina. 'The enemy outnumber us and most likely know we try to defend that once secret passage. But they not need it as they have my great defences at their disposal... *my* defences... the ones *I* created after Henrik and all men of old built that keep. Those bastards have control of the very gate to my keep and can lock the dungeon door!'

'Did you climb the old well easy enough?' Tariana tried to distract him from his growing anger. 'My gypsies said there was a rope of some kind.'

'It helped I guess,' Vlad sniggered. 'Radu must have set it down after climbing the well.' Vlad paused as he was clearly baffled. 'He must have learned my secrets after overhearing such... and from the well, he get open the dungeon door.'

'It was open when you...?'

'Yes, it was guarded by Turks until your gypsies disposed of them.' Vlad grinned as he gazed upon her, noticing her dark hair shine auburn in the firelight. 'With many of the enemy retired from exhaustion, it was just a matter of picking them off... making sure they were killed quietly.'

'But there be no evidence that your son be kept by them… locked away somewhere?'

'As I said,' Vlad was irritated again. 'They were everywhere… be like locusts in the plague… but with God's speed and courage we make it out alive.'

'You go search again if get more soldiers?'

'I find recruits somehow, and promise to take back what be mine.' Vlad directed his eyes to his dead wife's body to interject, 'but have to now report my loss to King Stephen… and my end of marriage could split our allegiance.'

'My gypsies tell of raids along the river so maybe many the enemy move south and abandon number in keep.'

'Even if that be true,' Vlad projected, 'with the many we saw, Poenari be taken by the enemy until I can avenge by number.' Tariana was about to speak, but saw Vlad hold up a hand to continue. 'Radu must have revealed the depleted numbers in my garrison and so our trick with the reversed hooves must have failed.' He tightened his fist and bit his forefinger in contempt. 'That bastard brother must have taken all pleasures in raiding my home after we so stupidly welcomed him.'

'He be cunning, but then you not know his true intent.'

'No and neither did she.' Vlad looked watery-eyed at Jusztina. 'But she had her suspicions and I should have listened.' He paused before glancing at Tariana. 'I guess you women have some sort of intuition.'

'I not know word… in…tu… tion.'

'It be some sort of perception… like your dreams, but probably drawn from a woman's nature to care for their children.'

'I not understand,' Tariana frowned. ''But know somehow my brother still be alive.' She moved close so Vlad could see the sincerity in her eyes. 'I be sorry that again our plans fail… that now you be without castle. Wish my dreams could have warned of such a future.'

'It be hard to say, but I would be at peace if I knew my son be dead like his mother… I will be tormented to think him subjugated to Ottoman rule.' He looked again to notice the gypsy girl bewildered. 'Surely that be a curse that even the Devil not put upon me.'

'We gypsies bury our dead so that the soul be judged before taken to the Heavens… even if our lives be cruel and unjust, our Lord consider forgiveness.'

'But my wife took her own life and that be sin.' Vlad spoke adamantly. 'So like Henrik she will be cremated so our Lord not judge her to the sin she commit.'

'Henrik not take his life on purpose.'

'I believe he did. That is why I cremated him.' Vlad stared at her hard. 'He wanted command on his life, not left at the hands of the enemy. And like Jusztina, she did not want those foreign hands to mark her fate.'

'But the Almighty be all seeing and forgiving… He would forgive her for her sin as she be a woman keeping her sanctity for one man.'

'But I be without wife now,' Vlad said sadly, removing her ring to hold it against his chest. 'And until I strengthen my army, I be without my only son too.' He glanced at Tariana to see her staring eyes near to tears. 'I promised you a deal to help find your young brother, but now need to find my son also.'

'Maybe they be captured, but help each other escape?' Tariana said excitedly, but paused to reflect on a gypsy boy and a young king being enslaved together. 'Maybe we never get to know their fate… your son or my brother?'

'My son would not be brave enough to take his life like his mother,' Vlad thought aloud. 'He be too young to… and would the Lord condemn a child for such a sin?'

'As I said,' Tariana interjected, 'the Almighty is all righteous and although He may set plagues and storms upon our lands for our sins, surely for those who believe in His name, the Lord forgives, even more if they be child.'

'I must get this done and give prayer,' Vlad said agitatedly, placing Jusztina's ring in a pocket and taking the reed torch from the gypsy girl's hand to ignite the pyre. 'My poor, beloved Jusztina… she was stupid but brave to escape the enemy. It must have been horrific to have no choice but to escape the enemy in such a way… leaving a note which she knew not whether I read… and not knowing our son be safe for my return.' The oil soaked wood took flame fast and within a minute Jusztina's body was engulfed by fire.

'If I do good and honour our Lord… lead a life of bloodshed I agree, but to be always a righteous man and defend our Christian ways… then why be it I loose so much?' He saw Tariana go to speak and so put up a hand. 'I lose many my men… good men like Henrik… I lose now my wife and mostly likely now my only son.' They both watched with amassing spectators behind, the pyre now ablaze and drifting downstream. 'And now I must get word to King Stephen of Moldavia that his relative be dead and cremated against his will.' He noticed Tariana's eyes open wide with a sense of fear. 'I not fear the man, not now. What can he do to me that has not destroyed me already?'

'You still have many these people, include those be us,' Tariana projected with optimism. 'We know your heart be good and you should keep it that way.'

Vlad stood silent apart from glancing aside to notice sympathetic faces watching the floating fire, now some distance downstream.

'Will not the enemy spot such a fire?'

'So what if they do,' Vlad said with disregard, 'we hide and camp, but keep guard of the entrance… Besides the water be fast and she be miles away soon. Let the flame cleanse all her sin as her skin be burned pure as not touched by enemy hands.'

Vlad turned to Tariana to see her in prayer with many other gypsies and so bowed his head to whisper his own secret words. This was different to his appraisal of Henrik; Jusztina was a forthright but gentle woman, and she would never have wanted such attention.

It was a minute before Tariana's voice broke the silence.

'So Master Vlad, what we do now, apart from camp in secret?' She looked at him expectantly. 'We can eat and shelter in the woods, but soon the nights be long and cold.'

'Have your gypsies camped up stream,' Vlad asked, wiping tears from his eyes and trying to control his grief, 'and be not far from Poenari?'

Tariana nodded in agreement but detailed, 'But we must camp light in case they…'

'I place guards on the entrance and give them notice to where we be.' Vlad rubbed his chin in disarray. 'Just hope we not need to vacate all of a sudden as they be lost to us.' He stopped Tariana in collecting her belongings to ask. 'Those you have camped upstream… is there many?'

'Yes my Lord, but if you suggest to what I think you want of them, they be too young or old, be frail or infirm… cannot be trained to fight.'

'I only want to take back what be…'

'I know,' Tariana interjected, 'and maybe one day you take back what be yours.' 'I be Lord and Prince… my people follow me,' Vlad said. 'But I be no good in

training many like Henrik.' He looked around as if dejected. 'I have not the numbers of men, and those I have be tired and weary… many injured. I can only protect that entrance so that one day, like you says, I be able to fight with hundreds, maybe thousands with my Wallachian army.' He raised his hands expressively with palms open. 'Maybe my allegiance with Moldavia can still grant me troops, but now she…' His sentence drifted into silence as he watched the distant cremation of his wife disappear. And then, after a minute, he turned to ask, 'So where be this camp?'

It was almost nightfall by the time they reached Tariana's gypsies but Vlad's garrison camped separate with some soldiers on high ground to keep sight of Poenari, its fires still burning in the distance. Sorin had returned from assisting the soldiers to make camp and was putting up tents for himself and Tariana, but she instructed him to erect another one some distance off. Vlad could see that Sorin was annoyed to her request, but after finding Vlad had been injured, it was that she wanted privacy to nurse his wounds. And after all, she contested; he was the Prince of Wallachia.

Not too far distant from Vlad's newly erected tent was a stream, where Tariana asked him to wash before she would treat his wounds, and as he was still bloodstained, lacerated and bruised, he welcomed the idea. But what Vlad did not know, as he splashed water against his chest and wetted his hair, was how inquisitive Tariana was to watch him bathe in the firelight of a reed torch. She squatted down in hiding to secretly watch this nobleman wash awkwardly in the shallow stream, the deepest part barely covering his ankles. She had ordered Sorin to comfort the tents and get ready some supper, but kept glancing around nervous, thinking her giant friend was looking for her. But as her excited eyes stared back to examine an almost naked Vlad, she realized that she had disturbed night creatures that scurried through the undergrowth.

For some time she crouched in silence to keenly watch Vlad wash his lacerated body, not realizing to how muscular he really was. But it was not until he returned with chest bare that Tariana saw how bruised and scared his body really was; marks large and small blemishing his arms, chest and back. However, this would not deter her from attending to his wounds, as she had nursed many an injured gypsy, Sorin being one big example.

Tariana had prepared his tent and left some supper aside to keep warm by a small camp fire. And as she asked him to sit close in light of the fire, it was here where she prepared concoctions that gypsies had used as remedies for generations. Although he had washed his wounds clean, Tariana prepared a potion known to sterile against infection and dabbed at his cuts; some still open and quite deep. He winced as she pressed the anointed cloth against his lacerations, and so had to hold his shoulder to steady him for her to continue. But then she paused for a moment, as this was the first time she had pressed strong against him, his touch excitedly still wet, muscles firm but skin soft. She gawped over his shoulders and back, secretly admiring his physique.

'Are you finished yet?' Vlad enquired in discomfort. 'The warmth of the fire soothes, but it hurts so.'

'Almost my Lord,' Tariana said, somewhat dreamy, 'Sorry master Vlad, but you have many scars.'

'Many the fights I have had against our enemy.' He looked around at her from over his shoulder, her hazel eyes glistening like dark jewels in the firelight. 'You be finished now?' He asked as he went to swivel round. However a delicate but firm hand stopped him.

'Your bruising must hurt,' she said, picking out another small dish of ointment. 'I rub into them mix of witch-hazel and willow root.'

It was then that she fully appreciated the firm but soft touch of his back and shoulders; the warmth of the fire drying the liniment, making it congeal shiny on his skin as she applied it. Although she had nursed wounds before and felt the skin of many a gypsy, the massaging of this fragrant ointment against *his* skin felt erotic. And somehow she sensed that Vlad had become aroused by her touch; her delicate but strong fingers sliding over sensitive parts of his spine and lower back, her fingernails leaving traces of impression.

'You have done this before to many a man?' Vlad pried with interest, trying secretly to control an erection squashed between his thighs.

'I have master Vlad, but you be different.' She paused for his reaction, but none came. 'It be pity your body be battered so, as it is beautiful and strong.' She glided her hands down towards his buttocks and for a while Vlad lavished her touch, but then stopped her hand with his. 'What be the problem my Lord? You have bruising lots of places and this…' Her sentence trailed off as Vlad turned around to face her, his fingers of one hand pressed to entwine with hers.

As he sat staring into her dark and sparkly eyes, he felt an overwhelming comfort from her that strangely suppressed his anxieties and pain. Maybe it was the warmth of the camp fire, or how its flames danced light against her face and hair, but Vlad was entirely mesmerized by this gypsy girl. And as he went to cup a hand around her cheek and remove straggles of dark hair from her face, he ignored her notice the bulge in his thin loin clothing.

'My Lord, I mean master Vlad,' Tariana frowned, 'I like you… a lot. But we cannot do this as you still–'

Vlad pressed a forefinger against her lips to silence her.

'My marriage is no longer and I need such beauty to quash my pains.' Again he cupped a hand around one of her cheeks. 'Besides I not feel this way to any woman before, even if you be…' Vlad looked away and into the flames of the camp fire. 'I not care, we all be equal in the eyes of the Lord, whether you be rich man or poor.' He clenched tight her still entwined fingers. 'Your hands be delicate but strong, your heart hard but pure, and your appeal wild and fiery like those flames.' He stared back into her eyes. 'I never met a girl with such wild but natural beauty.'

For a moment Tariana's fingers of her free hand stopped but then slid around to his waist to find his navel before working their way down to his groin. As his bright green eyes widened, she detected Vlad's excitement grow, but as he edged closer, he looked controlled, although obviously relishing her touch. And as her delicate and oily fingers of her free hand stopped to feel his growing erection, he groaned whilst removing her head scarf and unbuttoning her bodice.

Soon his one hand was inside the undergarments about her chest and caressing both her ample but firm breasts. As he stripped more her clothing to reveal her navel, she could feel a cold breeze waft about her chest and stomach. And although in the warmth of the camp fire the cold was discomforting, she could not ignore the exhilaration of his fondling hands. She stared into his excited eyes, wanting to stop and ask questions, but found herself wanting to give herself to him as she had wanted when they first met.

She retracted her hands to pull off her clothing, her doubts still strong but quelled by excitement. And soon they were close enough to entwine legs, the overlay of many layers of dressing removed to reveal her silky legs. She was petite, that was clear, but with ample bosoms and a curvy, full figure, Vlad's eyes glimmered with anticipation. And as he was practically, already naked, he eagerly stripped more her clothing, excited by his chance to see naked this irresistible beauty he had secretly liked for some time.

Soon they were sat with legs entwined, his erection almost touching her dark pubic hairs. But for a long moment they did nothing except hold their grasp on each other, savoring the moment as the camp fire came as vigorous as their passion. And then it was Vlad who overpoweringly reached forward to hug her against him, her breasts squashed against the lubricated skin of his chest.

At first Tariana felt like an animal was slobbering all over her face, but realized that Vlad was overly strong with passion, his teeth biting at her lips, his tongue reaching deep into her mouth. It was as though he thought her wild like an animal and retracted as she did not respond to how he had expected.

'Apologizes, my Tariana,' Vlad whispered, his eyes earnest, 'I be vigorous in love as I am in battle, but she never complained as I...' Vlad's sentence trailed off and Tariana knew this was how war had made him and that Jusztina had adapted to such treatment. 'I not know how you want me to love you.' He paused, hypnotized by the puzzlement in her gaze. 'That be if you want this man to love you at all?'

For a still moment, as they stared at one another, it was as though Tariana could see into his soul; his confusion a mix of tenderness and passion battered by years of brutality, his love wild but affectionate. Slowly she caressed his shoulders with fingers still wet with ointment and then smiled innocently, dimples in her cheeks becoming more profound the wider her smile. And then suddenly, with an uncontrollable urge, a wild and mischievous temperament took over.

Tariana pushed against his chest to force Vlad to the ground, her one leg swinging over to pin his groin against the earth with her buttocks sitting on top of his thighs.

'So master Vlad, you like it rough,' Tariana teased, her long dark hair falling over his face. 'Then I be a wild gypsy girl and play with you my way.'

With the palm of one hand balancing her against his chest, she moved her legs so her knees pressed upon his thighs. And before he could react, he felt her hand guide his erection into the wetness between her legs. At first he could feel pubic hairs tickle his penis, but then a warm stickiness pressed down over his erection until he realized all his organ was inside her. Slowly she moved up and down on him, sometimes side to side, erratic and then rhythmic, her perspiration making her thighs slap against his.

Vlad too was becoming rapturous, but found himself pinned down by her one hand. Excited by her eroticism, he was ecstatic, her palm now slippery against his chest. Unusually he was climaxing quite early; overwhelmed by her movements as her hazel eyes glared at him behind straggles of shaggy dark hair that fell over her face. She flung her hair against his chest and then towards the sky, but her eyes never left his gaze until she lowered to kiss his lips. Slowly she slid down on all fours but kept the tip of his penis still inside her, her face inches above his, her hair cascading all over his face.

'You like it this way my Lord?' she teased, moving slowly backward to push her buttocks down to take more of his organ. 'Or want to play like wild animals?'

Vlad felt her hand slip and so grasped her wrist. He then pushed himself up against her, his chest squashing her breasts.

'Play like a wild animal you want, here in the open?' Vlad declared, pushing her back but feeling himself still inside her. 'I take you like this, but we could be like dogs?'

'First on my back,' Tariana hissed as he coaxed her body back, her legs arched and open wide, 'but it be dirty here out in the nature.'

'I care not, and you like it that way,' Vlad professed, now moving his hips in rhythm, his erection sliding in and out of her vagina. 'You make me frisky like some wild dog.'

'Then take me that way instead,' Tariana teased, sliding back to remove his organ from inside her and coaxing him on all fours. 'Take me from behind then pull me back against you.'

Vlad conceded to her demands and for the first minute they mated doggy-style until he reached around for her breasts. And after clasping a breast in each hand, pulled her back against his chest, his penis forced more inside her. But as Tariana moaned uncontrollably, they heard noises. Maybe it was the camp fire wood snapping into cinders or night creatures again scuttling through the undergrowth.

They froze in their tight embrace; Tariana's back sweaty against Vlad's chest. In the still of that moment, they both noticed to how low the fire had got and its heat ineffective against the cold. With him still inside her but feeling anxious, Vlad slowly moved her off him and slid a hand around her shoulders to make Tariana face him.

'May be we should take our wild antics inside?'

Tariana agreed and after grabbing all her clothes, scuttled off towards the tent, her sleek but curvy body shining with perspiration against the dimming firelight. With his penis still quite erect and excited, Vlad grabbed all he had and followed her with eager anticipation.

Tariana had awoken late. Thinking of the sex she had last night in Vlad's tent, she was tired but still exhilarated, and certainly not eager to rise after returning back in the early hours. She had stretched and found comfort in her soft blankets, but her inquisitive mind disturbed her rest.

Was this just some fling that Vlad wanted because he had lost his wife… his castle, maybe soon his kingdom, or was their affair more to which Tariana hoped it would be? However, she considered; the Prince of Wallachia having relations with some poor gypsy girl… it did seem a little absurd. They had fought together well, his army and her gypsies, but she also felt she had failed him on numerous occasions.

She had pondered on many a thought, and it was these that had forced her to leave the comfort of her bedding, along with feeling quite sore as she had not had sex for such a long time. She had not pretended to be wild and erotic just to excite him;

it was just that her passion had quashed her usual inhibition to have sex. Of course she had found him handsome from the first day they had met, and somehow now she knew he liked her too. But would their differences interfere… he a lord and prince, and she a gypsy? Could this be their best kept secret, something intimate that would last, or just a memory Tariana would cherish as they go about their separate ways?

Although she was late to rise, after dressing in light clothing, Tariana left her tent to see that the morning was still crisp with a chill in the air. Stretching her arms high above her head, she squinted into the distance to where Vlad's tent was pitched, and so thoughts returned. Could she persuade enough gypsies to help in his campaign to take back Poenari? Would they be eager or fit enough to fight? Could he or men like Henrik train them? Could Vlad get other countries to help fight against this their common enemy? And would that king find out about Jusztina?

Whilst Tariana searched for her basic fishing instruments, she heard grunts as a large hand grasped her shoulder. She turned with a fright to see Sorin towering above her, his eyes suspicious and face troubled. She watched carefully as his other hand quickly gave signage to ask to where she was last night; it was that he had come to wish her good night, but she was not in her tent.

'Master Vlad and I had lots to talk,' she excused, pulling away with her fishing instruments after grabbing a shoulder bag. 'He was very upset to lose his wife, and his keep. And now he must find soldiers to fight for this kingdom on which we live.' She continued to talk, but trudged on towards the river, hoping Sorin would eventually stop in following her. 'And he lose everything now his son be gone.' She turned to see Sorin standing alongside her, his eyes still suspicious. 'You know what it be like. You know what losing my brother did to me. You know how I felt about that!' He stepped forward, his eyes still glaring. 'Ah, don't look at me that way. Go back and prepare me a camp fire,' she instructed, waving a hand at him. 'I go get fish for breakfast.'

Ensuring Sorin had turned and was on his way back to the main camp; Tariana changed her route to the river to check on Vlad first. Quickly and quietly she peeked into his tent, but noticed him still fast asleep. Once again she wanted to kiss his lips or just his forehead as she had when she had left. But seeing him so peaceful and thinking of their antics into the early morning, she thought best not to disturb him and so traipsed in the direction of the river.

But Vlad was not asleep and turned his head slowly to glance out of his bedding. Noticing Tariana had gone, he dressed swiftly to peek out of his tent, quickly searching the outside to see if she was still there. He stepped outside to search some more and caught sight of her strolling in the direction of the river.

After taking time to get fully dressed, Vlad had lost sight of Tariana until he stumbled upon her at the riverside. For several minutes he crouched in bushes and bracken to watch her cast lines to fish with earth worms, but then sat in cover of a fallen tree to admire her. She had pinned back her hair with some clip as it was bedraggled and wild, but Vlad was engrossed to watch her pull fish from the river. Yet again thoughts returned to him; ones he had contemplated after Tariana had left him in the early hours.

Surely he could never marry such a girl. He needed someone of royalty, a daughter or niece of a lord, nobleman, or king; someone such as Jusztina. And then guilt hit him about what he had done last night, just hours after losing his wife. What would happen to his allegiance with the Moldavian king if he learned of Jusztina's death and that he had had her cremated? And that now the Prince of Wallachia was having relations with some vagabond, gypsy girl?

For long minutes he watched Tariana fish as thoughts troubled him. Losing so much since he had met this gypsy girl, he considered: was she some beauty that had cursed him in more ways than one? Henrik had fallen for her like he had, but had died even before he had chance to truly befriend her. And what was it that Jusztina had said about this gypsy girl; too wild to be trusted? But then again his late wife was probably just jealous of Tariana's natural beauty.

As he watched her pull more fish from the river, many thoughts passed through his mind. He did not want to leave this dark and wild, beautiful girl, especially now he had no wife, but it was a fact that he had lost so much since he had got to know her. Nonetheless, she had saved him from that Turkish leader in that night attack, and many of her gypsies had fought strong and brave against their common enemy. He wanted things to work out, but he had to be realistic. And he knew she had to be also. He would need to regroup his soldiers and seek recruits from other kingdoms, not train weak and decrepit vagabonds, gypsies that could or would not follow orders.

Secretly he followed her back to their camp, to watch her gut the fish before spiking them to cook above a camp fire. And as a curious Sorin returned to ask more questions, she waved him away to prepare vegetables, but instructed him to save some hot water for her to wash. Gingerly Vlad approached but hid to watch her spike potatoes to roast alongside the fish. And then after she disappeared into her tent, he grasped an opportunity to steal what fish and potatoes looked edible. Two fish he quickly wrapped in parchment to eat later, but took the best roasted potato to eat on his way in cover of the woods.

Hiding in bracken on a woodland slope, Vlad paused to watch Tariana emerge from her tent and set up some sort of canopy. Strangely he felt guilty for stealing her food but smirked to watch her wave away Sorin, instructing him that no one should bother her. Taking a large metal bowl, she poured into it the remaining hot water and tested its temperature with her elbow.

Although he had spent such an intimate time with her into the early hours, Vlad became aroused again by simply watching her bathe. The sheet acting as some canopy was providing cover, but from the angle at which Vlad watched, he could see all. She had unbuttoned and removed her blousing to wash her breasts, them bouncing but firm as she frisked with the hot water, now pouring some onto her long dark hair. Vlad was entranced by noticing her face appear large against her long, wet hair that now lay flat against her scalp. And he could see her shoulders and breasts bare and glistening wet.

As he nibbled away the last of the roasted potato, he approached to get a better view, but sat in cover of the woodland, thinking of what best to do. Admiring her beauty and the way her athletic body moved, he recalled their wild antics early that morning, but contemplated on betraying his wife just hours after her cremation. Had this beautiful girl worked some witchcraft upon him, trying to snare him into keeping her so she would influence his future plans? But why, if he had always been such a righteous man, had his life been suddenly mired by death and corruption? Did he not deserve something different; a passion so natural but intense that it quashed all his grief?

But what of Jusztina; would she not go to Heaven now anyhow? Had she not committed such a sin in killing herself and so been cremated for it? Would the good Lord forgive her and allow her to join him in eternity when he died? Maybe not now he had slept with this strange but enchanting, gypsy girl.

Oppressed by all that had gone wrong, Vlad decided he could only do one thing; he must abscond with all the soldiers he could trust and erase this girl from memory, separating his army from the gypsies to find new recruits he could train to properly fight.

PART TWO

SEVENTEEN

Tariana noticed Sorin glance at her again and shake his head; his long, unkempt hair blowing in the dusty wind. He turned his head to examine the merchandise on the back of the cart, but as she pulled on the reins, Tariana knew he was making excuses to gawp at her. The scar across his left eye was accentuated by dust kicked up by the two bedraggled horses pulling the wagon. And as he rubbed his eyes with agitation, Tariana concluded Sorin was more frustrated to where they were going.

The gypsy camp they had left miles back had produced merchandise to sell, and knowing Braşov was such a good market town, they could make a little money or at least exchange their goods for other produce. With their harvests insufficient and ravaged by enemy troops, many gypsies faced the prospect of starvation through the coming winter. Indeed Tariana had spent weeks sewing and embroidering a collection of different outfits, but Sorin knew the other reason to why she wanted to visit Braşov.

Over the eighteen months or so since Vlad had fled the gypsy camp, taking with him many of his soldiers, Tariana had heard nothing of him since their night of wild passion. But now she had heard rumours of the Prince of Wallachia settling in the town of Braşov, and being so curious to why he had left without reason, she was determined to find out.

Sorin grunted again and cleared his eyes of dirt; Tariana also annoyed by the dust in the wind. She held herself from conversation, knowing if she lowered the scarf covering her mouth, the dust blown up from the horses' hooves would scathe her throat. But Sorin was becoming irritable, and she knew his grunts were to vent his dislike of Vlad. He had signalled his displeasure well before they had left camp and now was expressing his agitation. Nonetheless, Sorin knew well that their venture to sell or exchange produce was important to their gypsies, and so for another mile she ignored him. But as they approached within a few miles of Braşov, Sorin was angrily stabbing his dagger into the sideboard of the wagon.

'Sorin, you know we need to sell all this we carry,' she said after lowering her scarf, the track not now churning up so much dust, 'or at least return with foods that will keep.' Sorin grunted and shook his head, Tariana knowing his vexed mood without any hand gesturing. 'It may be that he not recognise me after it be so long. This be the second winter since...' At that she stopped to remember the pleasure she did have with Vlad, but now wanted to question him to why he had left so.

As she guided the cart along, she gabbled on some more about the past, muttering about the prospects of making her gypsies into good fighters and warriors, but Sorin knew she was just fantasising. Turning a sharp corner along the track and out of dense woodland, Sorin was glad to see Braşov in the distance; the town set kindly in the cradle of a pinewood valley, most buildings lining the flat land in the centre of the ravine. Soon he would be able to dismount the rickety wagon; it more uncomfortable than riding a horse long distance. And then he could free the numbness throughout his legs and buttocks.

Entering the town, Sorin was eager to stop at the nearest marketplace, but Tariana ventured on until they reached a larger and more central market area. And although the stalls were cramped and somewhat shabby, Tariana knew by the trodden earth, that there was much more footfall by both tradesman and punter. She guided the cart slowly to enter a passageway between stalls, thinking she could park and maybe just sell from the rear of the wagon.

But as Sorin disembarked wearily to tend to the horses and Tariana uncovered the tarpaulin, she heard a child's voice call. Ignoring it amongst all the pleas of tradesmen and the hectic discourse between market people, she went back to sort her merchandise. But then she heard a child's voice call again. This time it was near and undoubtedly directed at them; telling them that they could not set up stall there. She looked at Sorin and acknowledged that he had heard it too.

She looked about her and to the rear of the closest stall. Searching intently, Tariana saw nothing but an old, disabled man, sat up a corner and under shelter of the midday sun, overlooking a pair of shoes.

'You cannot sell there,' the young voice called again. 'It be our place to sell!'

Again Tariana glanced at the old disabled man, him now tending to the stump of his decapitated leg as he glared at them.

'Lady, this be our place to sell,' the girl's voice repeated with discontent. 'Grandfather pay lots to sell here!'

Tariana felt a sudden tug on the thick material of her tight skirt and so glanced down to see a little bedraggled girl with wild, unkempt hair, that reminded her of herself when she was young. She went to caress one of the girl's round, blushing cheeks with the palm of her hand, but the girl backed away.

'Lady, you cannot stop here to sell from that wagon… my grandfather…' She stopped to notice the giant figure of Sorin approach and then lean against the cart. 'Nor the man, if he be with you,' she affirmed, but somewhat a little more timidly.

'But what be it that your grandfather sell?' Tariana asked softly with a smile.

'Do you not see, he make all sorts of footwear,' the girl said, looking apprehensively again at giant Sorin. 'But he not sell much as winter be coming.' The girl looked at Tariana with a changed expression, her eyes staring expectantly. 'Do you wish to buy some shoes?'

'What be your name my dear?' Tariana asked, ignoring the girl's request.

'I not tell as you be strangers and grandfather says I must be...' the girl paused, glancing around to see her grandfather listening.

'We only need to set up and sell all that we have here, just for a day or two.' But the girl scrunched up her nose and shook her head with arms folded tight. 'It look as your grandfather not have much stock to display or sell.' Tariana looked around at the near empty tables. 'Why not we sell together? Surely we can make *some* arrangement?' Again the girl stood with arms folded, her face glum. 'Why not ask your grandfather my dear, as surely we can sell both our stocks together... clothes can sell well with footwear?' Again the girl looked uncertain, her eyes glancing back at her grandfather, who now stood leaning on a crutch. 'But here my dear, look at what types of things we have.'

The little girl stared up at Tariana, unperturbed by merchandise passed to her by Sorin, until she saw a dress. Suddenly the girl sprang forward to claw at a light dress and pull at it to admire its sewn patterns and embroidered sequins.

'You make this?' the little girl asked. 'Dresses that be both pretty and unique?'

Tariana caught Sorin staring at the girl until they looked at each other, both surprised by the maturity of such a child. Tariana grinned, realizing the young girl must have developed lots of experience to handle merchandise through her grandfather's trade. And at least now, she had hooked the girl's interest, and so played on it.

'Yes my dear, us gypsy girls camped many miles away, have made such.' Tariana fingered the detailed embroidery of the dress. 'These are, like you say, be unique… handmade by hours of delicate work.' She winked at Sorin, before handing more of the garment for the girl to feel, seeing her wide eyes not leave the golden dress.

'You can make one like this for me?'

'Why of course my dear,' Tariana said slowly, rolling her eyes at Sorin. 'But it be taking a few days, and need to be a little larger than you, otherwise you grow out of it fast. This I know, as I be the same as you once, when I was young.' Tariana smiled at the girl and saw her glance up, thinking her lovely, but a cheeky little mite. 'But if I am to stay and make such, we need to be acquainted.' She paused to point at herself and then her giant friend. 'I am Tariana and this be big Sorin.' The girl looked rather apprehensive as Sorin stepped forward into the sunlight; her thinking that Tariana was definitely right about him being big. 'What be your name?' Tariana asked.

'I be...' the little girl glanced over to see her grandfather nod his approval. 'I am Lydia.'

'And that be your grandfather,' Tariana asked pointing, 'who rent this place?' 'Yes that be my grandfather.'

'And his name?'

'His name is Andrei, but he not sell much. Only get a little off people as he be...'

The girl released her grip on the dress and paused to change her line of conversation. 'I go out and make people come but they not buy.' She went to retrieve a pair of light canvas shoes. 'I think these not sell as it be stock from summer and the cold weather will come soon.'

'You be right in saying that Lydia.' Tariana agreed, standing upright to stretch her back and place the dress back on the wagon. 'Why your grandfather should make boots like Sorin wear.' She pointed to Sorin's feet after swiping a finger along Lydia's little freckled nose. 'It look like he need new ones as those he has be tatty and worn.'

The girl chuckled to notice Sorin's laces were frayed and short, but then felt a hand on her shoulder.

'Grandfather,' Lydia said with a fright to stare at him leaning over her upon his crutch. 'These people… Tariana and Sorin want to know if…?'

'I could hear you talking, even from all over there,' Andrei declared. 'I may be regarded an old cripple, but my ears still be sharp.' He ruffled Lydia's shaggy, brown hair with his free hand and edged forward. 'My granddaughter be right in admitting we do not sell as not many come to buy. But it be not that which make us poor.'

'But you be a good craftsman,' Tariana said, examining some nearby shoes.

'It may well be,' Andrei confessed, his eyes wide with resentment, 'but it be the extortionate tax we have to pay just to rent such a small place. And now there be many Hungarians or others from foreign lands that pass through and trade without…'

'But that man was punished grandfather, even if he be rich and–'

'Lydia, I be talking now to…' Andrei interrupted his granddaughter, but silenced as he had forgotten their names. 'Sorry, but I not remember your… my age has been kind on my ears but not on my mind.'

'Tariana and Sorin,' Lydia spoke aloud, but backed away as Sorin edged nearer. 'That be correct, is it not?'

'Yes my dear, that be correct,' Tariana acknowledged but saw Lydia hide behind her grandfather as Sorin approached to grunt and signal whilst holding up leather and animal skins. 'But Sorin speak different in the land he come from.'

'And where would that be?' Andrei asked.

'A land of cold and ice,' Tariana explained whilst messing with garments on the wagon. 'Lands further north and east of mine, which be that way too.'

'And why can he not speak?' Andrei asked warily, noticing how Lydia glared afraid at the large Russian, 'or is it something I should not ask?'

'It be a long story to tell,' Tariana said, noticing Sorin stare at her. 'But he be punished by that our enemy.'

Andrei stood puzzled to watch Sorin grunt and signal again whilst holding up other materials.

'What is it he be trying to say?' Andrei held Lydia's shoulders firmly in his hands and could feel her trembling. 'Why can he not speak?'

'He be trying to explain how you can make good boots for the coming winter from our materials, whilst I make Lydia a dress.' Tariana smiled at Lydia and saw her return one, although somewhat uneasily. 'It will take a few days, if we can stay? But we have many materials… use anything you need.' Tariana noticed Andrei hold Lydia tighter as he looked anxiously at

Sorin as he grunted loud. 'Do not worry about my big friend, he be just as anxious as you.'

'Why can your friend not speak?' Lydia asked cautious and shy. Tariana glanced at Sorin to see him nod.

'Many year gone, my friend desert his lands as they be attacked by that our enemy. So one night he put up fight but get captured and be slave. With many that try to escape he get captured again, but not killed as he be big… useful as slave to enemy. But as punishments, they cut out his tongue… and he would have died if us gypsies not rescue and treat him right. Many of my clan and his be killed that night and we be lucky to escape… evade the enemy to travel south and west along coast of that they call the Black Seas.' She began to brush down and arrange garments on a nearby table. 'So it must be me who talk price and sell.'

'Your friend has a story much like mine, but my history go back well before this corrupt son took to govern Braşov after losing his keep.' Andrei continued a little before being interrupted. 'I fought with the first Vlad king and it was noble to…'

'I beg to ask,' Tariana interjected, 'but this son you mention, he be Vlad Dracul… the Prince of Wallachia?'

'Yes that be him, the son of the first and true king.'

'And he be in Braşov… ruling the lands from this market town?' Tariana interrogated whilst trying to ignore Sorin's stare and grunts of disproval.

'Yes, but he be not like his father,' Andrei said intently. 'I fought alongside the old king and he treated us like nobles although we be only infantry. This so be it prince have no honour since his wife sinned her death and his son got kidnapped. He takes his wickedness out of *all* people, although before I hear he be quite righteous and noble.'

Tariana was about to continue her questioning, but saw little Lydia step forward.

'But it be not just people who live like us, but nobles, merchants and rich men… they not steal the golden goblet as he test them so… like to the punishments my…'

Lydia stopped talking – a lump blocking her throat – her eyes swelling with tears as memories flooded back to what Andrei had told her a year ago. Shyly she recoiled to hide behind her grandfather, embarrassed to show her tears.

As Andrei held Lydia's shoulders to comfort her, he described more to what his granddaughter could not.

'The man you ask about… this Prince of Wallachia, he be righteous in some ways but cruel in many also.' He shuffled forward, pushing Lydia behind him. 'This Vlad keeps a golden goblet chained into the brickwork of the central well here in

Braşov. Anyone can use it to drink with… many vagabonds and the lame do, and so do travellers, even merchants, rich nobles and such like. I reckon it be his way to test the town's people of their trust. But I recall, as one foreign merchant left at midnight, he was caught trying to steal the goblet and he was…' He looked down awkwardly at Lydia, who grasped his free wrist with both her little hands. 'His goods and clothes were stripped to pay taxes to which he had not, and he was staked before being burned before a town audience.' He paused a while to see Lydia's reaction, but continued after recognising that she was deep in thought. 'I have heard rumours that this Vlad is trying to raise enough money from taxes and alike to amalgamate a large enough army to take back his castle. And many foreign and wealthy merchants, who market but do not pay taxes here, have been stripped of jewelleries and rich clothing as to provide payment. Some have been flogged for their incompetence or ignorance to his rule, and some… well a good number now over these months have been sentenced to a more terminal fate.'

'Yes, he a wicked man,' Lydia shouted. 'Lord or no Lord!'

'Actually he be once a very righteous and fair man to give justice,' Tariana conveyed. 'Maybe I can help him regain his Christian ways?'

'No, you cannot… he be wicked a man and cannot be changed.' Lydia stuck out her tongue but Andrei slapped her face for being naughty and disrespectful. She cowered behind her grandfather, tears of anger and pain now flooding her eyes.

'I can understand how this Vlad is distraught at losing his wife and son… if I lost Lydia now, being she is all I have… well.' Andrei paused before his eyes stared wide. 'But he let his boyar's torture people who be like us… people who try to earn just enough to get by. And when they are caught stealing to feed their hungry mouths, they be punished in the most horrible ways.'

'The Prince of Wallachia lost more than you know,' Tariana stated quietly. 'He be defending these lands from that our enemy for years.' She glanced at Sorin, who shook his head in disagreement to her preserving Vlad's name. And then she suddenly realized to why Andrei had taken responsibility of his granddaughter. 'What happened to Lydia's parents? Surely Vlad would not have ordered them…' Suddenly Tariana found it difficult to talk, and noticed Lydia shy again behind her grandfather.

'I agree that stealing be a crime and also killing livestock that not be yours,' Andrei confessed, 'but some of these boyars not get punished for their action simply because of their status or allegiance to this Vlad.' He shuffled a little nearer to Tariana. 'These nobles call such butchery a hunting practice… that this keeps them ready for real battle. But why kill for pleasure, whilst the likes of us go starved for such meat?'

Tariana glanced quickly at Sorin and swallowed hard before asking, 'Was Lydia's parents lost by punishments enforced by Vlad?'

'I did not see such happen but still hear their screams in my dreams.' Andrei continued quietly, 'His boyars boasted of their prince's generosity and rounded all thieves vagabonds, the lame or those carrying illness of the old plague, to offer shelter and food, but locked them in a barn not far from the church. And that be why they name it the *Black Church* as it too was set alight by such rampant flames.' Andrei paused to see the exchange of shock between the two gypsies. 'This be the reason there now be much spite between Vlad and the church hear in Braşov. It took many townsfolk to put out the fires and save that part of the church.' He took breath and then looked down at Lydia. 'I tried to put out the fires for my daughter and her husband, but we could only save the church. And from then on, I had to look after my granddaughter as she be such a young age.'

There was a long silence of reflection until Tariana looked at Andrei's incapacity and asked quietly, 'Is that to how you lost your leg… in the fire trying to save…?'

'Oh no my dear,' Andrei almost smiled. 'I lost this leg many a year ago fighting in the first king's army… he that was a true king and not this wretched son.' He paused to recall the many battles that had scarred his memory. 'I took one too many an arrow in the same leg as it was the side of my horse facing the enemy.'

'You can ride?'

'Can, but it be difficult now.' 'Can Lydia ride?'

'I wanted to teach her, but all our time be taken making this a living.'

'I'll teach her if you want.' Tariana pointed at Sorin. 'You teach big Sorin to make boots from our stocks here.' She grinned slightly and said jokingly, 'As it looks a lot like he need new ones.' With more sincerity in her voice she approached Andrei to state, 'That be if we can pitch here and sell our wares together… split sales by half?' She watched Andrei hesitate and look down at Lydia. 'But tell me first, if we can or cannot, how would I go about finding this Vlad, the son of the king you served?'

'I not tell you if I knew,' Andrei scoffed. 'I would not want a pretty girl to go get herself killed.'

'I be stronger a woman than you think,' Tariana puckered. 'Besides someone must get this Prince of Wallachia back to his good old Christian ways before that our enemy take these lands.'

'But you be from other lands, so why would you have any vow to this our country?' Andrei glanced to see Tariana lost for words and brooding. 'You can pitch here be that we sell fair our trades together, but come the day after next, you must leave.'

'At least give it time so I can make Lydia her dress,' Tariana pleaded, winking down at the young girl. 'And that you teach Sorin some your skill in making footwear?'

As Andrei leaned heavily on his wooden crutch to consider the gypsy's proposal, Lydia ran up to give Tariana a hug. And after lifting the little girl's frail, light body to hold her in her arms, Tariana heard Lydia say.

'That man be a nasty man and should be punished like my...' The little girl's face again expressed sorrow. 'But if one thing I remember father telling me when I be little to what I am now, was that forgiveness be the greatest thing to our faith.' She glanced back to Andrei before again facing Tariana. 'And grandfather tells that I must honour my father's wish... believe in God and be good a Christian.' Lydia glanced back at Andrei again after hearing him call for her. 'Grandfather believes not so much anymore, but that I must.'

'You must my child,' Tariana said placing Lydia down carefully. 'As I will try and make that friend of mine all good again.'

'I should not tell,' Lydia whispered, hearing Andrei call after her again. 'But that nasty Lord friend of yours meets men around noon at the church... but take care if you go, he punish people.'

Suddenly Lydia turned to run back to her grandfather, but Tariana caught the little girl wink at her first.

She had seen the golden goblet that Andrei had mentioned yesterday whilst refilling her tatty water flask, and had found her way from the central well to hide within the market stalls closest the church. From here Tariana could observe most activity; watching peddlers to noblemen stroll their way about the church, noticing how foreign merchants tried secretly to sell their stock, obviously fearful of the man she sought. And although she had the greatest of patience, it was the chance of meeting Vlad again that made her nervous. Was he now the changed man Andrei had described? And with it now being the second autumn since they had parted, would Vlad recognize her? Indeed, with all that Andrei had said, would it be wise to even approach him?

Tariana had been cramped in hiding now for over an hour and had to relieve the numbness in her feet, circling her toes to the exercises she used to do every morning. Surely by now it was past midday, and for a moment she considered whether to cancel her chance in meeting Vlad. But something inside her made her wait that extra minute. And then in her delay, she noticed a group of soldiers pulling along a vagabond woman. And behind them, accompanied by several boyars and noblemen, was Vlad.

Quickly Tariana raced across the gravel grounds of the church to meet the group who ascended a platform extension to the church. She paused in astonishment; surely Vlad would not punish the woman so close to the church… in the eyes of the Lord? And what exactly had she done to deserve punishments?

'What do you mean to do with that woman?' Tariana shouted as she tried best to approach Vlad, but was blocked by pike men guards. 'What it be that she has done?'

'It be no concern of yours vagabond wench,' Vlad said, but talked slow after recognizing her. 'Or should I say gypsy wench?'

'Shall we remove her m' Lord?' a pike man asked.

'No, let her know what this here wench has done,' Vlad stated holding his hand up to restrain his guards. The two pike men stood back but held pikes at the ready. 'I did know this gypsy girl once. Regretfully she bought on me curse after curse.'

'I helped you,' Tariana argued. 'We helped you battle the –'

'Silence woman,' a pike man shouted. 'You be in the presence of the Prince of Wallachia!'

'I know who he be,' Tariana snarled. 'And I hope he still have a good heart and be of Christian ways.'

'Such ways endorse laws that punish those for their wrong doings.' He instructed his soldiers to pull forward the vagabond girl and soon Tariana could see the terror in her eyes. 'This woman has been proved to have betrayed her husband… denounced him in marriage… and so will be punished accordingly.'

'To *your* rule,' Tariana questioned. 'Or that of a trial in the eyes of our Lord?'

'It be she who broke the laws of this land,' a nearby boyar stated. 'And our laws be Christian.'

'Shall we remove her m' Lord?' the pike man repeated.

'No the gypsy girl can watch the punishments of the vagabond's crimes,' Vlad stated inhaling a deep breath. 'It be an example to her peoples.'

'But I recall m' Lord,' Tariana stated, cynically copying the pike man, 'that the day after you lose your wife, you took comfort in someone else.' Tariana watched as Vlad's eyes bulged like she had never seen before and then continued although somewhat uneasily, 'And she be cremated against her ways before you took time with me.'

'The time with you was raw and exciting,' Vlad whispered, leaning over as close as he could to talk quiet, 'but the fish you cooked next morning be a finer taste and far more rewarding.' Vlad leaned back to watch Tariana's face tighten with resentment and continued with more vigor in his voice, 'I as a Lord do not recall any such time with this here wench, as it be against my decree.' He stared at her without the loving eyes she once knew. 'You should watch your tongue gypsy girl, or I be having one more punishment to conduct today.'

'Punishments like you caused for Lady Jusztina?' Tariana flared, enraged enough to oversee the consequences. 'Disposed of her against the ways of her lands?' She stepped forward but the pike men aimed their blades at her throat. 'Do you not have that passion anymore, like to what you showed me… and my people.' She glanced at people amassing around them. 'Instead I hear tales of you staking and burning innocent people who do nothing but try living off this the lands to which they be born.' A boyar shouted for her to be silenced, but Vlad put up a hand and simply grinned. 'Did you not promise m' Lord allegiances to my peoples, so that they live well upon your lands as they fought against that our common enemy?' She pulled Henrik's dagger from her clothing. 'That you gave me this in memory of our friend as we fought together?'

The pike men stepped forward, their blades almost touching Tariana's chest, and so she recoiled somewhat before noticing Vlad step forward.

'I shall have that removed if you do not discard it,' Vlad said, his eyes obviously recognizing Henrik's dagger. 'I shall have my soldiers remove it from your possession.'

'But it was *you* that gave it me!' Tariana glared anxiously about her; at the pike blades poking her garment. 'I have right to defend myself!'

'As you were supposed to defend that our posse and find safe passage through to Moldavia, but failed so miserably in your task?'

'That was because of that betrayal of a brother… the one I told you not to trust!' 'I had to entrust foreign mercenaries to escort me to see Stephen the Great.' Vlad

ignored Tariana's retort to explain, 'Someway the king found out about Jusztina's death, and the sin on how she went about it. And when he somehow learned of her cremation, he questioned our allegiance and denounced me as his ally. So I not get the wealth or infantry I desired as I came betrayed again.' He shifted towards Tariana, his angry eyes disregarding the dagger in her hand. 'Like many, I trust very few now, but have learned much. It be fear that govern laws… the severe the punishment, the more obedient the people.' He pointed to the vagabond girl as he backed away. 'This here wench knew the laws of marriage but defied them, and so she will be an example to a town audience.' He pulled his collar high from his tunic and armor, whilst inhaling strong. 'Merchants travel through here and scoff at me… pay no tax to their trades and do profit. Many live off this my land without contribution and so I cleanse my lands of such people and impose my authority.'

He glared at Tariana in a way she felt alien. 'Fear is the only way to scare people into submission, not kind words and good deeds.'

'If you punish your people without Godly justice, then you be no more a Christian than your brother.'

'All that live on these lands must obey the law of this my land… it be the only way to keep law and order.' Vlad sneered at her reference to Radu and continued, 'And it not just be the likes of your people… vagabonds like this here wench, beggars and lame and such like, but foreign merchants from Transylvania, Hungary, Moldavia… many who prosper from my lands but take their wealth back to their home lands… or even do deals with the Ottoman Empire.'

'You have not just a change in heart Master Vlad, but change in appeal.' Tariana shirked away a bit as she saw his temper flare. 'You gave promise to my peoples, as when you gave me this here dagger!'

'I cannot witness such common men live and pilfer off the sweat of others, whilst my army protects them from the enemy. All who dare to call this their lands should fight to keep it so!'

'My peoples did, and many died for it,' Tariana stated, her tear dimmed eyes exposing her emotion. 'Or have you forgotten such our past?'

'Less of this your insolence,' Vlad commanded lunging to quickly disarm her. 'You too have not changed... such a disobedient and wild creature!'

Tariana glanced in fear to watch her dagger bounce across the floor and slide towards the feet of the petrified girl. But before she could comprehend her vulnerability, she was dragged by her lapel to see Vlad's face breathing hard and down at her. With him so close, her memories shot back to when they had made wild but passionate love, but found him strangely different. Defenseless and in his grip, she cowered towards the ground, wriggling to find some escape, but now he gripped her with both hands.

'I see that you still have your courage, or would it be insolence.' He stared at her with contempt, but somehow she still felt that suppressed pain inside him. 'It may well be that you are not convinced of my command and royal decree?'

'I once loved a righteous man who happened to be some Lord and noble,' Tariana said slow. 'A Prince of Wallachia that I believed could rule one day as a great Christian king.' She felt his grip loosen and his eyes narrow as he recalled memories, 'A great king that would have the support of *all* his peoples.' She shook herself free a little. 'Not like the old, one-legged man that fought alongside your father in wars past... a friend that despises you now he be left struggling to raise a granddaughter because you deny his daughter and husband of life... a desolate but talented shoemaker who have nothing much after he pay for his keep.'

'What be all this nonsense?' Vlad ridiculed, but then grinned as he thought to make an example of his once gypsy friend. 'Your insolence be needing a lesson.' He stepped back, commanding two guards to secure her by each arm and then reached to retrieve the dagger. Before she could wiggle against her restraint, she saw Vlad pointing Henrik's dagger at her feet. 'If I remember you had such delicate and soft feet, but nimble as to the wild creature you be.' Vlad got kicked in the face as he tried to remove her threadbare sneakers and so retracted. 'We shall test you gypsy wench to your insolence in taking question against me.' He instructed a boyar to bring over a cane basket and had him tip out its contents by her feet. 'Would your shoemaker friend have such foot wears that would protect your feet from these collected from our enemy lands?'

Tariana stared petrified at the Turkish vipers that hissed about her feet, but could not escape from the encircling guards now holding pikes around her. At first she panicked as if dancing between the slithering creatures, but recognized that all but one were small; that they were young snakes dumped on the ground with their parent. The mother hissed at Tariana's feet and with surprising control she kicked it away to concentrate on the wild young. She knew from her many travels through the wilderness that young snakes were not just more vigorous, but released more venom with their bite.

Quickly she danced between the slithering young, and picking them off one by one, stamped a heel down upon the head of each, until again she had to kick away the mother who lunged at her sneaker. But now the mother had sensed the harm against her young and slid back vicious and resolute. It was just about to strike at Tariana's feet again when Henrik's dagger pierced its head.

Holding the dagger up to see how the blade had exited the shut mouth of the snake, Vlad gazed at it with allure.

'Evil but fascinating creatures, do you not agree?' Vlad inspected, turning his attention to Tariana, who grasped with relief. 'This one I could have let bite you, but I was curious,' He stepped towards her, holding up the twitching snake for her to see, 'Why did you kill the young first and not the mother?'

'I, I...' Tariana tried best to compose herself. 'I knew that the young be agile and bite with more poison... that they not control their bites...' She stared intense at him. 'But what you do against me be horrible trick!'

'Yet it be admirable that which you did... still have beauty and be smart.' Vlad looked at her longingly, his eyes examining her body. 'And strangely this mention of poisoned young relates to the matter we discuss.' Vlad noticed her frown, and so after removing the shake's head from the dagger and throwing the creature aside, explained, 'The same be happening to my governance over these my lands… that I must stamp out and discipline those who defy my rule… that if the young learn to fear my punishments, they not betray my future rule.' He chuckled a little, but then placed the dagger blade against her neck. 'These, *my* people, as you call them, will not deny me as heir to the Wallachian throne, once they learn the disciplines to my rule.'

'I prefer the first man I met,' Tariana said slow and soft, 'a Christian Lord who respected his peoples and honoured his agreements with *my* people.'

'My pact with your people be now annulled, as you failed in your task for me.' He slid the dagger into his belt and looked at her longingly again. 'I not need such help as I be declaring an allegiance with the Hungarian king… we have a common assertion to stop the Ottoman Empire conquering north and west.' Pinned to the spot by pike men blades, Tariana could not move as he slid his forefinger down her cheek. 'In my visit to see the king I may find myself another wife, but one that may not be as endearing as you my gypsy girl.' Tariana saw a glimpse of empathy in his eyes as he gazed upon her face. Somehow she recognized the memories flooding his mind. 'Yes it be a somewhat dirty trick I play against you girl, but had to prove a point.' Vlad scrutinized her for long seconds, contemplating the feeling he did once have for her. 'Let the girl go, and too the other one, as they have learned their lessons.'right.

The guards grumbled amongst themselves, questioning if they had heard Vlad

'You wish to let both go m' lord?' one brave enough asked.

'Yes, we should rebuke and be sorry for such pretty but pitiful minds.'

'I be sorry for young Mihnea as he be lost to us likes my brother,' Tariana stated calmly, noticing the guards retreat. 'And warn you that soldiers from the same lands as Henrik may not be as loyal.' She was joined by the vagabond girl who rushed to her side and held her arm. 'I was nothing but loyal to you Master Vlad.'

'Yes, but you see pretty gypsy girl,' Vlad turned to say as he smirked, 'you be once a good scout and have purpose, but these visions you said you had, never assisted in their predictions to warn me.'

Tariana knew that her last words had upset Vlad, and felt that the mention of his lost son and dead comrade brought back some humanity left inside his cold heart.

'I have vision that you be in danger again m' lord,' Tariana said, but saw Vlad ignore her to command his men to assemble. The vagabond girl held Tariana tight and glanced anxious at her, but Tariana directed her quiet words at the man she still somehow loved. 'But I not be telling you of it Master Vlad, as you treat me bad.'

EIGHTEEN

Tariana turned to go back to the wagon after sneaking through the undergrowth of the woodland to spy on Vlad. She had been trailing his garrison of soldiers for a day now and caught up with them passing Bran castle; pike men, archers and swordsmen marching steadily on foot to follow him and his boyars on horseback. And as it was getting dark, she had noticed them making camp and thought that she could do the same.

But on her return, she noticed Sorin throwing unsold merchandise about and digging his heels into them as they lay scattering the floor. Andrei could do nothing but watch Lydia run about gathering the garments from the muddy earth and shout for the big Russian to stop.

'What be the reason to this?' Tariana shouted.

For a moment all three froze to look at her, and then Sorin dropped all that he had to storm off and attend to the horses.

'Miss Tariana,' Lydia shrieked, 'Master Sorin go wild because he not like what we do... follow the bad man!'

'But we sell more than we thought,' Tariana stated. 'We have collected much coin and other wares. Should he not be grateful?'

'He moans as we did not get food for your camp and that we not sell all.' Lydia circled the area pulling soiled garments from the earth. 'He wants to go back to your camp.'

'We will, but we can sell the rest along the way.'

'Yes, but you follow this man we all dislike,' Andrei interjected, hobbling from his seat on a fallen tree. 'I thought we be returning to your gypsy camp?'

'We will,' Tariana said, helping Lydia collect the remaining garments. 'But first I must know where Master Vlad be going as I know he be in danger.'

'In danger with all those soldiers,' Andrei scoffed. 'Why follow a man that humiliated you?'

'I told you, if you not like where we go, you stay back in town.' She directed her voice at Lydia as she brushed past and stroked her hair. 'Maybe this our travels be too much for your grandfather?'

'We not stop in Braşov as it be too much a bad memory for Lydia… I explained this!' Andrei affirmed, his voice croaking to shout over distance. 'Besides my trade earns little with such overheads back there.'

'Your grandfather be stubborn,' Tariana said quietly to Lydia who stared back expectantly. 'I guess Sorin say same about me.'

'But it be your big friend that be most cross,' Lydia scrunched up her little, freckled nose. 'He say he should go back to camp with Kateryna.'

'Kateryna swore to help me as I stopped her punishments.'

'Yes from the very man you follow,' Andrei stated as he approached, his crutch slipping upon the muddy earth. 'Maybe I *should* go back to your camp with Kateryna and maybe Sorin.'

'I need Sorin and will speak to him.' Tariana glowered at each in turn. 'Besides, you not know the way and you need this our wagon for transport. We will return to camp once I be sure my visions not be true.' Tariana looked around but could not see the vagabond girl. 'Where be Kateryna?'

'She went to pick firewood and tell of making a camp fire.' Lydia replied softly. 'Good, we need a warm fire as it be getting cold now. We will make camp, sleep

tight and set off early on the morrow.' Tariana sorted through the soiled garments until she found a small, clean coat. 'Here Lydia, it will get cold at night so this be yours.'

'You not finish dress,' Lydia said timidly as Tariana wrapped the coat around her. 'They not suit each other.'

'Does it matter?' Andrei said bitterly, 'If we follow that man any more north, we will all freeze to death.'

'No we will not,' Tariana snapped sharply. 'Here, they return to make camp fire.' She wondered over to Sorin who dropped branches after snapping them in halves, but the big man turned away and plodded in direction of the wagon. 'I need speak with you,' she told him, but he just tended to the horses with his back to her. 'I know you not like what I do, but I ask of this one favour… apart from that you protect both Lydia and Kateryna.' Tariana recognised Sorin's resentment in his sullen face as he turned to sign. 'I know you not like this, but just this one thing and we go back with these our new friends, I promise.' He sniffled and grunted to show his disproval, but looked upon her with sympathetic eyes. 'I told Lydia to have my herb tea, but she not like, so it be yours if you want?' She recognised a glimmer of a smile. 'You know it soothes your nerves and helps sleep with you. I make it up with you when all this I want be done. But for now, we make an early start on the morrow.' She reached up to stroke his weary face and fingered with his scruffy beard. 'We be through too much to have now these differences my friend. Kateryna looks up to you and likes you to protect.'

'Do we not all?' a little voice declared from behind them.

'You should not snoop up on peoples,' Tariana told as she turned to see Lydia. 'I not know word snoop,' Lydia said looking bewildered.

'I thought you be scared of our big friend here?'

'He not so bad,' Lydia said fumbling with her fingers. 'He be like my big uncle.'

'There you are my friend,' Tariana stated, slamming her palm against the big Russian's chest. 'You be big uncle Sorin, how do that feel?'

Even Sorin began to chortle after seeing the girls laugh, but then signalled to Tariana.

'What does,' Lydia tried to copy Sorin's hand movements. 'What be it he say by moving hands?'

'He tell me that he will settle horses and after be alone to have my drink.'

'What, that horrible tea?' Lydia stuck out her tongue and scrunched up her face. 'It be horrible!'

'But it will help you sleep my child.' Tariana noticed Kateryna arranging a circle of stones to make the camp fire. 'And keep you warm now these nights be getting cold.' Lydia followed Tariana over to where Katerina was making a camp fire with twigs and branches. 'We will talk more around a nice, warm camp fire before an early start.'

After travelling several days, all but Tariana were getting grouchy. Sorin, although keeping with his chores to look after the horses, constantly grunted on the footplate to express his displeasure of trailing Vlad. Lydia and Andrei were repetitively complaining about the cold and the discomfort of travelling on a rickety wagon through perilous mountain wilderness. And although she kept herself busy with cooking after setting up camp fires, Kateryna felt anxious to them travelling so far north.

As the wagon banged and squeaked through the rocky, mountainous terrain, Sorin had decided to relieve the discomfort in his back and legs by resting on the remaining bundle of garments that Tariana and Kateryna had washed in a stream. With Kateryna resting also in the back, she and Lydia heard the big Russian start to snore and were secretly giggling. Taking the big man's place on the footplate alongside Tariana was Andrei, who kept glancing at her, obviously apprehensive to ask questions.

'You still dislike me following this man?'

'Well it be my leg,' Andrei replied as an excuse. 'The cold get into it and make it ache so terrible.'

'He most likely be miles ahead of us now,' Tariana admitted, but expressed her determination. 'But I follow the tracks and we catch up as they be fresh.'

'Why not just give up?' Andrei pained at rubbing the stump of his leg. 'We sold merchandise in that little town miles back and could stay there a while more.'

'But we lose sight and track of him.'

'But it come more a hazard the more north and high we go.' Andrei turned to see Lydia and Kateryna wrapped up in animal skins. 'Like you, they are young and take strong to it, but I...'

'And like me, they be girls and not moan much like you men.' Tariana turned to glance at Sorin asleep and snoring. 'And we be hearing him moan much, if he be able to.' She pulled on the reins to speed the horses up a stony incline, the ground now exposing fresh flurries of snow. 'Maybe you should have stayed in last town or from where you came?'

'It be Lydia I come along for,' Andrei asserted with a stern face, 'I want her to have a better future.' He then looked upon Tariana with sentiment. 'She takes good to you. You are like a mother to her... and in the coming days when I not...' His voice trailed off as he turned to look at his granddaughter again. 'But you follow blindly this man and his soldiers... most likely you have lost trail of them as this wagon be slow with all us on.'

'They not be far,' Tariana told with enthusiasm as the wagon came out of a pinewood forest and onto a mountain pass. 'See them there tracks... many marching feet melting fresh snow.'

'So where they be?'

Tariana ignored Andrei's concerns to direct the wagon through a gorge, which lead upon one of the lower pinnacles of the mountains. Concerned that the cart wheels could buckle or break, she guided the wagon down to less rocky ground. Although obscured by a narrow cluster of pine trees, she could hear voices some distance ahead. Gradually slowing the wagon, she snaked a safe path through the trees until she could hear the voices close.

On the edge of the woodland but under cover, Tariana stood on the footplate to squint in the direction from where she could hear voices. Before stepping down to disembark, she turned to acknowledge the girls and with a forefinger to her lips instructed them to be quiet. And then she signaled Kateryna to wake Sorin, but to keep him quiet.

Leaving Kateryna with Lydia in the wagon, Sorin paced quickly through the woodland to catch up with Tariana. And although limping slowly behind, Andrei followed, his curiosity too great. Eventually he caught up with both gypsies stooping to listen to the voices, but found them flummoxed by the discourse between the garrisons. Tariana stood and took a careful step forward, her one hand shielding her eyes against the low sun that shone against the powdery covering of snow. She had recognized Vlad and his banner men, his boyars and troops, but who were these others dressed in different armor and attire?

Both Sorin and Tariana turned sharp to see Andrei catch up from behind. 'Why you follow us?'

'I am curious,' Andrei replied. 'What you choose to do be affecting me and Lydia, do it not?'

'Yes but you cannot…' Tariana held her words as she heard raised voices and shouting, but could not understand the words from the unknown party.

'They be Hungarians,' Andrei declared. 'I know much their language, but it be a while since I talk such.'

'How can you be certain?' Tariana glanced at Andrei, after distinguishing bewilderment in Sorin's eyes.

'I know much their language but it be like Transylvanian.' Andrei rubbed the white bristles on his chin as he looked baffled. 'The armies of these banner men would not normally venture this far from their Hungarian borders… especially here!'

'Why, where be us… these mountains you said you know?' Tariana asked after Sorin signaled the question.

'We fought close to these here borders many years ago with the true king.' Andrei shuffled to find comfort against a fallen tree. 'These I know now as the Piatra Craiulul Mountains… and it be good that it be early… before winter sets in… as otherwise we be trudging through snows taller than your friend here.'

'But why meet here?' Tariana queried. 'Vlad say he was to do deal with the Hungarian king, but why meet here… it be so remote?' Tariana saw Sorin signal that it could be a trap. 'But he says they had arranged them a pact… for more soldiers against our common enemy.'

'Hey, so be quiet,' Andrei limped between the two and hunched forward to listen intently. 'I listen and see if I understand what is said!'

Tariana silenced and glared wondrously at Sorin, seeing that he too was amazed by the old man's interest.

'Vlad talk a little, but it is his boyar that talks in their language.' Andrei hushed both gypsies to be quiet so he could listen, and after a minute of silence, explained, 'The commander of the Hungarian garrison instructs that they are to escort the Prince of Wallachia to a keep at Visegrad under orders of King Matthias, but Vlad argues that he did not agree to this.'

'I have bad feeling about this,' Tariana exclaimed. 'Why meet them here in these mountains, so alone and high up… why not meet in town?'

'Hush lady, I listen more!' Andrei said.

But as Andrei heard Vlad protest, unsheathe his father's sword and display the crest of the Order of the Dragon, the prince did not notice another Hungarian garrison encircle his soldiers from behind and entrap them.

'What be happening?' Tariana asked impatiently.

'The boyar argues with the Hungarian, but the commander now owns up to some pretense that King Matthias wanted an alliance with Vlad. Instead the Prince of Wallachia is to be taken for trials and sentenced for many a crimes against the king's people… he read off many names of people and evidence that condemns Vlad to his crimes. His men are told to put down their arms and…'

Before Andrei could explain more, it all happened too fast; Vlad's men drew swords and raised their bows, but many were slaughtered before they could even protest. The clashing of swords continued for several minutes but with his depleted army, Vlad knew he could only give in. He jumped off his horse and stabbed his father's longsword into the snow-covered ground, declaring to be given a fair trial as he had been lied to and led on false pretense.

As the Prince of Wallachia and his remaining men were seized by the Hungarians, all three watching stared at each other in silence until Tariana instructed.

'We must follow but quietly.'

'You must be joking,' Andrei exclaimed, and seeing Sorin nod in agreement, continued, 'We cannot interfere with this any longer… it be political.' He saw that Tariana obviously did not understand his last word. 'He is to be taken to Visegrad for sentence to his crimes… and that be… miles into the borders of Hungary.'

'I not care,' Tariana retorted, 'we go but track in secret.'

Andrei glared at Sorin for support, but saw the big man just roll his eyes. Through all his time with Tariana, Sorin knew better than not to argue with such a stubborn, young woman. And as Sorin followed Tariana briskly back to the cart, Andrei hobbled along as fast as his crutch could take him.

Their arguments had subsided by the time they had travelled throughout the day to reach Sighişoara, slowly and carefully tracking the captured Vlad through snow powdered mountain hills, until they descended to less rocky ground. From what they had observed when close, there was no let up to Vlad's protests and many of his men found arrows in their back whilst trying to escape. And so when the Hungarians made camp at night, their prisoners were tied to trees or bound in lines and guarded.

As Andrei had fought alongside Hungarians against the Ottoman Empire, it came all too much for him to watch the two sides squabble, but muttered his protests in secret. Sorin too was troubled, wanting Tariana to forget this prince; a changed man who now had no want for her. But Sorin knew he was indebted to her, and now had other people to protect, friends he liked.

Kateryna was mostly quiet, but that night disclosed her knowing some of the Hungarian language as her father had travelled from the northwest to prosper in Wallachia. And so it was in Braşov that her father had met his future wife. Seated around a small camp fire Kateryna had made, Tariana asked more about the quiet girl's history, but Lydia was cold and more hungry than usual, the hot, herbal tea not helping her sleep as much. And so the little girl turned the conversation to more pressing concerns.

'I think me and grandfather should go back to that last town,' she said looking sheepishly around at everyone. 'Winter be coming and you drag us on through these mountains to… where we be grandfather?'

'We be nearing Bistritza… about a day's ride,' he replied to Lydia. 'It is not too late to turn back. But should we go on any further, then…?' he looked expectantly at Tariana.

'We not turn back now,' Tariana spoke adamantly. 'We come this far and will get to this keep at Visegrad.'

'If we not freeze up here first,' Lydia whispered angrily. 'It be so cold.'

'Sorin and I have travelled many lands and survived much the cold.' Tariana stated getting up to walk over to Lydia. 'We have good clothing now to keep you warm… and we make you little boots for cold feet.' She rubbed vigorously Lydia's back before sitting beside her. 'I make a different soup on the morrow… spiced to keep you warm.'

'It be many days ride to this keep at Visegrad and who knows who we will meet on the Hungarian border.'

'Who is this King Matthias Corvinus anyhow?' Kateryna interrupted Andrei. All sat quiet, staring perplexed at her until Tariana proclaimed.

'We could get supplies from this town Bistritza… maybe sell last of the attire?' 'No, I think it be best to avoid such a large town,' Andrei advised, scratching the

white bristles of his growing beard. 'If I remember, those north and west of Transylvania do not like travellers.'

'Then we stick to the hillsides and track from there.' 'But it be more difficult and slow,' Andrei countered.

'And it be colder in the high grounds,' Lydia interjected, scrunching up her nose. 'And as Sorin expressed his concern yesterday,' Andrei continued, 'the cart be

close to breaking and in need of repair.'

'Then I and Sorin will go to Bistritza with wagon to repair.'

'So what do we do,' Lydia groaned, 'wait in the mountains to freeze?'

'On return we be going north and west where it be warmer, and with repairs the wagon go faster on lower ground.'

'It will still take many days travel to the Hungarian border and a little more to Visegrad.'

'But you know the keep at Visegrad,' Tariana asserted with Andrei. 'You know the way in case we lose sight of Vlad.' Tariana huffed to see Sorin sign for them to lose track of the prince completely. 'We track around town, see to repairs and all be good.'

'We may not get safe passage through Bistritza and with only me and Kateryna knowing Hungarian, we may be challenged.'

'Then you teach me some their words so I can pry,' Tariana stated as she winked at Lydia. 'Besides this be adventure… better than struggle to live in Braşov.'

Andrei was tired of arguing, but knew Lydia needed a fresh start somewhere else; that he wanted to see her secure before his age and disability got the better of him. And of course with Tariana and her trusted friends, he knew his granddaughter was safe.

'I for one be glad we quit Braşov and leave behind that lying husband,' Kateryna said to interrupt Andrei's thoughts. 'I too do not like to go all this way, but Tariana must have good reason to follow this Vlad.'

'She must love him very much,' Lydia whispered.

'He deserves a chance to better himself again,' Tariana explained, glaring at each face to see them nibbling on stale bread. 'I know deep in heart he be a righteous Christian man… to again defend these lands against our enemy… he just needs help.'

'You must love him a lot,' Kateryna professed quietly. 'More than I did that husband of mine.'

'But to follow him day after day, as grandfather say,' Lydia moaned, disliking her stale bread, 'he not deserve it as he be guilty to the murder of my…'

Andrei had never known his granddaughter openly acknowledge the murder of her parents and so put his arms around her. She then snuggled her face within his chest to hide her tears.

'I cannot accept that he be fully guilty to such crimes,' Tariana professed before standing to stare at each in turn, her eyes eventually settling on Lydia who peeked at her from out of hiding. 'And did your father not say that forgiveness be the most Christian virtue?'

'It still be stupid to follow a man most of us hate and go…'

'Lydia and you know that we should forgive those whom trespass against us,' Tariana interrupted Andrei.

'You may love him, but I think he not love you like how mommy and daddy loved each other.' Lydia spat out her stale bread and threw the remaining crust onto the camp fire. 'We not have a good meal in ages.'

'We must use up what be left,' Tariana explained. 'We sell much in towns and buy foods, but need to keep enough to last.' She looked at Lydia wiping her mouth with the back of her hand. 'You could have had it toasted.'

'It be toasted now,' Kateryna smirked as she watched the crust burn in the fire. 'It be cinders soon.' But then the young woman stared up at Tariana with concern. 'There be five mouths to feed and we eat more as it be cold.'

'If there be good people on the outskirts of Bistritza, maybe me and my granddaughter could settle there… be less a burden on this your venture.'

'We be strong as a group as we be of help to each other,' Tariana responded and looked at Lydia. 'I promised to look after Lydia like her be my own daughter to give you peace of mind, and I stick to that promise. I shall always be there for her. We talked much about this and settle this many days ago.' Andrei looked upon Tariana with sentiment, knowing she was right. 'I tell you of my plans once we reach Visegrad. Once we oversee the keep, I can find a secret way in and…' Tariana's clarification trailed off as she watched Sorin sign his argument; that they come all this way without thought to some final resting place, and that she risks her life and theirs just to help some prince that is clearly now a broken man. 'Should we not rescue the man, who did us,' she directed at the giant Russian. 'He took us in under his wing; otherwise we get slaughtered out in wilderness.' She saw him sign that this was only because they helped to save him in the night attack. 'Still he made us safe, feed us and show compassion.' Sorin signalled his displeasure; stating that Tariana's obsession with such a Lord was wasted, as such a prince would never marry a simple gypsy girl, even if he did once love her. 'I not argue about any of this anymore Sorin… we travel before daybreak on the morrow…' But then she saw him grunt and sign that she was crazy and that he would refuse to go along anymore. 'Look my old friend, I know we be all tired after travelling day and night, but once we catch up with the garrison at Visegrad we can rest and make better ours plans.' She saw all others looking up at her, the glint of firelight in each of their eyes. 'We go on and things be better… get wagon repaired and sell last of merchandise for food.' She ran her fingers vigorously through her shaggy dark hair before sitting. 'We need to keep strong… we need to keep together!'

After days of carefully tracking Vlad's captors, they caught up with the garrison on the edge of a copse of pine trees, overlooking the keep at Visegrad. Although they had travelled over many rocky hillsides, the repairs Sorin had overseen to the wagon had been sufficient to keep it in good working order. And by selling the last of their merchandise to Hungarian locals on the edges of Bistritza, Tariana and Lydia had learned some of the language with from Kateryna. But by now their food resources were again running low.

As they rested in hiding of hillside woodland, to watch the garrison enter the keep, all eyes turned to Tariana. She could see by their concern that her task to get in covertly was going to be difficult. But as the sun set and dusk approached, she observed traders and farmers wheel stock in and out of the keep through an entrance aside the gatehouse. She also noticed several maids and servants come and go.

This gave Tariana an idea, but one which would require Kateryna's assistance. As Andrei was incapable due to his disability and age, Tariana would need Kateryna to translate any discourse that may prove vital in helping Vlad. But as it was Vlad that had prompted punishment upon her, it may prove difficult to persuade Kateryna to conform to her plan. Nonetheless she knew Kateryna was still obliged to her and so hoped she could coax her. But for now she would let her group rest and take camp for the night, making sure they were some distance away so the flame of a camp fire would not be spotted.

That night before they retired early and doused the camp fire, Tariana told of her plans, but again most in the group was not entirely convinced or enthusiastic.

Whether they had been lucky, or it just came suddenly convenient, next morning Tariana saw ale casks being examined by a guard before a cart was due to enter the keep. At first she thought they were all full to deliver trade, but noticed some empties to refill. And as Kateryna was quite petite and nimble like herself, she told her friend of her plan.

As the guard browsed over papers and questioned the tradesman up front, the two girls raced swiftly to the wagon, finally resting their backs against the tailboard, their eyes eagerly searching for people who may have seen them. As they watched from afar, Sorin silenced Lydia's questioning to see Tariana and Kateryna squeeze themselves into two empty casks, the girls holding tight the lids from inside. No sooner had they hid, they could feel the wagon moving. And after hearing the wheels grind over coarse gravel, Tariana knew they had entered the courtyard of the keep.

When the wagon stopped, Tariana whispered aloud for Kateryna to stay put, but then silenced to listen to distant voices. Tariana was the first to sneak out of hiding, and seeing it safe, slapped her palm against the cask in which Kateryna hid. Soon both girls were out and hiding in an alleyway beside a small alehouse.

But being strangers to Visegrad, Kateryna had to ask for directions to a place that was deemed as a court of law. Eventually, after flirting and convincing some nobleman to divulge, she was successful in finding the way to a building that they believed was some sort of courthouse. And as Vlad's horse was being held by Hungarian guards, along with his captive soldiers, the two girls were confident they were close.

Secretly they snuck around the side of the building, each looking out for one another as they searched for some sort of access. And as luck would find them again, Tariana noticed a partially open window, of which with help from nearby crates, gave them access. However, inside the courthouse they were nervous and at a loss where to go, but soon heard voices as they crept gingerly through shadowy corridors.

Suddenly Kateryna stopped Tariana by holding firm her shoulder; her face sharp and expectant after understanding discourse from a high, central room. The slim, attractive girl held a forefinger to her lips to signal Tariana to be quiet. She focused to listen on the heated conversation of which she deciphered was between Vlad, his translating boyar and many interrogators, one she deduced was the Hungarian King, Matthias Corvinus.

Kateryna explained quietly to Tariana that Vlad was being forcefully interrogated by many Hungarian boyars, including the king himself. The heart of the discussion was that they had heard many terrible accounts about the Prince of Wallachia torturing and murdering Hungarians just because they could not pay taxes or that he deemed them criminals. She silenced for a while to listen, but then told of the numerous accounts to which he was sentenced as guilty. At first Vlad calmly denied their accusations, but came aggressive; carelessly revealing that he had indeed been guilty of some.

Tariana shifted forward to take a peek at the proceedings, but was pulled back by a fretful Kateryna, her friend pleading as not to get caught. However, Tariana's glimpse of the courtroom was enough to catch sight of Vlad, and she grinned at Kateryna as the girl explained she would only interpret the Hungarian if they kept in hiding. Tariana agreed, but wanted to know what was being discussed as the conversation turned into shouting.

Kateryna listened and translated the discourse in bursts; that the king was decisive in his decision to imprison Vlad in a pit at Visegrad until he returned from travels which could take weeks. Although in shackles, Vlad lunged forward in protest and condemned the king for being deceitful, but the chains withheld him and he soon found the point of a pike at his chest.

As they overheard the king command orders and exit the courtroom, the girls could hear Vlad denounce the Hungarian king and that he had no authority to imprison him. As they left quietly through their secret window, Kateryna heard Vlad implore his want for laws and justices; that fear was the only way to control unruly people. And then, as he was dragged away, Vlad reminded all those about him, to who had for many years defended Christian lands from the Ottoman Empire.

From around the corner of the building, both girls spied to watch the guards hold Vlad captive as the king bellowed orders before riding off with his escort.

'How do we find out where he be held?' Tariana asked, staring wide-eyed at Kateryna. 'You mention something of a pit?'

'I have plan to stay in the keep a while,' Kateryna explained slowly as she thought. 'I will find out what be happening as I look for work. Maybe I get supplies to take back to our camp.' She hesitated to think again. 'I can try to get you in on the morrow.'

Tariana looked and pointed to Vlad's remaining soldiers. 'What will become of his soldiers?'

Kateryna shrugged at first. 'Maybe them boyars be spared, imprisoned like your Vlad… but the rest?' She then sliced her forefinger across her throat to signal their execution. 'Come on, we follow to see where he be imprisoned, and then you get back to the others.'

'You not come back with me?'

'No, I speak language and so can get work,' Kateryna grinned. 'Maybe get food and money.' She opened out the palms of her hands to express her suggestion, 'Besides someone has got to try and get you back in.'

'How will we know where to meet up?'

'Go through that side gate,' Kateryna instructed. 'I saw some maids and servants use it, so maybe they–'

'But when will you be there?' Tariana interrupted fretfully.

'I will try and get you through at daybreak as those deliveries are then.' 'You promise?'

'I promise,' Kateryna reassured as she winked. 'You want to see this *Vlad* again, do you not?'

Nineteen

It was still dark and gloomy at dawn. Not only was sunrise getting later due to oncoming winter, but the sky was as dull and overcast as it had been yesterday. Tariana had strolled down to the side gate that Kateryna had mentioned, trying her best to pretend to be some employee of the keep to await entry. But as she saw guards stare her up and down, she felt awkward and fidgeted. Although she had learned many of their basic words, when the guards questioned her and sniggered, she could only reply that she was waiting for someone. One guard scrutinized her inquisitively but then smiled; his interest in her obvious that he found her attractive.

For several uncomfortable minutes she toyed with her headscarf and necklace charm, not answering anymore questions and just smiling back. But then a voice from inside the gatehouse called out to let her in. The guard nearest the gate turned to see Kateryna approach and heard her proclaim that her cousin was to be granted access as she was to work with her in the tavern. The guard asked for some type of permit and Kateryna obliged by removing a rolled up piece of paper from a low-cut blouse. Indeed she made sure his eyes adored her bosom as he rolled out the so-called permit to find a note and a small bribe. At first the guard was unimpressed and snubbed her, but as she snatched back the note and described to what he would miss that night, the guard then looked at Tariana. Seeing her now quite close, the guard turned his admiring eyes from Tariana to notice Kateryna wink at him. As she described that, although it was her cousin's first day at the tavern, she would serve him free ale later if he obliged to let her in. As she went on to describe that her cousin was bashful but amorous, a crowd now joined Tariana to await entry.

After recognizing regular workers that bunched around her, another guard stepped forward to unlock the gate and let them pass, Tariana luckily one with them. And before the first guard could remonstrate, Kateryna had grabbed Tariana's hand and they were racing through the keep, weaving each way and that between buildings until they rested to catch their breath outside the tavern.

'I'm sure he be suspicious of me,' Tariana said. 'That's why he not let me in.' 'Why should he be so?'

'I picked the lock last night to get out, but my hairpin broke so I could not lock it before heading back to our camp.'

'How are our friends?'

'Alright, but still angry with me I guess.' Tariana changed the conversation to discuss the guards. 'Do the guards always ask for permits?'

'Not always… well until they get to know you.' Kateryna grinned wide. 'You should try my trick… the one I just did with that guard.'

'It makes you out to be some whore if you do that.'

'But it works though, does it not?' she countered. 'Besides they be easy to please these Hungarian men… quite stupid in a way.'

'Talking of men, and be it more important, did you find out where Vlad be?' 'He be kept on the west side of the keep, but have guards patrol the area.'

'Can you take me to him?'

'I will later,' Kateryna agreed. 'But first you must learn your work in the tavern.' 'What work, I did not ask for this?'

'You said you wanted to get in and out of the keep,' Kateryna replied stern faced. 'You take up this work and play my tricks on that guard… he let you in as he likes you, I can tell.' She smiled before announcing, 'Besides, I will not be working there soon and promised the innkeeper that I have you replace me.'

'But why,' Tariana was baffled, 'you only just started here?'

'I know, but that be another story.' Kateryna diverted her conversation to discuss other matters. 'I show you innkeeper and how to work there… then when you know the area… we go to see your man.'

Later that day, after Kateryna had shown Tariana the formalities of work and the gypsy had learned more Hungarian during her shift at the tavern, Kateryna directed Tariana to where prisoners were confined in pit cells.

'I not see him,' Tariana asked anxiously. 'Where be it he be held captive?'

'That one,' Kateryna pointed whilst wary of patrolling guards. 'They be like holes in the ground… square pits with high stone walls with only one route out – an iron grate that be locked and too high to climb or jump.' Tariana crept closer but Kateryna held her arm. 'You be better to stay in keep until tonight and try seeing him then.' Tariana's face was full of expectancy and so Kateryna advocated, 'You be best to try and see him at midnight as the guards not patrol so much.' But then her face went grave. 'But at night they have vicious dogs.' Kateryna studied Tariana's face as she looked reassuringly at her and toyed with a charm about her neck. 'I be sorry, as in future you must do this alone… I not stay any longer.'

'But you be of big help,' Tariana stated holding her hand whilst frowning, 'What come of me if I not know much this language?'

'You be alright,' Kateryna assured, 'you learn quick the language.' 'But why you not stay?'

'I miss those be at camp.' Kateryna pulled at Tariana's arm to make her follow after noticing guards nearby.

'That not be the true reason, be it?'

'Alright, I confess, so if you be asked, you can lie about me.' Kateryna detailed. 'I happened to take a little money after some nobleman got me tipsy, and so must avoid him.'

'You must not make with men like to how you be suggestive to that guard.'

'But he took dirty pleasure from my body, and so I take money as compensation.'

Tariana did not understand the meaning of her last word, and so asked, 'You slept with some Lord and took his money?'

Kateryna glared at Tariana before stating, 'And you would not sleep with this

Vlad, but for *free*?'

'That be different,' Tariana paused sharply to realize she had lied; that indeed she had already spent such a time with Vlad, remembering vividly her night of passion with him. 'I love him as a man, not to take reward from some strange Lord or noble.'

'Yes, I be sure of that,' Kateryna rolled her eyes before pulling Tariana along to hide them out of sight of the guards. 'You will watch them and get to know their patrols.' She glanced about quickly before continuing, 'Maybe you get to see your man, maybe you will not, but keep safe from the guards and try at night.'

'Can the grate be opened?'

'Do not even attempt it… it be locked solid,' Kateryna warned, but then winked, 'unless you can flirt with that guard to give up his keys?'

'But you cannot stay and help?'

'I do more than be good to help you my friend. Get you in and give you work.' Kateryna held Tariana's hand between her two. 'But I fret that soon I get known to that man, and be back in situation likes to where you saved me.' She smiled and hugged her tight before saying close to her face. 'I do more than you ask and now we be even.' She stepped away, but turned before heading for the side gate, 'I see you back with those camped west… await your return.'

'If I get caught,' Tariana pleaded, 'you look after Lydia like be a mother?'

'Wild gypsy friend,' Kateryna said before leaving, 'you be smarter than me… I just hope he be worth it!'

Tariana sensed a warmth grow inside her; to remember her group camped outside the keep and her flirtatious friend that had just left. But gradually she came sullen, fretful to be alone and to the risky task just to see Vlad. And had his already short imprisonment dampened his memory of her? Would he in fact want to be with her or even remember her? She was excited but anxious to see him, but as Kateryna advised, she would have to wait until midnight. More importantly, she would need to avoid the guards.

Awkwardly she shut the tavern door, trying best to conceal the bundle of food wrapped up in cloth. Carefully she stuffed it down between her blousing and leather jerkin before quietly racing through passages between buildings. She stopped at the edge of the guard's room and observed the two night patrolmen inside the shabby hut. With both inside and talking, she was confident that near midnight she could at least get half an hour before they strolled their patrol pattern again. But she would no doubt have to be cautious.

Quickly Tariana went past other cells, and in one had recognized the boyar who translated on Vlad's behalf, but was glad that he had not seen her or called out. Soon she was kneeling on sandy earth close to the iron grate of Vlad's cell, its bars no more than a thumb length apart. She lowered to whisper aloud and called to Vlad, but in response she heard nothing. Again she called, but there was nothing but a deathly silence.

'My dearest Vlad,' she whispered again. 'I forgive to what you did and know you be a righteous man… a good warrior to great Christian belief.' But again there was silence. 'I not forget or regret what we had together although you lost poor Jusztina… I be sorry for your loss, truly I be… but we need you to defend this *our* realm… I need you… want you be with me again… please be the same man I met after that night attack.' She paused and felt a tear escape one eye as she pushed the squashed bundle through the grill. 'I bring food but it may not be much.'

Again there was a haunting silence until she heard chains rattle. As the night sky cleared of racing clouds, a near full moon gleamed down upon her. And through the grill Tariana could see the shadow of a body appear and a hand reach to grab the bundle. She squinted to see Vlad's bruised and battered fingers try awkwardly to unravel the knotted cloth, his weak and lacerated wrists shackled with tight iron manacles, both which were joined by short, iron chains. And between the chains was a large rusty padlock that lolled about to hinder his attempt to eat.

'I not know why you come as I treated you unkind.' Vlad spoke, his voice coarse as he nibbled at the fine, fresh bread and cheese. 'I do not deserve such sympathy.'

'We shall forgive those who trespass against us,' Tariana recited, thinking of young Lydia. 'I know there be a strong soul within you Master Vlad and it be of goodness and honour, but I need that man to be with us again.'

'As you can see, I have no freedom to do such here.' Vlad choked to snigger on his food. 'I cannot even eat properly this you give.'

'Then be and take this,' Tariana said, throwing down a large hairpin onto the dirt floor of the pit. In the moonlight she saw his fingers reach and pick it up. 'Remember how I showed you to pick locks?'

'Yes, I remember' Vlad said slowly, 'but my fingers, I cannot...'

Tariana heard voices and so popped her head up to glance about; the guards were talking some way off, but would soon part to circle the area. She crouched down lower, hoping that she would have a least a few more minutes. And then she was delighted to see Vlad spring the lock to the padlock, but broke her hairpin in the process.

'You be free,' Tariana said, her voice somewhat loud. 'But keep it secret until I find...' Shadows of the guards were approaching.

'I have such the same on my ankles,' Vlad whimpered, 'but they be much the larger.' He grabbed the remaining food to retreat into the shadows. 'Why bother, they be no way out until the king return... and then I be...'

'You save some food for the morrow and the next day,' Tariana instructed. 'Hide it so the guards do not eat your foods themselves.'

'At least my hands be free,' Vlad said from a dark corner of the pit. 'I can mark the days until maybe I be free, or condemned to death.'

'You not speak that way Master Vlad,' Tariana tutored, her eyes searching the darkness and moonlit shadows in the pit. 'I get more food, but it may not be for some time.'

'But why would you still care?' Vlad called, shifting his body to glance up at her and see the moonlight gleam against her dark hair, her face stern but white like an angel. 'Why take pity on a man who be tortured and broken?'

'I fret the guards be close,' Tariana exclaimed. 'I return soon as I can. I have friends who be camped out west of the keep and its wall not be far.' She saw a guard turn towards the cells. 'I must go but will return, I promise.'

Vlad managed to find strength in his legs to stand and reach his hands up towards the grate. 'Please, I be needing more… I be weak and hate the stench of this place.'

'Better get used to it, you may be there for some time,' a deep voice announced as Vlad saw the shadow of a guard in the moonlight. 'Should you not starve first?'

The guard chuckled as Vlad envisaged Tariana's pale but beautiful face staring down at him instead of the guards.

'I prefer my friend's company,' Vlad said, not realizing he talked aloud.

'Your only friend down there old prince, be the darkness.' The guard chuckled as he stepped away.

It was not until she reached the side gate that Tariana realized that Vlad had used her hairpin. She cursed and fretted, thinking she may have to persuade one of the guards to let her out, and at such a late hour, they would probably grill her. She peered into the alcove of the small guardhouse and noticed the guard who obviously fancied her. But how could she lead him on; she could not act under pretense like Kateryna?

For a long moment she leaned with her back against the cold, stone wall, her body tense, but then remembered; surely she had another hairpin to hold up her hair. Searching her headscarf, to her relief she found one more, but would it be sturdy enough to spring the iron lock.

What luck she thought, as she toyed with it in the lock of the side gate, suddenly pleased to hear it spring open. Quickly she squeezed through a narrow parting, trying not to open it wide and make it screech against its hinges. Quietly she closed the gate, but attempting to lock it behind her, felt the hairpin break as it had before. Nonetheless, as she ran for the nearest tree, she amused herself; she had seen Vlad, freed his hands and given him food. And now with his hands free, maybe he would find ways to unshackle his feet. But still she fretted as she pondered to think; apart from returning with food a next time, what else could she do?

As she lost sight of firelights glimmering in the distance from the keep, Tariana found the countryside eerie and dark; the moonlight disappearing as clouds raced across the sky to leave the wilderness black. Her eyes constantly blurred as they tried best to focus on her path ahead; her route constantly thwarted by brambles and slippery undergrowth as she eventually snaked her way onto a woodland path. And as she recognized a large fallen tree (that her group had to meander the wagon around previous), she reconstructed her path back to where her friend's would be camped.

Through the darkness, she had stumbled against exposed roots and wiry brambles, but was confident to be on the right path. Sometimes she would navigate her way using the position of the moon, but mostly now it had become hidden by cloud. And besides, things always looked different in the dark. Suddenly ahead she noticed a glimmering flame and headed towards it, but stopped as branches snapped beneath her boots. What if they were enemy soldiers or hostile dwellers, she thought. It was a chance she would have to take, and so stepped ever so carefully closer.

It was not until the girl turned to place broken branches in a sack hanging at her waist, that she recognized Kateryna. But suddenly a hand grasped her shoulder to turn her unsteady on her feet. She grasped for her dagger, but suddenly realized that it was not there; that indeed the man she had just seen had took it. But then another large and powerful hand held her other shoulder to steady her. As her fright calmed, in the emerging moonlight, she could see Sorin, his eyes intense and his face a scowl.

'By joys it be you, big friend,' Tariana gasped as her pounding heart slowed. 'You be giving me a scare!' Sorin signaled his apology, but knew he had no way to warn her. 'I know my friend, but why do you not whistle or something.' He signed again but with some annoyance. 'Ah you cannot, as you have no...' Tariana tried to whistle and found her tongue necessary. 'Then just use your lips,' she exemplified, '*pssst... pssst!*' She pushed his hands from her shoulders and turned towards Kateryna, her thoughts now of worry, as she failed to lock again the side gate of the keep.

Within an hour Tariana was seated with her friends around a low camp fire. At first they were all glad to see her, but now as she described seeing Vlad and the condition he was in, they stared at one another, each with their own thoughts.

'He deserves to what he gets,' Andrei exclaimed unsympathetically. 'By what happened to Kateryna, I have no doubt he be guilty of some, if not all those be crimes.'

'He was nasty man when he murder mommy and daddy,' Lydia whimpered to say. 'They not get as he gets... what grandfather call, justice?'

'You must love him very much for one reason or be another,' Kateryna stated, putting another branch onto the dying fire. 'It must be better a reason than I ever had for any man.'

'Sorin tell some of your past,' Lydia revealed. 'I guess you love this prince to get wealth and fortune.'

'I not do it for that; I do such by heart and know this man's soul.' Tariana glanced around at each face before focusing on Lydia. 'How can Sorin tell such stories if he be...? She failed to state her last word.

'We draw pictures, me and Sorin,' Lydia smirked, wiping clean her scrunched up nose. 'I learn some words from his hands.'

'Is that so,' Tariana interjected. 'Not so afraid of my big friend anymore.' 'We all be puzzled to why you want to help him so,' Kateryna cut in.

'What else we be doing?' Andrei asked, nibbling on toasted bread. 'Carted miles over mountains and wilderness to a foreign land where we be sat not knowing one another's future.'

'I have work at tavern,' Tariana said. 'Get money for keeps, and can get foods.' 'Yes, after Kateryna managed to get it you,' Andrei countered. 'Risked herself for

this selfish exhibition.'

'You mean expedition,' Kateryna corrected.

'No it be an exhibition,' Andrei animated strongly. 'Be like some freakish show and we be puppets to her.'

'I try show you better the life,' Tariana stated aloud. 'Want us all to be better and so we must get on.' She rifled angrily with her hair. 'Just let me help some more and then we be moving on.'

'The way I see it, he not last much longer in there,' Kateryna stood to say before marching off. 'He will starve to death within a week as they not feed him.'

'I know he mean a lot to you, but I still not see what you can do,' Lydia said slowly. 'Kateryna tells us what them prisons be like.'

'If God wants his soul early, he shall have it,' Andrei interjected, 'if he not go elsewhere for his evil crimes.'

'Yes, you all have your beliefs; some show more the sympathy than others,' Tariana felt her body burn with anger. 'You not see the man in that there pit… a prince that once was… a future king that could save this and many other lands from that our true enemy.' She paused momentarily, standing to toy with her necklace charm. 'Now such a weak but good Christian man should starve to death by the very people he trusted to want to stand and fight with… men from the same lands as Henrik, but truly not the same.' She began to stride up and down aside the campfire. 'I felt there be a special bond between us before his wife die and son be captured. Poor Jusztina, no doubt she had no choice but to commit a sin in the eyes of our Lord to escape the filthy hands of that our enemy.' She sat again, but found that her nerves had not calmed. 'The only thing I be guilty for, be spending little and precious time with such a man shortly after…' Tariana lowered her head and interweaved her fingers together. 'I cannot let that man starve to death in such a pit, it be heartless.'

'But you not see all what he did; that be heartless. And not just Lydia's parents,' Andrei declared. 'Inciting his boyars to gather people and put on them unfair laws and taxes… incur suffering to not only foreign merchants and such like, but to them his own people.'

Tariana looked up to see Sorin grunting and nodding his head, but stared down into the flames of the campfire, trying to ignore him. And then she heard him grunt aloud and start trying to whistle.

'*Pssst… pssst*,' Sorin's lips vibrated to sound. '*Pssst… pssst.*'

Tariana looked up at Sorin to see him also quickly and repeatedly clicking his fingers. And then seeing he had caught her attention, started to signal that such the loss of Vlad's wife and son had made an already corrupt man as mean and sinister as that brother of his, Radu.

'Sorin, I believe that not be so,' Tariana directed to disagree with the Russian. 'I swear I will somehow rescue this man who was once a prince, so he govern as the King of Wallachia and defeat all those that be our enemies… keep these Turks from invading and pilfering our lands, and unite many other lands to stop those who want to defy us our faith.'

'It all sounds and be good, my dearest Tariana,' Andrei said, 'but he be locked to starve in a pit.' He looked up to stare at her in earnest. 'How do you propose in getting him out?'

TWENTY

Again Tariana cautiously closed the side door of the tavern whilst trying to conceal a bundle of food down between her blousing and leather jerkin. As she turned and looked around, she slung a water pouch over her shoulder and positioned it to lie beside her waist. However, what she did not notice was the figure behind, its pair of eyes watching her inquisitively.

She went to sprint and visit Vlad, but found her path blocked by a man; a familiar face to which she had come to loathe. It was the guard from the side gate who she knew now fancied her, but her pretense at being nice was wearing thin. And he kept asking questions to which country she had come from, deducing that her native country was anything but Hungary. To stop him from getting too inquisitive, she had bit her tongue to flirt like Kateryna, but it was obvious that he was getting the wrong impression.

'What have you there pretty lady? The guard asked.

She understood most of his words, but deduced what he asked by him staring at both the water pouch and the bundle of food.

'To take home for supper,' Tariana replied the best she could in his language. 'For me and my cousin… you remember her?'

'What be in the pouch?' He pointed to it hanging at her waist, whilst his eyes studied the curvature of her hips.

'Why, it be just water.'

'You could have your supper in the guardhouse,' he prompted, his eyes peeking at the half concealed bundle. 'I be alone a while and have hidden a bottle of wine.'

'No, thank you,' she said courteously whilst smiling, 'I must go, meet my cousin.

We have long journey on the morrow.'

'You be leaving your work here as bar maiden?'

'Briefly, I leave to comfort my cousin… she had loss in family,' she lied, but felt that she was getting better at it. 'I must get on as I be late.'

'That is a strange charm about your neck,' he said, again studying her face and bosom, 'A family heirloom?'

'Something like that,' Tariana was fidgeting again as she knew he was purposely trying to delay her. 'Please, I must be off.'

She scuttled around him to briskly walk in the opposite direction of the cells, but knew that once she was rid of him, she could double back.

'Maybe another time then, pretty girl?' He proposed as she sped off.

After skirting quickly between buildings and in the dark of a passageway, she stopped to ensure he had gone. And surely enough she noticed him saunter his way back towards the guardhouse. But now he had seen her, Tariana worried about getting out. What if she could not pick the gate lock with her last twisted hairpin and needed that guard to let her out? And after visiting Vlad for half an hour, he may have the question to why she had not gone already, if as she had said, she was in such a hurry. She clawed her confidence back. She had not seen Vlad for days and so he would need food. Another day late and she could well find him starved to death.

Avoiding the guards to sneak to his cell, she called softly down to Vlad, but again was greeted with silence.

'Master Vlad, Prince of Wallachia,' she called again. 'I bring food and a pouch of water, but hide it good and make it last.' She pushed the bundle of food through the grill and saw it hit the cell floor. 'I not be sure when I can return as the guards be getting suspicious.'

She squinted at the bundle of food to see if a hand would grab it, but instead from the shadows, a rat came sniffing. She cursed to see another appear, inquisitive of the smell, and so threw down the pouch of water; it being just slim enough to slide between the bars. As the pouch hit the cold earth, it scared the rats away, but soon she could see from the cascading moonlight, that again the rats came sniffing and started to nibble at the cloth.

'Master Vlad, you must take it,' she fretted, 'or those rats will get first.' She twisted to look around after hearing faraway voices. 'I take big risk to be here and so not come much.' She glanced down to see three rats now nibbling at the cloth. 'I fret I get caught and be punished. If I do, I cannot serve you.'

'Serve me?' a voice croaked. 'You not come for five days.' Vlad coughed to clear his throat as his hand reached for the water pouch. 'I know it be days. I mark it on the wall. I score each day with your hairpin.' He crawled across to swing his chains at the rats and after having to knock one off, grabbed the bundle. 'What food they throw me be scraps and be horrid… but I eat it directly as the rats get at it when I be asleep.'

'I provide more but take big a risk. I have to pick gate lock and have no more big hairpins.' She paused again to check about her. 'I fear guards will find me out as already I have left broken hairpin in lock.' In the gloom she could just make out that Vlad was drinking from the pouch. 'It be good the water? Maybe I refill, if I can return. But you must take only little a day. Make it last.'

'You be strange a gypsy, but a good woman,' Vlad croaked and coughed as the water soothed his sore and parched throat. 'You must forgive me to how I treat you, my mind be troubled since…' His voice croaked again, but Tariana knew he referred to his wife and son. 'And I be starved… be so weak and queasy.' He coughed again as he went to ask out of curiosity. 'How did you find out I be imprisoned here?'

'We followed you from Braşov to where you be arrested and taken captive in those snowy crags. Then we tracked you to be here, on the borders of Hungary.'

'We,' Vlad enquired. 'Who be with you?'

'You remember Sorin, the big man from lands north and east of mine… and now there be that shoemaker and his granddaughter, the one who had her parents…' Tariana felt a sudden guilt and contemplated to what she was doing there. However, she continued, even though the next person was also resentful to her helping him. 'And that girl you not punish… I help her and so she help me in return.'

'One good deed deserves another,' Vlad said quietly, but then raised his voice to ask, 'Where they be now?'

'They be camped west, not far from this keep… the outer wall be not far from your cell.'

Your cell, Vlad pondered, as he nibbled more of the food. *What a grave thought.* 'Where did you get the food?' He asked to rid bad thoughts from his mind.

'From the tavern, that girl help find me work there.' But Tariana came more curious to why he had been imprisoned. 'Why did that king betray you... put you in here instead of fighting alongside you against them our enemies?' Vlad was quiet, but Tariana saw him eating. 'Master Vlad, you must save some for the morrow... maybe next day.'

'I eat now so those rats do not get at it.' He glanced up to admire her face gleaming pale in the dark as she searched nervously around. 'If I reach the cell grill and get out, could you get me past the guards?'

'This grate be too high and fixed,' she stated and continued to explain, 'I use side gate, as do workers, servants and alike. I have to be careful as to avoid guards... it be daunting even for me, although I be light on my feet...' Suddenly she gulped to remember the snakes writhing about her feet back in Braşov.

Strangely he could sense by her abrupt stop, that she was recalling his trick with the snakes. It was as though they perceived each other's thoughts.

'Again kind gypsy, I must apologize for tricks I played against you.' He washed down more food with a mouthful of water. 'Your defiance proved not just a good show for my boyars, but to how strong you are a person. I was impressed. That be why

I let your friend go.' He glanced up again to see her long, dark hair just touching the grate and so came curious. 'Can you and your friend get me out… somehow move that grill?'

'It be stuck solid,' Tariana groaned as she tested it. 'It be bolted into the earth somehow.' She scratched at the earth to examine the sides. 'I cannot see any lock to pick.'

'I be guessing it be too difficult for you or your friend,' he moaned coldly, resenting his confinement. 'Be too heavy to lift open, never mind remove.'

'I may be a simple woman Master Vlad, but I not be stupid… I know how to pick lock and such like… make camp, cook and sew.' As a gypsy woman, she knew also that she would make a good mother, but this bought back the memory of the sex she had had with him. 'As my friends keep telling me, maybe I should not return… that night of passion you be forgetting, as it mean nothing to you.'

'I remember,' he croaked. 'It be different to anything with…' He could not say his late wife's name and crawled out of the shadows and into the dark. 'I confess, I not be the man I once was, but now be broken and without heart and passion to fight such wars anymore.'

'Yes you be nasty to me and my friends in one way or another,' Tariana gritted her teeth. 'But you have duty to this realm, be great a king and rule with Christian values against those our enemies.' There was a daunting silence as Tariana could just about hear faraway voices. 'You must carry on strong Master Vlad.'

There was no reply for a minute as Tariana searched again for guards on patrol. 'That not be what the voice tells me,' Vlad muttered.

'What voice?' Tariana asked in surprise. 'There be another in your cell?

'Not always, but at night I hear the voice from the darkest corner of the cell.' 'Do the guards be taking tricks with you?'

'No,' Vlad paused to reflect. 'He knows things of my past that only I be knowing… tells me that I be condemned for my past sins and will join him in hell.'

'But you be a man of good… fight hard for that our Christian faith and kill only them our enemies.'

'And all the others I have wrongly punished or sentenced to death.' Vlad was clearly feeling distraught. 'He mocks at me for what I have done, but seems devilishly pleased to do so.'

'If it not be guards plaguing you or another prisoner, who be it in there with you?' 'I not know, but he haunts me at night… takes pleasure in reciting all the evil I

have done.' Vlad slapped his head in temper. 'But how can he know such things?' 'Like what, Master Vlad,' Tariana stared, her face serious. 'What be it he say?'

'I be guilty of burning crops to starve the enemy, but it be our own that I starve… poison the water to kill many our enemy, but so kill those I be supposed to rule… burn people alive as to punish them of their sins, but without justice.' His voice was rising as his temper flared. 'Why he know so much… haunt me so that I rather be dead.'

'Maybe it be that you not eat,' Tariana suggested. 'That your mind be starved… play tricks upon you.' She heard voices from not far away and so came perturbed at the intensity of Vlad's voice. 'Master Vlad, please be calm… quickly hide the food and pouch… I fret I must hide!'

'Please you must not go,' Vlad pleaded. 'You must come back or I starve.' He kicked away a rat that had come sniffing at the bundle of remaining food and then took to hide it just as heavy boots resounded above. He kicked the pouch into a dark corner just in time as he heard a deep voice.

'Talking to ghosts again my prince,' a guard ridiculed. 'It may be that you will need more time with them, as our king be taking longer on his errands.' He stared down at the pitiful excuse of a man who was once the Prince of Wallachia. 'Not a Lord or warrior knight anymore, is we? Just a half-starved captive who be talking to oneself… it be a sign of madness, that it be… and deserved so… to a man guilty of killing many our people.'

Vlad crawled to a favoured corner, taking with him the pouch and bundle, hiding them against his stomach and out of sight of the guard. He heard the guard belittle him again, but hid in the shadows to wait for him to eventually leave.

After several minutes, Vlad felt the food he had gobbled down making him drowsy. Suddenly he awoke from a sleepy stupor to hear Tariana's voice calling.

'I return Master Vlad, but fret I must go for good.'

Vlad crawled into what light shone down into the pit to admire her face before she left.

'Please my gypsy girl,' Vlad pleaded, squinting up at her, 'may I have your

crucifix to remember you and keep hold of my faith… I believe there be evil at work down here.'

'I have not my crucifix, in case I be taken by that our enemy.'

'You would not survive, if you were,' Vlad muttered flatly. 'A woman pretty as you… what those bastards would do, I hate to imagine.'

'What you be saying, I not hear you proper,' she said searching for guards. 'I have only my pendant, but that be special to me… you know it be.'

'Has it brought you protection from devilish creatures at night?'

'When I be scared, I knock it to hear it sound, but not be sure it work,' she spoke as if thinking aloud and tried it against a bar on the iron grate. 'But when I have, I never have been…' Her voice trailed off as she whipped her long, black hair behind her ears.

'Then please, my gypsy friend,' Vlad called in earnest. 'Drop it to me and I promise I will treasure it so.' He poised to stare up at her to show his conviction. 'It will help me to remember you. I will give it back to you some day. Take promise and my riches will be yours and your friends.' He held up a hand as he struggled to fully stand.

Tariana looked down with pity but recalled to have heard such promises before. 'It may keep this evil away,' Vlad professed; his face now visible in the gloom. 'If

such a Christian charm protects you, maybe it will me? And I be in such a pitiful situation as you can see.'

Suddenly he noticed Tariana had disappeared, only to be replaced by another figure. It was the guard again, glaring down at him with scorn.

'What you be mumbling about now m' Lord and prince,' the guard sniggered. 'Still haunted by ghosts?' He kneeled down to study him in the gloom. 'Your madness will be a judgement for your horrid past doings against our people. I rather relieve myself over your face than take any pity.'

Vlad cowered away until the guard had left, but crept back to call softly up to the grill. But to his despair, Tariana had gone. He asked for her several times, but there was no reply. As he gawped at the dark skies above, tears escaped his eyes, to roll down his cheek, stinging cuts and grazes he had not known were there. Dejected, Vlad sat and gazed back up to watch the fast passing clouds through the grill.

His mind came full of questions that tormented him. *How long had he been in here now? Would Tariana return? Would these friends of hers even contemplate helping him?* And his biggest question: *Would he ever get out?*

Vlad heard rats shrieking behind and turned to see a couple of the rodents come sniffing at crumbs he had left. After eating the remains, they advanced towards the smell of the food bundle, and so Vlad crept after them.

'The food be mine!' he shouted and kicked out his feet at them, rendering one dizzy and twitching upon the floor. 'It be all I get, and she may not return!'

Quickly Vlad grabbed the rat and its hind feet scratched at his wrist, its bared teeth snarled as it tried to bite his fingers. Studying its budging, black eyes as he held it tight, he came nauseated at straw-coloured saliva that oozed from its chattering teeth. Denying the creature's aggressive attempts to bite and get free, Vlad trapped its head between his other thumb and forefinger and twisted its head.

'If I not get out of here, so you will not either,' he said, as his stomach sickened to hear its little neck snap and its body twitch. 'And none of you will have *any* of my food.'

He looked curiously to how fat the rodent was and considered whether such creatures, like wild squirrels, could be eaten. For a moment he pitied the creature for it being trapped down there like him, but realized the rodent at least had the ability to climb out, should it assail the grill? 'I put you out of your misery vermin creature, but I am still here to suffer more of mine.'

In a fit of rage, Vlad slung the creature's head against the stone wall of the cell. As he removed its crushed head from the wall, he then watched the rat's blood run down over his hand. With a hard root he had pulled from the earth and had previously sharpened against stone, he staked the rat into the ground.

'You will not escape,' he said aloud. 'Like me you be stuck here!' Vlad started to chortle as he noticed the other rat sniffing the air whilst on it haunches, its black eyes peering at him from a distance. 'You be next should you take what be mine!'

Vlad released the stake that pinned down the rat and wiped sweat entering his mouth with the back of his hand. Suddenly he licked his lips to taste the weird, coppery taste of blood; a vile and sickening fluid, but somehow rich and sweet.

TWENTY – ONE

He was not sure what time it was when he awoke, but the room seemed darker than before, with the air very cold against his face. As he stirred, he rolled onto his side to face the window, his ears gradually tuning into the groaning and shrieking sound that his son often made whilst dreaming. He could feel his wife wife's legs against his as he stretched to free the blanketing. Throwing back the covers, Vlad announced that he would tend to his son, as Mihnea was beginning to snort and gape for air.

But as he tried to move his legs, Vlad found them restrained, somehow numb from the waist down. He tried to pull himself up, but his arms too, were irrepressibly weak. He could now hear his son finding it difficult to breathe and tried desperately to get up, but to no avail could he lift his legs to slide them over the edge of the bed. Now hearing his son call urgently for his father, Vlad shivered uncontrollably, terrified to why he could not move.

Suddenly Vlad noticed Mihnea's face appear at the edge of the bed, his eyes level with the sheeting. As his son reached up to ask to join his father in the bed, Vlad looked in horror to see Mihnea's face and arms lacerated. He gazed upon his son's hands as they tried to reach him and found the skin torn away, the flesh bloody but dried to a clotted black.

As Vlad tried best to withdraw in horror, he noticed Mihnea's mutilated face contort in pain as blood oozed out from slashed wounds. The boy called for him, but Vlad was terrorised to look upon Mihnea's tortured body.

'Why you not look after me and mama?' Mihnea's mouth gargled saliva and blood. 'Why you not be there to save us?'

Vlad swung his petrified body around in terror to take comfort in his wife, but as his wife turned from having her back to him, she too was horrific. The living corpse of what once was Jusztina reached to grab Vlad's shoulder, its skeletal hand rotten but swollen from cold river water. He could feel her bony fingers through his nightshirt, the cold water wetting him as they slid across his skin to reach for his throat. He glanced at the woman he had gladly taken for his wife, but now saw a gaunt and rotting face, her eyes sunken and deathlike, but glaring with the fires of hell.

'You were not there for us dear husband,' the corpse spoke with water gargling from its throat. 'I commit sin and be condemned to hell as you not be there to save me.'

Vlad's arms felt as heavy as lead, but somehow raised them to resist his wife's brittle fingernails raking across his face. He tried best to restrain her putrid wrists but his hands failed to hold them, his fingers slipping against dead, sodden flesh. Again he heard Jusztina shriek to moan at his failure to save her and their son.

'You failed us husband, took refuge in others whilst we died.'

*　　*　　*

Suddenly Vlad awoke in a spasm of terror, his heart pounding and body hot and sweaty. Beads of perspiration ran down his face, but it was not this that made him smother his face with his hands; small creatures were crawling over him and in haste he brushed them off. He glared at cockroaches and spiders, wet and disorientated, trying best to escape. And then in his dismay, he slammed one hand down on a number of them as they scuttled about in disarray.

He glanced around to realize that he had been dreaming; most of the cell was dark except the center, where rays of moonlight lit up a square on the floor from the grate above. As his body calmed to feel the cold of the night, he could see more creatures scuttling away. Again he wiped his face with his hands, but this time it was to remove further perspiration that had beaded from the cold. He sat up and clenched his knees to bring them into his chest, unnerved by his dream and then a strange cold within his cell. And then his heart jumped as a voice announced from a dark corner.

'You kill those creatures without any remorse.' The voice was deep and unsettling. 'No wonder you have such disregard for your wife and son.'

'What be it you know about my wife and son?' Vlad asked anxiously as he peered to see the faint outline of a shadow in a dark corner.

'Well that be why Jusztina commit such sin, was it not… because you was not there to save her, or your son? Have you not just dreamed it?'

'How can you know about it?' Vlad asked angrily, but came hesitant as he noticed red eyes glow and then fade as if they were blinking.

'I know much about you, Master Vlad… Prince of Wallachia,' The voice made a low grumbling noise before continuing, 'the likes that your wife will not go to the one she prayed to, although you purified her by fire for her sin.' The voice seemed to echo around all corners of his cell. 'And poor, little Jusztina, so pure at heart, and like her son, will not join the one she believed would be her saviour.'

'What can you know of them?'

'Jusztina be dead and her soul condemned by her sin, but the boy, he is alive… but again not to join your beloved saviour.'

The voice continued mockingly. 'He is yet to be converted to the ways of them your enemies.'

'You speak words like how my…' Vlad paused to wonder if Tariana has visited. 'Your dear gypsy friend,' the voice surmised, 'that wild and beautiful girl that you

penetrated deep, not long after losing your wife?' The voice paused as if grinning. 'But her offerings of food and water will not last.'

'How can you know what she be like?' Vlad asked irritated. 'She be a Christian as I be and…' Vlad paused to cover his ears as the voice shrieked like some night animal.

'Her faith be the same as yours, that be true,' the voice returned to state calmly, 'but it be quashed by such ridiculous gypsy beliefs.' Its red eyes blinked again as the dark figure talked as if thinking aloud. 'Such faith span many centuries, that be true, but is quite incredulous.'

As the voice spoke, Vlad quickly snatched the bundle of food and the water pouch, but saw crumbs fall from a gnawed hole in the cloth.

'They ate the last of it while you dream Master Vlad,' the voice mocked before laughing. 'You kill them but still they take the last nourishment you have.' But at least Vlad could still feel some weight in the water pouch and took some gulps of water. 'And that not last long, as she not return to refill it.'

'She will,' Vlad said, wishing secretly. 'I think she be back soon.'

'Not when she learns more of your cruel past since your romantic escapade.'

Vlad sat in silence, perplexed to how the dark figure could know such personal information. But in defiance, he remembered to what she had said of their faith.

'I may have wronged her in the past, but she be a true Christian to forgive me for all that I did.' He heard the voice groaning, but continued, 'And if her friends help and be of the same righteous faith, they will all be rewarded.'

'And how will you be in a situation do that?' the voice chortled, as its blazing red eyes blinked again. 'You already are starved and be dying of thirst when that water runs out?'

'She will come and provide more!' Vlad shouted.

'Oh, I very much doubt that.' The figure stated, somehow shimmering as it shifted side to side. 'There is nothing more a wild gypsy girl can do for a *once was* prince.'

'She will come,' Vlad shouted angrily. 'And she will find a way to get me out!'

'I very much doubt that,' the voice derided before bellowing a haunting laugh. 'Tell me if I be wrong, but as I see it, you will be stuck in here with me, the next day and all days after that.'

'I will not!' Vlad shouted as he stood, taking a stone to throw at the figure in the corner. 'You will not haunt me anymore!'

'Still haunted by them ghosts, prince?' a guard questioned from above. 'Shout all you like, but no one be hearing you!'

Vlad glanced up to see the outline of a guard standing in the emerging moonlight, his face contemptuous. He turned quickly to stand over the water pouch to hide it from view, but found he was giddy and uncontrollably weak.

Vlad looked up again to see the guard had disappeared, and in the eerie silence, squinted over at the dark corner. Although peering through bleary eyes, he noticed that the dark figure had gone too. He rubbed his eyes and felt tears sting his face as late memories flooded his mind. And then eventually, he collapsed to sit heavily.

*   *   *

In the darkness all he could feel were soft hands gliding over his body. At first they slid up his legs and around his thighs until delicate fingers probed about his groin. He was still very nervous, but his tension had become excitement, his penis erecting to near full extent. Again he squinted hard into the darkness, but at first could not see anything, until a round face appeared quite pale in the shadows, its forehead crowned with long, black hair that cascaded over shoulders to fall upon his stomach.

Vlad could now make out Tariana's naked body; her pale shoulders gleaming pastel white against the shadows, her voluptuous breasts hanging, but nipples hardened to the cold. And her hands now slid all over his chest and stomach, until they explored his testicles and held tight his penis. For long seconds he held his breath to the excitement, but exhaled hard as one hand moved up and down his penis as the other cupped hard his testicles.

He glanced down at her again and saw Tariana's head hovering over his groin, her black hair almost invisible against the dark. And now as her mouth had taken in his penis, he could feel the hardness of her teeth but softness of her tongue. Overwhelmed by her moving up and down on him, for a long time he was totally transfixed. But then questions came to him; how had she got into the cell? If this was real, why did they not escape first?

Vlad reached down to stroke her long, dark hair to reassure him she was genuine. And as he did so, she looked at him, her wet lips smiling and eyes glistening like black jewels as she played joyfully with his throbbing penis. He gasped with pleasure as she returned to suck upon his erection, feeling the tip of his organ almost reach her throat.

But then as Vlad wanted to pull Tariana towards him, he realized his wrists were cuffed by manacles that restrained him from clasping her head. He pulled angrily at the chains to reach her but found them secured tight. Naked and vulnerable, Vlad twisted to free himself from restraint, but then heard Tariana scream.

He glanced down to where she had been playing so joyful with him, to see a skeletal hand grasp her hair and pull back her head.

'Master Vlad,' Tariana called, her eyes bulging with terror, 'save me from him!'

Vlad wrenched at his restraints, but found his ankles too were fixed tight. He glanced down to kick free his legs and saw the dark figure holding strong Tariana's hair as her body twisted and turned to wriggle free. But its skeletal hand twined her hair about its fingers and jerked back her head so her calls came garbled. And as its flaming red eyes blinked frantically in the darkness, its other hand came out of the shadows with the dagger that had once been Henrik's.

Before Vlad could writhe with one last attempt to contest, he saw the blade slide deep across Tariana's throat as her head was jolted back. Jets of blood squirted out from her slit throat to splash all over him; the red, warm liquid covering his body to flow in rivulets over his skin.

In total despair, all that Vlad could do was hear his gypsy friend choke as her hazel eyes slowly turned to a deathly glaze. Above her in the shadows, somehow Vlad could sense that the dark figure was grinning, its eyes glaring gleefully at him before blinking.

*　　*　　*

Again Vlad awoke with a fright, his body trembling with a cold sweat. As he felt his blood pulse heavy about his veins, he gasped at the cold morning air, his eyes staring at the grill where daylight shone into the shadowy pit. He then glanced over to the corner where that dark figure had scorned him, but saw nothing.

Inquisitive, he crawled over to examine the corner more closely, but squinted in the rays of daylight that now hurt his eyes; so long had they become accustomed to the darkness. He inspected all other corners of the cell, but there was nothing.

He looked back to where he had slept and found a damp patch on the earth. Had he somehow lost control to urinate? Thinking of the horrific dream and to what had happened to Tariana, he could understand why. Crawling back, Vlad noticed the cockroaches and spiders he had impaled with Tariana's broken hair pins, and the dead rat that was beginning to smell. He picked up the stiff rodent by its tail and flung it to the corner where the dark figure appeared at night.

'Here, you want death,' Vlad shouted. 'Take this and appear not again!'

But seeing the rat hit the wall and fall in the corner, he thought about how he had tasted its blood. *Could it be that which had made him ill? Maybe that was the reason he was becoming delusional, having such horrible and vivid nightmares? But the blood had been the sweetest thing he had tasted for days. How he longed for the sweet taste of wine and a heartily cooked meal.*

Swinging around to sit back, Vlad placed his hands to the floor for balance, but retracted one, thinking he had touched the damp patch. But as he smelt nothing from his hand and checked his groin, he noticed a rivulet of dried up water trace back to another pouch. Quickly he grabbed the smaller pouch to notice its cap different to the other and that this one had leaked. Frantically taking long gulps of what water remained, he paused to look up, wondering if Tariana was still there. He called for her several times, but there was no reply. *When had she visited him? Why had she not spoken to him? Had the guards seized her whilst he was unconscious?*

He glanced around and gleefully noticed another bundle of food, but lifting it saw one side gnawed by rodent teeth. Some crumbs fell to the floor, but as he unraveled it, he came delighted to find malted bread, an apple and oatcake, and a long slab of cheese. This, he was determined, would be made to last; if Tariana had been taken, he may never see her again. Suddenly the thought of his friend being seized by Hungarian guards ended his joy. *What would become of her, and of him, now he would be truly alone? Was this what his dream had foretold; that Tariana would be executed, but not by that thing that kept haunting him?*

Gradually as terrible thoughts crept into his mind, he felt tears sting his eyes as he glanced around at all walls of the cell, hating the impossibility of getting out. But then through blurred vision he noticed something glimmer from rays of sunlight that shone upon the floor. He stepped closer to view the glittering artefact. And then he recognized it as Tariana's necklace charm; the tuning-fork that she sounded to repel evil spirits. Snatching it from the earth, he placed it against his chest, his heart exhilarated.

'The Lord is my saviour,' he said aloud. 'But my Lord, I believe you have sent me another saviour… one that be of my own faith, and that forgives me of my wrong doing. I promise I shall never maltreat her again.' *But had Tariana already been taken and punished for trying to help him?* 'Lord Almighty, please watch over my loving gypsy friend,' he said looking up through the grill to the heavens of blue sky. 'Bless her so we can meet again.' Again he wondered if Tariana was still there, and so stood tall to call up through the grill, repeatedly whispering aloud her name until a tall shadow appeared to stand on the grate and block the sunlight.

'What names you be muttering?' the guard enquired, but continued without giving Vlad chance to reply. 'But it matter not what you say… as you will probably rot in there… our

King Stephen the Great has ordered the troops from here to go south against Turkish advance.' He looked around before kneeling down to tell more. 'Apart from a handful of us to keep guard on the gate, he has ordered this keep to be abandoned. I very much doubt those who be staying will take care to you, and why should they?' He sniggered as he stood and glanced down again before leaving. 'If they be anything like me, from this height, they rather relieve themselves over you.'

After watching dark clouds cover the sunlight from the sky, Vlad twisted around in anger, kicking at the restraining manacles bruising and cutting into his ankles. He cursed at the fact that he would never get out of the wretched place. And without Tariana, he would undoubtedly starve to death.

Whether it was his rage making him delirious, or malnourishment, Vlad turned to each of the cell corners after hearing some cynical laughter, but saw nothing of those blazing red eyes he envisaged blinking behind a dark hood. Quickly he placed Tariana's charm to hang about his neck and bundled the food and pouch in the cloth.

'I've got enough to last a while,' he shouted at all corners of his cell. 'And now I be having something that will protect me from your evils.' He scampered with his belongings to what he considered was his safe corner, where he had scored each day upon the wall with the worn hairpin. 'I be safe now I have faith in this and my friend.'

Vlad sat with his back up against the cell wall to examine the necklace charm. *Would using it to score days upon the wall affect its tone or render it useless? As much as he wanted to believe in what Tariana had told about it, surely it was nothing but some old gypsy heirloom... some pretty jewelry that tuned musical instruments of some kind. But he had to believe in something to keep his faith, especially if it deterred that dark figure appearing at night. He knew it was imperative to keep well his mind, his faith and dignity. Above all, he had to try and get out of the cell before he starved to death.*

And then, thinking of food, his stomach ached and rumbled, so he gazed over the slab of cheese.

'Just a little with some of that bread,' he muttered to himself. He looked at the tuning-fork again and how he could use it to cut thin and economically the cheese. 'Just a small amount for today... to keep my strength... the rest I will hide from them horrible rats to have more next morning.'

*　　*　　*

Startled, Vlad awoke, but this time not haunted by his dreams. He must have fell unconscious after eating, but now his stomach pained to digest the food he had consumed. Although his body ached all over, he could feel some reprieve from the delusive thoughts and blurred vision he had been having. *Had the food bettered his senses? But how long would it last? And how long would that little water last?*

'She will not come again,' a deep voice announced from a dark corner. 'If the keep is now abandoned, the gypsy will not get in.'

Now Vlad knew what woke him; it was the shriek of laughter that he had heard in his slumber. He stared in both fright and anger to see those red eyes blink again.

'She will,' Vlad responded zealously as he clutched tight the charm in his fingers, 'but if she does not, at least I be having something to remember her by… and it be keeping my faith strong against the likes of you.'

'But for how long, you have no escape?' the voice chuckled. 'Do those chains not keep you in here with me?'

'I got those off which bound my wrists together, did I not,' Vlad squeezed his knees into his chest and rubbed his wrists to ease the bruising. 'I just need a bigger hairpin… something that will not snap in such a sturdy lock.'

Suddenly Vlad took the charm from around his neck and tried to prise the manacles apart.

'As the Prince of Wallachia, you are not the brightest of noblemen, are you?' the voice again mocked him and sniggered. 'Do you really think damaging that feeble heirloom will free you of those chains?' Vlad stopped to consider that breaking the charm would render him vulnerable against evil, and that should he get out, he could never return it to Tariana damaged. 'It is not strong enough to even break a link on those there chains.'

Vlad loathed to hear the voice laugh again, but knew the thing was right; the steel of the tuning-fork was too soft for such an undertaking, and to be used as such a tool, it was too small and fragile. With regret he returned the charm about his neck and held it tight.

'I have a proposition that will get you out of those chains,' the voice said cunningly, 'but you need to rid yourself of that thing about your neck and the faith you have in it.'

'Never,' Vlad shouted. 'It be all I have and keep dear to the memories of such a friend… one that shares the same faith and passion.'

'Passion… passion?' the voice ridiculed. 'What do you know of passion, but to take pleasure in poisoning water and ravaging crops to see those poor of your lands die after they labour hard on such all year. And punish your peoples without trial.' The voice groaned like some animal. 'The time you spend imprisoned in here is the same justice you gave them.'

'I poisoned waters and such like to fight back against those that be our enemy,' Vlad snapped back. 'It be all I could do as we be outnumbered score fold.'

'But that was when you was a lord and prince… a noble warrior that led men into battle… men who fought at your side and would die for you… not some treacherous renegade that tried again to rule the lands once his, but now are not his right to rule.'

'Wallachia was my right to rule, as it was my father's.'

'But those days are now gone,' the voice retorted. 'The allegiance of the Order of the Dragon is long gone, as so is the faith it tried to preserve.'

'My faith be strong as long as I pray and keep comfort in the memory of my friend.'

'And how long will that last?' it questioned. 'Already you live awake at night and turn into some night creature, the likes as me.'

'I will not! Never will I be the same as you!'

'So how long will it be before you see your blessed friend again, and not wake every night wishing I was not here?'

'You taunt me to levels I detest, but I be strong while I be awake and not be haunted by the nightmares you set upon me.'

Vlad could hear the dark figure muttering, but could not make out what it said.

And then it started humming as if testing his nerves.

'Morning be coming soon and so you will be gone,' Vlad said, grinning. 'But does the light not affect your eyes as it does mine?'

'No, I be liking the sunlight on my face.'

Even though cramped up in the corner of the cell, Vlad could detect that morning was coming and so welcomed the first light. It was not just that daylight diminished the thing that taunted him, but he recalled many good memories of mornings spend with Jusztina and Mihnea; watching the sun come up over the horizon during winter months, a rainbow of colours that brightened such a bleak time of year. And although he could not wonder at the wilderness from the corners of his cell, Vlad envisaged the landscape and smelt the fresh air to the start of a new day.

But then the thing in the corner groaned like some animal to make Vlad return to reality. And so trying best to ignore it, he turned to consider how many days he had scribed upon the wall until the hairpin had broken. He peered up through the grill from the shadowy corner, content to notice the first rays of sunlight gleam upon its iron bars, although they hurt his eyes. After being cooped up for so long down in the pit, he longed to be out on fields and heathland, galloping his stead after a hearty breakfast. Instead, curling up in such a desolate corner, he felt so tired and rejected, knowing he was regrettably turning into some night creature, like the voice had said. And again he would need to dig another hole to cover the stench of his excrement.

As he heard the dark figure muttering, he held strong Tariana's charm, afraid to look over, but as he eventually peered to see what the thing was doing, he found it had disappeared. At seeing the thing gone, he turned to gleefully watch the sunlight grow stronger, but had to squint to appreciate its full glory. After relieving himself in a hole dug in the corner where the thing appeared, he settled down to get some sleep. At least he could be confident that during the daylight hours, that thing would not bother him.

But how would he scribe another day upon the wall once nightfall came? And what if Tariana visited with more food and water whilst he was asleep? What if she and her friends could get in the keep, if now it was abandoned? Surely, unlike to what that thing had suggested, an abandoned keep would have less security... maybe one day they would get him out? But regrettably no doubt, he would have to wait some time before that day would come. With so many questions his mind ached terribly, but eventually he fell into a twitchy, but not so haunted sleep.

*   *   *

Vlad awoke delirious again. He felt weaker than the previous day, and certainly the day before that. To how many days had passed exactly, he could not be sure.

He peered up at the grill to notice that dusk had come; that he must have again missed all those hours of afternoon daylight. Yet it was hard to tell, as those dark clouds of winter were gathering and he could feel that rain was in the air.

He trudged over on hands and knees to again grimace that all the food had gone and could only sip enough drops of water to wet his lips. Although the rats had nothing now to steal from him, he decided to keep all belongings close. And so together, before returning to sit in his preferred corner, he gathered the two water pouches, the stick he dug mess holes with, his wooden food bowl and even the gnawed cloths.

Fumbling with Tariana's charm, Vlad took it from around his neck and again went to scribe another day against the wall. Delirious by his weakened state, he accidentally slipped and felt the now slightly sharpened points of the tuning-fork gouge into the skin of his left hand. As blood oozed out from his wound, he went to lick it clean, again finding the taste of blood coppery and sickening, but somehow sweeter than that of the rat.

His mind came hindered by intrusive thoughts about drinking the blood of those rats to survive, but then felt rain drops fall against his outspread feet. With the cold droplets revitalising his senses, he shook his head to rid himself of such weird dread, and went to wash his wound with wetted strips of cloth torn from what remained of his shirt.

But surely if he could wet a strip of cloth to cleanse his wound, he could use it to soak up rain water.

Beneath the grill, where rain percolated through the bars, he placed his wooden bowl and all cloths he could stretch between digging sticks. Over time he could collect enough water to pour from his food bowl into each of the water pouches, and by wringing out the cloths, he could surely collect more. He rubbed his hands to see the rain fall a little more heavily and placed the bowl under a constant drip.

Content with his novel idea to collect rain water, Vlad returned to his favourite corner to inscribe the end of the day more carefully. Although in the dark it was difficult to examine the wall up close, he could see that where he had slipped, the scratched mortar had exposed the stone beneath. He inspected Tariana's charm to see how sharpened the squared edges of the tuning-fork had been worn, but thought that surely a little more wear would not harm it. Hitting it against the iron manacles above his feet, he heard its tone resonate strong and so began to use it to dig away more of the mortar.

Whilst scuttling to collect water, Vlad continued for more than an hour to carefully scratch away the mortar, scraping the tuning-fork at different angles as to evenly wear away the points and hopefully not lose its novelty. *After all, he did promise to return it to Tariana one day. But how could he do so if he could not get out? And now he had no provision of food, and only water if and when the Heavens blessed him with rain.* He glanced back at the wooden food bowl to see that again it was almost full and so poured its contents into a water pouch.

He found that the work not only gave him purpose, but lifted his moral; additionally, he took refreshing mouthfuls of water between scraping away the mortar.

Within a couple of hours, Vlad had not only removed a square of mortar from the wall, but had dug out cement from around a stone. With the padlock that once had bound his wrist manacles together, he hooked the clasp in his largest finger to slam its base against the stone. He glanced up to wonder if any of the guards would hear the noise, but after pausing a while, continued. After many attempts, he could see that the stone was working free from crumbling cement. With one last blast from the palm of his hand he felt the brick push inward and break free. Carefully using the tuning-fork to prise the stone free, he clasped it and pulled it at angles to shunt it towards him, until eventually it broke free. The square stone fell to the floor as Vlad's weak wrists could not hold it; his arms and body truly exhausted. But inside him grew hope, an excitement of getting rid of that thing that haunted him, and to finally escape the filthy pit.

Fetching more water while the rain still percolated through the grill, he gulped down more mouthfuls, but decided to rest. He peered over to the corner now knowing it had become night, fearing the thing might reappear. And then it came to him; he remembered to where the last rays of sunlight had shone before the sun had set. Trying best to envisage himself as a compass in the centre of the pit, he recollected that the final sunlight had indeed come from the same direction to where he had removed the stone from the wall. Therefore the wall was west and if he continued to dig in that direction, he would reach the outer wall of the keep.

What was it that Tariana had said about the outer wall of the keep being not far from his cell? But how long would it take to reach it, and would the guards become suspicious of his digging or his spreading fresh earth across the cell floor? But were there even any guards now to bother him? It was a great undertaking and something he had certainly never done before, but what other choice had he got, but to die in there of starvation? He again considered what Tariana had said about her group camped west. *This was not just a coincidence,* he believed, *but was deliverance by their faith in God. It was a blessed justice to them wrongly imprisoning him.*

Suddenly he thought he heard the thing groan in anger to his appeasement and so glanced to the corner. But the dark figure was not there.

Vlad was tired and weary, again fearing that the thing would haunt him during the hours of darkness, but with new determination, he began to dig away at another stone. *Say what you will... mock me as much you might... but I will get out of here and away from whatever you be!*

Into the early hours of morning, Vlad had dislodged several of the heavy stones and arranged them against the base of the wall, to be in the same order as they had come out. He could always stack them back into the wall should guards come and pry. And hide it with his body sat against it.

By now he could dig away the earth and scatter it across the cell floor with his feet. And by the time he had removed earth from nearly an arm length in, he noticed the soil had become moist and littered with dead roots. With several more scrapes with his cupped fingers, suddenly Vlad felt earth fall away and so eagerly glanced through the dark hole. Until the light of midday would light up the cell better, he could not see for sure what was beyond the hole, but after feeling a cold draft, he was confident it was some sort of tunnel, maybe a natural underground drainage of some type.

For another hour, although weary, but revived by gulps of rain water, Vlad dug away as dawn approached. Although not quite wide enough, he went to squeeze through the gap, but paused to glower at the corner to where the thing usually appeared.

'You cannot stop me getting away from you now,' Vlad chortled. 'It may take days and hard work, but one day I be finally rid of you!'

Even though he had lost a lot of weight, indeed it would take more work, as Vlad found the hole too small. But as he tested the gap, eager to see how more he would need to dig, he felt his legs restrained.

'You forgot about those, did you not?' the deep voice returned to state, before bellowing laughter.

Vlad flinched to reverse and fell back into the cell, his eyes again glowering at the dark corner to observe a pair of fiery, red eyes.

'Get through the hole you might… but any further?' Again the voice turned to hysterical laughter.

Vlad crawled to his preferred corner and curled up, grinding his teeth as tears stung his eyes. Desperately he covered his ears so not to hear the evil laughter and badgering mockery. But at least the light of dawn was less than an hour away.

Tariana paced up and down and scowled at the dancing flames of the camp fire. She had considered the idea after not being allowed into the keep; of the few guards who had remained, none knew her and so refused her entry. Therefore, she had secretly combed the west wall of the keep at dusk to search for other ways in. But as she had explained to the group, the only possible way she had seen, was through some sort of drainage tunnel that lead inward.

'I would go myself but I be too big,' Tariana avowed. 'Maybe I get so far but no doubt get stuck.' She turned to face Lydia. 'Can you not at least try?'

'I do not want to, it be…'

'But how would she get a bundle of food through,' Kateryna interjected sharply, staring from her seat beside the camp fire, 'and what about that container of water?'

'I know he mean a lot to you,' Lydia said slow and shy, 'and you make good me a nice dress and treat us kind, but...' The little girl coughed and so sipped more herbal tea. 'But that man be bad for what happen to...' Again she could not mention her parents' names. 'It be hard to forgive such a man, even if father told me to do so as it be our Christian belief.'

'But it be only this one time... just to see if he be alive?' Tariana implored. 'If he still be alive, he need food before he starves.'

'You should not impose such on a little girl,' Kateryna declared. 'It not be right.' She held her hands up in gesture. 'Besides... when her father returns, I know he not agree to such.'

'But at least hear me out,' Tariana requested as she sat with a stick to scribe the earth where there was a clearing on the ground. 'Look, here be a map of what it be likes.' Tariana etched a crude map into the earth using the point of the stick and continued to explain where things were located. 'Here be the wall and the gate... here be the wall west and his cell... not much a distance to where be this drainage passage. And here be...'

'I not want the man to die, but it be dark in there, and cramped…' Lydia started to cry. 'I do not like the dark.'

'Let her be, can you not?' Kateryna said annoyed. 'Why do you insist on such? Andrei will not agree to it! And it be dangerous for her… the tunnel may collapse. If she crawls through, how do you know that she be able to get in?' Kateryna fixed her stare on Tariana. 'The passage could be blocked by a grill or something?'

'If it be drainage, access must be close to those cells,' Tariana toyed with her hair. 'I be sure I saw such when I visited last.'

'You just be making it up to convince her to go… pretending that it be easy.' Kateryna stood and turned to notice Andrei and Sorin listening after their return. 'Andrei will not let her go.'

'You be right I will not,' Andrei spoke harsh as he pulled Lydia away, the little girl weeping and glancing sheepishly at Tariana. 'You may see well our group, but you not control my granddaughter.'

'But we cannot let the man die!'

'And why not?' Andrei snapped as Tariana saw Sorin also sign his disapproval. 'The man probably be dead already.'

'How can you all be so… cruel?'

'He was,' Andrei stated adamantly. 'Because of him, Lydia lost her parents.'

'He be harsh to me also, remember?' Kateryna added. 'He did not drag me, but he was in charge of those who did.'

'Then I guess it be me that must go, even if I get stuck in the blasted hole!'

'I suppose I could go,' Kateryna sat again to stare into the camp fire, 'I be smaller and slightly thinner than you.' She glanced up, grinning. 'And be a little more nimble.'

All faces turned to hear Sorin grunt and click his big fingers. 'What be it he say?' Kateryna asked.

'You do not need to know,' Tariana replied as she joined Kateryna beside the camp fire.

'He not like that we help the man,' Lydia spoke up. 'Is that not true?' They observed the large Russian nod to agree.

'Well at least come and see,' Tariana implored, fingering agitatedly with her hair. 'Can you not at least check the place out?'

Again it was almost dark by the time Vlad awoke. He hated sleeping through the daylight hours, remembering only short periods where he had peered up through the grill to squint at passing clouds. But it was his only chance to rest peacefully and not get tormented by that thing, or be haunted my horrific nightmares. Besides it was easier to ignore the dark figure whilst he worked on his escape, and the guards hardly patrolled at night so he need not worry about digging. And as he deliberated on how long he had been imprisoned in the dark cell, he remembered to how much his eyes hurt in daylight.

Another day he thought, as he went to scribe it on the wall, but stopped to examine the wound on his left hand. He had kept it clean will mouthfuls of spat water, but now with both pouches dry, he could only cover the wound with the cleanest strip of cloth. *How many days has it been,* he thought gazing at the marks on the wall, *or has it been months… is it winter yet?* He scribed carefully with the tuning-fork another line. *Better I get on digging while I have the strength and before that thing shows up.*

Although motivated by his determination to escape, Vlad knew he *was* weak and again grimaced to pick cockroaches, bugs and spiders from the wooden food bowl; swallowing them whole, so he had no time to retch. Without any rain water to collect, he stored as many as he could find, staking them with Tariana's broken hairpin only to use it also as a food pick.

As he fumbled around to find the tuning-fork charm, his stomach rumbled and ached as bile rose and tried to force him to vomit. But he had found ways to resist puking although it rendered him giddy; turning his head to the ceiling to stretch his throat whilst he took long, deep breaths. But his throat was terribly sore and dry, with only sips of his own urine as reprieve.

He lowered his head after the dizziness had gone and looked over to the dead rat he had impaled last night with the sharpened points of the tuning-fork. Gradually he recalled the harsh memories of the thing tormenting him about his confinement and hunger. So in his rage he had staked the rat and stripped it open, wanting to eat its flesh, but could only drink the sweet, warm blood before passing out. And now he noticed the blood that had stained his fingers, thinking falsely that it was from his wound.

By now Vlad could see that it was dark outside the grate above him, and so dismissing all thoughts of dread, ambled over to the hole he had made in the wall west. Muttering words of determination, he scrambled through the gap; it now just wide enough to squeeze his body through. But as he pulled on the chains to allow him more movement into his freshly dug tunnel, he again heard the deep voice.

'You will have to eat its flesh before long, if you want to survive.' Vlad peered through the hole in the wall to see the fiery red eyes staring. 'Not that you be getting any further with those irons about your feet.'

'I will find a way,' Vlad snapped. 'I will return her charm and make it up to her.'

'She is only a gypsy,' the voice ridiculed. 'But what would she make of such a depraved man now… a has-been who was once a lord and prince?'

'She is pure of heart and will understand.' He turned his back on the dark figure to work on the tunnel. 'She has lived in the wilderness and so will understand to how I have suffered in here.'

'You will not tell of how you talked with me?' 'Certainly not.'

'And how you killed those rats with her… *charm*?' The voice paused to snigger. 'That such a thing is useless now to its original purpose.' The voice poised to correct itself, 'Or would it?'

'She will understand as she have a heart of gold,' Vlad convinced himself, trying best to ignore the voice that muttered behind him. 'Only some gypsy you say… but she be something better that you will ever be!'

'You were right to poison the water and burn crops to eliminate that your enemy,' the voice continued in a serious tone as if thinking aloud. 'Certain sacrifices are required to win a war in such a cruel world as this you lead. But it proves that your soul can change and adapt to harvest such cruelty.'

Vlad stopped digging with the long, hard root; his arms aching and head giddy as he listened to the deep voice mutter on. He pulled on his chains to stretch his reach and dig further west the tunnel.

'And a sacrifice you could give to escape this place… deny your faith in that there charm to believe in me.' The voice groaned on as somehow it knew Vlad was listening. 'It is the only choice you have to rid yourself of them there irons.'

'I not listen to this sacrifice you speak of.' Vlad turned to shout through the opening. 'It be some trick… nothing but some curse… you haunt me too much already!'

'So you do but listen,' the voice growled. 'Must be that you have *some* interest in that to which be offered… how else will you escape those restraints?'

'I get out of here by my own doing,' Vlad shouted back, 'even if it takes breaking those chains or irons… I will find a way!'

'Well the best of luck with that,' the voice spoke cynically, 'as luck be something you have not much of lately.'

Vlad had had enough, and with the last of his energy, threw himself through the hole to swing his fists at the dark figure.

'Go, leave me alone,' Vlad shouted. 'Haunt me no longer!'

But as he swung his fists at the cold air in the dark corner, the thing had gone.

Having exerted such a rush of anger, suddenly Vlad felt himself faint and fell upon the cold earth.

TWENTY – TWO

Vlad rubbed his tired eyes to peer up through the grill and admire the diminishing rays of sunlight, but even the last of daylight now hurt his eyes. Blinded by the light, he cowered back to his favourite corner to scratch another day's end upon the wall, deliberating on how long it had been since he saw a passing guard. The last time he recollected, the guard had never even stopped to provoke him, never mind throw any food down.

He tried to remember the last time Tariana had visited, but unfortunately that was when he had missed her; all he could do was to be secretly grateful for the food and water she had brought. But how long had that been now... had she truly forgotten him? He paused to examine her charm after using it to again scribe the wall. With all its use, he noticed how the ends of the tuning-fork had worn away and were now quite sharp, like two needle points. He hit it against his manacles, testing to see if it still worked, and to him it still sounded the same as it did before.

He smiled, but then felt his anger intensify; thinking that if he did not get out in what could be the last of his days, he would never see Tariana again. And although he had secretly promised to never hurt her in any way, progressively he had become dispirited towards her. *But was this the result of that thing tormenting him; trying best to mock his friend and her heirloom, and last night, their Christian faith? Why did it demean her so much?* Again Vlad came disturbed by restless thoughts. *Yet, although the voice had ridiculed the gypsy charm, it seemed so curious about it? Maybe it was trying to persuade him to denounce it in order to get more at him? But how exactly did it protect gypsies from evil spirits? Had Tariana not told him everything he needed to know about it?*

Whether it came from his hunger, or indeed the revolting things he did manage to eat, he knew his mind was wavering, his sanity quite unstable. With his stomach constantly upset from digesting spiders, bugs and cockroaches, his only relief seemed to come from rat's blood. And now, as it had not rained for days, he had to sip at his cold urine to relieve his dry throat. But this too, he found nauseating and humiliating. However, before digging again, he knew he needed enough to wet his lips and sooth his throat and so crawled over to the small water pouch.

Vlad was just about to grab the pouch, when he noticed a dark figure scuttle along the floor. Another rat had found its way into his cell, most probably from that drainage tunnel to where he dug west. He watched it stop and rise upon its haunches, its whiskers twitching as it sniffed at the air. For a moment he thought it stared at him; its dark, beady eyes provoking him about knowing a way out. So as the rodent bravely approached near, Vlad reached for the charm about his neck and after removing it, clenched it in his hand, ready to strike. Still delirious in his attack, at first Vlad failed, but then in its panic the rat had no escape; the hole in the western wall now behind Vlad. As it scurried within reach, Vlad struck at the rat, the sharpened prongs of the tuning-fork entering the rodent's back neck. As it writhed and screeched in pain, Vlad heaved its body from the ground, turning it in view to watch the creature twitch in pain. And then, dismayed by seeing its eyes bulge, he slammed its skull against the wall, again closing his eyes and ears as so not to witness its death.

'Sorry, but it's a matter of survival,' Vlad spoke aloud to the now dead creature, 'and I be the far superior in here.'

He had killed rats this way several times by now, but always found it repulsive to break the creature's neck and slit open its throat. Most of the blood he would drain into the wooden food bowl, but could never wait too long to drink it, as it was never as good when cold. And then he did something he had never done before... he attempted to nibble at its flesh. He closed his eyes as his teeth tore into the creature, trying to envisage the rodent as just a piece of cooked fowl. After a few minutes he could nibble at the flesh no longer, his mind rejecting the ravenous act, although his rumbling stomach welcomed it. Sickened by the blood staining his hands, Vlad threw the rat's body to the corner from where the voice usually came.

'I'll get out of here,' he announced, but looked apprehensively into the darkening shadows of the corner. 'You finish him off if you want.' He sat with his head back again to steady his dizziness. 'I got work to do, so you need not appear.'

Again Vlad found himself digging west, but with his ankle chains now at full stretch and manacles cutting into his ankles, he needed to reach further with the longer root he had found. And it was getting harder to dislodge the earth, especially around the sides and above him, only the floor now wet from drainage water. He had found moist mosses and lichens, even some grass, and nibbled on them after remembering what Tariana had told him. After living as a gypsy in the harsh of the wilderness over so many years, she had learned many things; one being that such plants not only retained water, but that they had healing or herbal properties. And so to moisten his dry throat and to help him breathe during digs, he had kept in chewing them. He certainly felt that they had helped his stomach resist the vomiting that constantly aggravated him. For this he was again thankful to his gypsy friend.

Suddenly Vlad dislodged a clump of earth to release dirt that cascaded down upon him, hindering his sight and breathing. At first he panicked, but pushed away at the earth to roll on his back, his mouth now able to gasp at the air. As he lay there in a daze, it reminded him of the once when he had woken in the centre of his cell, a guard ridiculing him as he pissed over his face from above. Are you not dead yet, the guard had asked? How stupid, he thought of that Hungarian – how could he reply, if he was dead? He then recalled to how the guard had told of him leaving the keep and that none of them would even check on him anymore. But this determined him even more in his attempt to escape, and so he shunted himself towards the wall, to crouch low and transfer the excess earth through to his cell.

Vlad squeezed through the gap and busied himself by scattering the earth across the floor of the pit, but then realized that it was well after sunset. Fretfully he glanced at the dark corner of the cell, and then to the others, but as of yet, saw nothing. Soon he was back at full stretch and digging where he had exposed another opening, one that like the first had a cold draft. But this one had more draw and so he assumed the outside was near. But exactly how far had he dug? Was it enough to try and pierce the earth above?

He grimaced after a brief period of rapture, his body aching all over. Although his eyes had now accustomed so well to the dark, he could not make out to where the new tunnel led, and come next day, the noon daylight would not illuminate this far. He shuffled again to edge towards his new tunnel, using his digging stick to manoeuvre him forward. But feeling the pain of the manacles cutting into his ankle bones, he retreated to observe them best he could. Indeed again they were bleeding beneath the bandaging he had already wrapped tight about them. Suddenly, echoing all about tunnel, he heard that evil laughter that sent him to shiver.

'Are you the far superior in here?' the deep voice bellowed. 'You may be to those rats, but at least they are free to find themselves out of here.'

Vlad turned to glance through the gap, regretfully knowing to what he would see. And there again it was, the dark figure shimmering as the hood over its head fell back to expose those fiery, red eyes. And again it laughed.

'You not be there if I not think it,' Vlad shouted.

'But I am,' it replied sarcastically, 'and you are here because those manacles still refrain you from digging any further.'

'I will find a way to rid myself of them,' Vlad flared with anger. 'And rid myself of you!'

'But you cannot,' the deep voice chortled. 'Only I know a way for you to do so, and all but I know how you can do it.'

'I be free soon… very soon!' Vlad shouted as an overwhelming fit of anger took control of him. 'You will see I be finally free!'

Vlad took the tuning-fork about his neck and tried to prise open the padlock holding together the short chain between his manacles. In his mad failure to wrench open the padlock clasp, he then tried it against a manacle. But suddenly as he slipped, he felt a sharp pain, which along with his abrupt exertion, made him pass out.

TWENTY – THREE

At first he thought it was that evil laughter resonating about his cell, but as his ears listened more acute, he could hear weeping, as if a child was crying. And then suddenly he opened his eyes, realizing it was his son calling. Mihnea's voice was garbled and faint, but Vlad was convinced it was definitely him.

Rising from his stupor to look round, Vlad saw his son lying awkward on the floor of the pit, and so quickly crawled over to console him and see that his son's hands and knees were grazed.

'Dearest Mihnea, you be alive?' Vlad sat in disbelief as he cradled his son's head. 'But how you get to be here?'

'That man pushed me through there,' Mihnea explained, pointing at the grate above. 'And then he locked it. I heard him after I fell and hurt…'

Mihnea again started to weep as he tried best to shift his limbs from beneath him. Vlad kissed his forehead and examined his son's knees to which Mihnea rubbed with pain etched on his face.

'But you be alright now my son,' Vlad said trying best to comfort him as he pulled his son into his arms. 'We be united once and for all.'

'What if the man comes back?'

'He will not return,' Vlad scoffed, glancing up through the grill to see nothing but the dark of night. 'Besides it be no more his concern that we be together.' Again Vlad smothered Mihnea in kisses.

Vlad examined again his son's grazed hands and knees and looked around to find his items; the water pouches, the digging sticks and his many strips of cloth. But surprisingly all were gone. Stunned, he checked his chest for Tariana's charm, but that too was not dangling from his neck.

Confused he glanced up again, thinking if the guard had taken it. But surely the guard had not bothered to enter his cell; he had just shoved Mihnea in before locking the grate. Vlad grit his teeth in desperation, muddled to where his precious items were. He held tight his son, but pondered on how he was going to bandage his lacerations. As Vlad consoled Mihnea, his son continuing to whimper, he heard again that evil laughter, it echoing strangely about all corners.

'We must get you out of here!' Vlad said scared. 'That thing might return.' He glanced at his son, but noticed how Mihnea looked up at him in bewilderment. 'You hear that?'

'I hear nothing father,' Mihnea mumbled. 'You did not hear such wicked laughter?'

'No, I did not.' Mihnea pulled away slightly from Vlad's grasp to look up at him. 'You alright father?'

'I be… I be seeing things in here my son,' Vlad garbled a confession. 'It be my lack of food… having to drink rain water when it come… besides other things.' He glanced at his son to notice him even more baffled. 'I be starved and so see things that not be real.' Seeing puzzlement etched still on his face, Vlad ruffled his son's scruffs of hair and pressed his nose with a forefinger. 'Not to worry my son, at least we be back together again.'

Thinking that he had spoken too soon, Vlad heard a noise that rattled the cell from all four corners. Shocked to hold Mihnea extra tight, he glanced about in fright, totally confused to what was happening. It was only when he noticed a number of rats scurry across the cell floor towards the hole that he acknowledged to what was happening.

He glanced at the west wall and its hole, and then the wall east; both were as they should be. But the walls north and south seemed to be moving inward, a heavy grinding noise loud from each of them. Totally transfixed by their peculiar motion, Vlad at first sat in shock. But then as Mihnea too came frightened by the bizarre trap, Vlad pulled him to his chest to again console his son.

He knew he had to do something quick, as eventually both of them would be nothing but crushed flesh and bone. Stumbling as he rose to carry Mihnea in his arms, Vlad struggled to reach the hole in the wall west, before falling awkwardly. Mihnea bounced along the pit floor before hitting Vlad's arrangement of laid stones and then started to cry.

Vlad could see by now that their room in the cell was gradually becoming more confined; the walls not faltering against the mounting earth dragged up from the floor or being hindered by his pile of stones. He saw many of his arranged stones tumble as the northern wall advanced, his heart now racing with its incessant progress.

He saw Mihnea get covered by falling stones, but the boy wiggled free as best he could.

'Mihnea, go through the hole as quick as you can!' Vlad called, trying best to

reach the opening himself. 'I be coming and follow!'

By the time Vlad had reached the hole, he could see stones were being pushed up against the hole and it was becoming partially blocked. And with the opposite wall enclosing in on him just as steady, he had not much time. He watched Mihnea crawl through the hole to follow rats on their escape, and then the boy turned to outstretch his arm to reach for his father.

'Father, father, you must be quick, or...' Beyond the hole, Mihnea's little, terrified face appeared in and out of the shadows, his eyes wide and glistening.

Vlad crawled on all fours to reach the hole, but the gap was being barred by enclosing stones, earth and debris. He reached to grab his son's outstretched hand but only managed to fumble with his little fingers. Yet Vlad was determined to squeeze himself through the gap before the walls entrapped his body. And so, crazed with terror, he twisted himself through the gap, and was almost with his son when his legs got snared half way through. His son grasped at him to help pull him through, but Mihnea was too small to use any of his weight.

Vlad kicked and writhed, and all but his ankles had pulled through. And as he glanced back to see what snared him, he could see dark, ghostly hands grasping the manacles about his ankles. Strangely the body and hands beyond the darkness was not squashed by the enclosing walls, but Vlad knew that soon, his feet would be. He kicked again in desperation against the ghastly hands that restrained him, but staring back again into the darkness beyond the gap, he recognised those fiery red, glowing eyes as hysterical laughter again deafened in his ears.

*   *   *

Vlad woke in an instant, his mind wavering and body nervous. But most of all he could feel shocking pains in his ankle. Had the walls crushed his feet or did his strong iron manacles prevent irreversible damage?

With his mind clearing from the nightmare and his body cooling of sweat, Vlad crawled to sit up and examine his feet. The manacles were still there, and the chains binding them together, held still by the large padlock. But what he saw too was the tuning-fork stuck into one of his ankles, the two prongs imbedded just above the bone. *It must have been when I slipped, stabbing myself accidently before passing out. How stupid it was to try and break those irons with such a weak tool.* And there were now a couple of rats nibbling at his blood that soaked thickly into his makeshift bandaging. So Vlad kicked them away before painfully removing Tariana's once gypsy charm.

Vlad sat back against the wall he inscribed days on and took time to breathe. At first the pain had just been a dull ache, but now as blood flowed freely to soak more the bandage, he gritted his teeth and grimaced. Carefully he unwound the bloody bandage and flung it away, pleased to replace it with some strips that were somewhat cleaner.

But then that part of the nightmare returned; he had his things here with him still, but obviously no Mihnea. In anger he kicked again at the rats that shifted around his feet, recollecting how they escaped through the hole with Mihnea. *How much longer could I stand this torment… that thing not just making me harm myself, but torturing my mind about my son?* He checked again his throbbing ankle and tugged angrily at the manacles that still restrained him. *What must I do to rid myself of these? What be the point of digging that tunnel if I cannot go any further? What be it that that thing say about me escaping these things... what must I do?* He cursed the dark entity with mutterings and looked anxiously at the corner. *But I must carry on... maybe try now to dig towards the sky... maybe it be far enough to see daylight outside of the keep?* He wrapped more bandages around his ankles, not just to stop the bleeding, but to prevent further bruising. If he was to dig on, he needed as much protection as possible. *It be dark soon... maybe just another hour before dusk... and I do not want to be haunted by that thing again. Vlad, you must press on... dig as far as you can reach... but the pain?* He hesitated, as shifting about the pit intensified the hurt. *Move you stupid bastard... you may no longer be a lord or prince down in his hell like hole, but as a man and a Christian you will find a way... the Lord Almighty will watch over me!* Grimacing against the pain, but convinced with his escape plan, Vlad went to work more on his tunnel.

At first he had continued to dig west, as far as he could comfortably stretch his restraints, but then wondered if he had dug beyond the outer wall. *But would I have not reached some sort of foundations? Even though I be some distance underground already, would I have not seen something? Maybe even if I dig out but not be outside the wall, could I sneak past those pesky guards?* For a long moment he deliberated on the idea, before deciding to turn upon his back and dig upward. As he could not stretch any further, he thought he might as well. But after several minutes he hit clumps of earth that fell on top of him. And again feeling faint and claustrophobic, he panicked to clear himself of suffocating debris. *What I be doing? I have had nothing to be of sustenance? Again I must try and keep down some of those…* Again he hated the thought of eating such creatures, even though he collected many in the bowl every night before starting his dig. *I must go back. Besides I need to clear all this… scatter it across the floor of the pit.*

He could only eat a few of the spiders and cockroaches, before washing what he could manage down with sips of last night's urine. And yet again he had to control his attempts to vomit, breathing deeply whilst looking out through the grill at the near dark sky. Soon he felt tears stinging his eyes, eventually rolling down his cheeks, harsh against his dirty, scathed skin. How much longer could he keep this up?

Vlad had not heard any evil laughter or felt that unnatural cold, so as he detected the dark figure's presence in the corner, a shiver ran up his spine. But the thing was just sitting there, playing with its fingers as if pondering on its thoughts. So he approached as quiet as he could, to finally get some perspective to the thing's appearance. At first he thought he was losing his mind, as it just resembled some prisoner sharing his cell; a very small man with a hooked like nose peeking out from the black, heavy cloth hood that hid most of its face. And as Vlad advanced a little further, overwhelmed with curiosity, the thing was indeed dressed head to toe in black. But Vlad rubbed his eyes to clear his vision, as the figure constantly shimmered, as if trying to conceal its true form. And then, as he saw it's strange, hooved feet, resembling something like that of a goat, it faced him and beneath the heavy, dark veil, Vlad noticed those red glowing eyes start to blink. He backed away to his corner as he noted the thing grin at him.

'I know you are curious about me,' the thing's voice growled. 'But you will never comprehend who I am, or all that I can do.'

'You be nothing but a part of my imagination,' Vlad shouted, his throat coarse. 'I be getting so delirious you may as well be part of those dreams… in fact…' Vlad stopped to remember the thing's appearance in his dream with his son.

'Yes, I am haunting your mind even when you sleep,' the voice chuckled lightly. 'I am appearing almost anywhere… even in dreams your dear son be having.'

'You leave my son out of this!' Vlad shouted. 'He most likely be…'

'Dead?' the voice finished the sentence Vlad could not. 'But he is not, as I sense his pure, little soul… although I must regret to inform you that soon it be corrupted by those of your enemy.'

'How can you know he be alive?'

'I know… believe me I know,' the thing grinned wider. 'And you could have powers to take him back… such great, but dark powers that would neutralise those that be your enemy… it would be such a great revenge, would it not?'

'Lies they be,' Vlad shouted back, 'nothing, but deceitful lies!' 'But is your son not worth such an agreement?'

'My son be nothing but a dear memory to me now, so what can you know?'

'I know that he is alive,' the thing leaned forward, a gargling noise resonating from its throat. 'You could have powers that could take him back… and eliminate all those that are your enemy.'

'Lies, you speak of nothing but lies.'

'I see that you need a little convincing,' the thing fingered its mouth, although Vlad could not make out distinctly its face. 'What if I rid you of those irons that restrain your escape, would that convince you?'

'You talk more lies,' Vlad laughed hysterically. 'You may as well be one of my jesters… do tricks like that of my castle's magician… or be some sorcerer?'

'Tricks of the darkest witchcraft would be more appropriate,' the thing muttered knowing Vlad did not hear.

'What be it you say?'

'Like I said previous and repeat,' the thing blinked profusely, 'I can rid you of those chains so you can avenge all those who defy you… relish in all that which you have done bad or wicked, or take pride in all those you have killed or poisoned, burned or slayed.' It fingered its mouth again. 'It is but a small sacrifice.'

'Sacrifice,' Vlad enquired with scorn, 'what do you mean by sacrifice?'

'Denounce that which is from that gypsy… mark it with your own blood and surrender it to me as you will your soul… defy that which you call your Lord Almighty and believe in that which is my power.'

'No, never, that which you tell be deceitful,' Vlad held strong the charm which hung about his neck. 'She be all I have memory of now.' Vlad's voice croaked from his anger, remembering to what Tariana had told him about her charm; that a pure and righteous heart would protect the bearer from evil. 'My wife and son be gone, and that which was my castle… and soon no doubt all that which was my kingdom.'

'Then it is a way to avenge and get all back.'

Vlad stared with sore and hurting eyes at the dark figure, his mind wavering but strong to the precaution that the gypsy charm should not be cursed by evil. His heart warmed to recall their love and wild night of sex, but mostly her timid smile and the soft touch of her unblemished skin. And of course the promise he had made to return it to her once he got out.

'But what use is that charm but as some gypsy heirloom? You are left alone to die in here, so why resist? Soon you will be nothing but a dead carcass, left to rot in here.' As the thing spoke, Vlad shivered to how the thing could be reading his very thoughts. 'You are not any longer that noble prince that she wanted… that is why she abandons you in your very days of need.' The thing growled deep again. 'No longer does she bring you sustenance. No longer does she visit… and no longer does she care.'

'She cares,' Vlad felt tears again escape his eyes. 'It be because she cannot get beyond the gate, otherwise –'

'Excuses,' the thing growled aloud, shifting in the corner with impatience. 'Why do you make such pathetic excuses for such a vagabond girl?' Its voice calmed somewhat before continuing. 'If the keep is abandoned, surely she would make *some* effort to visit?' 'I have treated her badly many times,' Vlad reminisced, 'very much so in Braşov,

along with that girl who now be her friend.' Vlad stared nervous at the figure. 'But she forgive me like we Christians do and –'

Suddenly the thing howled with a deafening shriek that made Vlad cover his ears. 'You will not speak of such,' the thing shouted. 'How can such faith be of use to

you in here, if you die alone?' Its eyes blinked wild as it tried a less cynical and more persuasive tone. 'Defy that which you believe and I can grant all that you wish... avenge your wife's death and that of your man-at-arms, capture back your son, kill those gypsies for they are no good use in either war or crafts.'

'I not listen to your lies anymore!' Vlad struggled to get up, but managed to stagger over to the hole in the western wall. 'I have work to do.'

Vlad could hear the thing still muttering behind him, but ignored it, his determination to escape by his own methods somehow giving him strength. But again, as he had done for several nights now, when he returned to dig, he found he could no longer reach any further, either horizontal west or vertical. Even with his longest root stick, he had reached the furthest he could dig up in hope to the sky. Again he pulled on his restraining chains, but as taught as he could get them, still he could get no further. And now his ankles were hurting bad, not just from bruising, but from his accidental wound.

Vlad tried best to ignore the thing talking aloud to him through the gap in the wall, but it was getting all too much.

'It is no good Master Vlad,' it chuckled to copy Tariana's voice, 'you have got no further than yesterday or the day before that… and what day is it exactly… how long have you been down here… how long will you survive?'

In a fit of anger, Vlad bashed at his restraints with the long, hardened root and then again tried to prise them apart with the gypsy charm.

'I will get these free,' Vlad muttered to himself, but knew the thing would hear. 'I be free someday soon, you will see!'

'You had better not break that which is your dearest gypsy's precious heirloom,' the voice shouted like a supervisory mother, 'or she will be very upset.'

'How can you know what I be doing?' Vlad shouted back, perturbed by how the thing could see though the wall.

'Like I said before Master Vlad,' it chuckled again. 'I see all… your mind and dreams… those of your son… and memories of your dearest wife Jusztina.'

'You shall not mention my wife as I grieve still her memory.'

'Is that true?' the voice scorned. 'Was it not just the night after her cremation, you slept so wild with that gypsy girl?'

'I not listen!'

'But you have it in you to be such a wicked person… to use all that passion on revenge… it is such a powerful and great word… to avenge.'

'I just want to be clear of these irons that keep me from my escape,' Vlad shouted in desperation.

'Then do as I say,' the voice spoke aloud to him calm and slow. 'Bleed that which is your life's blood from your left palm upon that there charm and pass it willingly to me with an open soul.' The dark figure sat crouched in anticipation, its eyes staring wild. 'And those irons will restrain you no longer.'

Although he had tried to hit the dark figure before, Vlad's anger got so enraged he tried to inflict injury upon the thing. But as he raced through the hole and to the corner where it sat, he saw the thing shimmer even more as he attempted to punch it. Suddenly his arms and legs felt like lead, his fists clenched but weak as he found his movement restricted. Even his calls of abuse and defiance came stifled.

'You not listen because you are weak,' the dark figure stated. 'And you can see by my power that you cannot harm me.' Vlad could do nothing but stare at the thing, watching its eyes blink as his body stood wavering and frozen. 'But think of having such powers like mine… the darkest and most unbelievable powers to afflict on those your enemies… to fulfil your revenge?'

'You cannot do such things,' Vlad managed now to speak. 'Such powers do not exist!'

'So what is it that holds you there, Master Vlad?' Vlad glanced about him, conscious of the freezing air that somehow held him immobile. 'It is because of my will that you cannot move, but that I allow you to speak.' The thing stopped blinking to glare directly at him. 'What have you to lose but to surrender a little of your blood… if you do not yet believe in such things, then believe your own eyes when you escape those irons that bind your feet.'

'How can I believe in such,' Vlad fell back giddy but scampered back to his corner. 'These chains will only break to allow my escape, should *I* break them!' He pulled with all his might against the chains and the padlock locking them, and then he tested each manacle.

'It is but a small sacrifice to grant you freedom and to gain such powers.'

'I cannot,' Vlad felt tears escaping his eyes to roll down his cheeks. 'It be against what she told.'

'But she is not the one who starves, and is shackled and imprisoned to die down here.'

'She will not forgive me for such a deed, even if it be to make my escape.'

'It is your decision,' the voice stated slowly, 'and one you must make with an open mind… an open soul… Bleed on the charm and sacrifice it to me and our pact will be done.'

'I be guessing you leave me with no other choice,' Vlad chortled hysterically. 'I be dying without food and water now she not bring it… have chains preventing my escape… and be forgotten by all that know I be here!'

'Yes, you do seem to have no other chance of escape,' the voice spoke slowly his assessment. 'You do seem to be abandoned by that gypsy girl.'

In a rage that left him quite giddy, Vlad took the charm from around his neck and pushed the two sharpened prongs of the tuning-fork across his left palm. Eventually they sliced the skin of his emaciated and dirty palm in two parallel cuts that oozed blood. After swapping the charm to his left hand he painfully squeezed his fingers until his strength gave out.

'Do as you will,' Vlad shouted at the thing, clearing his mind to only think of escape. 'Just set me free and I will reap back all which was once mine… avenge all who betrayed me… seek out all those that conspire against me.'

Vlad opened his tightly shut eyes to stare at the dark figure shimmering in the corner. Although his vision was blurred to his anger and weakness, Vlad threw the charm in the direction of the corner where the thing sat.

Suddenly Vlad heard the bellowing of laughter and with open, glaring eyes witnessed those fiery, red eyes grow larger and larger, somehow grossly enlarged to fill the whole of his cell. Quickly he shut tight again his eyes, but cowered to the corner, his stance wavering as he covered his ears to the most horrific laughter.

Eventually he fell to his knees with eyes closed tight, hands still over ears. But in the darkness behind his eyelids, he could see memories tormenting him; flashes of his past that were horrific... the burning and slaughter of innocent people... the beggars' and thieves' hands he had amputated as punishment, the disembowelment and staking of deceitful women or ones accused of witchcraft, the lines of heads on spikes... and all so many battles he had fought over many years.

It was as though the devilish thing was reading his memories, replaying them in his mind to recall all the evil he had done. But some things he had not... many things he had not... not yet anyway.

TWENTY – FOUR

Exhausted and confused, Vlad woke with the light of late afternoon shining through the grill and onto his face. He needed to move as the daylight was blinding his eyes, and found his body sprawled awkwardly upon the cell floor. After manoeuvring his weak arms up to his head, he managed to rub careful his eyes before sliding along on his stomach. He crawled out of the square where daylight shone against the floor of the pit and searched the corner to where the thing usually appeared. As it was still daylight, he realized that the dark figure would not be there.

Gradually recalling to what had happened, Vlad noticed Tariana's charm lying on the earth in the now empty corner. He crawled to reach the tuning-fork and at arm's length managed to snatch it without getting too close. Sliding back towards what he considered was his safe corner, not far from the hole in the western wall, he started to laugh; a little at first, at believing such rubbish that the charm repelled evil spirits. And then he laughed hysterically at being so gullible in believing the dark figure, thinking of how surely the devilish thing was just some part of his deluded imagination, as for days now he had been malnourished.

He examined the tuning-fork as he turned over on his back, still giggling to see how sharpened the prongs were. *You be no good as any charm for me*, Vlad deliberated. *Probably would never have kept that thing away like she said. The only use this thing will be is to help dig me out of here.* He snorted as he giggled, finding the air quite stale. *Let's see if you can do that?*

Vlad scrunched up his body to pull in his legs, but stared in disbelief. As he went to test the sound of the tuning-fork against the irons about his feet, he saw that he was indeed free of them. Not only had the padlock been opened to release the chains between them, but his ankles were free of the manacles, and so he could walk unhindered. *What be it that happened,* Vlad questioned as he rubbed his sore ankles, retightening his makeshift bandages. *Did I manage to prise each manacle apart with this thing? Surely it was not that...* He glanced to the corner, but saw nothing. *Even if that thing did set me free, surely I can get out of here now before it reappears?*

After placing the charm back around his neck, Vlad collected the water pouch that did not leak and after several sips of urine, climbed through the hole to reach the furthest part of the tunnel. *Now I be free,* he thought with a wide grin etched across his face. *Whether that thing did it or not, I be out of here before it wants anything else of me.* Vlad chuckled again as he dug into the earth with the charm and scooped the earth out of the way with his wooden food bowl. *I be out of here before nightfall, you will see!*

Although in a terribly weakened state, Vlad was ecstatic at being free of his manacles and so he dug as energetically as he could, taking breaks to catch his breath in the stale, dank air of the tunnel. He did not care that his hair, face and body were filthy, his knees, elbows, and face scathed and lacerated, and that his fingers bled from digging; he knew without his restraints, he could soon be free. And so from dusk and into the early hours he dug, laughing now and then at his naivety at believing either Tariana or that devilish thing that haunted him.

With his stomach aching and rumbling, Vlad came weary from his initial excitement and so knew he had to eat something, maybe take more gulps of urine just to relieve his dry throat. And so on his return through the hole in the wall, Vlad crawled around his cell, dreadfully chasing anything he could swallow without retching. There were a few more spiders that had crawled in from the cold due to oncoming winter, and a few more cockroaches. He had even taken up cleaning earth worms in his urine to suck them down in one go. Aggrieved to urinate in the leaking water pouch, Vlad suddenly came cold, and after noticing the dark of night outside, anxiously looked to the corner with fear.

There is was, like a spectral image at first, but as it stopped shimmering, its outline came more defined. Quickly he picked up his bowl and good water pouch and rushed through the hole in the wall.

'You are free of those irons I see,' the voice said as Vlad squeezed through the hole, 'be it with my help of course.' Vlad paused not to look behind him, but sensed those fiery red eyes glaring at him. 'So do you not believe me now?'

'It be something I did,' Vlad protested. 'I pulled them apart in a fret of anger.'

'I do not think so… a weak mortal as you would not be strong to do so,' the voice affirmed. 'And yet you not thank me for your freedom.'

Vlad hurried to start his digging again as to ignore anything else the voice said, trying frantically to close his ears without covering them. As the voice mumbled on about the pact not being complete, Vlad dug on frantically, wishing morning would come sooner than the few hours that he anticipated. Somehow, even though he was imprisoned in the darkness of his cell, he could sense the arrival of morning well before the sun rose in the east.

Gradually Vlad's hopes of escape diminished the more and more he dug away earth that revealed a large rock. He dug anxiously around it in hope that it was nothing too big, but as he hauled away the earth with his food bowl, his assurance to rid himself of his claustrophobic world diminished.

'You did this?' Vlad shouted back at the devilish thing back in his cell. 'You knew this would happen… that be why you not grant me powers… you toy with me… not let me escape… you knew this would happen!' Vlad took gulps of stale air to relieve his dizziness. 'You play with me you bastard!'

'Now then Master Vlad, it is not that,' the voice announced. 'Did you not say that there are foundations below the outer wall of this keep?' Vlad could not understand to how the thing could know about the rock blocking his escape and so stopped to listen. 'You should have more faith in the powers of darkness and not in those pitiful beliefs you had before.' Vlad gulped at the musty air, his ears ringing as he tried desperately to listen, subdued now to his hopeless predicament. 'You have yet no control of your situation, and as I said before, you must surrender too your soul.'

'You want me to die here, is that it?' Vlad spluttered out. 'Take my soul in death without reaping the rewards you promised?'

'I believe that rock be part of no foundation and can be moved. But only your belief in the darkest power can move such a weight.'

Feeling all over weak and claustrophobic, Vlad was losing any patience he had left.

'You get me out of here you bastard,' he hollered. 'You just want me dead so you can take that which be my soul.'

'Blaspheme means nothing to me Master Vlad,' it teased to copy Tariana. 'And I did not get you into this predicament. It is but your choice to honour that which be our pact.'

'Curse you, you bastard, I can do this no longer… be toyed with in such a way.' Tears ran from his eyes to his ears as he lay on his back. 'It be better I be dead than be tormented by you!'

'You have no need to die, but to surrender that which is your soul.' The voice paused for a response, but Vlad kept desperately digging. 'I bestow on you dark powers, but you not yet know how to use them.'

'Then I want proof that such powers exist… move this there be rock and I shall believe such!'

'Vibrate the tuning-fork against the rock and watch it break,' the voice declared. 'It will be but dust to allow your escape.'

Vlad paused, deliberating the thing's instructions, thinking it was madness but what other choice had he?

After twanging the tuning-fork against the rock, he felt the whole ground around him reverberate as wicked laughter came from the thing back in his cell. As the laughter escalated to a deafening roar, Vlad covered his ears, but witnessed the great rock before him crack and crumble into nothing but gravel and dust. But with nothing to support the earth to where the rock had been, the earth about him collapsed in on him.

In terror of suffocation, Vlad panicked to clear all debris around him, but was struggling, as earth was in his eyes, his ears, nose and throat.

'You do this to kill me,' Vlad hollered after spitting out dirt. 'I see that which be your power, but know you want only my soul.'

Although trapped by clumps of earth and choking, Vlad paused to listen, but could only hear wicked laughter. He kicked back soil, he cleared best his face, but the air was stifling, his consciousness growing faint. Gulping at the stale air, he managed to free his arms to place the charm back around his neck and found his food bowl to clear more earth.

'If I am to die,' Vlad spluttered with tears streaming down his cheeks, 'then take that which be my soul… have done with me, and leave me in peace!'

Suddenly the laughter stopped and then he heard the voice announce in the distance.

'Give your soul you will,' the voice resonated through the blockage of earth between him and his cell, 'but you not yet know the powers you now bestow.'

Vlad was truly suffocating, his breath frantic to gasp any air he could. And with oxygen depleting every second within such a confined area, he knew he had not long before his consciousness would leave him.

However, he found the last of his strength to fight as if it was his last battle, kicking and scraping at the earth, hollering curses at the thing that he could hear back in the cell muttering the same words over and over. He banged at the earth and yelled to what he thought now was to be his earthly coffin; trapped underground in the tunnel that was to be his escape, his salvation to the outside.

Slowly he felt he was losing consciousness, but could hear other sounds, as from above more earth fell against his face. He shook his head in one last attempt to keep himself alive, but knew his lungs were starved of oxygen, his arms heavy as lead, and his legs and waist trapped by heavy soil. He tried to wriggle but the weight around him held him immobile. Now only his arms were able to reach out to try and drag along his body. But starved of energy and oxygen, and in such an enfeebled state, even this proved futile.

It was then he thought he had passed out and was dreaming; thinking his arms were being pulled upon and his body tugged at. But in the total darkness he could see nothing, until a blinding light shone upon his eyelids.

And yet all the time all his ears could hear was that voice repeating the words…

But you not yet know the powers you now bestow…

…you not yet know the powers you now bestow…

PART THREE

TWENTY – FIVE

Tariana tried to push Sorin aside, but the giant Russian had heard the Hungarian guards checking the entry gate and so hid. She nipped into the alcove with him, thinking if they could not see him, surely they would not see her.

Waiting a minute or two to ensure the guards had moved on, silently Tariana and Sorin crept around the outskirts of the Visegrad keep, trying best to hide undercover of the wall. But as it was difficult for such a large man to remain undetected, Sorin signed to Tariana for them to return to their wagon as in a couple of hours it would be dark.

'We be having a little more time yet,' she replied grouchily, 'besides I want to check that drainage pipe.' But Sorin signed his disapproval as they might be spotted, especially if moving the wagon. 'Then go and hide the wagon within that clump of trees as they be opposite that wall.' Tariana pointed to the western horizon. 'The west wall be the one the sun be shining against before it sets.' Sorin rolled his eyes and signed that he may be clumsy but not stupid. 'Go then… go and be quick!'

Sorin ran to the wagon and quickly whipped the horses about to head in the direction of the copse of trees. At the same time Tariana crept slowly around the base of the outer wall of the keep, heading towards the west side wall in search of the pipe.

It was not until she saw the drainage outlet again that she realized how narrow its diameter was, and how Lydia would struggle to get through, never mind herself or Kateryna. Carefully she stepped back to inspect the height of the wall, gingerly walking along its base to scan for other possible ways of entry, but the drainage pipe seemed the only access. Somehow the western wall looked even more steep and sturdy than the others, probably because of the prison cells, she assumed.

Soon she found herself back at the drainage pipe, peering into its darkness and grimacing at requesting such a young girl to crawl inside. And now she knew it was an impossible task, especially for her or Kateryna. But surely there had to be another way she could get a little food and water to Vlad?

A tap on her shoulder startled her to shudder, before spinning around to see Sorin towering over her.

'You test my nerves big man,' Tariana said, her knees still trembling. 'What have I told you about…?' Tariana cut short her sentence to see Sorin sign and point angrily at the drainage hole. 'Yes, I realize such now, it be too small for Lydia never mind…' He signed again with even more irritation and conveyed his want to leave. 'But Vlad be starved in there… he want only this little food and water.'

Sorin held his arms to the sky and grunted loudly to express his displeasure, eventually turning to traipse back to the wagon, but stopped abruptly. As he stood motionless, Tariana approached, her dark eyes searching his face, perplexed to his pause. And then he turned back to face her, his expression full of curiosity.

'What be it?' Tariana stepped close to him. 'Why you not let me help the man who gave we sanctuary at his keep… the castle he have now lost?' Sorin signalled for her to keep quiet. 'Why, do the guards still patrol, as I see no…?'

Swiftly Sorin took Tariana in his strong arms and held one hand to her mouth to silence her. At first she wriggled to try and set herself free, but as Sorin signalled for her to listen and pointed to the ground, she calmed so he would release her.

'What be it you hear?' Tariana silenced as Sorin grunted at her to be quiet, again pointing at first to his ear and then to the ground. 'But I hear nothing!'

As Sorin signed to clarify how his hearing had become more acute over the years, Tariana could now hear something like a knocking. Sorin signalled that it sounded like a knocking of wood on rock, but Tariana could hardly make it out, never mind detect from where it came.

'Where be it come from?' Tariana's question went unanswered as Sorin searched the area, stooping to listen at the ground.

The big man stepped around in bewilderment, traipsing back and forth until he paused over a small embankment very close to the wall. Tariana observed him turn and focus on the sound, his stern face searching the long grass beneath his feet until he again pointed to his feet.

As Tariana stepped close by, she noted Sorin signal that the sound was beneath their feet; that strangely it was resonating from under the ground.

'Maybe it be noises from that drainage pipe?' Tariana saw Sorin shake his head. 'It could be some animal... moles or rats?' And then she too heard the moaning. 'It sounds like some dog trapped... maybe in that drainage tunnel?' But again she noticed Sorin shake his head.

Together they sat on their knees, both searching the long grass and trying to locate from where the noise came. And then suddenly Tariana saw Sorin wield the axe he kept across his back and strike it into the ground. At first she saw nothing but clumps of grass and weeds, but as his powerful arms swung the axe deep into the earth, she noticed him displace soil. Carefully avoiding his axe at work, she scooped and kicked the earth away from the hole, so he could dig deeper. For short periods Sorin paused to listen more intently, and then excavated in another direction, trying to locate from where the sound was coming.

Soon Tariana could hear wailing, the sound intensifying the deeper Sorin dug. And then it sounded like a voice hollering and cursing, until suddenly it stopped as the earth below them caved in to reveal a tunnel below.

'Sorin, stop with your axe,' Tariana called as she spotted the body of a man buried in the earth. 'There be a man buried and stuck in the hole.' Quickly she scooped away as much earth as her hands could excavate. 'We must get him out or he die from no air!'

Sorin moved Tariana aside and with his long and powerful arms reached deep into the hole, his big hands trying to grip what remained of the man's clothing. But as the clothing constantly tore, Sorin located both of the man's wrists to heave his body out by pulling both arms. He slid the man out onto the grass verge, eventually turning him onto his back for Tariana to inspect.

Tariana stood aghast as she wiped away the dirt from the man's face. It was Vlad, but she could not see that he was breathing.

Quickly she asked Sorin to stand him upright, and with the large Russian supporting Vlad' back with his arms around his waist, Tariana poured the contents of her small water pouch all over Vlad's face.

Abruptly Vlad's eyes shot open as he gasped eagerly for air. With his mind suddenly awakened from such haunting images, and his ears still tormented by that voice, Vlad's body startled into panic. With his wooden food bowl still clenched in one hand, he swung it at the figure in front, lashing out against the blinding rays of low sunlight that hurt his eyes. But then he lost grip of his bowl as he turned to face something that held him from behind. And as his blurred vision made out some enormous figure holding strong now his shoulders, Vlad struggled before reaching for the charm around his neck. As he struggled to pull free of what he thought was some large, devilish entity, Vlad jerked the charm from around his neck and struck it at the enormous figure.

Vlad felt rivulets of hot liquid flow over his right hand and down his arm, before being shoved backward. Distraught to shield his eyes and face from sunlight that seemed to burn his skin, he ripped open what remained of his shirt to cover his head. And then as he cowered into the long shadows from the wall, Vlad's eyes accustomed to see his right hand covered in blood. And still he held tight the tuning-fork, its two prongs also covered in blood.

Vlad glanced up, his ears also now tuning into the sound of heavy groaning and the stamping of heavy feet. He could feel through his bare feet, the weight of the large figure stumbling about as he again tried to focus against intermittent rays of blinding sunlight that shone through distant trees.

It was then, as he hid the shadows, that Vlad could now see the big Russian he recognised as Sorin, Tariana's large henchman. The giant man writhed in agony as he held his one large hand to the side of his neck, blood seeping through his thick, chubby fingers. Sorin threw his axe to the floor as he inspected his hand to be covered in blood. The large Russian bore a most wicked stare at Vlad and began to advance toward him in haste, his anger so fervent he did not notice the hole that he had dug. Suddenly Sorin dropped to the ground, his one leg falling into the very hole from where he had pulled Vlad. Sorin tried best to pull out his leg, but found it snared by roots and rock. And gradually he felt his enormous strength slowly draining with every pulse of blood that squirted out from his neck. He wailed at Vlad, but his curses were just loud snorts and grunting as his eyes fixed on him with such anguish.

Cautiously Vlad approached the trapped Russian, but found the last rays of the setting sun still harmful against his vision. He fell back against the wall, first glancing at his bloody hand and then at Sorin, the big man's body snared like some animal in a trap. And he could see now, as his eyes focused out of view of the setting sun, that Sorin was losing consciousness from lack of blood.

Confused to what had happened, Vlad froze in his dilemma, trying to differentiate between the haunting images and what must have been his rescue. He glanced around in bewilderment to see Sorin stuck in the hole with his neck pouring of blood, the axe stained with grass and earth. And then he recalled the feeling of his arms being pulled…

Vlad gradually came to envisage what must have happened, but he knew that trying to help the big man now could put him in danger. What could he do, but watch the large Russian drift into unconsciousness? If he approached Sorin after such an accident, such a big man could spring back at him in hatred; some reflex before dying. But surely he could not watch him die, if the man had genuinely tried to rescue him?

As he glimpsed to see the sun finally set over the western horizon, Vlad felt guilt come over him. But as he wiped dirt from his face and tasted the blood on his hand, all that guilt was strangely replaced with a malicious, unnatural hunger, as if darkness now swirled about him, poisoning his mind with evil thoughts. He licked again his hand. Oh how sweet was that life giving blood? At first it was a disgusting coppery tang, but now his demented and ravenous thirst craved for it. And now he could hear again that voice…

You not yet know the powers you now bestow… but also the sacrifice you make… and to what you will become… drink that of only the blood of life… or you shall weaken and perish…

Suddenly Vlad found himself arched over the big Russian's dead body, sucking and licking at the hot blood that oozed from Sorin's neck wound. At first he felt sick and disgusted at his act, but found that with every swallow he took, his body came invigorated, somehow energised with a dark and strange power. He paused to look at the charm, its prongs sharp like two needles, which were what made the deep incisions into Sorin's jugular vein. And then he had to drop it.

It was not right to kill the man who pulled him from near death, never mind kneel there and drink his blood like some ravenous night creature. But it filled him with an abnormal and euphoric power, one he could feel run through his own veins. And although he knew he still had the scrawny, emaciated body from surviving weeks in that cell, he felt cold but animated... so alive. But what had he done to himself? What was this pact that the dark figure had induced on him? Is that why his humanity seemed to be ebbing away... replaced with the need to drink blood from this dead man? And why did he have to drop the tuning-fork, as its metal suddenly seemed to burn his skin?

Sorin had been a gypsy traveller, Vlad recalled; a friend of the gypsy girl he had found so enchanting. And then he remembered Tariana. But where was she?

Vlad pulled himself away from the giant Russian's dead body, spinning around to stand and hold his head in his hands, feeling the cold of night enclose about him. As he sensed twilight give way to the darkness of night, at first he shivered, but then welcomed the cold of the night. As so many emotions flowed through him, he felt dejected to sense that somehow his humanity was leaving him. He tried best to fight against it, erasing that image of those terrible fiery eyes, to remember his best of memories... of Jusztina and Mihnea... his long friendship with Henrik... the many soldiers that had fought to the death alongside him... long summer nights in Poenari. And then it came to him the memory of his beloved gypsy friend, Tariana. But where was she if Sorin was here dead?

Vlad opened his eyes, the light of day almost gone, replaced by the shadows of night that oddly he could see beyond. Moreover, he could hear the rustle of trees, the wind and night creatures scurrying about in the undergrowth a good distance away. What was happening to him?

Perturbed and giddy from all his new experiences, Vlad stumbled along, turning back now and then to see if Sorin could still be alive. But somehow he had sensed his death a while ago. What were all these new strange feelings... these abnormal senses he had attained?

Suddenly his naked feet caught against something at the bottom of the embankment. And as he steadied himself, he glanced down to see another body. He stooped to turn it over. It was Tariana.

He remembered now to what must have happened. And there she now lay, unconscious and bruised from the swipe he had given to her head with his food bowl. At first he looked upon her with pity and felt his heart ache, but gradually the cold of night seemed to ebb away his love and want for this gypsy woman. And then as he closed tight his eyes and tried best to shake haunting thoughts from his head, he could again envisage those fiery eyes and the voice that spoke with them.

You are not any longer that noble prince that she wanted… that is why she abandons you in your very days of need. Vlad opened his eyes to glare down at Tariana sprawled in the long grass. *No longer does she visit… and no longer does she care.* He shook his head and gritted his teeth. *Why do you make such pathetic excuses for such a vagabond girl?* He approached near to look upon her pale, but beautiful face. *No longer does she bring you sustenance. No longer does she visit… and no longer does she care.*

Vlad looked away towards the gypsy he had already killed, although accidentally. Sorin's corpse was propped up like some half-fallen statue, its one leg bent at the knee and the other submerged. He glanced back at Tariana, wondering too if she was dead.

In his mind the voice spoke again.

…kill those gypsies for they are no good use in either war or crafts.

'No…' Vlad bellowed, his eyes closed and releasing tears. 'I gave my soul for your pact, but I will not harm her if she be alive!' He glanced at Tariana again before touching her face, slowly rolling her head from side to side. 'Should she still be alive?'

For a long minute he knelt to look upon her, his heart and mind rejecting this new, strange influence. And as he was suddenly relieved to see that she was breathing, he wet her lips and forehead with water from her pouch. But as she stirred and spoke slurred words, he glanced back at Sorin, knowing that she would have questions.

'What happened to me Sorin?' she murmured. 'Did you get the wagon?'

Quickly Vlad tore off his bandaging from around his wounded ankle to bind Tariana's wrists together behind her back. And as he saw her eyes flicker with activity, he tore a strip from his emaciated shirt to blindfold her.

'Sorin what happened?' she repeated to ask. 'Get the wagon... we... we go back to camp.' As Tariana struggled to get up with her hands tied, Vlad pushed her firmly against the ground. 'Why is it I cannot see?'

'It is me Tariana... Vlad.' He paused to find an excuse for blindfolding her. 'I not want you to see me like this... but you must travel with me until the time be right.'

He stood and glowered down at her as she wriggled in the long grass. At first she was quiet, but then she came agitated, her questioning becoming louder and louder.

'Why you bind my wrists, I cannot free them?'

Vlad had no choice but to gag her too with another strip from his shirt. It was then as she mentioned again the wagon, he squinted to look into the darkness of night to spot their wagon enshrouded by a copse of trees. As she wriggled hopelessly, fraught with her mouth gagged, Vlad paced through the long grass to retrieve the wagon.

By the time he had pulled the wagon alongside her still wriggling body, he could distinguish her murmured questions.

'Why you gag my mouth Master Vlad?' 'You need to keep quiet.'

'Why?'

'The guards.'

'Where be Sorin?'

'He went…' Vlad glanced up to study the big Russian's body again. 'He went to distract the guards… we meet up again later.'

'But Kateryna be waiting at camp,' she coughed against the tightness of the cloth. 'Lydia and Andrei, they wait too.'

'You need to be quiet,' Vlad repeated. 'I shall load the wagon to get away from here, but you must be quiet.'

With surprising new strength Vlad lifted Tariana and sat her on the wagon. Next he emptied a sack full of clothing to conceal Sorin's dead body, eventually laying him on the rear of the cart. It was then that he found some clothing for himself, including a long and dark, velvet robe with a thick hood, ideal for hiding much of his face. Surely he could use this during the daylight hours to hide his face and shield his eyes from sunlight.

Standing on the wagon, Vlad could hear Tariana murmuring again, but paid no attention as he was searching the area. At first he saw Sorin's axe, and then Tariana's water pouch and food bundle. Quickly he stepped down to retrieve the items, which if left, he knew could be used as evidence to trace him.

In his one last sweep of the area, before hastened to leave, Vlad saw something glittering near the hole from where he had dragged Sorin's body. He stepped nearer to identify it as Tariana's tuning-fork charm. Indeed he had promised to return it to her, but for some reason wanted to keep it himself, at least until he found out why that thing back in the pit, wanted it as part of his pact. But as he went to pick it up, he found that the silver metal burned marks into his skin. And so with another strip of cloth from his soiled shirt, he wrapped tightly the cloth around the handle so he could hold it again properly.

Vlad heard Tariana murmur questions to what he was doing, but ignored her, eventually whipping the horses about to speed away from the Visegrad keep and towards a lane that cut through woodland. As he headed in what was to be a long haul back to his keep at Poenari, Vlad heard a voice calling from a camp fire, but set the horses to gallop as to escape a young gypsy girl who ran following.

As he rode as fast as the horses could gallop, he glanced back to see the girl running behind, but noticed her eventually stop, stooping forward to hold her knees as she was clearly out of breath.

'That be our wagon you steal,' Kateryna called. 'You be hanged, you thief!'

Vlad glanced at the blindfolded Tariana beside him, wondering if she had heard what Vlad deduced was the friend she had mentioned. But then he realized that somehow his hearing had come more acute, even better than that of the once Russian mute, whose dead body now lolled about in the cart behind him.

TWENTY – SIX

When she awoke Tariana found that again she was blindfolded. But feeling herself bounce against jolts from the wagon, she deduced that she was now lying in the back of the cart. Although she was not now gagged, at first she kept quiet and listened to her surroundings, but all she could hear was early evening birdsong and the heavy grind of wheels as the wagon raced upon rocks and gravel.

'Master Vlad, why do you drive this wagon so hard?' There was no reply, but she was sure she heard him snigger. 'Where is it that we be now?' She heard him sniff and cough. 'How long have we been travelling… you reach soon your keep?'

'Be quiet gypsy girl,' Vlad instructed. 'Be soon approaching the river if we continue with haste.'

'Why Sorin not travel with us?'

'He went back to your camp in those woods,' he lied, grinning to see the dead man's large body roll around not far from her. 'In the end he be unlike those our enemy in size, but be the same in cowardice.'

'That not be true, he be one of the bravest men I know,' Tariana retorted, struggling to get comfort from her bound wrists and ankles. 'Why he go back to camp… he usually follow me?'

'Maybe he would have,' Vlad chuckled quietly and then said aloud, 'He insisted in going back to camp, maybe for that other girl.'

'You mean, Kateryna?'

'Yes, if that be her name,' Vlad pretended, glancing again at Sorin's big body bundled in the wagon, concealed in the heavy sack. 'Maybe he liked her more than you?'

'But we be best friends,' Tariana went on to tell, not realizing Vlad had spoken in the past tense. 'We have been through a lot, so it be strange he not come.'

'Again gypsy girl,' Vlad snorted, 'things can change so all of a sudden, especially if your precious love be involved.'

There was a pause for a long moment until Tariana came curious again. 'Why be it I am now in back of wagon?'

'You must have passed out, so it was good that I grabbed you before you fell off.' Vlad sniffed and again cleared his throat. 'Besides, I not have to make excuses if people see you blindfolded up here. And so it is best that we travel by night.'

'I not see that it be night… you not answer me to why you blindfold me?' She waited for an answer, but none came. And so she wondered to why she could have fainted. 'Me passing out like that, it must be an after effect from being knocked out…' And then she stopped to remember. 'But it be you that hit me… but why?'

'I told you to be quiet.'

'But you can answer me at least this one thing… why hit me so?'

'I awoke as you pulled me from what I thought was to be my early grave,' Vlad described slowly. 'I panicked and so lashed out. That be the truth.' He again cleared his throat. 'Now be quiet, we travel with haste back to Poenari.'

'But surely enemy soldiers still hold your keep,' she proclaimed, 'and you have no army to defeat them.'

'I will have soon,' Vlad said soft and slow. 'You ask too many a question gypsy girl.'

'My name you know is Tatyana… or should I say, *Tariana*.' She raised her voice as she came irritated by her restraints. 'Why tie me and blindfold so I do not see? Why treat me so?'

'It be for your own good until we reach the river.' And then it was Vlad that came unsettled, his thoughts recalling all those arduous nights in the cell. 'You treated me kind at first, to that I agree, but raised my hopes only to forget me… left me to rot in that filthy cell night after night, tormented by that fiend.' Tariana went to interrupt, but he spoke on. 'I was left alone in such filth and darkness, and so had to find my own way… dig west towards the sunset as you told of the outer wall being not far. I scribed the end of each day against the wall in hope that you would return, but you did not. And so I used it to dig as it was useless for anything else, until…'

'That not be true,' Tariana injected. 'It work but only for the righteous… only a pure and Christian heart can make it warn off evil spirits.'

'Is that true?' Vlad sniggered. 'I thought it be nothing but some old and decrepit, gypsy heirloom.' But then he came quite curious because the dark figure had wanted it to do his pact. 'So what would happen if a soul took hold of the charm for such evil purposes?'

'I hate to think, but I was never told such,' Tariana paused, trying to recall things told to her years back. 'But why ask such of this?'

'I was just wondering,' he said as an excuse.

'But what be this dark figure in your cell,' she asked, 'this fiend?'

'It be nothing,' Vlad pretended and changed the subject to announce, 'We be reaching the River Argeş soon so give up this idle chatter as I be having work to do.'

'Work,' Tariana asked, ignoring him, 'What work be that?' But she too was ignored as Vlad kept silent, and after several minutes felt the wagon slow down and swish its way through water until it stopped on rocky ground on the other side of the river.

'Where we be,' Tariana asked. 'I hear the river and that you went through it?'

'We travel day and night to get here with haste,' Vlad responded. 'Mainly travel by night to avoid enemy soldiers and those Hungarians back there.'

'How long I be tied up on here?'

'Several days, but mostly you be asleep.' Vlad jumped down from the wagon and dragged out Sorin's body, watching it fall against the shoreline with a thud. 'And I was wishing you would be still asleep and quiet now.'

'What be that noise?' Tariana heard the thump of the heavy sack, but paused to listen. 'Now I hear the river.' She heard Vlad moving around but could not distinguish to what he was doing. 'Are we at the base of the mountain that supports your keep?'

'Good guess gypsy girl,' Vlad said as he sat on the edge of the cart and pulled her body around. 'But that be all you be knowing for now, so be quiet.'

'But let me see,' she pleaded. 'Untie me and I promise I not run.'

'I not think so,' he said slowly, his face not far from hers after cutting the binding around her ankles. 'You be scampering like a rat if you see me now.' Vlad was truly distraught with how he looked but this strange new power overwhelmed his grief. 'It not only be my body you deserted in my time of need, but the nights alone in the darkness of that cell played devils with my mind, and the time with that fiend has somewhat changed me.'

'You said there be a stranger in the cell with you, but there be no one there when I visit,' Tariana responded, feeling his breath upon her face. 'The Hungarian king insisted that you be imprisoned alone. So there be no fiend as you tell. It be nothing but your imagination!'

'And how did you come to hear such words from the king?'

'That girl and I heard them talk in council as Kateryna know their language. But that be the first visit. I could not again visit after, as I could no longer pick the gate.'

'Yes, you left me after giving me hope... abandoned me when I needed help most!'

'You still be chained by wrists if not for me,' Tariana retorted, wriggling against

her wrist restraints. 'Be best if I did not, as you could not hit me like you did!' And then she held strong her breath, detecting his face close to hers. 'But how you free them *your* ankles?'

'I be free now to avenge them my enemies… whether it be that deceptive bastard of a king or those small and cowardly Turks. I also have vengeance with that brother.'

'But since you left me… us, that night,' Tariana could still sense Vlad hovering over her. 'Apart from those who take troop with you to be ambushed, you have now no army or any of my gypsy comrades to help in this your revenge… not that we would do so now anyways as…'

'But gypsy girl, I not need the weak and vagabond peoples of your camps,' Vlad interjected to laugh aloud, feeling power from the dark of the oncoming night. 'Nor do I need other foreign allegiances.' He stooped close to her so that his breath expelled against her tight lips. 'I have a new allegiance that commands the armies of the night… that fiend in that cell will become my greatest ally, as he promised me powers to do things no man can comprehend… I feel it now… it fills me so…' His mouth was so close to Tariana he could have kissed her lips. 'And so these powers that fill me shall take revenge on those my enemies and all who have defied me!'

'I be afraid and sense that you have changed, Master Vlad,' Tariana said solemnly. 'Not just it be your tone of voice but…'

'Yes on that you be right my gypsy girl,' Vlad interrupted. 'My looks may not be as appealing as before.' His bony, cold forefinger smudged a tear that escaped down her cheek as it was not absorbed by the cloth of her blindfold. 'But do not pine for me, as it be not tears of sadness that you should now shed, but that of joy that I have an almighty power to avenge them my enemies.'

'What be it you have done to get such power?' Tariana disbelieved the story Vlad had mentioned earlier as there was no one in the cell when she visited. 'And what will you be doing with me… I be your friend, remember?'

'I not need such friends and comrades in what I do now.'

'Then take off this blindfold, return me my charm and I go without word or deceit.' Tariana felt a sharp, cold touch of metal slide down her cheek, over her chin to her neck, before slowly gliding down to her chest. 'If that be it, why it be sharp?' And then she felt it cut and rip at the ties of her bodice about her cleavage. 'What be it you still want from me?'

'But if I let you go, I will miss that which excited me.' One of Vlad's cold hands pulled at her clothing as the other explored beneath her bodice, manipulating the breasts of her heaving chest. 'Never have I been so besotted by such beauty, and that night… that night you were wild like an animal of the night. It was such bodily pleasure… a desire of the flesh.' He looked at how the blood pumped through the veins of her taught neck. 'What wild perverse you have… but such innocence.' But now he could feel that she was trembling. 'Not that I will ever hurt you as to that I laid promise… and why should I, as you open my mind to such superstitions when I said there were none…

but it be true my friend… there be an entire dark truth to it all… and I thought you as a witch, but it be that gypsy curse that now darkens my heart. It is he to whom I gave my soul, and it is he who is not just some tormentor in my cell… but he is…'

'You do not have to succumb to such a curse,' Tariana bawled. 'Surely such devilishness can be reversed if you take back and be the man you once were?'

'But it is the Dark One who I drew such a pact with.' Vlad's cold fingers moved over her shoulders, pulling down her blousing before again molesting her breasts. 'I regret that I must give up these pleasures of the flesh, as my desires be augmented to retribution… that now my soul crave not this beauty that you have gypsy girl, but the magnificence of revenge.' Suddenly he dropped the charm as its silver had again somehow burned his long, skeletal fingers. 'But maybe this gypsy curse has secrets to protect it so.'

'I implore you Master Vlad,' Tariana said fearfully, 'if it be that you do such with my charm, it will not end well, as mothers before our mothers insisted it be only used by a righteous person… someone who be good and pure of heart.'

'Like you, gypsy girl?' Vlad disputed, but went on to contend his past. 'But what has being such a righteous man brought me?' Vlad questioned heatedly. 'Praying to that which be your God has bought me nothing but grief.' He held Tariana strong by her shoulders, his icy, cold hands a deathly touch upon her naked, pale skin. 'Now I have no army or comrades. I have a wife dead with sin and condemned to hell, a son no doubt to be corrupted by that our enemy, and a failed legacy to honour the Order of the Dragon. Instead of endeavouring a duty to my father, I was sent a brother who betrayed me and sides with that of our enemy.' He shook her by her shoulders. 'Why should I be some righteous man? *This* is now the only way to seek revenge.'

'But it will not end well,' Tariana whimpered, 'as without men to fight at your side, you will only get yourself killed.'

'And why should you care?' Vlad spat out to interject. 'No doubt you gave up on me as soon as you saw my predicament.'

'That not be true,' Tariana cried, more tears escaping to roll down her cheeks. 'I just could not get in… I tried but… the gates be locked and there be…'

'You gave up on me, as you see me no longer a prince,' Vlad shouted, pushing her back against the wagon. 'A nobleman and a gypsy… as if that would earn respect?'

'It would be of respect,' Tariana muttered quietly, 'if someone loves another no matter who they be… that be why I still love you although you hurt me so.'

'You would not love me if you laid eyes on me now,' Vlad chuckled. 'It was a good thing that I knock you out.'

'Has the man I once loved changed so much whilst he be in prison?'

'It be not just my mind that be changed as the time has defiled me.' He again approached close enough to kiss her lips. 'But it also taught me a way to seek revenge.'

'Take off these blindfolds and I be the judge if I still love you now or not.'

'I think not,' Vlad withdrew to gather Sorin's body in secret. 'I am withered and unkempt… I am now but a fraction of the fine man I once was.' He flung the Russian's heavy dead body upon a shoulder as if he had the power of ten men. 'Now I am no prince of this realm, or that mighty warrior I once was, but I will gain back that which was once mine without an army of men.'

'But Master Vlad, how can you do such without soldiers to command?' Tariana listened intently although her body was sprawled awkwardly against the cart. But all she could hear now was the whoosh of water, distinguishing Vlad pacing through the river. 'And what will become of me, I not eat or drink for days now?' She was feeling dizzy but called again. 'I be hungry and thirsty… it be days now. Untie these bindings!'

As Vlad's traipsing through the water faded, Tariana gave up calling as she was truly feeling giddy.

She shifted about and felt her foot kick something, and so fell off the wagon and onto her knees to try and discover what it may be. And although she had felt her legs brush against it, it was difficult to locate it with her sight impaired. As she wriggled along like a snake, she rolled over and managed to grab the object between her fingers. And swivelling it about in her fingers, she realized that it was in fact her charm, but the tuning prongs were now pointed and sharp, its handle now bound in cloth. She tried to pierce the binds that entwined her wrists, but winced as all she managed to do was to prick her skin. Gradually she gave up, but decided to hold onto it, as after all, it was formerly hers.

Listening to waves that rippled against the shore, she wriggled down towards the sound of the river and joyously felt the cold water touch the cheeks of her face. Slowly she dipped her mouth to take sips of the water until in her desperation of thirst she took gulps that also washed her face. Suddenly she gulped at what she thought was weeds and so spat it out. Again she gulped at the river water, but became sick with such an empty stomach. Tariana sat up trying best to steady her dizziness, but with such hunger and dehydration, she passed out upon the shore.

Although in her weakened state, when Tariana awoke she knew her charm had been taken from her grasp. And as she was still blindfolded, all she could do was listen to her surroundings. But now she could feel the cloth that bound her wrists being replaced by rope. She knew it was Vlad, as again she recognised him sniff and cough. But why now were his strong hands so gaunt and cold, his fingers shaky as he clamped her wrists together?

From lying in the back of the wagon, Tariana was suddenly lifted and carried towards the sound of the river, after which she was sat, her legs crossed, her bound wrists resting on her lap. She listened to the snap and crackle of a campfire as the heat from its flames warmed her face. And then suddenly her blindfold was removed.

At first the bright flames of the campfire blinded her vision, but as she blinked to focus on the dark of night, she could see a figure dressed in a thick, dark-velvet gown; a garment resembling a monk's habit. She deduced it was Vlad; recalling that the habit had been one of the garments left in the back of the wagon.

She glanced about to notice that they were close to the water's edge, and then squinted to try and identify him. But as Vlad's figure moved to hammer a wooden peg into the ground, she saw him shimmer against the flames and oddly cast no shadow along the ground; it being as though the firelight shone right through him, as if he was not there at all. She rubbed her eyes to better scrutinise him, but now he towered above her, his face hid under a heavy hood.

'You may fish and reap berries to eat, but the rope will only permit limited movement.' Vlad's coarse voice went on to instruct, 'And do not test my patience should you try and burn the rope or dig out the peg to escape, as I be giving you only this one warning.'

'Why you be treating me like this?' Tariana peeked to make out his pale, gaunt face that emerged now and then from beneath the heavy hood.

'Things are different now, as you will find me changed,' Vlad moved stealthily, but with weird, rickety movements. 'And you will not look upon my face until I feel I have your trust.'

'But why not,' she asked whilst testing the rope that bound her wrists in front of her. 'I can still love a man even if he be a little changed?'

'I am changed more than you think,' he declared with a deep voice of regret. 'I feel my soul ebb away each passing night.' As Vlad turned quickly, she noticed to how haggard his face looked, but could not define his features. 'But every passing night, this strange power fills me more and more.'

'I not care to what you think you have become,' she remonstrated, 'but can help you if you let me.'

'I am beyond help in such the way you speak, for my soul is taken to a pact with the Dark One… this I did to escape such fate in that prison.'

'But surely it not be too late?'

'Concern yourself with your own problems,' Vlad professed as he threw down her pouch of fishing tools. 'Go catch fish to cook like you did that morning I left you.'

'I will catch enough to feed us both,' Tariana stated, trying to peek at his hidden face, 'and have sweet potatoes to bake from our wagon.'

'Do as you wish,' Vlad pronounced, 'but I will not need such sustenance.'

'You not like my cooking,' Tariana grinned at him, trying to humour the situation, or was it because she felt so tense and uneasy? 'I still have my special herbal tea?'

'I not need anything from you.'

'But you need something to eat, surely,' Tariana queried, standing to step and approach, but felt the drag of the rope on her wrists, 'build enough strength to recruit armies and fight to honour your father's legacy?'

'Avenge I will,' Vlad distanced himself from her. 'But there be no more love in such honour… only the magnificence of revenge and slaughter.'

'Does love mean nothing to you now,' Tariana ran forward to grab his long sleeve, but he backed away. 'Does *my* love mean nothing to you now?'

'I am passed that point of return,' he grumbled low, grabbing her wrists with icy cold fingers. 'You will not like me as I not be the man I once was.'

'I shall be the judge of...' Tariana quickly retracted one hand from his grip and pulled away his hood.

In the time before he stepped back to replace his hood, Tariana saw now that Vlad was indeed different; his face long and gaunt with eyes sunken into dark sockets, his skin a deathly greyish blue, his eyes – although still that piercing green – were bulging bloodshot red. Oddly, his nose and ears looked enlarged against the gauntness of his face, with his head balding. As he raised his hands to push Tariana to the ground, she saw how withered they looked, his skeletal fingers strangely elongated with fingernails as long as bird talons. But with the strength that had left her breathless and sprawled upon the shoreline, she sensed him now having an immense, strange and abnormal power.

But then Vlad turned to approach, his one hand holding his hood to hide his face. 'It was true on that night, I had never felt such passion, but all that be gone now.'

Although she could not see them, she could feel his eyes glaring at her. 'You be the temptress that make me which I am now... gave me that which the Dark One now controls to curse me... possesses me more and more each night.'

'I gave you my charm to keep your faith in our Lord,' Tariana contested as she sat glaring up at him. 'It be not my fault if you did wrong with it. I thought it may protect you and help you move on from all that has happened.' She paused to observe again how his body shimmered in front of the camp fire as he stepped towards her, his figure casting no shadow from the flames. 'I thought we could move on through all of this together.'

'Have you not forgotten all that happened to me… why I have become like I am?' He pointed out across the river. 'It was this river to where I sacrificed Jusztina's body to the flame, to cleanse her of her sins… after being betrayed by my brother and lose my keep.' He stood with his back to her as he looked out across the River Argeş. 'And now any love I had will be consumed by this evil until it cast me to hell to join my wife.'

'But surely you can reverse this curse before it takes hold of you?'

'It has consumed too much of me already,' he described stepping swiftly towards her. 'I am afraid that soon I will not be able to resist hurting you.' He yanked her to her feet, almost dislocating her arm from her shoulder. 'Now do your fishing and find berries to eat.' He dragged her to the riverside so they were perched by the water's edge. 'But remember what I said about the rope… do not test my patience.'

As his icy, cold fingers let go of her wrist, she looked across the vibrant, glittering water of the river, until her eyes came back to observe the calm water of the shore. In this still, dark water, she observed her reflection and the stars that twinkled above her head, but to where Vlad stood, she saw that he cast no reflection into the water, his body not obscuring any of the mirrored stars above. For a while Tariana found it hard to swallow as all spittle had gone from her mouth, but then spluttered out a request.

'It be hard to fish by night, but I be hungry, so will try as you say.' She approached close to him, but Vlad turned his face aside. 'I have no knife to gut the fish as you took my dagger... the one you said would be mine after we lost dearest Henrik.'

'Do you take me for a fool?' Vlad snapped. 'Think I will hand you back that dagger so you can cut free of that rope.'

'I promise I will not,' she blabbered, trying to observe again his face. 'I have not yet the strength to escape you, never mind find my ways back...'

'What be that?' Vlad interrupted sharply.

'I hear nothing,' Tariana paused to listen, but could only hear the rush of water and night creatures, 'only owls and such.'

'It is far distant, so only I can hear it.' Vlad paced around trying to locate the source of distant footfall. 'It be soldiers on the march... most likely a garrison of the enemy tramping towards the river to make camp for the night.' Vlad rubbed his long, spindly hands together with excitement. 'Maybe I get to try out my new strength against those worms… see what benefits this curse be having?'

'I have a campfire to cook, but how do I gut the fish?' Tariana kicked the earth in dismay. 'Guess I be having just a sweet, baked potato for suppers.'

Whilst she looked glumly at her feet, suddenly Vlad tossed the charm down by them. After seeing its silver pongs glimmer against the emerging moonlight, she glanced up at him.

'Use that to gut your fish,' Vlad instructed, 'but its prong be not sharp enough to cut rope… and if it does, I will not be far behind you on my return.' He took paces towards the woodland, but turned to speak again. 'I will avenge those that be my enemies, but to you gypsy girl I have no quarrel, unless you deceit me so.'

'But why is the handle wrapped in cloth?' Tariana asked as she stooped down to retrieve her old heirloom. 'Will I not be able to keep it when…?'

She stood tall and glanced over to where Vlad had given warning, but in such a short time, he had vanished.

TWENTY – SEVEN

Tariana knew it would be difficult to fish from the river at night, even if it was only early evening. Moreover, with her wrists bound together by rope, her endeavours were always going to be hard. And as she had not caught a thing, she baked her last two small, sweet potatoes, turning them intermittently on spiked wooden skewers just above the flames of the campfire. Fortunately, the skewers proved more than adequate to roast the potatoes and retrieve them to eat. But at that moment, as she tried best to bite away the charred skins, they proved to be still too hard and raw.

She looked hard into the darkness of the river, and then across it, into an eerie woodland. *How long would Vlad be? Had he gone to ambush the enemy; if so how could he possibly do it?* She looked all around her at the dark landscape; somehow strangely fraught by spectres she imagined hiding throughout the shadows. She had camped out in the wilderness mostly all her life, but alone things felt different; there was no Sorin to support her, or any other gypsies she usually made camp with. She looked pensively at the rope that bound her wrists together, until finally staring into the flames of the campfire. *Surely he would never know where I be should I cut free these bindings*, she thought. *He would never know which way I went?* She recollected to what he had said about never being far behind her, should she betray him and escape. *What would he do to me if he caught me after my escape?* She shuddered to the thought after contemplating him now such a changed man. Or was he indeed a man now, as he looked more like some living corpse? *I must at least try? But first I need to eat these even if they still be quite raw.*

Tariana grimaced to bite into the uncooked, but scorched, sweet potatoes. However, she munched away ravenously as she did not know when her next meal would come. With her gums and lips still tingling and somewhat singed, she rose to her feet to find her charm. But then as she retrieved it from her fishing pouch, she heard in the distant darkness from upriver, the sound of marching feet. Quickly, thinking these were enemy soldiers, she tried to cut the rope binding her wrists with the prongs of the tuning-fork, but at such awkward angles, all she could do was cut her skin.

She ran over to the peg and fell on her knees. With one hand scooping away soil and the other digging the prongs of the tuning-fork around the peg, Tariana worked frantically, but was getting nowhere; at the same time the marching feet of the garrison resounded nearer. Panicked and annoyed to her fruitless attempt to free herself, she pulled on the rope not knowing that it had circled and got caught in the campfire. Again she tried to pull tight the rope, and then looked back to where it had snagged against the crossed branches that supported her skewers. *How stupid*, she thought, *why not use the fire to burn the rope?* And indeed, by the time she ran back to her campfire, the flames were indeed eating away at the twining of the rope.

But now the sound of marching feet was but a short distance upstream.

Tariana pulled repetitively on the rope until eventually the burned and weakened part snapped free. Darting about to grab her belongings, she returned to the campfire to extinguish it, but firstly grabbed a well-lit branch to use as a fire torch. Her worn boots came scorched and she could feel the heat burn their soles, but ran to the water's edge, eventually cooling them in shallow pools as she ran down stream and away from the marching garrison.

But then, standing on the shoreline of the River Argeş, she paused again to listen, as another garrison of marching feet proceeded towards her from downriver. Again this must be another enemy group, probably ordered to strengthen the other. If she was to be sandwiched between them, what could she do? She could not attempt to wade across the river, as although this part was relatively shallow, the current was fierce and could sweep her away? Surely her only escape was to hide in the dark of the woodland, maybe wait until the enemy had passed. Or maybe, she could scout around them?

It was then that she realized that she was on the side of the river that led up to Poenari, or at least the highland it stood on. And on this side was that secret entrance, a cave concealed by a waterfall that cascaded over and into a stream that met shortly the river. As she heard the echo of marching feet now from both sides, she was at a panic and so darted to the darkness of the woodland.

Hiding within its depths, but just enough to watch the enemy garrisons meet, Tariana glanced behind her into the shadows of the woodland and then up and down river. Her thoughts of the enemy going to reinforce their capture of Poenari was disturbed by a strange, dense mist that flowed towards her, through the woodland and towards the river's edge. At first she was worried, that if she got enshrouded by it, she could lose her way; maybe end up running straight into the enemy. But as she paused to watch this strange, thick mist, it glowed intermittently as it meandered its way towards river.

She traipsed swiftly along the shoreline in cover of the edge of the woodland, trying best to keep out of sight of the enemy whilst she searched for that waterfall and cave. And then, as she stooped to take breath, exasperated to see the waterfall not far, she watched how the mist lingered on the edge of the river, hovering not far from the amalgamated group of enemy soldiers. *How strange,* she thought. *Never have I ever seen a fog bank move towards a river and linger so... surely the cool draft from its flow would push it down stream?* For long minutes she hid behind a large fallen tree trunk, baffled to watch such a thick assemblage of mist dawdle beside the shoreline, as she observed too the enemy. However, she required better hiding and so raced towards the waterfall, covering her fire torch as she ran beneath it and into the cave.

Peering back through cascading water, Tariana could just observe some of the enemy, but realized that her makeshift fire torch was almost dowsed. She placed it down, out of the way of sprays of splashing water, and in its diminishing firelight, tried again to remove the rope binding her wrists and its tail wrapped around her arm. Eventually, but after taking a number of cuts to her wrists, she cut free her binds and used the rope to wrap around the flame of the fire torch. Gradually, as she watched the enemy soldiers move upstream, she smiled to see that the flame had ignited the rope to burn brighter.

Spying to watch the garrison march past, she backed further into the cave, hoping that these enemy soldiers knew nothing of its entrance. But then she realized that some of the enemy must be protecting the passageway up to Poenari; that Vlad had mentioned its passageways to be ominous and deadly, but not impassable. She remembered too, then how Vlad construed that this must have been the way the Turks had besieged Poenari, but to how they got past the dungeon door and assailed the keep, he was baffled.

She poised then to remember Vlad being so handsome in the firelight of their night of passion, but suddenly chilled to a breeze, and felt that someone or something was watching her. Turning swiftly to face the dark passageway that led further into the cave, she took fright and dropped her fire torch. It was then the realization of how Vlad looked now, that almost made her heart stop.

Although most of Vlad's face was concealed by the thick, velvet material of his hood, Tariana could see his pale, haggard face from the flickering firelight of the torch on the ground. She could see now how withdrawn his jaw and cheekbones were, his eyes bloodshot red and withdrawn into dark sockets, his nose now hook-like against such gauntness. And then she felt icy-cold fingers grasp tight her neck, her breath short of air from restraint as well as shock.

'My dearest gypsy girl, Tariana,' Vlad spoke slowly, his voice gasping somewhat. 'I am very disappointed in that you broke that which you promised… to try not and escape those ropes that I put on you.'

'But I… I be…' Tariana stuttered after observing more of his gaunt face. 'I had to do it, or the enemy be murdering me!'

'Is that so,' he muttered, his breath short, but from previous exertion.

'And there could be more of the enemy in this passage, as did they not take –'

'There be none here now,' Vlad laughed and sniggered, 'as I be taking care of all in here.' He tightened his grip on her rasping throat, 'As I will too be taking revenge on those that march outside.'

'But surely you…' Tariana groaned, her throat compressed by his elongated and bony, cold fingers. 'We could escape through here... and now to your keep?'

'I think not,' Vlad instructed, knowing that Sorin's unburied body was not far. 'We must face that our enemy outside.'

'But we be captured… that be why I escape… but not to dishonour you.' Tariana choked and so Vlad released more of his grip. 'I be trapped and so killed.'

'And raped and butchered before that,' Vlad smirked to describe. 'But what be it I do with you now my dear... such a wild, but beautiful gypsy girl?'

'But if you talk that way, and I see you as you are now,' Tariana fretted, 'I not sure what be my worse fate?' She then watched him revolve her one wrist with his other hand to ponder over her blooded cuts. 'What be it you want and do with me now?'

As she saw Vlad's eyes glare at the dried blood from the cuts of her left wrist, she panicked in the need to be free and went to strike him with the tuning-fork held tight in her right hand.

But Vlad was freakishly fast, his hand releasing her left wrist to whip up to clench her right wrist, the tuning-fork halted not far from his face.

'You should not test me in such a way gypsy girl,' he said with discontent. 'The enemy be out there!' Releasing her throat, Vlad grasped the charm from her right hand, but dropped it as it burned again his long fingers. 'This your charm will prove worthy in my revenge, but its metal have still curse against me.' He picked it up from the ground with cloth and again wrapped its handle so he could hold it properly. 'But I shall keep it now, as your intentions seem to be against me.'

'But I be afraid,' Tariana spluttered after coughing. 'You be a changed man. And I not know...' She paused again, observing the change in his face. 'I not know what you want or do with me?'

'You should not be afraid of me, but that of our enemy... like those soldiers that be outside. They are the ones who would butcher all your people.' Vlad sniggered again, his nose quivering. 'But they will not be there for much longer, as I devised a plan long before they approached.'

'You still promise to keep safe those that be my people on these lands?' 'I keep no more promises, as you did not yours.'

'But I be murdered like you said, should I have been still tied to that peg?' Tariana was pulled aside and dragged further into the tunnel. 'Where be it you take and want of me?'

'I take back that which was mine,' Vlad rasped briskly, 'my keep at Poenari.'

'But that be where those soldiers mostly likely be heading… to secure more your keep.' She grimaced as he pulled strong her arm. 'Maybe you assassinate easy those that be in this tunnel, but there be too many a number out there?'

'Like I said, I have devised my own plan.' 'But you have no army?'

'My army fills the night… is the night… and all that comes with it.' He pulled her close, his eyes wild. 'That enemy outside might be of number, but be vulnerable to the elements and creatures of the night… like that mist which can disorientate them in their movement… the trees of the forest… the beasts in the dark.' He saw that she was either perplexed by his words, or just scared. 'The power of your charm was told to me… as with an evil heart, the tone that keeps away night creatures, can now summon them.' He sniggered a little, seeing that she was stunned by such knowledge. 'The very opposite to which *you* kept it for my dear.'

'How can you know of such?' she fretted. 'How can you know where the enemy be going?'

'The darkness of the night may blind those who be mere mortals such as yourself and those soldiers… the mists controlled to lead them astray… the creatures and elements of nature summoned… but their eyes be my vision… their will to kill be mine.' Again he noticed Tariana either horrified or confounded by his words. 'It be like your dreams… your premonitions to envisage the future.'

'My dreams… my visions,' Tariana contended, 'they be a gift by gypsies of old and from my country, but they have no control over what happen… no one be having such control over animals and the forces of nature.'

'So you be unconvinced of this power which was granted me by the Dark One in my cell.' Vlad dragged Tariana by her wrist, and on reaching the waterfall, pointed his free hand to the cascading water above and flowing over them. 'Observe my friend… can your dreams do this?' Ensuring she followed his waving hand, she watched the cascading water part so he could pull her through without getting wet. 'And that be not all.'

Tariana glanced back in disbelief to see the waterfall return to normal, but then with both her wrists now clenched together by Vlad's cold, skeletal fingers, she felt herself being lifted and drift towards the river, her feet but inches from the ground. Shocked by Vlad's calm, but supernatural strength, she was too terrified to question him, her eyes bulging wide as he glided her to the shoreline of the river. It was not until they both lowered to set foot again upon the sandy shoreline that Tariana stuttered to ask.

'But how can… how be it you do such?'

Although Vlad's face was still quite hidden by his heavy velvet hood, she saw him simply grin at her. And then he pointed again, waving his hand at the dense mist hovering on the other side of the river.

'Watch gypsy girl,' Vlad scoffed. 'Observe of how that mist will now surround that our enemy and confuse them in their march to my keep.' He stared menacingly at her as his hand somehow grasped control of the fog bank. 'And they will not reach Poenari if the elements of nature and the creatures of the night be summoned.'

'A mist cannot kill enemy soldiers,' Tariana stammered to contest. 'Surely they will still reach your keep to take refuge?'

'You listen not to what I say, or what I show you.' Vlad grasped her wrist tighter to watch her wince. 'The forces of nature be stronger than you can imagine… winds and rain to gather storms… move the trees of the forest… these are but many things granted to me by my pact with the Dark One. A small sacrifice I have done to bestow such powers… but now have to live indifferently to the way you do.'

'What be it you sacrificed?' Tariana fearfully asked, but then remembered his previous statement. 'You have surrendered your soul?' She saw him nod in agreement. 'But what be this difference of living… can you never love again?'

'I cannot eat or drink as you… only blood is my life.' He released her to explain, knowing her curiosity would prevent her from running. 'I look withered like this as my soul now belongs to the Dark One… but my strength would match that of any army… and I be having now these great powers that you have just witnessed.' Scared stiff, Tariana could ask no more questions but stared at his strange, hypnotic glare. 'I will show that my revenge begins this night and all nights thereafter. But first I see that our enemy have crossed the river.'

Again Vlad clenched Tariana's wrists together with his long, cold fingers. And before she could attempt to wriggle free, she found herself drifting across the shoreline, until her feet glided just above the spitting torrent of the fast flowing river. She trembled to feel the cold water spray her tatty boots and shivered to see Vlad glaring wild at her. As they reached the calm pools of the opposite side of the river, again she glanced down at her feet; her reflection standing just above the dark water, and at her side there was no reflection of he who carried her. She glowered up to see if Vlad still held her there, and after noticing his bloodshot eyes, saw blood begin to trickle from both his nostrils.

Gradually somehow his grip on her was diminishing, until not far from the misty edge of a woodland, they both collapsed to the ground, Vlad kneeling in pain with blood flowing from nose, eyes and mouth. Tariana gasped in horror, as although she found it hard to contemplate all that he had just done, she could see he was hurting.

'Why you bleed so… nose, eyes and mouth?' Tariana stood; glad now to be free from his freezing grip, but concerned. 'Why be it so?'

For a long moment, as he fumbled about in some weakened state, she felt pity for him whilst trying to take in all that had happened. But then she saw that he had dropped her silver charm. Quickly she raced to grab it from his side and stood close, stooping to watch blood trickle down over his mouth and cheeks.

'It be rightly mine,' she said resolutely, holding high her charm before clenching it tight against her bosom. 'I gave it to keep you from harm… not use to wicked ways!'

'But you have no use to it now,' Vlad groaned as he struggled to stand tall. I need it to kill that there our enemy.' He saw how she held it strong, as now it had no rope to place about her neck. 'But why should it hurt so… and this crossing of water?' He stood tall and wiped blood from his face, eventually licking clean the ends of his long fingers. 'Must be some other curse that be put upon me.'

'I have…' Tariana fretted to look to escape, but knew Vlad had regained his strength. 'I have nothing to do with such a curse, you know that!'

'Yes, gypsy girl,' Vlad grinned to explain, 'but you should stay… as do you not want to see to how I take revenge on those our enemy?'

'I just…' Tariana's eyes looked to the river, but knew of its ferocity. 'I just want to be back with my peoples.' Her eyes looked to the woodland, but exposed to Vlad that she was considering an escape. 'I just be wanting Sorin and Kateryna … Andrei and Lydia… that be all!'

No sooner had she turned to race for the woodland, her little feet running as fast as they could, she saw a mist flow and collate dense around her. She looked up and down river, before glancing back at Vlad. As she saw him glower at her with bloodshot eyes, she felt a strange and freezing cold envelope her body until she could move no longer.

Twenty – Eight

'What is happening to me, why can I not move?' Tariana bawled; her heart pounding as her eyes stared in terror. 'What is it that you do to me?'

She stood frozen, watching Vlad advance towards her, his eyes glowering and quivering strangely.

'I described to you these, my new powers, and still you discredit them… want to escape without witnessing the true glory of my revenge.' He stood close, grinning, somehow feeding off her fear. 'I know you fear me now, and yet you still be curious… want me to be the man I once was.'

'I not know how you hold me here so, as this be no magics of my elder gypsy mothers.' Tariana took deep breaths to prevent her from fainting and took courage to divulge. 'But yes, I want the man back I once knew… I not bother if he be prince or noble lord, but just Vlad… *my* Vlad.' But then again she took sight of his gaunt features and almost cried. 'Free me please from this your spell and I promise not to run.'

'You have broken promises already and will no doubt do such again.' Vlad scowled at her in thought whilst he arched his long, bony fingers together. 'You will witness that which I shall do to that our enemy, as they are your enemy too, be they not?'

'Please Master Vlad,' Tariana begged, tears falling over her blushed cheeks, 'I just want to be free... go back to my gypsy camp.'

'Where be the fun in that my dear?' He gazed at her intently from head to toe, as if admiring a beautiful stone statue. 'You be the one who unwittingly bought me the very thing that bonded my pact with the Dark One.' He stepped forward a pace or two to hold out one gangly hand, his fingers strangely elongated as too were his fingernails. 'I want back that which you just took from me, as I can then start my revenge.'

'It be mine and not to be used for such dark magics.' Although she could not move her feet, Tariana clenched best her charm against her chest with both hands. 'It be handed down to me from many mothers of my gypsy clan.'

'Then sound its bars and see if it works for you now? See if it protects you from such evils?' Vlad teased, his hand still outstretched. 'I guess not, as such a gypsy have little godly power, or be practiced in witchcrafts as I first thought you were.'

'You thought of me as a...'

Before Tariana could finish her sentence, Vlad shot near to loom over her, his eyes glowering down into hers. 'I'll take it… and *you* can simply watch.'

Vlad snatched the tuning-fork from her grasp and stood back a little to admire the heirloom, but careful not to touch its silver metal. Carefully he rewrapped tight the cloth around the handle before pulling out Henrik's dagger.

'Do you remember this my dear?' Vlad teased, as he held the charm in one hand and Henrik's dagger in the other. 'It was once a gift to you in our pact between our peoples, to rid us of those our enemy… but now we be helped in a different way.' Vlad then sounded the prongs of the tuning-fork against the blade of Henrik's dagger.

At first Tariana heard nothing after the high-pitched tone. And then gradually a queer resonance wavered in her ears, before fading to make her feel somewhat deaf. She shook her head for a moment and pouted at Vlad, pleased to feel that her hearing had returned and that nothing else had happened.

Tariana turned her head to see what Vlad was gawping at, and noticed again that abnormal fog bank glowing and hovering on the edge of the woodland. But then strangely, without affecting the dense mist, a strong wind rustled the treetops and blew about her hair and face. She could have sworn she had heard voices in the winds that blew about her, but could not grasp whether they were shrieks of suffering or laughter.

Abruptly, as she went uncontrollably cold, all that stirred went quiet, and all she could look at was Vlad's partially exposed face, his eyes staring wild, his grimy teeth grinning. And it was only then that she realized the dried blood stains about his mouth and chin; had he lived off freshly killed animals? But her thoughts came disturbed as she saw Vlad point out into the direction of the woodland.

Again at first, all she could see was that strange mist lingering and swirling, unperturbed by the wind that blew about the treetops, but then through the fog bank and out from the dark depths of the woodland, she noticed a pair of glistening white eyes appear. Scowling to wonder to what creature they belonged, she then noticed several others, until she realized it was a pack of large wolves. And then as she observed Vlad raise a hand to the sky, she noticed the trees blacken with a colossal mass of dark birds; ravens, crows, and magpies… all types of birds of prey that gathered from all around.

As the black mass of birds engulfed to fill the swaying branches of every tree, she watched them blot out her sight of the moon and the fast-moving clouds that ran across it. She tensed with fright; not just mystified by a mass of different birds flocking together, but now without the light of the moon, the woods and landscape became dark, even the trees seemed to have an unearthly power, their thick branches moving without force of the wind. And as she turned to gawp at Vlad, his eyes quivering strangely in some hypnotic stare, she could sense the very evil he bestow on everything, even the tendrils of ivy and undergrowth that spread the ground. She spun her head away as not to look any longer at his staring eyes, but felt cold fingers turn her head back.

'I will show you that which I have now become,' Vlad growled, his voice hoarse, 'so you see this power that the Evil One has granted me. And it be because of this, your ancient gypsy heirloom, that now I be accursed.'

'But it be you that consent to such evil and abuse my charm,' Tariana whimpered, dismayed by still being somehow frozen. 'But deny such evil and free yourself to live like me… with me… it be because of such that you look…'

'Haggard… ghoulish… a freak,' Vlad gestured, pulling straight his heavy hood. 'But I cannot now lead the same a life as you, as I surrendered my soul to reap these powers to take my revenge… and this I will do… that be certain.'

'But it may not be too late… please, Master Vlad..?'

Suddenly Vlad's face appeared not far from hers, his eyes staring hypnotically into hers as he pulled back his hood. It was then, as she realized the true nature of his gaunt face, that she felt herself being carried along to be pinned against the trunk of a tree. She glanced down, feeling her wrists being wrapped and pulled by vines of ivy, the plant abnormally entwining her ankles too, to entrap her tight against the cold and sodden bark. Again she took deep breaths to stop herself from fainting, trying best to control her heart from pounding so fast. But then, as Vlad stepped back to again admire her some sadistic way, she noticed the huge head of a wolf come sniffing at her legs, her thigh, and then her fingers.

'It be a good thing that he likes you,' Vlad smirked, 'but then again you said you had always been good with animals, had you not?'

'Please Master Vlad,' Tariana begged, again feeling tears run down her cheeks, 'I be sure it be not too late… please do not hurt me!'

'I promised never to hurt you gypsy girl, but you must witness my revenge as I have no one now, do I?' Tariana saw Vlad's hand wave at the unusually large animal, his gesture somehow in control of it, until the wolf back tracked into the dark of the woodland. 'And I will show you all that I can do, to take back that which was mine.'

Suddenly, as Vlad loomed close up against her, all she could see was his bulging, bloodshot eyes. But then as they quivered into some hypnotical glare, she could see a bloodied mist enshroud her. She blinked wildly to reject his mesmerising gaze, but felt herself dizzy as if entering some horrific dream. And what she was about to witness, became just that.

At first, as if in a dream, it was as though she was looking through the eyes of a raven, flying just above the fiercely blown treetops to observe the movement of that strange, dense mist as it drifted swiftly up river. And then in the distance she could see its destination – the combined garrisons of the marching enemy.

As the fog bank sped towards the soldiers to obscure their way and surround them, all they could do was stop and gaze in amazement, wondering to how a mist could appear so. Watching to how it glowed, a peculiar musty yellow, they were then pushed off balance by violent winds that blew out their fires and lanterns. Some men huddled together in armed circles, holding their swords and shields in defiance, whilst others ran, only to either fall into the river or stumble against bracken and undergrowth. And each of these Turks, who found themselves momentarily incapacitated, were subjected to the most bizarre manifestations of evil that the woodland could bestow upon them.

At the riverside, water spurted up from dark, vibrating pools to smother soldier's faces, making them choke and gasp for air, many eventually falling into the river with drowned lungs, their bodies bashed against rocks and the riverbed as they were taken downstream by the fast-flowing current.

The sudden onslaught of fierce winds and the freezing mist spooked many horses so that their riders found them hard to control. From some invisible terror that frightened the beasts, many horsemen were thrown from their saddle and in their weighty armour they battered the ground. They glanced about in a daze, only to be horrified by wild ivy and undergrowth, of which vines shot to them like wiry tendrils, wrapping about their limbs to pin them against the earth. And as rats appeared from the shadows of the woodland floor, the furry black creatures scurried quickly to cover the soldier's armoured bodies, biting and gnawing at their vulnerable openings until they tasted blood. One horseman removed his helmet to scoop away the bristly rodents, but found something else assailing his face.

Tariana envisaged through the eyes of the raven, its dive to attack the fallen horseman, shuddering in her spellbound state to witness the bird's hefty beak peck at his eyes and mouth. And then it tore into one eyeball, as another joined it in its ravenous feast to penetrate the other eye; the Turk's face left torn and shredded, his eye sockets nothing but bloodied, gaping holes.

Suddenly Tariana's sight came to ground level, as though she was running through the woodland on all fours. Gradually as her vision pictured racing images of tree roots, bracken and scrub, she sensed by the snarling and heavy panting, that her eyes were now that of a wolf. Running with her through the forest were many others; unusually large wolves with enormous heads and powerful jaws, racing to a disbanded and confused garrison of Turkish soldiers, their faces terrified to see such wild animals leap to attack at them. And now Tariana winced at the taste of blood as she saw the teeth of her wolf tare into the throat of a fallen archer, the strength of his doublet and light armour no match for the wolf's sharp teeth and powerful jaws. As the archer coughed bloodied spittle and swiped at the wolf, it bared its teeth at his hands, nipping off his fingers as if it were pulling daises from their stems. And soon the soldier's defiance was lost, his mind drifting into unconsciousness as his torn throat pumped steaming blood over his chest.

And as Tariana witnessed the onslaught from all others of her pack, now the light from the moon was totally shaded by flocks of all different birds of prey; their black wings outstretched to swoop down to ravage at more incapacitated soldiers, their peaks pecking vigorously at any exposed limb or face. She saw many soldiers running to escape, but many did not get far, as when the ravens and crows scratched at their faces and rendered them blind, they were pounced upon by hungry wolves.

Although she had witnessed the aftermath and death of war many times, with such ferocity and brutality of the slaughter about her, she felt herself becoming sick and so blinked her eyes in frustration. But somehow spellbound by the hypnotic state Vlad had induced upon her, she could not shake free all images, and so she called out.

'Please Master Vlad, pity me and stop this horrid nightmare!'

'But it be not just some nightmare that be in your mind,' Vlad's voice echoed strangely from some distance, 'this be what is happening… the start of my revenge against that our enemy.'

'But I cannot be witness to anymore of this, please…'

'But I *will* you to watch them die… *want* you to see them suffer, like they make me suffer… made *us* suffer all these years… and be amused at how they understand nothing of the power of nature and how such evil can control beautiful creatures of the night.'

'Please Master Vlad… no more of this I can take!' 'But feel its power and you may wish to join me?'

'No, never… this be not right… it be inhuman,' Tariana cried. 'The beauty of nature should not be used in such a way!'

'And what be it *your* God has granted you, but much beauty and a voluptuous body?' Vlad sniggered with cynicism before continuing, 'You have nothing of value, live wild without fixed abode and have to scrounge and scrape each day your meals?'

'At least it be what I choose.' Tariana could feel herself wavering, her mind oppressed. 'You can choose too… surely it be not too late?'

'But it *is* too late,' Vlad explained, his voice echoing from her one ear to the other, as now her vision darkened. 'And why should I change as I have nothing now… you of all people now that.'

'But please…'

It was then that Tariana's vision darkened totally, as her body slumped, unconscious.

TWENTY – NINE

In fright of hearing a scream, Tariana woke from her unconsciousness. Glancing down to see that her wrists and ankles were still bound by twines that pinned her against the tree, she knew that this was reality; or at least it was some normality to what she had been subjected. And by the taught vines of ivy that indented her skin, she could feel numbness but pain, her eyes too trying to focus from her blurry slumber. The cold, dank bark of the large oak had sodden the back of her clothes, but as she heard more screams and yelling, this was the least of her worries.

As her sight accustomed to the shadows that were cast by moonlight shining intermittently through the lingering mist, she squinted into the darkness to see figures of men running and yelling. These she recognised, were more Turkish soldiers, the last of the garrison who had survived. Until now that is.

She noticed a swordsman darting around in terror, trying to find his way out of the thick mist that swirled about him. He almost cut down another soldier as they collided, but before they could both share their dismay, the first saw the second get grabbed by his throat. Tariana was as much in shock to see the soldier's arrest as the swordsman; both of them witnessing the Turkish bowman's neck get rapidly entwined, as a snake would writhe around its victim. But the thing choking the bowman's throat was no body of a snake, but that of a thick tree branch. The swordsman lifted his sickle sword and struck several times at the tightening branch, but found he only sliced bark until regrettably it got stuck in its wood. And then as the bowman was raised from the ground, the swordsman lost grip of his weapon and stood back aghast to watch his comrade get lifted to a great height. As more branches entwined to hold the bowman high in the night air, other branches were stripping each other of bark and snapping each other as if to create splintered stakes. And it was one of these that was thrust into the bowman's back with such force that the splintered branch shot out from his stomach, fractured and bloody.

The swordsman froze to witness such a strange and horrific death, but grasped his senses to try and escape. But as Tariana watched in disbelief, other trees swayed now not by the breeze, but with their own movement. Two trees either side of the swordsman reached to wrap twigs and branches about each of his arms until they were stretched apart. Held just above the ground, as if to be crucified, each tree pulled at the swordsman's arms as if to play a tug-of-war with his limbs. Somehow testing the Turk's strength, the trees seemed to argue, swaying and crackling, until each arm dislodged from the soldier's body. Swinging their bloodied prizes to great heights, the trees grabbled for other potential victims and Tariana thought she could be next.

As she noticed the swordsman's body finally topple to the ground, Tariana started twisting eagerly her wrists to get them free, but had to squirm at the pain. And now she wished that all this was some nightmare – one that she could wake from – and all would be fine. But as she whispered a secret prayer to God, she came to realize that only evil prevailed in this madness, and it would have to be by her own doing, that she would escape. She kicked and pulled her legs, trying to relieve the stiff and numbness that had overcome them, and luckily one ankle snapped free of its restraints. She knew that she needed to free her wrists, but the ivy fronds persisted to be taught and strong.

Grimacing at the pain, as she tugged at these abnormal fetters, she stopped to observe a Turkish soldier race towards her, his face full of terror. He paused to gaze upon her, pondering to why she was tied up there, but then heard distant screams and elevated his sickle sword in readiness to defend himself. Suddenly a long black arm grabbed for his helmet and as it was not fixed, it was pulled off. But before the soldier could swivel round to take horror at this extraordinarily long arm, his head was now held with another, as the dark figure of Vlad shot close to loom over him. And after both hands gripped his head to twist and snap his neck, the soldier slumped into Vlad's arms. Carrying the soldier's body, as if it was as light as a child, Vlad's now unnaturally tall figure flew to stake the Turk against another protruding branch. And then Tariana witnessed a glimpse of Vlad's wide grin as he returned to impale the dismembered Turk's body upon another tree branch.

Tariana constantly pulled at the ivy vines restraining her and managed to free one wrist whilst glancing now and then into the depths of the shadowy woodland. She could see Vlad in the murky distance, racing about in some bizarre rapid flight, to kill and impale remaining Turks. She kicked free her other ankle and felt she would collapse with her legs somewhat weak. With one hand now free, she yanked at the vines restraining her other wrist, but could not take her eyes of Vlad's abnormally tall body; his dark figure shifting swiftly through moonlit mists to impale more bodies upon tree branches.

Eventually she snapped the last resilient ivy vine, but fell with weakened legs to slide down the large trunk and roll upon the dank, woodland floor. With legs still tingling from free flowing blood, she crawled at first upon the sodden ground, her arms heaving her forward, her hands slipping against dank leaves and undergrowth. But now she was free and to that she sensed a little relief. But what would happen to her… would Vlad do on to her, as he had done to these Turks? But surely they were the enemy and not she… he had stated that himself?

Tariana hauled herself up to stand, and at first stumbled about like a newly born calf. But with life coming back into her legs, she traipsed the woodland as speedily as she could, squinting at the dark ground so as not to trip. She had covered some ground and paced a little faster, apprehensive still to what could happen to her. But then suddenly she stumbled against bracken and fell upon twigs and scrub, luckily the ground soft enough to cushion her fall.

It was then, as she looked up and wiped leaves from her face, that she noticed a young man – a Turkish soldier not yet older than his teens – lying face-up on the ground, his glazed eyes fixed with a deathly stare up into the night sky. And then she winced, as Vlad's tall and dark figure pounced down beside the young soldier; he obviously not realizing that she had escaped her binds and was there lying hidden within the thicket. She heard him mutter words of the soldier being so young, but about his blood being that of a foreigner. However, to what she witnessed him do, repelled her idea that the man she once loved, could be again the man he once was.

Raising her head enough to see, but not to be seen herself, she watched Vlad pierce the neck of the young soldier with the sharpened prongs of her tuning-fork, until when released, blood poured out from two small holes. And then she saw him crouch over the teen's body, his mouth at the neck, slurping and swallowing the steamy blood as it spurted out.

Tariana could not listen or watch any longer, but if she moved she would reveal herself, and what would he do then? So she shut tight her eyes and put her hands over her ears whilst whispering yet another prayer. And then she asked herself, *why has my charm corrupted him so much?* Her body ached, but she dared not move. *Why has something deemed to protect me, now be used in ways that be so evil?* Tears escaped her eyes as she could still hear Vlad slurping at such a young victim. *If the Dark One be in control of it and him, then why do its silver burn his skin... and why does he come weak to travel across water?* There were too many questions for Tariana to consider, and so as her mind ached and body soaked against the sodden woodland floor, she released yet more tears and sobbed.

Finally she captured enough bravery to glance up at him and saw that his eyes were again a bloodshot red. But the only blood that ran this time was from his lips and over his chin. It was as though this time, the blood that fed into him, made him somehow stronger; whereas last time, after he crossed the river, Tariana had witnessed him lose strength by losing blood from both his eyes and ears. But it was too much too comprehend.

Suddenly she grimaced to see two Turkish soldiers race at him from behind, and although she felt nauseated by his act, she pitied him and wanted to call and warn him. But somehow, as if Vlad could see with eyes in the back of his head, he was conscious of their approach and turned to meet them. But before he gripped strong the Turk's wrist that swung a scythe, the blade had slashed into Vlad's shoulder. Yet Vlad did not flinch and twisted quickly the soldier's wrist, before kicking out at his other assailant. With abnormal power, the second soldier was flung away, as if tossed against a tree like a ragdoll. And then Vlad clung onto the first soldier's broken wrist, whilst he removed the scythe from his wound. He then simply smirked at the Turk after glancing at his injury, after which in Vlad's grip, the scythe's blade split the face of the Turk, making him stumble back in agony. As the Turk fell back and writhed in pain, trying to dislodge his own weapon from his face, Vlad laughed hysterically before his bloodshot eyes narrowed to locate the other.

By now the other soldier had picked himself up from the woodland floor and was glancing on which way to go. But Vlad had other ideas. As the Turk turned to sprint, Vlad's arm again elongated to an unnatural length to grasp his head, before he soared to his side to grin at him. The Turk peered at Vlad, terrorised to what this man had become. And now as this new dark prince paused to contemplate the soldier's fate, the Turk hit his fists at him. But as Tariana witnessed, all the punches he hit Vlad with were somehow quashed; the towering dark figure of what was once the Prince of Wallachia stood unwavering, his gaunt, pale face smirking. And just before Vlad's long and spindly fingers twisted the soldiers head, Tariana noticed something shiny fall in their scuffle.

As Vlad returned swiftly to feed again upon the young soldier, Tariana sneaked undercover, to seek that of which she thought maybe her charm. And as she approached to see the dead Turk lying against a bush, his head rotated to face backward, she winced to kneel down past him and grasp for her charm. But no sooner had she stood with her gypsy heirloom in her grasp, she noticed Vlad hovering over her, his spindly fingers gesturing her to hand it to him. Again she clenched it against her bosom in rejection, knowing that he knew it was hers. But Vlad scowled at her, saying nothing but thrusting his hand more towards her.

Tariana was almost in tears as a group of soldiers accosted Vlad, their Turkish swords slashing at his unusually tall figure, their shouts denouncing him as some ghostly warlord. But Vlad turned again, his strength and speed too much, even as the group attacked him strategically, trying to poke their pikes at him from all sides. Tariana turned, knowing this could be her only chance to escape. But even as Vlad was hampered in dealing with his assailants, she somehow knew he could track and find her. Nevertheless, she sped to a woodland glade, where the mist lingered so light that she could find her way.

As she paced quickly but gingerly along a wide path, tall trees either side of her, Tariana grimaced to look up at them through the dissipating mist. As decorating the trees, were hung dead bodies of Turkish soldiers, their ribcages ruptured by many splintered branches, their faces frozen to expose the terror they had suffered by their sudden death.

She could now hear screams from where she had run from, and guessed that Vlad was relishing in his revengeful game with those remaining Turks that defied him. But somehow she knew they would be the ones who would suffer and die. They would end up like those above her, who hung like ungainly, lifeless corpses, with no purpose but to feed the ravenous birds of prey that she had once seen through the eyes of.

She walked with less vigour, stepping careful against the woodland floor as she noticed bloodied weapons and ripped costumes sprawled across the ground. Somehow this display of butchery and misery drained the life and love from her, her resilience to keep faith, to keep strong in her beliefs. She held out before her the charm and prayed again that it would be to what her gypsy mothers had told, but sadly she had seen the damaged it had caused. Yet as she held out the charm before her, she noticed the cold, strange mist fail to glow and swirl from her presence. Did it still have the fortitude to harness the power of a righteous, Christian heart? Why was it, that she could hold tight the silver metal unlike Vlad? Could it still protect her from these evils… maybe save Vlad if it was not *too* late? Again, as she plodded along, her boots dragging from exhausted legs, her mind ached in deliberating over too many a question.

It was then, as she sauntered along without direction, her mind wavering, that she stumbled against another dead body; a Turkish soldier, one that had escaped the horror of being impaled upon a splintered branch, to be staked and hung high above her. She glanced down in pity of this enemy, even though for years they had raided her camps, raped her gypsy women and took many of their children. In temper and defiance she kicked out at the body as watched it turn over, the soldier's eyes glazed still in terror.

And as she went to circle the body, not sure in what direction to go, she looked back to see a large raven come to peck at the dead man. She stood in bewilderment to reflect on how big the bird truly was, and how its black eyes revolved to blink with a dull sheen over them. It flapped its enormous wings to bounce upon the soldier's chest in order to get a better point at which to peck at the soldier's face. Its body shimmered such a pitch black, but with wings outstretched, exposed deep lines of dark blue. It was then, as its large black beak pecked and pulled out one eyeball that Tariana, feeling her throat dry and coarse, almost retched. Glancing at the man's now bloody gouged eye sockets and hearing the bird shriek to devour more his flesh, Tariana could witness no more and ran.

For several minutes she ran until her heavy legs could only plod her along, her sight of the woodland sometimes escaping her to envisage again, the sights she had seen through the eyes of such a bird as the one back there. And in the distance she could still hear the odd scream that undoubtedly lead to some soldier's demise. And then she remembered Vlad, the change that had become of him; not just to his haggard face, his tall body and elongated hands and fingers, but to his change of character, his neglect of love and compassion, his rejection of all else in his want of one purpose... a man besotted with revenge.

Again she heard another scream and startled from her stupor, kept moving without thought of direction, her legs sauntering her along by instinct. And as uncontrolled tears again escaped her eyes, she heard another sound... the rush of water... the fast flowing river. She stopped to catch her breath, and feeling her throat so harsh against her heavy breathing, Tariana etched a smile to the relief of a drink. But more importantly, if this was the River Argeş, she could find her way back to her original camp, maybe find Sorin and Kateryna, Andrei and Lydia... surely they would have returned there after knowing she was lost to them?

With hope she felt herself a little revitalised and plodded in the direction of the river, finally finding its shore not far from the edge of the shadowy woodland. In the dark of gloom all seemed weird and ominous, but through all that she had experienced, the still night was welcoming, especially as she rushed to the shore of the river to cup her hands in the cool water to relieve her parched throat. *I will get back to them by daybreak,* she reassured herself. *I will find all of them there.* She felt her mind wavering as her stomach rumbled to the fill of water. *And we shall travel on. Unless he can change and somehow be the man he once was, surely I have no reason to stay... have I?*

Suddenly, Tariana fell from kneeling beside the river, her one cheek lying in a shallow pool of water, as again her mind exhausted into unconsciousness.

THIRTY

Rather sheepishly Tariana approached a group she knew from her gypsy camp, but stood for a moment to reflect on the last time she had seen them. With all that had happened since the five of them had travelled to Visegrad on that cart from Brașov, she pondered on how they had all been surviving, and who may now be in charge. As the gypsies had frequently moved along river to avoid enemy soldiers, she had often questioned many people on her travels, but only a few had been friendly enough to give directions. Yet after travelling on foot nearly all day to get to them, now here she was, but what would be their reaction?

She stepped towards their camp fire set in a glade of the darkening woodland just before dusk, and seeing Petru, Remus and Simion she smiled, but felt guilt at being away for so long.

'Have any of you seen Sorin,' Tariana asked, having to appoint a brave face, 'I lose him many days ago, when we go to rescue…?' Suddenly she stopped, as not to reveal her encounters with Vlad, knowing these men did not like him much. 'We get separated some days ago, but...' Again she stopped to muse at their staring eyes.

'We not see him since you squander off with them others,' Petru answered, his eyes now squinting at her with disdain. 'The last we see of him is when he took that wagon with you.'

'I thought he would return here as we got separated you see.'

'No, he not be at this camp,' Simion said, 'but we be moving lots as the enemy be marching up and down river.'

'We thought he was still with you,' Remus told, 'and them others we saw with you, before you travelled north.'

'So Lydia and her grandfather not return here eithers?'

'They did, but only to thank us and collect what be theirs,' Simion informed, 'then they take another small cart to travel back to some place they had passed through on travels with you… some village in…?' Simion could not recall the country.

'It be Moldavia, or on the borders of,' Petru explained. 'That country we travel through about a year back, but they be going more north and west.'

'And Kateryna,' Tariana probed, 'she go with them too?'

'Yes, all three took off because they not like it here,' Petru told, 'Andrei be frail and Lydia young and be scared. It be now many days since they left.'

'Lydia be scared,' Tariana asked, 'scared of that which be our enemy?' 'It be not just that,' Remus interjected as Petru went to speak.

'No, it be this place… these forests that border the river,' Petru took charge of the conversation again; Tariana perceived him now to be the leader. 'Even that girl Kateryna, she be spooked. But it be not just from raids, or of being captured, tortured or raped… no it be eerie along this river from that keep up on the mountain down to that big city south.'

'Bucharest,' Tariana interjected, 'the river that stretch Poenari to Bucharest?' 'If that be what it be called,' Remus said, poking the fire to make it flare.

'I thought they would return and stay,' Tariana scowled. 'I asked them to stop here until my return, should we ever get separated… and we did get so… but they returned just to desert the camp again?'

'Maybe you should not have taken them in first place,' Petru declared, turning skewers above the flame of the camp fire to cook pieces of meat, 'going off on errands to find that owner of the keep… him that took us in, but now have lost it.'

'And where be that wagon,' Simion asked, 'do you not return with it?'

'No, it got taken,' Tariana articulated, but which was no lie. 'I have had to travel here by foot and be tired.'

'Do not think you can have any of this we cook,' Remus said defensively, 'we be hunting all day but only get little reward.'

'I not want your food, but maybe just boiled waters,' Tariana stepped closer to see what other supplies they had. 'I just be disappointed Sorin not here, and that my friends leave without any telling.'

'How can they, if you not get back until now,' Petru told. 'To them you could have been killed by enemy or by fiends that haunt this place.'

'It not just be wolves or bears that ravage our camps at night,' Simion added, his eyes fearful.

'What do you mean by that?' Tariana directed to the men encircling the camp fire, but Sabina, an old gypsy woman stepped forward with a walking stick.

'This place be accursed for sure,' she said, her old wrinkled face surly as her eyes squinted at Tariana in the firelight. 'Not just by enemy soldiers or wild animals, but ghosts and apparitions that kill both us and the enemy. Even the trees seem to be alive to haunt us in our nightmares.'

'It not be that bad,' Petru ridiculed the old gypsy woman, 'you be some more superstitious than many of us.'

'Yes, but we be less safe without them troops from that keep,' Simion disputed, 'or the keep itself to protect us. I had less a nightmare whilst we stayed within them walls.'

'And the foods be better.' Remus tried to take a skewer but Petru slapped his hand to tell that it was not ready.

'Yes, but that owner, or what once was… that so be prince, he be no mighty warrior any longer as he have no more an army… and be that of a changed man.' She hovered over the three men around the campfire, her eyes cloudy, but twinkling in the firelight. 'His heart now be darkened by not just grief… I saw it before that Kateryna tell of what he did to his own peoples of that town.'

'I be lying if I not confess that Vlad be succumbed to strange ways, but he be promising us that no harm come to we gypsies.'

'You cannot trust that man any longer girl,' Sabina told, stepping close to point a finger at her, 'and you be stupid in believing in him from the start.'

'It was good of him to protect us in his keep as we needed to take refuge,' Simion said. 'For once in my life I felt safe.'

'Yes, but that be the least he could do,' Petru intervened. 'Did we not help fight off the enemy when he got ambushed?'

'He would not be living now if it not be for us,' Remus added. 'Many of our peoples died that night!'

'He would not be alive if it was not for me,' Tariana muttered, her memories flooding back to when she first saw him about to be murdered by that Turkish leader. 'I saved him and to me he promised to slay not one gypsy upon his lands.'

'Yes but child,' Sabina interjected, her old voice croaking but strong, 'I heard from that Kateryna friend of yours, before she left that be, that the man you make promise with be dark now in his heart… punish wickedly many of his own peoples… take no pity to those that be old likes me, or be feeble or have illness. His answer to rid us of plague was to burn peoples alive. And now this plague seems to haunt us again, but he be the one bringing it.' Sabina did not see the three men sitting below her roll their eyes, as they knew she tended to rant on. 'There be a new evil that haunt us from the dark reaches of this forest…'

'But you not see, the Prince of Wallachia,' Tariana interrupted, 'this *Vlad*, have lost so much from his keep and army to wife and son?'

'That maybe true,' Sabina answered, 'he be a changed man from losing his wife who died from the sin she committed. But do you not recall that this be the very woman that called you a witch and wanted you burned as one.' The old woman scowled again at her. 'Why you sympathise with such a man's problems, if at all he be a Christian.'

'That man took us in, he feed us and gave water, train and give us new skills,' Tariana fortified, her anger making her quite giddy. 'He loose so much as be his castle, these lands, his wife and son… said he would help find my brother.' She stepped around the group of men to look at each of them in turn. 'Be he a changed man or not, he seeks now to rid us still of our enemy… these soldiers that make you move camp to avoid being butchered.'

'So that be why we decide to move on… one final time,' Petru announced. 'We go back to lands north… be they cold or not.'

'At least they be safe,' Remus interrupted.

'This place… these lands have good earth for crops and with the river it be thought ideal.' Petru wiped his face with both hands in frustration. 'But we be nothing but nerves in fear of the enemy and now this forest fill our minds with evil… we be haunted by nightmares that appear in shadows that linger in mists and the dark…'

'And those deathly horrible noises that we hear at night,' Remus added.

'We dare not stay any longer than need be and have it agreed by all to leave as soon as we can.'

'I maybe old and frail my dear, but in fear I cannot stay,' Sabina explained. 'We all be haunted by horrible nightmares and screams in the night.'

'But together we be strong,' Tariana said. 'If Sorin be here, he be not running.' 'Be it Sorin not return with you?' Tibor interrupted to ask; the only remaining Russian that travelled down from the north with them. 'Where be Sorin, as I hoped he would return. Is he not with you?'

'No, I be but confused to where he be myself,' Tariana told.

'I think he secretly go north with that girl Kateryna as he like her a lot,' Simion interposed. 'Both take off with Lydia and her grandfather.'

'Did you have fall out?' Tibor asked Tariana.

'Why no,' she answered thoughtfully, 'I be last seeing him…' She tried to recall the past best she could, but her mind was tired and confused.

'Maybe he had enough of your deluded love or pity for this Vlad,' Tibor grunted with disapproval. 'Get away from all this death and gloom to befriend someone who treats him better.'

'But it be me that saved Kateryna.'

'Yes, from the very person who you be somewhat besotted with,' Tibor turned away to sharpen his large dagger on a worn whetstone. 'At least that girl thinks more of him than you do… probably met her on her travels with that little Lydia and grandfather.' 'I be nothing but good to Sorin,' Tariana protested. 'It be me who save him from

losing his tongue and learn him a way to talk.'

'So why you take off to help this Vlad,' Sabina interjected to ask, 'and take Sorin along with those two?'

'They all wanted to come… at a chance of bettering their life.'

'Well maybe they do now,' Tibor contested, before disappearing into the shadowy woodland, 'as they not take you along this time.'

'They did not take to liking the way that man treated unkindly his people,' Sabina babbled on. 'He be just some rich lord almighty playing pretence of justice as a way to cover up his deceit.'

'But you not know how he was betrayed,' Tariana argued, 'not only by his brother to lose that which was his keep, but by that king up north, when he was promised soldiers to help defeat that which be our enemy.'

'Then he should trust us or that of his own people,' Petru claimed. 'We proved good assassins and fight strong, but he mocked us, told we be small in numbers and have no understanding of war.'

'But he train me some good… he who was his commander,' Remus said. 'He showed me how to wield correct a sword, and hold shield.'

'You talk of Henrik,' Tariana said with pride, 'he from who I had been given his scabbard in our pact to fight with Vlad.' She paused to reflect on all that had happened since the large Hungarian man-at-arms had fallen to his death; staked upon a splintered branch, similar to how Vlad now impaled his enemies. 'Yes, he was a good man… strong and honourable.'

'Not now like that lord you chase after,' Sabina disputed. 'He be somewhat crazed since his wife die with sin.'

Tariana turned aside to think, but listened to the old woman – and now the three men – condemn Vlad. But as her feelings of love and pity wanted to defend Vlad in his absence, she could not neglect the visions and depravity she had witnessed in him killing all so many. It was not just all those enemy soldiers impaled and staked upon trees to hang and rot, but to the stories she now heard from these gypsies; the old woman reiterating her concern for the young members of their camp after children had gone missing.

Suddenly a shiver ran down Tariana's spine, as she recollected the vision of Vlad stooped over that young soldier, puncturing his neck to drink blood… and the words Vlad had said about blood was now his life. But surely his word and promise would prevail; that he had not taken any gypsy children as Sabina had feared? Now she could hear them ridiculing her and her long absence from camp; to lead astray an aged Andrei and young Lydia, to take Kateryna on some pretence of a better future. And then Sabina interjected to continue and condemn the Prince of Wallachia, her eyes frequently staring at Tariana to make her feel guilty for leading them into this predicament.

Tariana could take no more, and so sped off in temper to make up some makeshift bed beneath the cover of a tree, but as she busied herself with the task, she noticed Petru approach with caution.

'Many believe that you should not now be our leader, and so they look to me,' he revealed with some degree of pity in his eyes. 'And that old hag never much liked you anyways. But, I be proud to what you have got us through this past year, as many be dead if we had not took refuge in that keep, be it when the enemy be strong and many. And it be because of you that we could take refuge there, protect and shelter young or old.' He took hold of her shoulder with one hand. 'If you stay, I for one will be sorry should we lose you as leader, but I cannot condone your quest to save this man who be corrupt and wicked.' She went to speak, but he put a finger against her lips. 'I understand his grief at losing all and such, but have not many of us… you included, with your brother.'

'He promised to help and find him,' Tariana muttered, 'and with his army strong, I thought I have good chance.'

'I should not tell you this,' Petru confessed, but gripped tight her shoulder, 'but we spot that brother of Vlad riding amongst an enemy garrison marching north from that big city south… Bucharest I think you said… for a while he be camped, but should he travel north alongside the river, he be seeing true and unexplainable horrors.'

'What do you mean… what horrors?'

'We did not venture too far south, enough only to spy on the enemy, but returning north we see the horrors of enemy soldiers staked upon trees and poles, their corpses rotting as flocks of big, black birds tear flesh from them. The smell was as horrid as be its sight.' He glared at her with concern. 'What man could do such to peoples? I agree, it still be good that he kill our enemy, but to butcher men in such ways, it be devil's work!'

'He said he want his revenge,' Tariana said quietly, 'and after all he go through.'

'But why torture men so… many still hang there half alive?' Petru grimaced, obviously recalling what they had seen. 'They be the enemy, but we took pity on some… put many out of their misery.'

'Was it truly the brother of Vlad… that small and fair-haired man?' 'Yes it be him.'

'Can you be sure?'

'Yes, I remember his face from our time in the keep,' Petru disclosed. 'An annoying and horrible bastard that thought himself lord almighty.'

'Was that enemy leader with him,' Tariana questioned eagerly, 'that Sultan?'

'I not be sure,' Petru confessed, but came excited to recall another thing he had seen. 'But there was a boy tied back-to-back with another seated on a horse. Maybe that be this Vlad's kidnapped son?'

'And the other, could he be my brother?'

'I not be sure,' Petru scowled in thought, 'I not remember good your brother, but he be older than these on horseback by now, surely.'

'If there be a chance to finding him, you know how important it be to me.' 'Yes, I know.'

'So could you take me to him, just to identify if it be him?'

'No I be sorry, it be too risky,' Petru told adamantly. 'Besides we must be ready to leave as soon as those enemy garrisons meet up and hopefully move on.'

'Then I will go alone and spy to find out myself, if you can please give direction,' Tariana said with wide eyes, but yawned. 'But it be on the morrow as I be tired.'

'I will try and draw map to leave with you and wish you luck.' Petru held strong both her shoulders to show his loyalty. 'But remember the enemy may have moved on from that camp and could now be any place, but most likely be marching along river to meet those who thwart our way north.' He looked away at the others around the campfire, but then returned to gaze at her with sincerity. 'I wish you luck and to be safe, hope you can find out if it be your brother. And if it be him, maybe we can help rescue him once we be settled north… but you know how short in number we be… and that some in our camp now take a dislike to you.'

'I will find a way,' Tariana replied, her eyes tearful. However, was it from his kind words or that she was just so exhausted?

But Tariana knew she could get other help, if asking Vlad did not put her in anymore danger.

She had only slept about an hour or two early that evening, when unexpectedly Tariana felt little fingers prodding her cheek. As she opened her eyes slowly and rubbed them, in front of dim firelight from a distant campfire, she could see the shadow of a small girl. At first she thought Lydia had returned and so rose quickly, but found that it was Alina, Mariana's daughter; a little blond girl a couple of years younger than Lydia.

'Miss Tariana, I cannot sleep like you,' the little girl said, her blue eyes wide with anxiety. 'Your big friend not be here to rock me asleep since I loose father.'

'You talk of Sorin,' Tariana inferred, twisting to sit up properly. 'No he be missing. Some think he go with Lydia… meet up with them to travel north.'

'I miss Lydia as well,' she moaned, but etched a half-smile to remember playing with her. 'Why both of them not be here now?'

'I not be sure about Sorin, I miss him too since we got separated.' Tariana poked the little girl's nose like she used to do with Lydia. 'I just hope they be safe and keep well on their travels north. Petru told she went with her grandfather along with some others, including my friend Kateryna.'

'Will they be safe and away from all these horrible things that happen?' 'Let's be hoping so, shall we?'

'I do not like it here any mores,' the girl sobbed. 'All my friends be busy or missing and I cannot sleep without his big, safe arms to rock me to sleep.'

'Maybe you meet up with them, Lydia and all. Petru tells that you be moving north too… maybe follow them to the village we passed through some time back.'

'Do they have charm to keep them safe likes you?' Alina asked, pointing to the tuning-fork heirloom hung by thin rope about Tariana's neck. As she grasped at it, luckily its sharpened prongs had got stuck in her bodice; otherwise Tariana could have been cut.

'I think not, as this be special… it be handed down to me from many my mothers.' Tariana pulled it from her neck, her long hair catching it awkwardly as it came over her head. 'I be hoping it keep me safe as was told to me.'

'Lydia worried that you might be dead… got killed by horrible men.' Alina revealed as she watched Tariana place her charm down by her bed clothing. 'Do you not wear it to stop horrible dreams?'

'No, I be afraid, I do not,' Tariana smiled, but then frowned, 'only it sounds to warn off...' Somehow she could not say the word 'evil', as she thought it would frighten the little girl. 'It be just like a good luck charm.'

'Why be its ends be pointy now,' the girl asked and frowned, 'it not be likes that before when I see you with it?'

'It be used to dig... and used now like a fork to eat instead.' Tariana was not lying, as she thought to how Vlad probably used it to dig out from that prison cell. 'But you must go back now, try getting some sleep like me... as I be very tired.'

'Can you not rock us both to sleep?'

'No child I cannot,' Tariana was still exhausted, and although she did not want to upset the girl, her patience was wearing thin. 'Alina, go back to your mother as I have long journey on the morrow and need my rest.'

'Can I borrow your charm to keep me safe to sleep?'

'No Alina, go back to your mother as she be concerned to where you be, I need my sleep.'

'Mother tells that the night be filled with terrors, but I see nothing in the dark.' The little girl stood from kneeling and looked into the shadowy woodland.

'Alina, go back to your mother and stay away from the dark, keep in sight of the campfire.'

'If I do not dream, the terrors cannot hurt me, can they?'

'Go find your mother,' Tariana said, as she snuggled down to sleep. 'Mariana be looking for you.'

'I do not like the dreams I be having since being here.'

Tariana heard the little girl's feet pace slowly away, and as she glanced back, she was pleased to see her heading for the campfire.

However, from a distance, Tariana could hear little Alina now mumbling. 'I wish big man Sorin was here to rock me asleep.'

*   *   *

Somehow she knew she was dreaming, but it felt so emotive and vivid. And being a little girl again was so surreal. Tariana felt the youth and energy she had as a child, but now as she ran through the darkening forest, her little legs were tiring as her lungs gasped for air. She slowed pace to glance back. What was that thing back there in the dark?

...the night be filled with terrors, but I see nothing in the dark...

She stopped at hearing noises, but realized that they were just night creatures; a hoot of an owl, screeching night birds... was that a fox or a wolf? Surely you did not hear things like this in dreams?

…if I do not dream, the terrors cannot hurt me, can they…?

But the trees of the forest looked ominous as they cast eerie shadows with the dark of twilight. Her mother would be cross with her, but somehow she had got lost whilst going to the river for water. And back there she had dropped that heavy bucket, a sudden fright making her petrified only to watch the water spill out over the earth. She had done the trip so many times, fetching water through all seasons and weather, but this evening had been different; somehow the last light of twilight was quickly being consumed by the dark of night.

She stood still to listen to the sounds around her, looking too for the flickering firelight of their gypsy campfire. But soon she came frightened to see mists flow towards her, hovering to pause and linger, as if watching to anticipate which way she would go. For many reasons she did not like it here any longer and would tell her mother. Thinking herself lost, she felt she could cry, but she had been told to be strong and keep faith in the Lord, that a secret prayer would keep her safe.

…I do not like the dreams I be having since being here…

And where was her brother, he had only gone to collect firewood?

She felt her heart racing again, her legs turning to jelly as she watched the mist now thicken into some glowing fog bank. She felt it watching her, as if waiting to follow, whichever way she would run. But she had to try. And so deciding her path, she ran as fast as her little legs could carry her. Father had told her to confront her fears, but mother said running from danger was best; cower and hide this day, but at least you will be alive to be brave on the morrow.

Terrible thoughts flooded her mind as she raced through bracken and undergrowth, hearing twigs snap underfoot as she went. Suddenly one of little Tariana's feet got caught in a bramble and sent her flying. At first she was shaken and winded, but rose on hands and knees, using one hand to wipe dirt from her clothes. She looked at her bodice and skirting to see how soiled it was; her mother would be even more cross. And then she looked ahead of her and came puzzled to how the charm that had been heavy about her neck had come off and was lying there. But even more puzzling, was the big pair of boots that stood beside it. After she tilted her head to follow the legs up and see the face of a stranger, she located her charm to grab it.

'That be a much curious thing you take back there,' the somehow familiar voice said. 'What be it?'

Tariana slowly rose but the man still towered above her, his green eyes sharp but somehow kind. She took a couple of steps back and clenched strong the charm against her chest.

'Sorry little girl, but we not be introduced,' the man said. 'Do you have a name?'

She stood, her body tense, her hands grasping the charm tight as she peered shyly up at him.

'Mother say I should not talk to strangers,' she bravely mumbled. 'And I must get back to her.'

'But I be no stranger,' the smartly dressed man declared. 'I be Vlad, the Prince of Wallachia… I be noble lord of these lands.'

'Well m' lord, I must get back to camp… and back to mother.'

'But what be your name child,' the man stooped to regard her more closely. 'Should I know that, I may be able to guide you on your way?'

'Tatyana,' she replied shyly. 'I be Tatyana, and lose my way.' 'Then shall we venture on and find that which be your camp?'

'I be not sure which way to go now,' Tariana bent down to rub one knee, 'and I hurt myself.'

'Shall I take a look?'

'No you not touch me or mother get cross.'

Young Tariana backed away a few paces, but Vlad lunged forward to snatch the charm from her small fingers.

'Give that back,' she ordered, her temper taking precedence of her manners. 'That be mine!'

'But what a curious object it be, and obviously very precious to you,' Vlad said standing tall, the object way out of her reach.

'And why be its prongs be sharp like so, surely it be some sort of musical tuning-fork?'

'It not be like that just,' she frowned and came anxious to him having it. 'What you do to it?' Tariana was again pained by her knee and so stooped to rub it.

It was not until she looked up at the man again, that she had noticed the most remarkable change. Instead of seeing a smart and handsome nobleman, with piercing green eyes looking sympathetically down at her, she saw now a somewhat taller man, his face although shrouded by a thick hood, was gaunt and pale, his eyes bloodshot red and sunken dark into their sockets. His body was covered head to foot by a dark velvet gown that resembled a monk's habit, but his exposed hands and fingers that clenched onto her charm, were gangly and long and as too, were his fingernails.

At witnessing his sudden change, Tariana's heart pounded strong within her chest and she wanted to run, but the thing that once was Vlad, had her charm.

Suddenly all the exhaustion and pain that had tormented her body now exploded from her neck, as in the split of a second Vlad had swung the charm so its sharpened prongs pierced her little neck. And soon she was on the ground, with him stooped over her, his mouth slurping red with blood.

*   *   *

Tariana woke with a start, her body sweating but cold, a shiver shooting down her spine. But what annoyed her most was something prodding her neck. After she brushed it away and sat up from her bedding, she saw it was some cooking utensil, and the person at the end poking her with it, was Petru.

'You take some waking girl,' Petru chortled, 'twitching you were.' He stood from kneeling beside her and smiled. 'Had one of those dreams that foresee the future?'

At first she did not answer him, her mind perturbed by the dream, and that his prodding of her neck was what had made Vlad's attack feel so real. And she sat silent for a while, just regarding him as she puzzled over what the dream could mean. Obviously it was prompted by her talk with Alina, as she remembered the little girl's words.

'Thought you be gone by now,' Petru inferred, 'said you were to leave early.' 'So why, what time it be?'

'It be well after our luncheon... getting on for mid-afternoons.'

'Then it be that I overslept,' Tariana concluded, 'must have been more tired than I thought.' She then stared at him in earnest. 'So why be it *you* have not moved on?'

'We wanted to early this morning as we all be prepared,' he stated, 'but those enemy soldiers have moved only to block our way… probably await those others to join them from the river before all move on… that brother to Vlad included.'

'Then I will go and scout on my way,' Tariana affirmed, 'and if you not be gone by my return, I shall move on with you when they do.'

'But I promised we move out as soon as we can,' he affirmed. 'We cannot wait if we not know how long you be gone.'

'My scouting should not take long,' she said thinking, 'but I might need to return after nightfall or on the morrow.'

'We could move around them, but with wagons and horses, we had better wait.'

'Then I have an idea,' she professed, thinking on her feet as she quickly collected her valuables and got fully dressed. 'I might just know a way to scare them off, or have all of them killed.'

'But how,' Petru asked, bemused. 'How can you ensure those soldiers move on and be back here before we move out?'

'Leave it with me,' she asserted. 'If you can wait for me at least to the morning, I shall see that your path be cleared.'

'But how,' Petru again was baffled to how one gypsy girl could do such a task. 'How can you be so assured of clearing them of our path north?'

'Because, after my plan,' Tariana avowed, 'they most likely all be dead.'

Petru went to grasp her shoulder to question her more, but she raced past him whilst bagging all her belongings. For a moment she turned to glance back at him as she comforted the bagging on her back.

'Just be here on my return,' she asked, winking at him. 'I not want to lose my gypsy friends and be left alone.'

Tariana heard Petru voice more his concerns, but she was already setting a quick pace away in the direction to that waterfall, and its once secret passageway to Poneari.

But in her confidence that Vlad would be delighted in avenging his brother, she could not neglect the fact that she needed to know that he had not hurt any in her gypsy camp; that the stories of children disappearing was not to his doing, as if true, he would have broken his promise. And if she could stop him, no way would he hurt any more children.

Although she knew her way by remembering countryside landmarks, her eager pace soon slowed to her sauntering along, her body already exhausted and stomach grumbling hungry. And knowing the afternoon was rapidly disappearing with miles to go, she came vexed that it would be nightfall by the time she reached her destination.

But now, as she watched the sun set beautifully between steep forested hills, she recollected how Vlad only ever appeared during nightfall, and of how he had hated even the firelight that flickered from her fire torch. And in that time within the cave, before he unnaturally floated her across the river, she sensed something malicious about him, or that something evil now controlled him.

As she followed the river south, wondering to where Radu's army could be, the twilight was already upon her, and hearing night animals welcome the dark, she came quite scared. But why, she asked herself, she had journeyed and camped all her life in the wilderness? Yet along the other side of the river, lingered that strange mist, that which made her shiver, remembering it in her morning dream.

How could such a man, if indeed Vlad was still by human form, be controlling creatures of the night, and the trees of the forest to the winds and mist that stirred them wild? He had explained such by this devilish pact, but even to a gypsy told of ancient superstitions, a man with his ability and power was unbelievable… unconceivable? She could again question him more, but after telling of his brother marching north, surely he would become obsessed with only revenge.

Tariana's heart ached, as all she wanted was Vlad back to the way he once was.

But she knew sadly that now there would be little chance of that.

Thirty – One

It was nightfall by the time Tariana reached the part of the river Argeş where she could see the waterfall cascading over the entrance of the cave. Luckily she had followed the river downstream on the correct side using the light from the moon as it rose ever higher to cross the night sky. As she paused by the shoreline to remember whether she had flint to ignite a fire torch, she squinted through the darkness to scrutinise the entrance. Although it was dark, the night felt sharp and crisp, and with that clarity she noticed something square and bulky hidden a little distance from the waterfall. And so she traipsed across rocks and scree to investigate.

Although covered with branches and foliage, on her approach she recognised it to be the wagon the five had travelled north and west with. Obviously Vlad must have camouflaged it for hiding after he had stolen it from herself and Sorin. As she pulled away the foliage and tossed aside branches, she pondered on what had happened to Sorin, as he would have never given up such a thing that he had repaired so many times. She paused to consider that that should be another question she would have to ask Vlad. But what would be his response? Would he just lie or deny he had any knowledge of where her friend was?

With most of the wagon uncovered, she hopped onto the back, and although it was dark, in the moonlight she recognised stains of blood over a large sacking and across the wooden boards; probably from the poor horses he may have slaughtered. But would the horses not be any use to him now, she thought? She certainly could do with one, to ride back in time and catch the gypsies before they moved on. Again she had so many questions, but how would she ask him?

She approached the cave to see how the waterfall that cascaded over it now flowed less, as the last few days had been dry. Nevertheless, if she was successful in igniting a fire torch, it may still get extinguished, even if she rushed under to get into the cave. But surely that fire torch was still inside the cave, she thought; the one Vlad had knocked out of her hand before taking her across the river? But was Vlad even inside the cave? There was only one way to find out.

'Master Vlad, Master Vlad,' she called out, revolving continuously to shout in all directions, 'I be having news about that brother that betray you, but if I reveal such, you must promise not to hurt any of my peoples.'

She paused to observe the beauty of the glittering moonlight on the river, and apart from its rush of water, Tariana was greeted only by an eerie silence. She felt so stupid and it awkward to shout out to nothing but the shadows and darkness, but tried again.

'Master Vlad, Radu marches an enemy garrison north along this river and I be guessing they meet another to take back your keep.'

As she squinted to examine all about her, Tariana suddenly came perturbed by an unnatural cold of the night, something that she knew did not come from the river. But then she noticed that strange mist again as it swirled and condensed just on the edge of nearby woodland.

'If your brother besieges your keep in double the numbers, you may not get it back again.' She studied the drifting fog bank with unease, noticing too how her breath exhaled to a mist against the sudden cold. 'You could take your revenge and move them on, as my peoples be needing their path north clear.'

Tariana stood freezing, the sudden cold biting at her hands and face. And all that she could observe was that lingering fog bank and to how it crept unnervingly towards her. She glanced up at the moon to try and take comfort in its bright light, but started to back away from that now glowing fog bank that drifted towards her.

'Master Vlad, I know you hear me, I know you do,' she shouted, sensing him have control of that strange mist. 'Your brother may too have your son and my brother, but I not be certain.' She edged her way towards the cave entrance, but then thought it a trap. 'I not likes to what you have become Master Vlad, and that I guess you will never again be that man I once loved, but take pity on my brother should you take your revenge.' The mists were almost upon her now, but she stood strong in defiance. 'Just promise not to hurt any of my peoples, especially if it be my brother.'

Again Tariana was greeted with nothing but silence, but gradually made out a tall shadow standing quiet in the mist. And as it stepped slowly towards her, the drifting mist followed it to obscure her vision. But she knew it was him.

She stepped cautiously but quick towards the river, after remembering how Vlad somehow lost strength to travel across water. And now, as she trod through rock pools at the riverside, her boots standing precarious upon slippery stone, she had to balance herself as not to slip. Clenching tight her charm hung about her neck, Tariana spoke out bravely as she hoped her boots would keep their grip.

'Take your revenge Master Vlad,' she called nervously, 'kill them all and your brother, but leave my brother alone if it be him... and leave alone my peoples... make sure you not harm the children.'

'I have not harmed yet any of your peoples,' Vlad croaked deep, as the silhouette of his figure came more visible. 'My powers be used but only on that our enemies.'

Tariana stepped carefully upon rocks to wade more into the river, thinking it would provide more protection, but came scared of the deeper waters and the ferocity of its current. She managed to keep glancing at him and wanted to believe his words, but again shuddered to what she had experienced and to her predicament.

'So why risk that the river could take you and that you could drown,' Vlad said slowly. 'Why not join me in my revenge, as it be your enemy also?'

'I not be sure you be the man I once trusted,' Tariana shouted fretfully, constantly glancing between him and the fast flowing river. 'You not be a Christian any longer like my gypsy folk, and if I were to die, in Heavens be where I would want to join them.'

'But likes me,' Vlad replied cynically, 'your God has failed you throughout your life, as you be alone without your brother and those parents the enemy butchered.'

'What do you know of my brother or that of my parents?'

'I can now sense such things, like you be having your visions,' he explained, his tall, dark figure standing at the water's edge, his eyes glaring at her from underneath his sagging hood. 'It be another strange power I now bestow.'

'My parents were murdered,' she jabbered nervously. 'This I was told when only young. And that be the time my baby brother was taken.' But then she stammered to ask bravely, 'You sense that my brother not be dead, as too be your son?'

'They both be alive, but what can I do if I rescue Mihnea?' Vlad flared with anger and swirled the mists around him. 'I be now who I am and can no longer father him… I sense him still alive, but after such a time he be now moulded to their ways and custom.'

'I could take them both and look after them,' Tariana suggested, attentive to keeping grip on the slippery rocks. 'We gypsies could take him in and they grow old to be none the wiser.' Tariana bravely asked another question. 'You say my brother be alive, but does your brother have him?'

'I can only find out by spying on them, or my scouts could go.' As Tariana could see Vlad was considering his options, she presumed his scouts were black ravens, like the one she saw from the eyes of. 'You say Radu marches his garrison up this river from the south to meet another north by my keep?'

'Yes, that was what my peoples told, as their path to travel north be hindered by the enemy.' She stepped closer to the shoreline; a little more confident he was only after information to plan his revenge. 'Maybe both armies meet to take back your keep.'

'But surely they not yet know that I killed all that guarded it, and have the dungeon door bolted.' He extended his arm to point at the cave entrance. 'I guard that access so can kill all by surprise. I merely climb that old well and unlock the dungeon door. I see that they will never break that down.'

'But how did they raid your keep in the first place?' Tariana stood poised on a rock by the edge of the river, thinking that showing her interest would calm any bad intentions he might have towards her. 'Did your brother know of that access and how to open such a heavy and armoured door?'

'That be something I might just torture him in telling, as it be the one thing that evades me.' Vlad grinned at Tariana, his eyes constantly studying her precarious stance on the slippery rocks. 'Killing all will be my finest deed yet… but torturing my brother to why he betrayed me so, will be the ultimate.'

'But Master Vlad, do not forget, do not harm my brother if he be with him.' Tariana traipsed back onto shore to follow Vlad in the mist, but had to shout after noticing him leave unexpectedly fast. 'And you be never to harm them my peoples!'

Tariana ran from the riverside to where Vlad had disappeared into woodland, but came uneasy to follow after noticing the mist linger somewhat. At first it swirled thick as if to block her, but suddenly retreated as if inviting her along a clear path. Suspiciously she entered the woodland, thinking if this fog was controlled by Vlad, he must now want her to follow. But after a minute or two, the mist had returned to flow about her and condense quite thick, her sight of her surroundings now obscured. For a moment, as she paused to listen, uncannily the sounds of all the usual night creatures were quiet. She looked up only to see the dim haze of the moon as the treetops above her were all enshrouded in mist. Suddenly she heard the sound of a twig snap, the rustle of bushes, and a movement through the undergrowth. Was it Vlad?

She froze, her heart beating fast, as again she felt the bite of cold air circle around her. At first it was a pair of eyes she saw in the mist, but then others could be seen glistening silvery bright. And then she saw their silhouettes gradually approach, huge dog shapes pacing slowly towards her through the mist. These were obviously the large wolves she too had seen through the eyes of, but in her vision she had not realized on how big they truly were. As they strode lightly to circle around her, she came frightened and considered twanging her tuning-fork. But what would it do in such a situation, as surely by now some evil had control of it? Standing brave and still, all she could do was to hold it tight against her chest, as her mind raced to think.

'Master Vlad,' she called out in desperation, 'you promised not to do any harm against me.' She stared at the wolves still padding through the mist to circle around her. 'And not let these creatures harm me eithers?'

Perturbed as one wolf stopped to approach and stare at her, Tariana's head spun with decisions; whether to try the charm, call again for Vlad, or simply just run for it. It was told by her elder gypsies long ago that such a high-pitched tone from the tuning-fork would tame such animals, but could she trust such fallacies. And besides what would she use to ping against it as Vlad had taken back Henrik's dagger. As she could probably make it to the river just before the wolves caught up with her, this was her gut instinct and the one she chose.

Tariana ran as fast as her already tired legs could carry her, glancing back at the wolf silhouettes following through the mist. It was just like that dream she had had before Petru woke her, but this time she was not so young, and this time it was real. Her heart pounded in her chest as she ran to the shoreline, her ankles now hurting from twisting and turning to balance upon the pebbles and scree, her boots sinking now and then into sandy pools.

By the time she crouched to balance on a large rock surrounded by fierce running water, the wolves were upon her, but stopped as she hopped onto another rock further into the deeper centre of the river. The wolves padded into the river's edge, but could only lick at the calmer waters, their senses knowing not to advance any further into such a rapid current. Apprehensive that they could not get to their prey, many of the wolves paced up and down the shoreline, their snarling proving their disgruntlement.

As Tariana watched the wolves saunter, between establishing her feet on slippery rocks, she remembered the old metal bar that she coiled fishing line about, and luckily it was in her leather pouch. Stooping to keep her balance and retrieve the metal bar from her backpack, she managed to get it, but as she twanged the bar against the tuning-fork, she lost grip of her backpack to watch it fall into the river. She gasped with fear to lose it, but luckily one of its straps caught against a trapped branch. But how long would it hold before the fierce current would take it?

Placing the charm back around her neck, Tariana stretched out an arm to try and recover her backpack, but it was just a little too far from reach. She waded out a little more from the safety of the rocks, but stood precarious in her stance to reach out further. Although with sudden delight of snatching back her backpack, one of Tariana's half-submerged boots lost grip upon a slippery rock and she fell into the water.

After feeling her head hit something to leave her dazed, she was taken with the current, but held tight onto her backpack. For a dangerous minute or two she was washed turbulently downstream, but eventually came to calmer waters near the river's edge. As she struggled on hands and knees to drag herself and her backpack to the shoreline, she whispered a secret prayer; that today she was not drowned and lived to fight another. And crawling soaked from the river, gasping strong for breath; she glanced up in fear of those wolves, but found that they had all gone.

It was then that again she lost consciousness and felt her face hit the ground.

THIRTY – TWO

'How much further along this river be this keep,' the Turkish commander asked Radu. 'It seems that we be travelling all day?'

'I press on hard so we meet up with the other garrison before nightfall,' Radu replied, his eyes squinting at the Turk as they rode aside each other on horseback. 'But I think the sun be setting within the hour.'

'Then should we not camp soon,' the Turk suggested, glancing back at his garrison marching on foot. 'The other garrison will not move until we meet, so what be the hurry?'

'I want to see it captured and in my hands for good,' Radu poked again his nose in the air. 'I will govern there with some of your army as you stretch others to conquer north and west.' He stared at the Turkish commander with some concern. 'I believe now it be only that Moldavian king that be of any threat.'

'Or those Hungarian armies,' the Turkish commander sniffed strongly at the air, 'although I hear that now they be somewhat depleted and may surrender to an agreement for peace. Probably beg for some truce. But believe me Sultan Mehmet will not…' Again the Turk sniffed at the air, and then scowled. 'What be that stench… that smell… do you not smell it too?'

'Yes, it be the smell of a dead animal… could be a rotting carcass from wolves or so like.'

'A pack of wolves would not leave any scraps,' the Turk indicated. 'But are there not bears here in these lands?'

Riding steadily along they heard behind them Turkish soldiers muttering about the stench too. As both Radu and the Turkish commander turned a corner to where the river meandered alongside woodland, they disturbed flocks of large, black birds that screeched as they took to the air. Watching masses of ravens and crows take wing and fly in all directions, they almost blocked out the setting sun that shone dim just above the treetops. As the birds departed and their horses trotted fast to approach, it was then that they saw the first of them.

Some were spiked on makeshift poles, branches sharpened to pierce either their spine or up through their rectum. But the majority of dead Turkish soldiers were staked upon splintered tree branches, their corpses rotting from days of being hung high in the late autumn sun. And as the garrison marched along, their eyes wide with fear and mouths a gasp, it was the rotting stench that added to such horror.

'Surely this cannot be the butchery of some Wallachian army,' Radu surmised. 'My brother hardly survived imprisonment, never mind trains such a large army to do such.'

'Did he not have assistance by common folk... trained many a farmer or carpenter to hold a sword and fight?'

'That be just his associate, some Hungarian renegade,' Radu told, turning his nose up at the pungent stench. 'But he got killed some time back... fell over a ravine to be impaled on...'

As they rode past corpse after corpse, spiked on poles in the ground or upon splintered tree branches, Radu glanced from one to another to wonder how Vlad could have copied the death of his Hungarian commander. But surely Vlad would be dead by now, or hiding like some vagabond pedlar in some gypsy camp? He may have even been caught again by the Hungarian king and sentenced to death. But he had not heard any news of that.

'I not know anyone who butchers men in such a way.' The Turkish leader looked at the dead bodies left rotting and then glanced back to see the reaction of his men on the march. 'Many be left alive like that and take days to die.'

'And you not have horrible customs to torture the enemy,' Radu sniggered, 'bury Wallachian soldiers alive with just their head above ground?'

'That be to ensure their soul not return to haunt us.'

'Be part of your strange religious belief no doubt.' Radu saw the Turkish commander stare hard at him. 'I be sorry if I be having different ways, but we share common a goal here.' He looked up again at many other corpses as he passed by, some birds undeterred in scavenging dead flesh. 'It just be so unsightly and uncommon... surely these must be buried, if not to rid us of the smell.'

'We have not the time,' the Turkish commander said, his eyes glowering at the number of corpses that lined the edge of the woodland, 'and my men need rest... but it not be here.'

'By their look, this sight of butchery will make them afraid, and a frightened soldier be a weak one.'

'You doubt my men, but want some of this army to reinforce your hold of your brother's keep?' The Turkish commander narrowed his eyes at Radu. 'Maybe I could see that your purpose in assisting our Ottoman Empire in this war could be terminated.'

'Apologises my Turkish commander,' Radu bit his tongue. 'This butchery be but such an unsightly and grotesque sight, not just for me but obviously for your men.'

'This can only be revenge done by that crazed brother of yours.'

'I very much doubt it,' Radu sniggered again, but grimaced still at the dead corpses hanging from tree after tree. 'I heard that Vlad be starved near to death by his imprisonment, so he be not having the strength to lift a sword, never mind train some Wallachian army to take his revenge.'

'Maybe he be having now new contacts with other lands,' the Turkish commander frowned, 'this be something we need news about?'

'I very much doubt that,' Radu smirked, his nose glad to sniff at fresh winds that blew from a different direction. 'My brother be nothing now but some forgotten and once be prince… he be reduced from being a lord to one of those vagabonds he once associated with.'

'I will not worry myself about that so called brother of yours,' The Turkish commander stated. 'As you say he be of no concern to the Ottoman Empire any longer… as there be no such Order of the Dragon.' He brushed aside Radu to get his attention. 'But this garrison needs rest and it must be soon as night approach quick in these lands. And it gets awfully cold at night.'

'But my commander, I thought by now, with all your experience here in Wallachia, that you be used to the cold of its coming winter.' Radu again sniggered, but looked with concern to see the Turk was not impressed with his sarcasm. 'But we shall find some place soon to camp. It be somewhere alongside this river for water supply, but out of sight of those horrible dead soldiers.'

'Yes, to whoever did this,' the Turkish commander stated adamantly, 'they will suffer the retaliation of the Ottoman Empire. And we will bury all but their heads in the ground.'

'Unless my brother turns up with some miraculous new army,' Radu chuckled. 'Your brother, if he be alive, be no worry to our concerns,' The Turkish

commander glowered at Radu. 'We stretch to conquer all north and west, even if there be many our soldiers butchered in such a horrible way.'

'Maybe it could be some army of the Moldavian king,' Radu surmised. 'Maybe he thinks it was the Ottoman Empire that killed that Jusztina? Apparently she took her own life as not to be a captive to you, but her body was never found.'

After their horses lead the garrison on for another half hour, Radu saw the sun had set and dusk was upon them.

'Here my commander,' Radu said, dismounting his horse, 'it be here that we make camp for the night to be fresh on the morrow.'

'So we meet up with the other garrison first thing?' the Turkish commander also dismounted.

'Yes, unless that brother exists to somehow miraculously train some new army to stop us reinforcing out hold on Poenari.'

'It be getting darker quicker than I thought,' the commander glanced around to see his troops settling to pitch down for the night. 'And be colder a night than the previous.'

'Well we have been travelling north,' Radu declared, rolling his eyes, 'and it be soon winter.'

'The weather be strange here,' the commander said, pointing over to the edge of the woodland that bordered the river, 'I not see a fog bank of such like ever before. It be so thick and moves against the downwind of this river.'

'I be no expert when it comes to such, but it can never harm you… not unless you want to wander off and get lost in it, especially now it be getting dark.'

'Twilight not last as long here as it does in our lands,' the commander stated, removing his saddle and attending to his horse. 'Never seen it get dark so quickly.'

'Another thing you obviously must get used to here in Wallachia.' Radu narrowed his eyes at the Turkish commander. 'Seeing the bodies of those your men, must have spooked you more than you thought.'

'They should be burned or buried, but we have not the time…' the Turkish commander glanced up to notice the fog bank now hovering near, but then heard the screech of distant carrion birds, as a flock of all types circled above them like a swarm of bees. 'What in the… they be the birds we saw south, if not but an hour ago… and what be it…?'

Radu stood from lighting a camp fire to watch with the commander the Turkish soldiers get accosted by a great flock of birds. If carrion hungry birds of all kinds did not flock together, at this twilight they did. And these large, black birds now seemed unperturbed by the men swinging swords and shields at them, their pitch black eyes glistening wide to attack for warm flesh, sweeping down to attack in droves to cause mayhem for the Turkish garrison. Here and there, pockets of men ran about, trying all attempts to fend them off, but most tried to take cover in their makeshift tents.

As several large ravens attacked the commander, Radu picked out the best branch alight from the campfire and swung it at them, but the birds simply squawked at him as if crazed. As Radu's attempts to thrust the fire lit branch at the birds to scare them off eventually paid off, he then shouted at the commander to saddle again his horse. But the commander just looked aghast at him until Radu turned to see what the commander was really afraid of.

As a large wolf padded close and began to snarl at him, Radu thrust the fire lit branch at it. Glowering at him with glistening silver eyes, it backed away somewhat, giving Radu chance to retrieve his crossbow mounted upon the saddle of his horse. But before he could aim with some accuracy, the wolf launched at him. Although he fell back and lost his crossbow in the wolf's attack, Radu heard the animal yelp and saw it retreat with a limp, the bolt fired and lodged deep within its hind.

As he searched the area to eventually retrieve again his crossbow, quickly Radu mounted his horse whilst shouting to the commander to do the same. But the Turk's horse was panicked as another large animal reared on its hind legs to accost them. The horse bolted in fright of the bear's advance and holding tight on its reins, the commander was dragged along to eventually be swiped by the bear, its large talons slashing across the Turk's face, almost tearing the commander's head from his body. And then as it started to maul the dying Turk, Radu steadied his horse in attempt to load and aim his crossbow. But it was then, as he was about to fire a bolt at the bear, that some strange and swift, dark figure took Radu from the saddle of his horse.

Although sore against the ground and dazed from his fall, Radu could see the bear continue to maul the now dead commander, the Turk's bloodied limbs contorted at all angles. And his sight of the horror intensified; witnessing men get attacked by wolves, their sharp teeth eventually tearing away at protective leather, armour and chainmail. Soldiers ran in all directions about him trying best to escape the mayhem, but Radu could see that birds blinded their way as the wolves pounced to tear out their throats.

He reached for the reins that dragged along the floor from his horse, but the beast was jerking to decide in which direction to gallop. Scampering to get to his feet, Radu clambered to retrieve his crossbow with one hand, as his other grabbed for his horse's reins. And just as he lunged to grasp the reins, the horse bolted, taking with it Radu's cumbersome body. He held on for as long as he could, but the gravelled ground bordering the woodland tore into his legs and thighs, so after just seconds in entering the cover of trees, Radu let go.

Dazed and confused, Radu rolled over to retrieve his crossbow, aggrieved but grinning to see that the bolt he had placed earlier was still loaded. Squinting in pain at the dense mist that swirled about him, he could hear the mayhem still in the distance; the growling of the bear, the snarling of wolves, and the squawking of birds. And now and then, he recognised the ghastly shouts of Turkish soldiers, their calls brief and sharp before being suddenly silenced.

Radu rolled back over, his crossbow in hand as he tried to sit up on his knees, but frowned at a dark figure not far away from him in the mist. As it approached, he could see that it was a man cloaked head to feet in a long gown, the head obscured by a thick hood. But what made Radu grimace, was how gangly the tall thin figure was, the man's hands and fingers unnaturally elongated as they pressed at his sides. Could this be his brother Vlad? Had he survived his imprisonment in the keep at Visegrad?

Quickly and without any want of an introduction or dialogue, Radu swivelled his crossbow and aimed, the bolt soon sent flying towards the strange dark figure. But in his disbelief, Radu witnessed the figure move aside with unprecedented speed to avoid the bolt and see it get lodged in a nearby tree. As he watched the strangely elongated fingers of the dark figure pull the bolt out of the bark of the tree, he squatted backward to find his legs and thighs hurt and bleeding. Cowering backward to scrabble away, Radu came fearful to watch the figure strangely drift in its approach, as its long fingers snapped the bold into two. And before he knew it, the figure was upon him; Vlad's piercing green eyes bloodshot and glowering at him beneath his heavy hood.

With his pale and gaunt face, Radu did not recognise his elder brother at first, but as Vlad grinned to peek at the crossbow bolt he had snapped in two, he knew it was him. Radu went to babble questions, but wavered on what he could possibly say as so Vlad would not harm him. But before he could string a sentence together, Radu felt an almighty sharp pain in his one boot and glared at his feet. As Vlad turned and twisted the arrowhead to thrust through Radu's boot, he eventually pinned Radu's foot to the ground. 'How did you first take my keep?' Vlad commanded, his spitting mouth exposing bloodstained teeth. 'How you get all those Turks past the great metal door?'

Radu screamed with pain but stared at him in defiance. At first he would not answer until he responded, spluttering sarcasm.

'That be something of a secret big brother,' Radu tried to pull his foot from the floor but failed, and then trying to dislodge the arrowhead was agonizing. 'The Ottoman armies hold your keep so that I will govern there… and they be moving north and west until your lands be taken… but I will have this land of Wallachia… they will give me ruling over Poenari.'

Radu again tried to remove the crossbow bolt Vlad had shoved through his boot, but felt his brother's spindly but strong and cold fingers press down on his.

'You be staying there until you answer to how you got them in.' 'It not matter now as they be in control and you have nothing.'

'All those in Poenari be dead and pinned along the battlements,' Vlad revealed, his emaciated mouth grinning somewhat. 'They be staying there on pikes as a symbol to my new power… and you will join them.'

'You have nothing of any power,' Radu spat out his words in pain. 'You have nothing now… no army… no keep… no wife or child!'

Radu yelped again as Vlad pushed down on his hand grasping the bolt.

'On those things you may be right,' Vlad released Radu's hand but took grip around his throat, his spindly, elongated fingers oddly powerful. 'But I turned my life to the Dark One… turned my back on that Christian God as he depict me a life of eventual ruin. And neither Christian God nor Muslim can have a greater power to that of the oldest religion. The Dark One maybe the one who now controls my fate, but he fills me with strength and power to kill you all… to seek out my revenge.'

'You have nothing of the sort,' Radu stated obstinately, but could not ignore the unnatural strength in Vlad's spindly fingers that clasped around his neck. 'Such things only exist as old vagabond women who profess to be witches, or warlocks and medicine men that would poison you for your money… they be telling their lies to heal, but cannot.' He clambered to get free, but could only hammer at Vlad's arms without any affect. 'Now let me be free, as you have no power to battle the Ottoman armies that come.'

'I will be killing all these until all are spiked liked that Commander I once had,' Vlad assured as he retreated but still towered over Radu. 'And I shall do the same to that garrison north and up river. I know all where they be.' Vlad pointed a gangly forefinger at his younger brother. 'Should more

Ottoman armies come, they will all meet the same fate. And I will line their bodies along this river as a reminder to that Sultan.'

'You be deranged if you think that alone you can do all that you say.' 'Did you not see already those lined along the river?'

Radu paused, his face contorted in agony with pain from his foot, but glared up at Vlad in recognition.

'But it not be true that you hold Poenari... it was and will still be mine.'

'I not know how you got in to let Turks past the dungeon door... or how they found their way through those passageways to assail my keep, but...' Vlad paused to smirk and hear deathly sounds emanate around him. 'You may just as well tell of how you did it, as I believe you may die.'

'If there be one thing that goes with me to my grave,' Radu replied full of spite, 'that be it!'

Radu clambered again to get up, but as he stood to try again to release his foot, he glanced around only to see Vlad's dark figure hovering somewhere within the mist.

'You be going now, I presume,' Radu shouted at the figure he could see of his brother. 'Leave me to fight off these *friends* of yours... lucky they not tear out *your* throat!'

'But a sudden death would be too good for you little brother,' Vlad appeared abruptly at Radu's side, his one hand clutching his throat, the other holding a broken spear. 'I will ensure that you will not only see these *friends* of mine kill for me, but that I can massacre many to ensure my revenge!'

As Radu stumbled about trying to free his foot, he watched Vlad ram the broken spear into the earth, forcing it down into the ground with immense strength, before he was again grasping at his throat.

'What is it you be doing,' Radu stammered with fear in his voice. 'No you will not… no you cannot… not your own flesh and blood?'

'Flesh and blood like mine you may be,' Vlad stated viciously, 'but stained against our fathers you will ever be.' Vlad clenched tight at Radu's throat and grasped tight his arm.

Suddenly Radu felt himself being lifted and strangely floated above ground to hover through the mist. As clouds of mists swirled about him, he realized to where he was going. Vlad's unnatural power drifted him towards the broken spear, staked solid to point up from the ground. And then with excruciating pain Radu felt the splintered part of the spear pierce his rectum. As Vlad released Radu he watched him slide agonisingly down the pole, gravity taking a slow but prevalent affect. Radu screamed and shouted at Vlad but his tall dark figure just stood silent and grinning in the mist, his bloodshot eyes wide to watch his younger brother squirm in pain.

Although suffering excruciating pain, as the pole pushed through his stomach, Radu witnessed Vlad shoot about the mists with unnatural speed, murdering Turkish soldiers with all manner of cruelty and slaughter. With eyes shut tight in pain, he could feel the spike of the pole about to pierce his heart and for seconds his mind was fading, until for one last moment he glanced at what could be his last sight of life.

Standing tall and smirking in the mists, Radu could see the thing that was once his eldest brother. But now this was not the Vlad he remembered; this was some gangly and gaunt, but immensely strong disciple of the Dark One, a devilish servant that would stop at nothing to seek revenge and go on killing. Radu watched Vlad's dark figure pull away his heavy hood and start licking the ends of his strangely long fingernails, his fingers too abnormally elongated.

'I should not taste the blood of the enemy as it may contaminate me,' Vlad said slowly, his eyes glaring at Radu. 'Maybe it be best to leave such doing to those *friends* I be having.' With a guttural bellow, Vlad chortled aloud, his bloodstained teeth grinning as he stared intensely. 'Argh, but here be one now... a raven of many to take feast.'

Although he could feel his heart about to burst, Radu felt talons stretch and scratch upon his head. And then other pains ruptured his face, as the large raven pecked viciously at his skin. Suddenly Radu could only see Vlad now with a blurred vision of one eye, as the beak of the large bird tore free his eyeball from its socket and tugged at the optic nerve. As the bird took wing but struggled to snap free the optic nerve, it flapped profusely until with immense pain, the fleshy cord snapped.

'You do not deserve such a quick death dear brother, but you be looking slightly more handsome in this that be the last of your life,' Vlad stated sceptically. 'But let them feast... let all my creatures of the night feast and help me avenge those all my enemies.' Again Vlad chuckled loud and strong. 'But now I must leave you dear brother, as I be having lots more work to do.'

THIRTY – THREE

Again Tariana had been dreaming, but as soon as she awoke all she could recall was that her dream had something to do with water. As her blurred vision cleared to look around, she gathered that her dream had been influenced by the fact that she was slumped at the water's edge of the river, her face and hair sodden.

She tried to pull herself up from the sands and gravel that had sunken to her body, but found herself uncontrollably weak. But then a sudden fear of realization hit her; had Vlad gone on and harmed her and punctured her neck to drink her blood as he had with that young soldier? Surely if he had, she would be dead by now. With her strength gradually returning, she heaved herself up from the shoreline and felt her neck for injury. Relieved, she found herself unharmed. It was just her body that was weak.

Sitting to brush herself off of dirt, she glanced around at the riverside to see that all was fine. But what had happened to those large wolves, she pondered, how come they had not harmed her? Had she collapsed on the opposite side of the river? And how long had she been there… what time of day was it… was it morning? On her travels back to her gypsy camp, she vindicated, she would have to check the height of the sun against the near winter sky.

Swivelling on her haunches to try and stand, she glanced curious to why her charm was in a riverside pool. Clumsily again she reached to her neck, as the last that she could remember, it was tied about her neck and shoved in her bodice when she bobbed about in the water after being washed downstream. And then she remembered those mighty big wolves staring at her from some distance. Maybe she had removed it to pray that they would not harm her, but to that, she could not recall. As she stretched herself to stand tall, she thought that maybe she would remember things as she headed back to camp, but would the gypsies still be there? Aching and weak, but determined, she would again follow the river the several miles that now was becoming familiar to her.

Again Tariana was apprehensive to approach those in the gypsy camp, but the smell of cooking enticed her as it wafted into her nostrils. And what she deduced as some sort of broth was simmering in a pot placed low over a campfire. Not far distant away and rifling through her belongings, she noticed the old woman Sabina, muttering words to herself as she always did when moaning.

Behind her, Remus and Simion were also sorting possessions, but with faces scrunched with concern, their conversation expressed impatience and fear. As Tariana slowly approached, she hid a while to listen to what they were debating. The two men were deliberating the old woman's warning that the Black Death had returned and that it was taking the young, old or frail, but the men knew some other strange evil had been at work before dawn.

'I tell you boys,' the old woman turned to point a finger at them, 'my dreams never be so disturbed by such dark forces… this be again some sort of plague, but this time it be somehow evil and corrupt.'

'It be just the battle between armies,' Remus told, folding up a makeshift tent, 'and without that Prince of Wallachia, we have no more to do with it.'

'Yes, but that man be known now as some sort of evil, seeking revenge against his brother.' Simion stared at his colleague from sitting on a log. 'His commander may have trained us to do good in battle, but I never hold a sword to fight for these lands again.'

'That commander taught us well,' Remus admitted, 'and things was good then… that Vlad was good to us… gave food and shelters, but things be different now… I have seen strange things at night outside of this camp.'

'You have not seen anything,' Simion jested as he busied himself with slicing cooked foul. 'You not venture outside that tent of yours as you be too scared.'

'If he be scared, I not blame him,' another voice joined the conversation as Sabina and the two men glanced around. 'I be seeing all horrors at night, and it not just be battles between soldiers.' Petru paused to stare at each of them in turn. 'I be seeing many a man murdered in all terrible ways… lifted in strange mists and impaled on stakes by some dark figure… their bodies left to die an agonising death… and we must not be here to experience such a minute longer.'

'What be it you see Petru?' Simion asked with concern.

'It be the plague again,' Sabina interrupted. 'But this time it be more evil.'

'I not sure what I saw last night,' Petru answered, trying best to ignore the old woman, 'but it be like some tall, thin shadow, jumping and flying about, torturing men in all manner of ways… it be like this thing take a pleasure in murdering all.'

'All I know, I be hearing such horrible screams that come from the dark of the forest at night,' Remus told, 'so I too will not be staying any longer than need be.'

'Yes, we must all leave as soon as it be…' Petru glanced at a figure that approached the group from out of the trees.

'But those men,' Tariana interjected as she strode boldly forward, 'they be not gypsies, but only those that be our enemy… they be Turkish soldiers.'

'I cannot say that this thing be killing only enemy soldiers as we be taking losses too.' Petru saw Tariana frown at him. 'You not know?'

'I be travelling up and down that river and all I have seen be dead enemy soldiers as was promised.' Suddenly Tariana stopped, her words coming without thinking because of her tiredness.

'Promised?' Sabina inquired, her eyes peering wild at her. 'What you mean

promised?'

'That not be of any concern. More important is that you will find your path north now clear.' Tariana looked at each as she swept back her long but matted hair. 'I be guessing that those that was killed last night be Turkish soldiers… those that were with that Radu, Vlad's brother who side for the enemy.'

'How can you know such,' Petru asked frowning, 'we not move yet as we thought his troops would make the garrison north even stronger?'

'By now both garrisons be most likely dead.' Tariana looked eagerly at the broth that smelt so good. 'So your path north be clear.'

'How can you be sure,' Petru quizzed, his patience wearing thin. 'Have you just seen this back from your travels?'

'She could be lying, so we must scout and take look,' Remus suggested.

'More likely she foreseen such in one of those funny visions she be having,' Simion jested. 'My guess is that she still sides with that man, that so be prince.'

'I do not lie.'

'If she know such from her travels, then that be it,' Sabina shuffled to be in the middle of the group. 'But I think she side for this man as she still be besotted by him, although I think him just as much an enemy to us as them be foreign soldiers.'

'I do not side for Vlad,' Tariana tried to explain, 'but told him about those troops and his brother to get them removed so your path north be clear.'

'How can one man rid us of so many troops?' Sabina contested. 'And how be it that you not get hurt in anyway, either by soldiers or by this dark fiend?'

'Like you said,' Simion interrupted Sabina, 'she be besotted with him, and so he probably takes pity on her.'

'She be stupid to take any more want of him, as no prince would ever commit marriage to such a gypsy.' Remus reverted back to his duties after seeing Tariana glare at him. 'Lords and nobles have always treated us with such contempt.'

'But he has not harmed any of you,' Tariana queried to get confirmation. 'Has he not only murdered those that be our enemy?'

All stood quiet for a moment as they glanced at each other, until a female voice broke the silence.

'I disagree,' Mariana sobbed as she stepped to stand beside the group, her little daughter held in her arms. 'My Alina was told not to venture outside the camp at night, but must have been looking for Sorin.' Suddenly she flopped down on her knees and cried uncontrollably. 'She be having marks like the other children we found.' Simion and Remus took Alina from Mariana's arms and laid her down as Petru placed a blanket beneath the little girl.

'What happened dearest Mariana?'

'What do you think has happened,' Sabina interrupted Remus as she pointed to the little girl's neck. 'Evil has been at work again, and it be because she brought us here, because of *that* man!' Sabina glared at Tariana, but she just stared back in amazement.

'You cannot pin guilt on Tariana for an evil deed such as this?' Petru protested. 'Surely she have no knowledge of such or would have warned us.' He glanced at Tariana to see her shrug her shoulders.

'I did not know children had been taken and harmed in such a way.' Tariana's eyes swelled with tears as she trembled nervously. 'I had no idea that…' Her voice croaked and so she cleared her throat. 'I remember warning little Alina to stay in camp by the fire or to be with Mariana.' She glanced over as Petru pushed Alina's long blonde hair aside to expose two puncture marks that were similar to those Vlad had made on the young Turkish soldier.

'What type of evil can do such a thing?' Petru asked, looking up in confusion to all staring down. 'If it be a snake or animal, there be poison or she be mauled… but it be like all her blood be drained.'

'It be told before the Black Death that creatures fed in such ways that brought on such plagues and disease,' Sabina advocated, stooping to examine the little girl's wound. 'This I reckon be the work of a vampire!'

'But they be nothing but old folk legends and fables,' Petru denied the old gypsy woman's declaration. 'They just be said to scare children into doing as told.'

'Looks like it did not work for this poor little mite,' Sabina said. 'Maybe we should tell such things again as more like this could die.'

'No more will die,' Petru turned the girl's head straight and placed a hand on Mariana's shoulder. 'We will bury this our girl with proper gypsy burial and then we be gone from these accursed lands… follow Andrei and Lydia, and Sorin if he be with them.' He glanced at Tariana. 'You can show us the way they went now that you say our path north be clear.'

'She should not stay any longer with us in this camp,' Sabina demanded, her wild eyes peering at Tariana. 'She be the one who brought all this on us!'

'How can she be,' Petru argued as he stood, 'she has only just returned to tell of our path north being clear?'

Tariana heard the others intervene to convey their own thoughts; the men rejecting the old woman's want for her to be extradited, but that they were confused to Tariana's motives. As of late, she had to agree, that a whole lot of evil had been done.

As she pondered to think about her charm, she stuffed it down between her breasts to hide it in her bodice. Surely she had had the charm on her possession overnight, and so Vlad could not have murdered little Alina with it? But then she remembered it being in the riverside pool that morning and not secure about her neck. Even if the silver of its metal somehow harmed him, could he have taken it from her to return it in the rock pool before dawn? But why murder such a young and innocent gypsy girl? Was young blood from enemy soldiers not good enough? The worst of it, apart from seeing Alina dead, was that he had broken his promise not to hurt any from her camp. And would he do it again?

'Why you look as though you have seen a ghost girl,' Sabina said to Tariana.

'What do you expect,' Petru replied, 'she be as shocked as us to see this happen to such a young child?'

'I just say, she look so pale all of a sudden.'

'I be shocked, that be all,' Tariana projected in her defence. 'But I will confront this Vlad to find out the truth behind this evil.' She stared down at Mariana in particular. 'I know it will not bring her back, but I promise to avenge the death of poor little Alina.'

'You do as you wish,' Petru declared, 'but we not wait here another minute, as I not want to witness any one more such cruel and evil death. We will scout north to ensure our path be clear and you can join us beside the river at foot of the keep.'

'But she could give away our secret passage north to this Vlad and he could follow.' Sabina looked despising at Tariana. 'He could kill more of us.'

'I cannot imagine it be him that could do such evil,' Petru contested. 'We were once all in alliance to rid these lands of a common enemy.' He went off to gather his possessions and command others to do likewise. 'It not matter now if we move out... so we go and rid ourselves of these lands.'

'If you go see him,' Sabina scorned, 'I make sure you never be again welcome in this our camp.'

'But I know the way Petru wants to go,' Tariana rebuked, trying to withhold her dislike for the old woman. 'And if it not be for me, your path north still be blocked by many an enemy soldier.'

'Still, if you go on after that man,' Sabina avowed stridently, 'I do my best to make sure you not follow us north.'

'That be not for you to decide.' Tariana glanced over to see Mariana lift and carry her little daughter's body towards the campfire. 'We must at first bury that poor little girl and leave aside all disdain to grieve. We must be strong as gypsies for Mariana in her grief.' She stepped over to sample some of the simmering broth and take a little food, but the old woman followed to continually deride her.

'All you be interested in is filling your belly before you take off!'

'I be hungry that be all,' Tariana disputed. 'You want me to starve after all I have done for this group?' She loaded up her own possessions and took a couple of apples for her journey. 'I be off once I see buried that poor little girl.' She stopped Petru in his busy duties. 'I shall meet up with you again at the foot of the keep.'

'Do you really have to seek out that man again?'

'I want answers… like to how that little girl got killed,' Tariana spoke adamantly. 'And only *that* man can give me the answers I seek.'

'Then I must wish you luck and to stay safe.' Petru looked upon her with unease. 'But if it be him that do all this, I want you gone after you show us the passage north.'

'You should rid us of her now!' Sabina shouted, spitting out her disapproval. 'She will side with him, as she be as evil as he be!'

'No, I be leader so I be deciding such,' Petru instructed. 'She has been a great asset to us for many a year and guide us gypsies through many a hardship.' He pointed at Tariana, his eyes sympathetic but sincere. 'I not know why you seek again this man and think he may take harm against you, but we will wait until dusk on the morrow… camp by the river at foot of the keep.'

'I will get answers and deliver them on to you,' Tariana professed, hiding well her nerves to think about entering that cave again, 'even if I must deceive he who I once loved.'

THIRTY – FOUR

Travelling relentlessly through the night, Tariana had eaten all her food and was tired, but her emotions were enraged in remembering the little girl. A couple of hours before dusk they had buried Alina with what was their best attempt at a gypsy funeral. Tariana had gone early, but heard Petru state that he wanted the gypsy group by the river Argeş, about a mile north of Poenari, before nightfall.

She pictured Mariana still sobbing at the small, flowered grave and imagined her reluctance to leave her only daughter, although she had agreed to move on to track Andrei and Lydia's route to the town they had so liked. In a way Tariana was now glad Lydia and her grandfather had left before things had turned hostile, but so missed too Kateryna and Sorin.

Maybe as hoped, once she had vented her anger at Vlad and got the answers she wanted, she would meet up with the group that Petru now led. Sabina, the old woman, would despise her, but she had no worries about that; she just wanted to know if and why Vlad could have done such a thing. Why murder such an innocent gypsy girl, when there were so many enemy soldiers to butcher? And trying to ignore the many rotting corpses still staked upon splintered branches alongside the river, she had grimaced to why he had butchered them so horribly. Why did this evil he had agreed a pact with curse him into having to drink blood? Could he not now reject this devilish pact and somehow reverse all his want to do such evil? Whatever Tariana could try and change about the man she once loved, she could never bring back Mariana's daughter. And could she get killed herself? With her anger ever more prevalent, Tariana strode on until, in the hours just before dawn, she reached the cave.

She frowned to notice the wagon had gone, but was pleased to see that the waterfall now had gaps she could go under, as rains from the mountains had not replenished it of late. Frightened and without thinking, Tariana ran into the dark entrance of the cave, trying best not to get wet from the cascading water that eventually meandered its way to the river. Standing alone in darkness, she suddenly shuddered to contemplate on what exactly she was doing there, but visualized all the horror she had witnessed, especially to the burial of that poor little girl.

As she paced gingerly into more of the cave, she could feel her eyes grow wide as they adapted to scrutinize the darkness, her mind trying to recall the memory of its layout. But it was getting darker; the far reaches into the tunnel almost pitch black. How could she possibly follow those chalk markings

Vlad had described indicated the way up to that dungeon well? If she miraculously found her way to it and climbed it safely, would Vlad even be in the keep? She paused to tremble to the chill of a breeze, the grim thoughts of getting lost and starving to death adding to her unease.

She stepped forward a little, thinking to strike the flint she carried just to expose her way in a flash of a second, but realized she needed something a bit more substantial. Fumbling in the dark to identify things in her backpack, it was then that it came to her; what about the fire torch she had dropped just before Vlad had taken her across the river? And backtracking best to remember where she had dropped it, accidentally she kicked it, but after hearing it roll, located it to pick it up.

It took several fine strips of torn cloth to ignite with her flint piece, but once she had a flame, she nursed it until it illuminated most of the passageway. Not only was she relieved to be able to see what lay beyond the dark shadows, but welcomed greatly its warmth. As she paced gingerly but determinedly through the passageway and more into the cave, she noticed the ends of other side passages piled with rotting bodies; Turkish soldiers tortured and staked as some assemblage of revenge ritual, some pierced against the rock, others left hanging to bleed dry from the ceiling. Grimacing to hold the fire torch before her, see grasped her charm with her other hand and ambled on whilst whispering a prayer.

Suddenly on the turn of a corner, a cold breeze stirred the flame and she shuddered to watch it nearly blow out. Spooked by some ghostly dark figure, she again shivered to a cold breeze that brushed past her, and paused to consider whether it was Vlad. Was he with her there in the shadows of that tunnel, his now devious and evil mind wanting to play tricks with her? Or in the confines of such a cold and dark place, was it simply her imagination running away with her? She called his name and demanded that he show himself, but all she heard was the echo of her voice, and then finally just a daunting silence.

Determined to go on, it was then as she snaked her way through the passageway, that she stumbled against another corpse. Quickly she thrust out her fire torch to identify it, but stood aghast and giddy to recognize Sorin's enormous body. Although his features had deteriorated somewhat, Tariana knew it was him by the scar that ran vertical from his cheek and up across his eyebrow, his clothes still the same as when she last saw him. And now she knew Vlad must have killed Sorin when he pulled him from the suffocating earth. It was now so obvious to what had happened; the tuning-fork she had gave Vlad to provide consolation, cruelly used to puncture her giant friend's neck as he did to Alina. She herself, as she recalled, was knocked unconscious, to be blindfolded and transported on their wagon. To that memory she shuddered, remembering something alongside her that rolled and bumped against her as she lay blindfolded. And thinking it Sorin, she realized Vlad must have transported both of them to that cave entrance. But luckily for her, she remained alive… but for how long?

In that moment, whilst grimacing at her giant friend's withered face and clouded eyes, she called aloud again Vlad's name and shouted questions to why he could do such… to kill Sorin as they went to save him… to haunt her gypsy clan and murder Alina? And how many others had he butchered that were not his enemy?

Again she dropped the fire torch as a strong, cold hand grasped her throat from behind. For a moment Tariana just glared at Vlad's pale, gaunt face in the flickering firelight, but then punched at his arm to get free. For seconds he simply grinned at her and watched her struggle in vain, until eventually he released her.

'I not know why you want and follow me here,' Vlad spoke, his bloodshot eyes staring from shadowy, withered sockets. 'You know I am not the man I once was and can never be again.'

'It not be right that you come such a dark and recluse man…' Tariana paused, she could not get dragged into the feelings she once had for him, but wanted answers. 'Why you go and kill that little, innocent girl Alina from my gypsy camp… it must be you… you took this my charm to kill and drink her blood, and then returned it beside me as if nothing had happened… why you do such evil… why can you not be that righteous man you once were?'

'To reap and endure such powers bestow to me… that which grants me great revenge… this be the sacrifice to the Dark One… and so must live off much young blood.'

'But you promised not to harm –'

'I promised nothing,' Vlad enraged, 'but that I would seek revenge against those our enemies.'

'And a little harmless gypsy girl be such an enemy?'

'I drink not the blood of the enemy as they be contaminated.' Vlad stepped away and turned his back on her. 'I not know who be or is not from your gypsy camp.'

'You may not have seen her before,' Tariana angered, 'but you killed Sorin the same way too.' She pointed down the tunnel to where she had identified his body. 'He lies there with the same marks that killed Alina!'

'That was at first an accident,' Vlad groaned, glaring back at her from the corner of his eye, 'until this evil filled me and make me ravage the nourishment of blood… as blood is now my life.'

'But how can you do such after I told of your brother… told of where they be and his army marching north.' She paused to see him stare unnervingly again at her, but angered, tears now filling her eyes. 'What type of reward be that you murder one of my clan… and such a young, poor little girl?'

'Like I said, I did not know.' Vlad turned with wild eyes and grasped hard her shoulder. 'But I need not answer to you… a petty, vagabond, gypsy girl whose prettiness once captured me.' He shook hard her shoulder, her long, matted hair quivering. 'Instead of hiding from the enemy by daylight in this cave, I will fortify that keep that be rightfully mine!' He finally released his grip, her eyes glaring at his strangely elongated fingers. 'They may make their plans and be prevalent by day, but at night I be master… kill whoever besiege Poenari!'

'But why you kill such my peoples,' Tariana cried. 'You promised no harm would come to us?'

'I promised nothing as now I be a changed man.' Again he turned to walk away. 'And if you not like what I be, then go… move up river with those gypsies of yours, now that *I* clear your route north.' He took another few steps away from her into the shadows of the tunnel. 'I live only now to seek revenge and to kill all those that be my enemy. Now that I have avenged my brother's betrayal, I will go on and kill all from Bucharest to the coast of the Black Seas.' He scraped his long fingernails to score lines across the rock walls of the tunnel. 'And nothing and no one will stop me!'

For a moment there was nothing but a daunt silence, a change of attitude between them as Tariana rubbed her choked throat and loosened her traumatized shoulder.

'So you not remember all that made you such a good man?' Tariana braved to shout. 'Fighting not just for your lands and lordship, but for the love of your wife and son… your commander and all those men who battled brave with you… and our night of passion… all that compassion mean nothing to you now?'

'There be no such compassion… or any love for that matter… not since my imprisonment… my soul be committed to the Dark One so I can reap his power.'

'But you promised to find my brother if not your own son too?'

'That which once was my family be now gone,' Vlad's face contorted, his hands covering his face to hide the last remnants of compassion. 'Jusztina be lost to Hell and my son lost to the enemy.'

'But get him back,' Tariana projected, bravely stepping forward, 'along with rescuing my brother.'

'Is that all you want me for?' Vlad grasped at her neck again, his strength unbearable about her throat. 'Want to use me as some puppet to redeem your wishes?' Suddenly with great power he flung her to the ground. 'Spare your own life and leave, and not look upon me again. I cleared your path north as promised, but did so as part of my revenge.' He stepped back into the shadows once more and placed back the heavy hood to conceal most his head. 'I took much pleasure in taking revenge upon Radu… along with many others.'

'You would have never known the whereabouts of that brother of yours if it not for me. You could at least confess it was you… you owe me such that I can tell that poor girl's mother!' There was no reply as Vlad's figure disappeared into darkness. 'Go then… be alone, hated and cruel… hide all your days in that keep!'

Again Tariana was left alone in daunting silence. As she retrieved the fire torch, her anger intensified by the fact that Vlad would not even confess his guilt; he had killed Sorin as maybe some accident, but little Alina had been purposely murdered. How many more had he killed from her gypsy camp that had not been accounted for? She stepped forward in pursuit of Vlad's figure, but paused to think; it was good that her group were moving permanently up north, as if they stayed by his keep, more could get killed. But what would happen to the people of his own land – farming children, sons and daughters of townsfolk – was these children not all at risk from his ravenous need for young blood?

'You not kill anymore our clan as we go north,' she shouted in the direction to where his shadow disappeared, 'and you not kill any those that be once your peoples!'

'You should be glad that I not kill you, gypsy girl,' Vlad's voice spoke faintly from a distance. 'You once filled me with your passion, but now all be different.'

'But maybe you can change all back,' she cried, 'redeem all you have done… make amends and find love again in your heart.' She continued her sentence, but quietly whispered to herself. 'Find love in your heart again for me?'

'There be nothing now in my heart but the want of revenge… and blood.' Vlad's voice was now, nothing but a distant murmur.

Tariana looked longingly into the flame of her fire torch, its flames making her recall her night of passion by the campfire with Vlad; remembering its warmth, to how it soothed their naked bodies as they made love out in the wilderness and beneath the stars. But then Tariana felt tears run down over her cheeks, as she came to realize that Vlad was now lost to her forever.

THIRTY – FIVE

Through the shadows and cold of the tunnel, Tariana followed a dark figure that she thought could only be Vlad. But as she turned a corner and held out the fire torch to light her way, she came engulfed in a chilling fog; swirling mists which seemed the same as those of which had lingered near the riverside. Determined to go on, she shouted out questions as if Vlad was still there; arguing to why he had become so evil and corrupt, to why he had killed Sorin and little Alina after promising never to harm her people. But stepping cautiously on, she was greeted with nothing but silence.

Suddenly the dread of becoming lost overwhelmed her as the daunt quiet came only disturbed by her footsteps and the sound of the torch flame as a strong breeze blew against it. And gradually she realized to how it was getting dark as the flame of the torch was diminishing. So at a junction of passageways, Tariana stood the fire torch up against a wall to lift up her skirt and tear strips of thin material from her underskirt. Then after retrieving the fire torch, she wrapped around the strips of material, carefully watching each melt within the flame.

Comforted by brighter light, but apprehensive on which way to go, she held tight her charm in the other hand.

She circled around to look down each of three passageways, but pondered on whether her charm was now itself an essence of evil, even if *she* held it with such deep faith. For a while she was all in denial of her beloved faith and her Christian God, but as her fire torch blew strong to the draft from one passageway and mists cleared to reveal a chalk mark, a smirk stretched across her face as her tenacious, natural willpower returned. And then, before striding forward through the dissipating mist, she remembered Vlad's conversation that revealed his secret about the chalked markings, ones that would hopefully guide her through the correct tunnels and to the bottom of the old well.

Again, as she stepped swiftly through the dank, contracting tunnel, she noticed a dark figure ahead, and thinking it Vlad, followed quick but cautious. She considered whether to shout out again her questions, but realized if she followed him in silence, maybe he would lead her to the bottom of the well beneath those dungeons. But what was it that he had said about climbing the old walls inside the well? Trying to recall her memories of their conversations, Tariana strode on, but came perturbed by how the tunnel was now becoming so narrow, with its ceiling also tapering to such a low height.

Following the chalk markings through one tunnel to another, after about half an hour Tariana found herself in a low ceiling cavern. This she gathered, by looking across its watery floor, must have been the original reservoir to the old well. And stooping to stride forward, she could feel a cool draft flow across her face and disturb her now, nearly extinguished fire torch. Using the draw the draft had on the flame, she came anxious to follow in the direction from which it emanated, as soon unless she tore more strips from her underskirt to feed the flame, her only light would be gone.

Squeezing her way through an area of an even lower rocky ceiling, she eventually came out to a circular area to where she could stand. Not only could she stand up straight, but after raising the fire torch way above her head, she could see the circular walls of the old well, its bricks laden with mold. And there they were, a stepping distance from each other as they rose like a spiral staircase, each brick jutting out just enough to take a footing. But as Tariana stood the nearly extinguished fire torch against the wall and tried the first brick, she found how slippery they were. With the weight of her backpack, there would be no way she could climb such slippery footings if carrying her fire torch. She glanced at how its flame was almost out, but luckily gave just enough light to locate the protruding bricks. And then she looked wistfully to the top of the old well after noticing the slight flicker of candlelight, or was it light from reed torches set into walls? Nervous but determined, she took a deep breath and after placing her charm back around her neck, she started her ascent.

She was trembling at first, but as she got half way, she froze to hear the sound of water, or was it the rush of air? She did not want to look down, even if to see whether the torch had gone out; Tariana just looked longingly but apprehensive to the top of the well. And then as she held on for dear life, almost at a height ten times of her own, she heard that noise again, even more loudly as it emanated from the bottom of the well.

Tariana clutched onto the protruding bricks circling above her head and stiffened her feet to glance down in horror to see a surge of black bodies hurtle up towards her. In terror she held on, her body stiffened rigid as she had never seen so many bats before; the sudden appearance of their little black bodies and flapping wings making her hold her breath as hundreds rose up and past her, and out the top of the well. Again she felt herself trembling and her heart racing as she hung on and looked up to hope the bats had disappeared. Relieved to see the creatures suddenly gone, Tariana again forced herself to steady her nerves in order to climb the rest of the well. Several times she almost lost her footing as she circled the well to climb its walls, but gradually she was winning, determinedly looking at the dry of the well's top circling wall in order to ignore her fear of falling.

As she reached the top circling wall of the old well and cocked over one leg, the relief overwhelmed her and suddenly she found herself giddy. Quickly she lunged to roll over upon the timeworn dungeon floor, to avoid reeling the other way and maybe fall down the well. Pained with her backpack digging into one side, she wriggled free and squatted upon her haunches, just thankful she had made such an ascent safe and well. She stood and peered down the dark of the well and shuddered, the flame of her fire torch at the bottom, now hardly visible. As she looked around, she noticed the flickering light of reed torches dispersed just enough to enlighten the gloom, and in the distant shadows were dungeon enclosures, many now dilapidated, there metal doors rusted and bent. And dotted about the rock and sandy floor were bodies, some his men, but mainly butchered Turks, their throats twisted and gouged, their cloudy, dead eyes fixed in a stare of terror. She could not look upon their ghastly faces any longer and so weaved her way through cavern passageways until she noticed the casting and metal works that Vlad had boasted about.

Though somewhat battered and lodged stiff against the floor, Tariana noticed the reinforced metallic door that she remembered led up a turret stairway to the keep, and although it was stuck ajar, her slim, petite body passed easily through it. And as she slid through the gap and squinted at the stony staircase circling above her, she felt a chilling breeze against her legs and hands, and thought she heard ghostly voices call from a distance. Trying best to ignore a chill against her face, tentatively Tariana began to climb the stony staircase, her hands cold against the walls whilst having to steady herself upon the steps in what was all but darkness.

It was not just because the climb was steep and so her weary legs ached that she took deep breaths at the top, but paused to peer out a narrow window from the turret, relieved to see the first light of dawn appearing over a forestry horizon. And with this stretch of emerging daylight, she could see more about her; a dim corridor that led off to adjoining rooms, its adorning reed torches dowsed or damaged, but its shadowy reaches revealing more dead bodies, many sprawled across its floor. She glanced again at the increasing daylight emanating beyond the trees and hills, and stilled with calm to hear the distant call of dawn birdsong. But with determination, she wanted to go on and get answers from Vlad, and to see if now he had took back his keep.

Wearily Tariana paced through the corridor, meandering left and right to inspect each of the rooms. At first most rooms were enshrouded in darkness, but here and there was now the odd window baring the first daylight or a faintly burning reed torch. As she progressed to examine each room, she noticed how they were mostly ransacked as if upturned by pillaging, some again containing a dead body or two.

And it was then, in one particular bedchamber, that she stopped to pause at its door, her mind puzzled at a strangely designed arrow bolt that was wedged into a leg of furniture. And a short distance at its rear, an attached rope had been crudely cut off. Gingerly she stepped inside and towards the narrow window to look apprehensively down at the river some distance below. Had this been Jusztina's bedchamber, the very window she had leaped out of to commit suicide, but to escape the marauding Turks as they besieged the keep? For a while her eyes filled with tears to remember Vlad's wife – the pyre on which she had been cremated and set down stream – and although Jusztina clearly despised Tariana, she could only feel pity for the woman.

Bravely putting her emotions aside, Tariana ventured on through the corridors, noticing the place totally ransacked and despoiled. Quickly as she passed through a large banqueting room she noticed to how the highest most windows now welcomed the first rays of daylight, and so she ran on to enter what was the archway of another castle turret. For a moment she poised to notice how dark it was and apprehensively looked down the corridor and beyond to decipher to where it led.

Decisively she strode on down the dim corridor, gradually realizing that on the roof must be battlements lined with weapons and armory, as above her were trapdoors set in the ceiling. It was then, near the end of the passageway and blocking the only doorway, that Tariana noticed a pair of silvery, glistening eyes staring at her in the dark. For a moment she knew not what it was, but as she made out a big, shadowy head, she remembered the same eyes staring at her from the riverside. At first she clasped tight her charm in one hand, hoping she still had her allure with animals, but as the large wolf appeared out of the darkness to unnervingly stare at her, she came anxious to its size and to why it was alone. *How did this wolf get into the keep? Do wolves not hunt in packs,* she thought. *What a prospect to consider… more of them… and this one looks big enough… and not very friendly at all.*

'I will not harm you if you not harm me,' Tariana spoke nervously as she held out her charm as some protection, but backed away down the corridor. 'I be going now and find another way, so be calm big wolf.'

Anxious, Tariana stepped back swiftly, but slowly enough as not to startle the wolf into attacking her. But with her eyes fixed on those staring eyes, she did not see the body of the dead Turk behind and almost tumbled back over him. The fright made her shudder, but once she navigated her way around the soldier's body, she tried best to calm herself. It was then, glancing at the soldier's feet, that she noticed the pike; a spear that had small blades that resembled hooks pointing back towards its handle. Quickly from the shadows beside the dead Turk, she snatched the weapon and held that tight instead for protection. But now the wolf padded slowly towards her, his whole body in view for Tariana to realize to how big he truly was.

'You stay there and not come any near,' Tariana spoke firm but nervous, holding out the spear before her. 'Again I say… I will not harm you if you not harm me!'

Abruptly the wolf stopped, but only to stare at the length of her new weapon.

Walking back into shadows, she could not now see the wolf properly, and so came nervous to hear it begin to snarl. As she backed away further, a little way behind her, she again noticed one of those trapdoors set in the ceiling. It came to her in an instant – probably as things did when she was scared – she lifted the pike to hook against a handle in the trapdoor and after several failed attempts managed to unhook it.

Although the first light of dawn was somewhat dull, Tariana came relieved to notice the light spread down to a square in front of her, its expanse enough now to properly see. But with the wolf still hidden somewhere in the dark, its growling still unnerving, Tariana had no plans to wait for the creature's reaction. And so she leapt up, using the pike to launch her through the opening and out upon the battlements. But in an instant the strap of her backpack got caught and snapped, her belongings falling into the corridor below.

As she winced to realize to what she had lost, she glanced back down into the dark opening of the trapdoor. Staring back up at her, as the creature constantly growled, was the wolf's pair of eyes, glistening silver in the half-light.

THIRTY – SIX

It was almost dawn by the sight of the brightening eastern horizon, but Tariana had no time to peer through the narrow slit windows, as she wanted to question Vlad. Finding her way along the battlement walkways, she was determined to explore the upper reaches of the castle, thinking she could retrieve her backpack once that wolf had gone.

But striding along, again she noticed dead Turkish soldiers, probably those who not long ago guarded the keep, their bodies spiked on stakes that lined the battlement walls, their eyes glazed in terror and disconcertingly staring down to follow her every move. She shuddered at the sight of so many, young or old; as if Vlad had butchered and lined these men against the walls as some exhibit to his revenge.

Most were already dead; their bodies spiked up through their anuses with the tapered end jutting out bloody from their mouths. Some however, were simply pinned against the walls, their wrists and throats staked with long, metal nails, as if Vlad had crucified them in denial to his once precious and

Christian God. Averting to look only at her feet, Tariana could not gaze upon them anymore, until she heard someone groan.

The Turk was only a young man, barely out of his teens. And as Vlad had failed to crucify him properly and had not impaired his throat, he called out at seeing Tariana pass by. She stopped to pull back his head and noticed him open his eyes again to gaze at her. But she knew he was beyond saving; his loss of blood so ruinous and injuries too devastating and beyond repair. *But why should I show any sympathy for such a young man*, she thought. *He is but a soldier of that of my enemy, those the Ottoman Empire that murdered my parents and kidnapped my brother, leaving me so young to survive the wilderness alone and lead such a harsh life?* Eventually she let go of his hair, hearing a creak from his neck as his head fell.

She stood from crouching to examine more the keep. Many battlement walkways meandered off to access other turrets or wooden armory storehouses, some having ladders that lead to higher ramparts. These were the very top walls of the castle, where arrows would be fired or fireballs and bricks would be launched from catapults fixed into the stone. As she paced steadily along the one battlement walkway, Tariana came to pause at the sight of one particular part of the castle, at where the upper wall had been damaged. Vlad had not educated her with the conduct of battle and its consequences, but gathered that cannon balls had ruptured holes in parts of that upper wall. *Maybe*, she thought, *it was that side of castle that was easiest to assail. But how did such a well defended keep get besieged… had Vlad truly lost that many of his troops?* Her thoughts, whilst glancing around to grimace at more spiked bodies, came troubled by another occupant.

It was again that wolf… or was it another? The creature looked even bigger in the increasing light of dawn. And as its sleek body padded slowly towards her along an adjoining walkway, she fretted on how to escape from it again. For a while it stopped to study her from a distance, its caution somehow not perturbed by the height of the narrow path it walked upon. And as it again regarded her with silvery, glistening eyes, it sniffed at the air, as if to taste for her fear.

However, Tariana had already studied the upper parts of the keep, and a ladder was near, one which led to that top battlement wall that had been bombarded with cannon balls. But with the creature wandering around below her, even if she kicked down the ladder, could the wolf jump up to attack her? And being on one of the highest ramparts of the castle, would she be able to get safely down without walls collapsing? Another option was to jump down that only open trapdoor, but would that other wolf be patrolling there? And how would she get back there if she kicked away the ladder? *Were there two wolves now in the keep,* she mused, *or had the whole pack from the river got in?* She could not be sure as she had not seen if the castle gates were demolished and so open.

Noticing the wolf again start to stride slowly towards her, Tariana felt that she had no other option but to climb the nearby ladder and try to escape the creature, maybe discover a place of hiding or find safety at such height. Again she contemplated to how this was one of the highest ramparts and to how its blasted walls might be dangerous, but surely now she had no choice.

As she ran for the ladder, the wolf began to pick up speed, its stride lengthening as it trotted steadily along the walkway. It almost reached her as she quickly started to climb the narrow, wooden ladder. And turning to sit, once she reached the top, she glanced down to see the wolf place its giant front paws upon the bottom rungs of the ladder.

Tariana came so scared that quickly she kicked away the ladder and tensed to watch it fall. Suddenly the wolf backed away, its wide eyes watching the ladder now tumble over the edge of the walkway and fall into the grounds of the keep.

Tariana stood slowly to examine each way along the narrow rampart, but then looked back at the wolf. Strangely the creature had suddenly disappeared. *That be strange*, she pondered nervously, *where he go to vanish so quick?* She scrutinized all around, puzzled to where the wolf had gone, but concluded that it must have somehow squeezed through the opening of that trapdoor. But now without the ladder and her backpack amiss, surely she had no way to get back down, and so must venture on.

At first she took careful strides to walk along the narrow rampart walkway, holding a wall level to her shoulders to steady herself. This was one of the highest and the outermost wall of the keep. And as she glanced through the crenel gaps of the outer wall, she could see the first rays of sunlight glimmering through the treetops. But she did not realize to how high she really was until she came across the battered wall. Through parts of where it had been shot away, she glanced fearfully down at the treetops of woodland some distance below, a dark gloom still evident beneath. Even if she had that rope from her backpack, its length would not be enough to climb down. And moreover, even though she was not known to be scared of heights, it would be terrifying to even contemplate such a descent.

She glanced down again to assess the height, but came nervous at the view, and so grasped at the wall. Quickly she had to retract her hand as some bricks dislodged to tumble and fall into the woodland below. *I have no chance getting past this way,* she concluded, realizing to how damaged and unpassable the walkway was. *Looks like I will have to go the other way or maybe find another ladder... or a plank of wood that will hold my weight?*

Suddenly as cold and spindly fingers grabbed her neck from behind, Tariana had something else to fret about. As she swiveled around in alarm, the first thing she noticed was Vlad's tall, dark figure; his gaunt, ashen face hidden beneath that heavy hood, but his piercing green eyes glaring hard and bloodshot. She tried to rush past, but he grabbed at her arms. In turn she struck out, her hands flailing until she pulled away his hood, tearing seams of cloth at the neck. And then she backed away towards the damaged wall, the terror of seeing Vlad's now corpselike face, superseding her fear of the collapsing wall.

Vlad glowered at her, his eyes bulging extreme from such dark and withdrawn sockets, his face almost skeletal if not for his pallid and withered skin. His bloodstained lips parted to expose gritted teeth as he went again to lunge at her. As his spindly long fingers again went to grabble for her neck, all Tariana could do was to stumble backwards against the already crumbling wall.

At first she could not understand to why Vlad cowered away and fretfully tried to replace his hood, but then noticed him blinded by sunlight; the first rays of the sun at dawn emerging as the uppermost part of the wall collapsed and fell. With the foundation upon what she stood unstable, Tariana had to grasp at what she considered was the safest brickwork, but glanced again at Vlad to watch him shield the sunlight from his eyes.

Tariana realized then to how after such a long time in the darkness of that prison cell, Vlad's vision had long accustomed to the dark of night, and that was why he only appeared after dusk. For a moment, as Vlad tried best to move and focus to locate her, she pitied him over such imprisonment, her heart almost reaching out to him in hope to gain him back. But as she stared upon his monstrously gaunt face and deliberated on the things he had done, she came suddenly overwhelmed by hatred; her soul telling her to neglect this now evil man, forget this once proud prince and noble warrior that now had become some hellish disciple of a corrupt and evil power.

Snapping off the charm strung about her neck, Tariana lunged at Vlad's tall figure as he cowered low, but he was fast to clench the wrist that held her makeshift weapon. In their struggle, Vlad swiveled Tariana around to be out of the sunlight and suddenly stood tall in temporary shadows clenching tight her wrist. But with sunlight reflected from the silver of her charm, Vlad's eyes came blinded by bright light resembling the sign of a cross. And as Vlad cowered away after releasing her wrist, she stood amazed to look upon her charm as it reflected the sign of the crucifix; an unusual but effective protection from her Christian God, the Almighty God that Vlad had rejected to become corrupt and evil.

Briefly Tariana rotated her wrist, trying best to amplify the bright sunlight to reflect upon his face, but withdrew her hand to hold high and to lunge it at Vlad's chest. As soon as the sharpened prongs of the tuning-fork stabbed into his chest through his gown, Vlad stumbled back and into the sunlight. Stumbling about in terrible dismay, Vlad cowered into shadows still cast from a tall part of the wall and tried best to remove the prongs that dug into his chest. But as he grasped at the handle and winced to pull the charm out from his chest, his spindly fingers stung against the pure of its silver metal.

Although with his power weakening, determinedly Vlad wrenched at the tuning-fork, the very one he had misshapen in his attempt to escape the wretched confines of that prison cell. And eventually, with his hands strangely burning, he pulled the prongs from his chest and dropped the charm with great relieve. But seeing Vlad now glare at her in anger, Tariana recoiled back as much as she could against the disintegrating outer wall of the keep. And now she was quaking at two things; in seeing Vlad stand tall in the shadows to glower at her, and knowing she leaned back against such unsafe foundations.

She could feel the large bricks of the castle wall dislodge as she trembled against them, but knew she could not escape, unless she could rush past this changed man, the one that she once loved. Maybe if she ran in the exposure of the first rays of dawn sunlight, she might evade he who now had nothing but an evil heart and a monstrous vendetta. But for some reason she could not move, his glare somehow hypnotic enough to keep her there against her will, stunned like a fly bitten with spider venom.

'You never answered me to why you kill my peoples,' Tariana flinched and shook her head as not to look upon his gaze. 'Why murder Sorin who tried to help… and that little girl, Alina…

why murder those of my people, when you gave promise not too?' With every shout of anger, Tariana felt her will and faith return as if God himself gave her strength. 'I gave you that charm to help you, but now you make me use it to defend myself!'

She shivered uncontrollably to await Vlad's reply, but he just stood there staring at her, his one gangly hand holding his chest as his other replaced his hood.

'I was condemned to this life and so now must live it,' Vlad growled as he paced towards her. 'And to reap such powers I must feed off the blood of the young and virile.' In a tall and gangly stance he paused to study her, glancing around to ensure he was in the shadows. 'Now I be weak, and so must feed before the sunrise.'

Vlad scrutinized the rampart walkway in order to locate the very thing Tariana had stabbed him with, but the gypsy girl knew his intention and so tried to rush past. With frightening speed Vlad flew at her and grasped at her neck, his strange elongated fingernails scraping down the skin of her neck.

'I had you in life, but that was love,' Vlad snarled, his eyes bulging to stare at the veins pumping blood through her neck. 'And now I take that life from you, as so I not die.'

Tariana struggled to push away Vlad's advance, but dug her heels into the foundations of the crumbling wall, her boots slipping but kicking back to find better footings.

It all happened within seconds. Suddenly the upper part of the outermost wall keeled over. And as many large bricks dislodged from the part shadowing Vlad, it crumbled to expose him now to the rising dawn sunlight. Although he had replaced his hood to shield his eyes, the low rays of sunlight powerfully blinded him into disarray, causing him to lose his footing and slip against the crumbling mortar and dislodged bricks.

In one last attempt Vlad went to lunge at Tariana, or was it to cower from the rays of the rising sun? Whatever, Tariana recoiled again against the crumbling wall, her eyes shooting from glancing at Vlad to examine the now collapsing wall. She winced back in horror to watch another part of the wall disintegrate; taking with it Vlad's flailing body.

Within seconds Vlad's dark figure disappeared over the edge along with bricks and rumble, and for a moment Tariana came relieved. But a crack along the foundations was shooting towards her and she thought that she would fall too. So as it disintegrated beneath her, she lunged for another section of the wall, but was this other part safe?

It seemed an eternity as she held on to the edge of the wall, her fingers slipping against the gritty pieces of mortar, her heart pounding with the fear of falling. She shifted herself along, clutching best onto what part of the wall looked safe.

But then her right hand slipped and lost grip as another part of the wall disintegrated.

Tariana had always been light and nimble and this certainly helped in her last, desperate attempt to swing a leg over the wall before her other hand slipped. As that part of the wall collapsed from her fingertips, she retracted her hand to grip another part; luckily the foundations of this section were more secure. In one dexterous motion she cocked her other leg over and rolled upon the grit and fragmented mortar fallen upon the remaining part of the battlement walkway. After turning over onto her stomach, she rose to crawl on all fours along the rampart, to glance down over the edge to where the wall had disintegrated.

At first she had to squint to focus from such a height, trying to scrutinize the distant woodland below. Increasingly the depths between trees and the ground below were being illuminated by the rising sun, its powerful rays percolating through leafless branches to glimmer on the wet, fallen leaves of autumn.

And then she saw him.

In the distance and upon the ground of the woodland, Tariana detected Vlad's body lying face up, but sprawled over a large branch. And as he had crashed through trees to fall to the ground, he had become impaled against a splintered branch, the fractured piece of bloody wood sticking upright and out of his chest.

Tariana winced to see Vlad spiked so horribly, but then recalled to all the cruelty and evil he had done.

Staked like all those he had tortured and killed, she contemplated, her eyes swelling of tears. *His chest impaled after falling to his death like Henrik.*

Eventually, tears escaped Tariana's eyes. But were these for the man she once loved who had now turned evil, or was it remembering all the friends she had lost, and the chance of never finding her brother?

EPILOGUE

The sunlight glimmered quite bright through the gloom of the trees by the time Tariana had reached the woodland to where Vlad had fallen.

She had crawled her way back along the rampart walkway to luckily find a plank of wood sturdy enough to slide down and reach the inner battlement. But it had been a struggle to find her way back down through the trapdoor and through the keep.

Wandering through the barracks and courtyard, she had witnessed many of the horrors that Vlad had done to enemy soldiers, and although she had refused to show any sympathy for the enemy, she knew her Christian heart ached with remorse.

She had traipsed the mountainous terrain of woodland to shadow the high walls of the keep, but as Tariana approached the clearing to where Vlad had fallen, she looked around perplexed to where he was. She glanced up at the high walls of Poenari castle, and to the wall that had crumbled from the bombardment of enemy cannon fire.

Baffled, she trudged through bracken and undergrowth to circle the area, ensuring that she was beneath the wall that had collapsed. She had noticed fallen debris scattered about the woodland floor from where the wall had disintegrated, but there was no sign of Vlad.

Then, as she turned and glanced down from following the path of fallen bricks, she saw the bloodied branch to where Vlad had been impaled. But now his body had gone; all that remained was the broken end of the splintered branch with blood running down to gradually congeal.

How could...? Tariana's thoughts were but of confusion. *Surely he would have died from such a...*

She glanced around after hearing something growl, her breath turning to vapor in the early morning air.

There it was again, that enormous wolf, its silvery glistening eyes glaring at her as it snarled to expose its teeth. And from its gleaming teeth came misted panting, as it too breathed the cold air of early winter.